The
Solid Gold
Circle

The Solid Gold Circle

Sheila Schwartz

Crown Publishers, Inc.   New York

In Gratitude

I wish to thank my beloved children, Elizabeth and Jonathan; my mother, Sylvia Frackman; my sister, Lucille Becker; my friend, Rhoada Wald; my agent, Liz Dahransoff; and my editor, Carole Baron, for their compassion, love, and encouragement.

Any resemblance in this novel to persons living or dead is purely coincidental.

Inquiries should be addressed to
Crown Publishers, Inc.
One Park Avenue
New York, New York 10016

Printed in the United States of America
Published simultaneously in Canada by General
Publishing Company Limited

Library of Congress Cataloging in Publication Data

Schwartz, Sheila.
The solid gold circle.

I. Title.
PZ4.S3998So 1980   [PS3569.C5674]   813'.54   80-12486
ISBN: 0-517-541637

10 9 8 7 6 5 4 3 2 1

First Edition

Dedicated to
My Beloved Daughter
Nancy Lynn Schwartz
1952–1978

AUTHOR'S NOTE

*M*y daughter, Nancy Lynn Schwartz, died on September 3, 1978. She was twenty-six years old. Had she lived, we would have written *The Solid Gold Circle* together.

Nancy was an extraordinary girl. Many people thought she had everything: beauty, brains, figure, sweetness, integrity, compassion, social and political conscience, and amazing success at a very young age. People called her a golden girl.

She was generous and had a vast army of friends at every age level. Those of like tendencies immediately recognized her as an exceptional, superior kind of human being, witty, vital, vibrant, totally devoid of envy or malice, fun to be with.

Her short career in Hollywood was a remarkable one even in a town famous for its meteoric successes. She wrote four of the ten episodes of NBC's "Wheels" miniseries, the screenplay for my novel *Like Mother, Like Me,* the pilot and plot outline for Robert Stigwood's *Charleston,* and a first draft for a nonfiction work on the Hollywood blacklist and the Screen Writer's Guild to be published by Alfred Knopf in 1981.

At the peak of her success, out of nowhere and without

warning, she developed a terrible headache. Her doctor put her in the hospital for tests. The next day it was diagnosed as a brain tumor. Two weeks later, she died.

Nancy and I had written together from the time she was seventeen. We had an extraordinary affinity, love, respect, and communication with each other. We were so similar in tastes, ideas, and perceptions that we used to joke that I had cloned her.

In the hospital she asked me, "Am I going to be all right, Mom?"

"Could I be functioning this way if you weren't?" I asked.

"No," she said, and she was comforted.

We had planned to write this novel together but we never could have dreamed there would be no time. And the day after Nancy's funeral, instead of dying too, I got up and started to work on *The Solid Gold Circle.* During the year and a half that followed, whenever I was filled with despair at her loss, I would look at her picture and hear her telling me to go on.

So here it is, a book that we should have done together, written by me and dedicated to the memory of my dearest friend, my beloved daughter.

The
Solid Gold
Circle

PROLOGUE
1946

The streets seemed absolutely safe at night. During the days, in safety, children roller-skated and played stickball. There was no crime, vandalism, mugging, or drunkenness. This was Borough Park, Brooklyn, the next stop upward for immigrants after the Lower East Side. For these immigrants, life here was comfortable; not luxurious, just good. To them, Borough Park was an address to be proud of in 1946.

Although it looked fine to recent immigrants, it was, in reality, a gray, grimy, lower-middle-class Jewish enclave which lacked even one handsome building to lift the spirits. On the north, it was bounded by elevated subway tracks which separated the Jewish community from the Italian ghetto as completely as if it were a frontier of high, impassable mountains.

Ellen Graetz lived with her parents in a respectable two-family house between Fourteenth and Fifteenth avenues on Fifty-first Street, a modest location in which her mother took unreasonable pride. Mrs. Graetz was certain there could be no finer address than her own. She was, in fact, positive of this. But then, she was positive of most things. As Ellen progressed through life

1

and even when she reached the stage at which she mingled with the wealthiest and most successful echelon of American society, she never again found anyone who was as certain of so many things as was her mother. Never again did she find anybody as consistently certain . . . or as consistently wrong.

It was difficult for Ellen to determine the source of her mother's unassailable information. Ellen had never seen her read a book or a newspaper and Mrs. Graetz thought movies were only for children. Television was still an experimental toy and the Graetz social life, apart from regular attendance at the local conservative temple, was nonexistent.

And yet, Mrs. Graetz knew, was certain, was unshakable, and woe betide anyone who challenged her opinions, which were as uncompromising as the Ten Commandments and were unswervingly applied to her family's daily existence. These opinions had been imprinted indelibly on Ellen's consciousness.

One: concerning marriage. A woman without a husband and children might as well be dead. Two: concerning sex. The ultimate evil when engaged in, a powerful weapon when withheld, given to women by God as the bait with which to ensnare a husband. Women who gave in before marriage had only themselves to blame for subsequent disgrace or spinsterhood. Three: concerning friends. Nobody was really your friend; everyone was basically no good and out to get you. The only way to keep from being fooled was to give as little as possible to people and to ask even less of them.

Four: concerning family. Relatives, apart from her husband and daughter, were a necessary evil. Relatives were maybe a little more trustworthy than friends, though even relatives could not be fully trusted. But relatives didn't really matter anyway. Once a woman got married her only real family was her husband and children. Five: concerning clothing. No decent woman walked around without a girdle and stockings. Cottons and light colors were not worn until June and a lady wore white gloves in August. Six: concerning education. Fine for boys but a stopgap for

2

girls. "Pray to God, Ellen, that you'll never need to use it." Seven: concerning responsibility. A child's major responsibility was to honor her father and mother and come directly home from school. Eight: concerning reading. Too much of it was not good for you. Boys didn't like girls who were too smart and besides, it would ruin your eyes. Nine: concerning politics. Every Jew should kiss the ground of the United States, never think disloyal thoughts, never criticize, and vote Democrat. The threat of Communism, now that World War II was over, was the primary danger to the stability of the world and any people even vaguely identified with left-wing causes did not deserve to live in this country when they were so ungrateful. Ten: concerning minority groups (this especially applied to Italians). They were all no good and the wisest thing any Jew could do was to have nothing to do with them.

These were Mrs. Graetz's ten assumptions, delivered with the certainty of commandments, and always summed up with her final philosophy of life: "Life is no picnic and whoever said it should be?"

It was bad enough that she held her opinions from the vantage point of ignorance. But even worse was the fact that if her husband and only child were to live in peace, it was essential not only that they repress their own opinions but that they appear to endorse each pronouncement vigorously. After seventeen years of home life, Mrs. Graetz had succeeded in convincing them both that they were ignorant fools and incompetents, heavy burdens, who would fall apart without her guidance.

"Look, Ma," Ellen would protest when her mother started her usual daily complaints, "you work so hard, please let me make my own bed."

"All right, Miss Know-it-all, let's see how you make it."

Nervous, fumbling, Ellen would make the bed. It was never good enough. After the last wrinkle had been smoothed and Ellen had adjusted the spread with sweating palms, Mrs. Graetz would look up to heaven, shrug with martyred acceptance of her idiot daughter, strip and remake the bed, while Ellen would stand by weakly protesting, "Oh, Ma, what do you care? I sleep in it."

"You sleep in it!" the shriek would begin. "You sleep in it, but it's my house. When you have your own house you can be a slob. Until then, show a little respect."

The bedmaking complete, Mrs. Graetz would straighten up, put her hands on her hips, complacently survey her domain, and ask, "See the difference?"

When Ellen would stand there sullenly, not answering, Mrs. Graetz would continue, "Don't give me those looks. At least treat your *maid* with respect. Some girls your age are already out contributing to their families. We ask you for nothing. So the least you might do is be grateful."

"Thank you, Mother." Ellen stood there hating her mother and, what was worse, confused about whether she really was as bad as her mother indicated. Was she wrong to think it didn't matter how a bed was made?

"Maybe," her mother's litany would continue, "someday you'll learn. God knows, I must be killing myself for some purpose. If only you marry Mr. Right someday, I'll feel it was all worthwhile."

"Yes, Mother," Ellen would sigh.

Mrs. Graetz's major campaign, however, was against Ellen's passion for reading. Her daughter's habitual escapes into literature seemed a purposeful affront to her mother, which, in part, they were.

"Always with her nose in a book," Mrs. Graetz would mutter to heaven.

Then, to Ellen: "When I was your age, I liked to read, too. But my family was more important. When you have a family, you can't be so selfish, you can't spend all your time doing exactly as you please. I kill myself for you but when I want to talk to you, your nose is in a book."

Whenever possible, Ellen would flee. She had a refuge—her beloved library, a quiet, serene, small understocked storefront.

4

She loved the quiet, the retreat into the mind, the absence of guilt she found there. Ellen also adored the women who worked there, so neat, uneffusive, unemotional, so ritualized as they stamped the books, filed the cards, and wrote in the symmetrical printing they had learned at library school, printing Ellen tried to emulate at home. Someday, she promised herself, she would have a home like the library, a home full of books, full of quiet grace, devoid of hysterical shrieking.

Ellen's years in high school passed in a dream. Scholastically, she always did very well. Mrs. Graetz's ten assumptions had produced the model public school student—a polite, repressed, docile, hard-working, frightened girl. Her papers were immaculate. Sometimes she would do them over many times to achieve the proper degree of neatness. Her handwriting was a credit to the Palmer method. She never talked in class, never fooled around in the halls, was always prepared, handled her books with respect, dressed in unobtrusive, somber colors, wore bras under her sweaters, did not flirt with boys, answered correctly and deferentially when called on, and brought her teachers lovely gifts at Christmas, which her mother said Gentiles expected.

At odd moments, Ellen felt rebellion surging up in her, but she quickly repressed it. How could rebellion help her? She had heard stories whispered in the lunchroom of how parents beat, starved, and neglected their children. Many of her schoolmates worked for eight hours a day when they finished with school and were constantly berated by teachers for being stupid or sleeping in class. Most of them would never get the chance to go to college. But not Ellen. She was warm and well fed, took vitamins, got good marks, and was cozy and safe from evil. But because of her mother's hysteria, this feeling of safety was always accompanied by a vision of the world around her as a jungle filled with quicksand and beasts, waiting to destroy her if she failed to obey her all-knowing mother. Her mother was a pain in the neck but, listening to the other kids, Ellen knew there were far worse parents.

In March 1946 she was seventeen years old, not pretty, her

breasts a little larger than the norm, her head a mass of dark curls, her body slightly overweight. She was a senior at New Utrecht High School, where she had managed to get through three and a half years without offending anybody and without making a friend. Her marks were good, teachers liked her, and she was not unhappy.

On a balmy spring night, Ellen followed the routine she had gone through hundreds of times before. She finished drying the dinner dishes, took her library books, and happily walked the twenty blocks to the local library. The placid librarians greeted her with quiet affection; she walked around taking more books than they would let her borrow, then sat down in her usual corner to decide which to take with her.

Lost in pleasure, she sat reading one she wouldn't take home, until the warning lights for closing flashed on and off. Her books were stamped at the desk, she bid the librarians a fond goodbye, the library door was locked behind her, and she started the walk home. When she saw the gang of boys coming toward her, she did not think anything of it. This was a peaceful neighborhood. As they came closer she noted that they were the leather-jacketed, black-haired boys who hung around in the schoolyard. She had no connection with them or they with her. Or so she thought.

As they approached, she moved toward the buildings so they could pass her on the deserted street. They reached her, but they didn't pass her. Suddenly they surrounded her in a ring, jostling her, rubbing up against her, pinning her against the cold stone of the building. This must be a mistake, she thought. They must think I'm someone else.

"I don't know you," she stammered out in fear. "You must have me confused with someone else. Let me pass."

"Not yet, baby," one of them said as he reached out and caressed her breast. With that one gesture she understood that she was lost. Here was the chasm, the danger, the abyss her mother had always warned about. Here were the Cossacks, the Nazis, the

6

monsters who lay in wait for good little Jewish girls in every corner of the world.

She couldn't move. Her knees were melting, she was afraid she would urinate where she stood, could feel herself perspiring under her arms. She felt choked, dizzy, paralyzed, unable to say a word. Hugging her books to her chest, her carapace against evil, she made a futile gesture to push out of the ring but she never had a chance.

One of the boys grabbed her, spun her about, and tied a dirty handkerchief across her mouth, reminding her wildly of the children's parties at which she'd played "Pin the Tail on the Donkey." She gagged and suffocated, reached to pull the hand-kerchief away and her books fell to the street. She was dazed, in a dream, watching this happen to someone else in a movie.

She bent to pick up her books and then they were upon her, a pack of wild dogs, rending, tearing, snapping, and pulling at her. Two of them pinned her arms down and a third ripped down her panties. And then they did it to her, right there in the street, in front of the closed shops, banging her body against the cold ce-ment, doing it there on the dirty, cold, hard, abrading street. A sharp pain and the first was finished. And then the second, the third, then the fourth. In a dream she heard the grunting, felt the weight, the rhythm, the pain oozing from between her legs. One of them ripped the handkerchief away from her mouth, tossed her panties on her, and they were gone.

She lay there shivering for a few minutes, then stood up and pulled on her ripped panties. In the dark, she felt for her books, picked them up, and weeping, hugged them to her. What was she going to do? In an instant, her life had been ruined. How could she deal with this horror? How could she face her mother?

She stood there shaking and weeping. It never occurred to her that this nightmare might be concealed from Mrs. Graetz. Her mother had once told her that if she ever slept with a man before marriage, it would immediately show in her face and be evident to her mother. Ellen knew what would happen. Her

7

mother would blame her. She'd say, "You must have done something to invite it," "These things don't just happen," "Why you?" "No decent man will marry you now," "How could you do this to us after all we've done for you?" and, "I warned you what would come of all this reading."

Maybe her parents would throw her out and declare her dead. This had happened to a neighbor's daughter who had married a Gentile. For eight days, the family had sat *shiva* for the dead, mourning, sitting on little stools, rending their garments, tearing their hair. When it was over, the girl was considered dead and when she'd tried to see her mother, her very own heartless mother had driven her away with a broomstick. If this happened to Ellen, what would she do, where would she go, how would she live? She had no money, no friends. There would be no solution but to kill herself.

She heard a footstep and started to shiver again in terror. Were they coming back?

"My God" — she heard a boy's voice—"what happened to you?"

"Who are you?" she asked between trembling lips.

"It's me, Saul, Saul Greenberg from your civics class."

Oh, yes, Saul Greenberg, that bright, thin boy in glasses. Some said he was a Communist. He was a nice, pleasant boy.

He stood there with her until she was able to talk, to say the horror, and the saying of those words was one of the most difficult things she had ever done. She could only tell him in a shocked whisper. She had been attacked. She didn't tell him how many boys there had been because she wasn't sure. Was it four, six, five? She had been attacked by wild beasts. He listened, nodded, then protectively put his arm around her.

"I live near here," he said, "come with me. My mother will help you."

Her teeth chattering, her vagina scalding, she walked the few blocks with him to the first tenement she had ever visited. She held his hand while he pulled her up three flights of stairs,

8

down a grimy, bad-smelling hall, to the unlocked door of his little apartment.

The apartment seemed to have only two rooms, the kitchen and a small bedroom. A gray-haired woman, her hair in braids wrapped around her head, sat at a rickety kitchen table, smoking, drinking tea from a glass, and reading the *Daily Worker*. Saul led Ellen to the couch in the kitchen, covered her with a blanket, and told his mother what had happened. The woman was beside Ellen in a moment, rocking her in her arms, giving her warm, natural human consolation.

"Where is the bathroom?" Ellen asked at last, when she had stopped crying.

"It's in the hall," Saul said. Ellen limped to the door, peered out at the dark hall, and started to cry again.

"Sha, sha, don't cry," his mother said, "I'll go with you." She waited outside the door while Ellen went to the bathroom. There was no sink in the stall, just an ancient pull chain toilet that filled with her blood, her pain, her ruination, then flushed with a gurgle. They walked back inside the apartment.

"Where do I wash?" Ellen asked. Saul went into the small bedroom and shut the door while his mother took Ellen over to the deep sink which apparently served both as tub and clothes-washing basin for them. She gave Ellen a soft, warm, soapy rag and Ellen scrubbed and scrubbed, trying to wash away the horror. All the while, Mrs. Greenberg made comforting, soothing, gentle little sounds to reassure her. Then she threw Ellen's panties in the garbage can and gave her a clean pair of her own.

"I'll return them," Ellen said.

"Such a thing to worry about now," Mrs. Greenberg said kindly.

Ellen put on the panties, far too large for her, and Mrs. Greenberg tightened them with a safety pin. Ellen stood there, as docile as a baby being diapered. Then Mrs. Greenberg took another soft cloth and washed Ellen's face and hands the way one would for a small, hurt child. Ellen sat there passively, in shock.

Finally, Mrs. Greenberg gently brushed Ellen's hair. "Very pretty," she said, giving Ellen a hug and patting her face. "Nothing shows."

Mrs. Greenberg called Saul back into the room and he sat down with Ellen at the kitchen table while Mrs. Greenberg made hot chocolate. She put a large marshmallow in each cup and Ellen was somehow comforted by this remembered ritual from her childhood.

"Can you listen now?" Mrs. Greenberg asked after Ellen had taken her first sips. Ellen nodded.

"What do you want to do?" Mrs. Greenberg asked.

"I don't know," Ellen mumbled.

"This is my advice to you," Mrs. Greenberg said. "Don't go to the police. They're always on the side of men. They'll say you invited it. You'll get no help, so there's no point in going to them. Don't tell anyone. Gossip about this thing can only hurt you. Your only protection is secrecy."

"What will I do if I get pregnant?" Ellen shuddered.

"You can worry about that when the time comes," Mrs. Greenberg said. "There's nothing you can do about that tonight, but your parents must be worried about you. Saul should take you home."

"No, no," Ellen sobbed. "I can't go home. My mother will kill me if she finds out what happened."

"So don't tell her," Mrs. Greenberg said.

"She'll know," Ellen wept. "She'll look at me and know. She always told me that if I slept with a man she would only have to look at my face to know. So how could she not see this right away?"

"That's crazy," Mrs. Greenberg said, repressing a smile, "nobody can tell anything like that from your face."

"You don't know my mother," Ellen said. "She can just look at a girl and tell if she's still a virgin."

"Old wives' tales," Mrs. Greenberg said. "Old wives' tales mothers use to keep their daughters virtuous. You can't tell from looking."

10

"Are you sure?"

"Absolutely, darling. Please believe me."

They finished their hot chocolate while Ellen thought about what to do. The only solution was to go home and brazen it through. God help me, she thought. I never was a good liar.

"Here are your books," Saul said. "They're not even damaged." He handled them as reverently as she did and she liked that.

It was midnight, two hours later than she had ever arrived home from the library. Her father would be asleep. If her mother was not asleep, she would be frantic. Well, maybe she would be asleep, too, and there would be no confrontation until morning. If only Ellen could get some sleep, she might be able to deal with things.

Mrs. Greenberg kissed her goodbye, told her not to worry, and she and Saul set out for her home.

For ten minutes they walked together in silence. Ellen ached with every step. He kept trying to start conversations but she was so abstracted that he kept faltering. Finally, outside her house, he summoned up his courage.

"Listen," he said, "I'd like to see you again. Could we make a date?"

"Why would you want to see me again?" she asked.

"What do you mean, why?" he said uneasily.

"Is it because," she burst out, "you think that now that I've been raped I would sleep with you?"

She was ashamed of herself as soon as she had said it. How could she return his kindness in this way.

"Oh, no," he said, embarrassed, "I just thought maybe we could be friends. I've seen you in school but I never got around to talking to you before. It's just that I'd like to see you."

"Why should you want to see me anyway," she said bitterly. "I'm damaged merchandise."

"That's a hell of a way to think of yourself," he said indignantly, "as merchandise . . . damaged or undamaged. You're a person, not a thing, not a piece of merchandise."

"I know what I am now," she said, crying softly. "No decent man will ever marry me now."

"A decent man would feel compassion for you," he said, "and you should never marry anyone who doesn't feel it."

He was a nice boy, she thought, but naïve. It was evident to her that he did not understand the workings of the real world. She understood, as he did not, that the only way she could ever again be safe would be to hide her terrible secret.

"You won't tell anybody," she begged, knowing she need not ask but unable not to.

He shook his head, hurt again. "I'll see you in school," he said as she turned to go inside. "Okay?"

She made a gesture which was halfway between a shrug and a nod, opened the front door, walked softly into her house and scanned the kitchen. Thank God! They were both asleep. She took off her shoes, tiptoed into the bathroom, locked the door and filled the tub. Bruised, sore, her entire body aching, she lay in the tub wishing the horror away. Well, she could get to sleep without seeing her mother and she was grateful for that. But in her stomach she felt a leaden weight of fear, fear of the future, of pregnancy, of disease, of her mother's wrath. After a while the tub lulled her a bit and sleepiness began to dull the edges of her anxiety. She felt steady enough to brush her teeth and go to bed.

Quietly she opened her bedroom door, felt for the chair on which to drop her clothes, dropped them and switched on the light. She almost fainted when she faced into the room. Her mother sat there grimly, her mouth a tight, hard line, her arms folded over her chest, her eyes those of an avenging angel, black with wrath. Ellen felt so weak she leaned against the wall for support. Shaking with terror, she then stumbled over to her bed, nervously got under the covers, and said, between chattering teeth, "I have to get to sleep now, have to be up early for school."

"Bum, tramp," her mother hissed at her. "As if I don't know where you were. I was watching from the porch. You were with a boy, you good-for-nothing."

"I wasn't with a boy," Ellen wailed. "Honest, I swear to you, I wasn't with a boy."

"Liar. I saw you from the window. What was that? A girl?"

"I was visiting a girl friend," Ellen said, her teeth still chattering, "he's her brother."

"All right. A girl friend! Give me her name and I'll call and ask her parents."

"They don't have a phone," Ellen improvised desperately.

"Another lie," her mother said bitterly, "another lie. You were with a boy, you bum."

She pulled the covers from Ellen, yanked the girl up, and started to slap her rhythmically back and forth across her face.

"Don't think you can fool me, you bum. I can see it in your eyes. You've ruined your life, you fool. You've ruined your life and you've ruined mine. You were with that boy. I saw you. No matter what you do, I'll never forgive you for what you did to me tonight."

"I didn't do anything," Ellen wept, trying to shield herself from the blows. If only her mother would take her in her arms, comfort her, love her the way Mrs. Greenberg had.

Now her mother was weeping. "A viper in my bosom. All these years I've nurtured a bum. Why has God punished me this way? What did I do to deserve you?"

"Please, Mother, I have to go to sleep or I won't be able to get up for school tomorrow."

"You want to sleep," Mrs. Graetz wailed. "I suppose I don't need sleep. All day rubbing and scrubbing to keep this house clean! Is this what I sacrificed my life for? A bum? A tramp? Let me tell you, my fine lady, you'll go to sleep when I know the truth and not a minute before."

Oh, God, Ellen thought, what could she do to get rid of her mother? What should she tell her? What lie would be so horrendous that her mother would forget about sex? What did Mrs. Graetz hate as much as sex? Suddenly Ellen knew. Her panic subsided, she looked at her mother with a sincere expression on her face and uttered the lie that would convince.

"All right," she said, "I was visiting Communists."

A wail rose up from her mother. "Communists!" her mother said, in a voice reflecting death and dismemberment. "Communists! We're done for. How did you get mixed up with Communists?" She rocked and moaned in grief.

Ellen had been right. Sex had flown out of her mother's mind at the mention of the Red menace.

"No lies now," her mother said. "Where did you meet them?"

"I met the boy in school," Ellen said, "and then I ran into him in the library tonight. He invited me home to meet his mother."

Then, to really clinch it, Ellen added, "She was reading the *Daily Worker* at the kitchen table."

A fierce intake of breath from Mrs. Graetz. "A woman like that is not fit to be a mother. What business does she have being a Communist? She should be grateful to be living in a country like this."

"Please, Mother, it's past one and I have to be up at six. I have to get some sleep."

"Not until you promise me you'll never have anything else to do with those people. My God, you'll ruin your life. The FBI keeps files on all Communists. Once you get on their list, you never get off it. Promise me you'll never see them again and I'll let you go to sleep."

"All right, all right, I promise."

Satisfied at last, her mother left the room and Ellen finally sank into the sleep she so desperately needed. But she couldn't get up for school the next day. Pleading illness, she stayed in bed for two days, sleeping most of the time, and then, on the third morning when she got up she found that her menstrual period had begun and a flash of sheer joy ran through her entire body. It was one of the most extraordinary moments of happiness she had ever known. Oh, thank God, thank God, she wasn't pregnant.

14

Now if she didn't develop a disease, nobody would ever have to know what had happened to her. Nobody! Only Saul and his mother and they would never tell.

She was not afraid that her attackers would know who she was. Because she had barely been able to see their faces in the darkness, she was sure they would not recognize her either. She hadn't been a face to them, just a body, an object to attack. No, the rape was over. She would never tell anybody about it and she hoped that gradually it would fade from her memory so that she could pretend it had never happened.

The next day she returned to school and went on seemingly as before. But she had made a decision that would now dominate her every thought, her every action, for the rest of her life. The thing she now wanted desperately, more than anything else, was protection. Her future goal was to be safe and the kind of safety she wanted could come only through marriage to a husband who would protect her. She had to find that kind of husband.

Several times before graduation, she had lunch with Saul in the school cafeteria, but she would never visit his home again. When he pressed her, she told him the truth.

"I don't want any reminders of what happened to me," she said. "I could never feel easy with someone who knows the truth."

"It's because I know the truth that you should be able to be friends with me," he said. "I really like you, Ellen. I'd like you to be my girl friend. Someday, we might even want to get married."

"There's no future for us," she told him, trying to be gentle. "I don't want to hurt your feelings, Saul, but you're poor. Your family is even poorer than mine and you want to be a teacher. Teachers are always poor and they have no power. Teachers can hardly protect themselves, so how could a teacher protect me? I want someone to protect me."

Saul looked at Ellen with compassion. "Let's drop the subject. You're still in shock from what happened. In time . . ."

But Ellen didn't let Saul finish his sentence. "You're wrong,

Saul. You don't even know how I feel. I'm afraid all the time now. I'm afraid when I walk home after school and I haven't been out at night since this happened. I never even go to the library anymore and I start to cry at strange moments. I don't feel safe anymore and all I think about night and day is how to be safe. If I didn't live in this poor neighborhood this would never have happened to me. I want to be rich. I want to marry someone powerful, a businessman with an office and a car and lots of money and power who can protect me from anything bad ever happening to me again. That's why I say there's no future for us even though I really like you a lot and I'll always be grateful to you."

Now Saul looked at her in puzzlement. His eyes were kind as he peered at her through his thick glasses, his thin shoulders hunched forward, trying to understand. He struggled, in his characteristic way, to be fair.

"I don't want to seem as if I'm criticizing you, Ellen," he said, "but your feelings will change. They're not realistic."

"But they're my feelings," she snapped.

"I know, I know," he assured her, "but what I mean is there really isn't safety anywhere in the world. Look at Europe, look at Spain, look at China. All over the world people have had bad things happen to them. People have been bombed, tortured, murdered, lynched. In Rumania, the Nazis cut the throats of ordinary decent Jewish men, all the while they were killing them making jokes about making chickens kosher. In the South, right here in America, a Jewish businessman, Leo Frank, who never did anything wrong, was lynched by a mob. In the concentration camps people were frozen to death, beaten to death, had terrible experiments done on them. These people weren't different from you. One day they were safe in their little apartments and the next they were lying in mass graves. But even the people who got out of concentration camps went on living. They couldn't have lived if they'd kept looking back, remembering."

"Oh, easy enough for you to say," she said bitterly, "but I'm not interested in politics."

16

"What—what do you mean?" he stuttered. "How can you not be interested in politics? You're part of politics. Do you think all the Jews who died in Europe were interested in politics? No, they thought they could pray in *shul* and God would take care of them. They thought they'd be safe if they prayed. What a laugh. Their idea of safety was as crazy as yours, Ellen. How can you not be interested in politics? All there *is* is politics. Politics is the water you drink and the food you eat and the air you breathe. Politics is life."

"Shussh, someone will hear you." He was making her uncomfortable.

"Sorry," he said, flushing. "I guess I was getting carried away. All I mean to say, Ellen, is that you're not alone. You're part of a whole world of people who've been raped."

Ellen froze at that word. Icily she said, "I'm not going to see you anymore, Saul. You're a good person and I'll always be grateful but you're always going to remind me of what happened. Your ideas have nothing to do with me. I'm not somebody else who was tortured. I'm me, one person, and I have to live inside my own body with what happened to me, not with what happened to someone else. Even if every girl on my block had been attacked it wouldn't make me feel better. Their problems would still be their problems and mine would still be mine.

"You say there's no safety anywhere," she continued, "but that's not true. Rich people are safe everywhere. In Europe, even in Germany and Japan, rich people lived out the war in safety and they escaped and now they're right back in power again, living in their castles and châteaus, and the rich people were not the ones who were imprisoned and murdered."

"Except for Jews," he noted.

"Yes, yes," she said irritably, "but that's over and this is the United States and even here the rich ones, Jew and non-Jew alike, were the ones who got enough gasoline and nylons and meat and sugar, all through the war. They were the ones who could afford the black market, who never felt the war.

"No, Saul. I'm going to find a rich, strong man who can protect me against everything, and then I'll be able to forget what happened to me."

"So," he said heatedly, "your future plans are to sell yourself, like some kind of prostitute."

"No," she responded with equal anger, "like some kind of wife. I'll be a good wife. I won't marry anyone I don't love but the one I marry will have to be rich and powerful."

"What makes you think you can find someone like that in Brooklyn?" he asked.

"I'll take my chances," she said. They sat there for a moment in angry silence. Then he tried again to reason with her.

"You don't have to marry someone to keep from being raped," he said. "Honestly, Ellen, statistically I would think the chances of its happening again are remote."

"Will you stop saying that word," she hissed. "Somebody will hear you. You don't understand. I'm not only afraid of that thing happening again. I'm afraid of everything now. I have to be protected."

Ellen stood up to leave. "Goodbye, Saul," she said.

It was no use arguing with her, but Saul got in the last word. "You need a psychiatrist, not a rich husband."

She stalked away without looking back.

PART
ONE

1

The fear was still with her seven years later. Ellen gazed across the sunken living room of her home in Freeport, Long Island, and could hardly believe her luck. A fireplace, a real wall-width fieldstone fireplace, just like in the movies. And a bar from which she could serve drinks to guests. A bar, a fireplace, a home, a child, and exactly the best kind of husband to protect her from danger. So much for Saul's predictions. She was secure and safe. It was true that her nightmares persisted no matter how hard she tried to ignore them, but she felt as though she were a planet away from Borough Park.

Her first house: two bathrooms, two bedrooms, a large kitchen, a screened-in porch, and an enclosed backyard for three-year-old Jennifer. It had cost a staggering twenty-three thousand dollars, twenty thousand dollars more than her parents had been able to amass in a lifetime. But Jeff had calmly assured her that they could swing it and he was right about most things. Jeff Sheldon, her husband, her savior! Even after four years of marriage she still felt overwhelming gratitude to him for her safety, for her rescue.

Jeff Sheldon, wonderful Jeff Sheldon, handsome, tall, successful, the kind of husband anyone would want, anyone would envy. So strange to think that the first time she met him she had actually thought he might send her to jail, had thought this white knight of hers would be an instrument of doom. So strange to think that she would not have met Jeff had it not been for Saul. Another thing she now owed Saul! She pushed that thought from her mind.

After that bitter lunchroom confrontation with Saul, she had thought she would never see him again. She didn't want to. He was an endless reminder of the brutal night she had tried to forget. But in September, when she began classes at New York University, Saul was there, in every one of her classes. He was a scholarship student. She was surprised because her field, elementary education, was composed almost entirely of women.

"Isn't it a little peculiar for a man to be going into elementary education?" she asked him.

"I had to study what I could get a scholarship for," he said, "and I really like children."

But he didn't expect to teach for long. Because of the postwar baby boom there was a great need for elementary school principals and these jobs usually went to men. He would probably become a principal immediately. Any male in education could write his own ticket.

"Besides," he said, "if I don't like it, I can take my M.A. and doctorate in another field. I'm attracted to psychology, too."

"What would you want your doctorate for?" she asked.

"College teaching."

"It's hard for Jews to get college jobs," she said.

"Things are changing," he grinned. "By the time I'm ready for them they'll be ready for me."

So she started to see him again. He was so friendly, so decent, it was hard to push him away. And to what end? Even on the first days of college orientation it was evident that there were not many options for male companionship in elementary educa-

22

tion. There were twenty women to every man. She was not jeopardizing the kind of relationship she hoped for by being with him. There was no reason why she couldn't be friends with him, as she would be with any classmate. When she met her dream man, she could again sever this relationship.

The truth was that she enjoyed being with him. He was fun, kind, generous, and he went out of his way never to touch her, except in the most neutral, brotherly fashion. It pleased and reassured her that his knowledge of her secret did not make him think he had a hold over her.

In addition, he was completely nonmaterialistic, absorbed only in ideas, culture, all kinds of knowledge. He was always excited about ideas: literature, music, politics. His passion was buying books and every minute that she was in his company she was learning through him.

Unlike Ellen, he did not suffer from the stigma of being poor and living in Brooklyn. He never seemed to think about things like that. He said he would be ashamed to own a Cadillac while there were so many hungry people, and he really meant it. He didn't brood, as she did, about not knowing how to ski or play tennis, about not having a country home, about not having the correct clothing for every occasion. He was totally indifferent to status symbols.

Ellen also liked the way he related to people. He never held back from making friends because of fear of rejection. For the first time, through her association with him, she felt popular, accepted, part of a social group. Wouldn't she be foolish to throw this away before something better presented itself?

They became inseparable, traveling to and from Manhattan together on the subway each day, going at night to hootenannies to hear Woody Guthrie and Pete Seeger, attending lectures at the Jefferson School, concerts at Lewisohn Stadium, jazz sessions at coffeehouses on MacDougal Street, and browsing by the hour in Village bookstores. Saul was a jazz enthusiast and he took her to jam sessions all over the city. They went to hear Billie Holliday and Dizzy Gillespie on Fifty-second Street, Willie the Lion Smith and Anita O'Day at Birdland.

Saul had endless enthusiasms. He was wild about foreign films, *The New Yorker, New Masses,* I. F. Stone, and the street scene along the Lower East Side. He dragged her all over the city to demonstrations: demonstrations against the new loyalty oaths, against teacher firings, in support of the fur workers, and to march in May Day parades. He ate up New York City and his enthusiasms made her feel alive. But all the time, in her heart, she knew that she was only biding her time until she could find the man to keep her safe.

Her mother was, of course, furious about her constant association with Saul. Ellen learned to ignore the screams when her mother yelled out at her, from the front door, calling her "The Queen of Greenwich Village." If Saul was offended because she never dared to bring him home, he did not show it. Probably it never occurred to him.

During their junior year, Ellen became increasingly nervous about the closeness of their relationship. He was constantly bringing her petitions to sign, continuously involving her in left-wing politics about which she did not give a damn. She was too concerned with her own well-being to worry about other people. The country had become increasingly crazed on the subject of Communism, bringing about a mass hysteria unequaled since the Salem witch trials. Her nightmares grew worse and in her dreams her rapists were the policemen she had seen clubbing the striking fur workers.

The idea of "guilt by association" terrified her and she knew that their friends assumed she was a Communist merely because of her close association with Saul. She kept trying to pick fights about trifles in order to dissociate herself from him, but he was unfailingly amiable and understanding. Her attempts at self-preservation were also weakened because she hated to hurt him. If she were really to admit the truth, she knew she loved him. But it would never work. She couldn't shake the fear. With this in

24

mind, she applied for a summer job as a camp counselor. If she could get away from him for the summer, maybe she could maintain that distance when she returned to college in the fall.

One afternoon, shortly before the end of the spring semester, she returned home to find her mother sitting in the living room, talking to two strange men. Instantly, Ellen knew who they were, what they did, and what they were there for. She'd seen these men around the fringes of demonstrations, in courtroom scenes in movies, in newsreels. She could feel her stomach contract and her knees begin to tremble. She felt the same terror as the night of the rape.

One of the men, tall, fair, with beautiful blond hair and warm, sincere hazel eyes, was the handsomest man she'd ever seen off the screen.

The other man was dark-haired and also handsome. Fred MacMurray and Dan Dailey; not a wrinkle in either shirt. They wanted, of course, to ask her about Saul. She sat there trying to look calm, hating them, nauseated with fear. Her mother had been basking in their attention and was now oozing tea, cookies, and flattery at them.

"I told them you had nothing to hide," her mother urged, "that you would tell them anything they want to know."

"I don't know anything that would interest them," Ellen said, her mouth so dry she could hardly speak. She was afraid she'd blow it all by crying. She struggled, digging her nails into the palms of her hands and trying to think of something funny, to keep from crying. Keep calm, she told herself. They're not going to rape you. But they *are* trying to rape me, she answered herself. She lifted her chin and clenched her teeth to look defiant.

"What can you tell us about Saul Greenberg?" the dark-haired robot asked.

"What do you mean?" she answered in a whisper.

The fair one smiled. Condescending, supercilious son of a bitch, she thought. The dark-haired one started to question her. No, she didn't know anything about Saul's politics; all she knew was that he was a good, loyal American, the best kind. No, she was not interested in politics herself. No, she knew nothing about the politics of his friends. No, he had never discussed Communism with her. No, they were not engaged, not even sweethearts. They were merely classmates, platonic school friends. No, she had no knowledge of his future plans, no idea of what he did or where he went when she was not with him.

Finally, the dark-haired one looked at his watch and the two men started to leave. Ellen looked at their faces anxiously, trying to determine whether or not she had given them any information that might be harmful to Saul. She felt ripped apart with anguish at the thought that inadvertently she might have said something disloyal. The dark-haired one started to walk out but the fair, handsome one held back a moment and stood before her, looking down at her from his imposing height.

"You're a pretty brave girl," he said, "and a bright one, too. Your friend Saul is lucky to have you on his side."

She flushed. How did one respond to compliments from the enemy?

"But listen, Ellen," he said in a confidential, ingratiating tone, "you're keeping bad company. Any Jew who's a Commie nowadays is a fool. You should know how they treat Jews in Russia. They were better off under the czar. Wake up! This is a great country and it deserves the loyalty of all of us."

He patted her shoulder, flashed her a toothpaste smile, then nonchalantly, self-confidently, sauntered out.

"Now that's a *mensch,*" her mother said.

"Why don't you just shut up, you quisling, you," Ellen said, and she started to cry. She was furious with herself for having cringed in her soul, for having been so polite to those two. They had no right to come barging in that way. She called Saul and told him what had happened. He was more concerned about their upsetting Ellen than anything else.

"They shouldn't have bothered you. I know how frightened you get. Try not to stay upset."

"But what about you?" she asked.

26

"Don't worry. They're just fishing. Actually, in a way I'm flattered. I never thought I was that important."

Oh, Saul, you dear person, she thought.

"I may have said some wrong things," she whispered, "even though I tried to be careful."

"Please don't worry," he repeated. "There's nothing to worry about. If they really wanted me or had something on me, they'd get me, no matter what you said or didn't say. But I don't think they'll bother me. I'm too unimportant. Was your mother there?"

"Yes," Ellen said.

"I *am* sorry," he said. "She must have been pretty angry."

"Well, you know my mother."

"When are you leaving for camp?" he asked.

"Day after tomorrow."

"Can we get together tomorrow night to say goodbye?"

"Sure," she said. Saul was working in a cleaning store for the summer. She met him at the Chock full o'Nuts across from NYU and they strolled through the Village together.

"I hate to see you go away, Ellen," he said. "I'll really miss you."

"I'll miss you, too," she said, "but I'll be back in two months. We'll go back to school in September. Everything will be the way it was before."

"Well, listen, hey, don't meet a boyfriend at camp."

"Not likely," she said, feeling a little guilty because she really hoped she would, also feeling guilty because she knew she could never see as much of him in the future as in the past. It was too dangerous. He was her dearest friend but encounters with the FBI had nothing to do with what she wanted from life. She hugged him and kissed him lightly on the cheek. "Don't be sad," she said, but in her heart she knew she was saying goodbye.

She liked being at camp even more than she could have anticipated. It was the first time she had lived in the country and every smell and sight delighted her, the mists rising in the early

27

morning, the moon reflected in the placid lake, the hugs and kisses of her little charges. She spent long hours reading to them, playing with them, enjoying them, congratulating herself on her choice of future profession. During her free time she would take a rowboat out into the middle of the lake and sit there reading, feeling completely safe, completely at peace. For the first time in her life she was free of her mother and she dreaded returning to her tension-filled home.

But her respite from fear was short-lived. Ten days after she got there, on a Friday afternoon, standing in front of her bunk with her happy, shiny-faced, spruced-up children, waiting for evening services, she saw the tall, fair FBI agent who had come to her home walking toward her. She stood there in shocked, hopeless horror.

As he advanced, she said goodbye to all her dreams. Her mother's dire warnings rang in her ears and she ached for the memory of the past happy ten days, the only period she had ever known that was free of either tension or fear. What would she do now for a job? What would be the point of continuing to train as a teacher? The Board of Education had been purging all suspected left-wing teachers. Once they knew the FBI was on her tail, there would never be any possibility of getting a job. She willed herself not to tremble.

Oh, you fool, she mourned to herself. You've wrecked your life, you've wasted your life . . . and for what? What was the point of the sacrifice? Hypnotized, paralyzed, filled with resentment of Saul, wishing she had never met him, she waited. And then the FBI man was standing directly before her. She inclined her head like Anne Boleyn offering it to the executioner.

Then she heard his voice. "I don't believe it, what are you doing here?"

My God. Not an executioner. Just an ordinary person and it was evident that he was as surprised as she.

"I'm a counselor," she said with forced gaiety. "What are you doing here?"

"Visiting my kid sister. Do you know her?" He mentioned a junior counselor from another bunk.

Her sudden relief made her feel faint. Reprieved! He wasn't after her. The paranoia of the cold war era was contagious. She sank down on the grass, trying to look natural. The children, despite their Friday evening clothes, followed her lead and sank down with her. Ellen smiled weakly up at him and he joined them on the grass.

"I know who your sister is," Ellen said, "but I've never actually spoken to her."

He was beaming at her, liking her, acting friendly. "Would you like to come out with us tonight to celebrate?" he asked.

"What are you celebrating," she asked, "putting somebody in jail?"

He laughed uproariously at this, not the slightest bit offended.

"I don't do that anymore," he said. "That's what we're celebrating, my new career. I've just bought half of a PR agency."

"Then I'd love to go out with you," she said. "That's a great thing to celebrate."

In the back of her mind there was a tiny grain of suspicion. Perhaps he *was* still working for the FBI. Perhaps he was just trying to disarm her and worm more information out of her. No, that was ridiculous. He really had been surprised to see her. Anyway, she had nothing more to say and no matter what his motives, how often did she get a night away from camp? Just the thought of an alternative to camp cuisine—the endless parade of starches, mystery meat, and overcooked vegetables—filled her with anticipation. So she got one of the other counselors to cover her for the evening and met Jeff and his sister, Mimi, at the parking lot. His car looked very old and not American, though it was in superb condition.

"What kind of car is this?" Ellen asked.

"It's an old Renault," Jeff said. "I bought it from a fellow who brought it here before the war on one of the Cunard liners."

Then he looked at her directly. "Hey," he said, "you look great."

Ellen blushed, glad that her appearance pleased him. She had spent a lot of time tweezing her eyebrows, setting her hair, and experimenting with makeup borrowed from another counselor. She had chosen her most slimming clothes and she thought that she didn't look all that bad.

She slid into the front seat while Jeff held the door for her. His sister sat by the window. As they drove to the restaurant, Mimi chattered adoringly about how Jeff had found this old wreck of a car and made it look almost new. Ellen murmured occasional comments, glad that the conversation was being carried by someone else. She was still a little shy, worried that Mimi would resent her presence.

While Jeff drove, Ellen studied his handsome profile. She had always adored blond hair. What exquisite manners he had. No man had ever before opened a car door for her. Saul didn't have a car, of course, but even so, Saul didn't bother with what he called, "bourgeois formalities," such things as holding doors, holding chairs for women, the sort of polite behavior that Emily Post considered absolutely necessary in society. Ellen was also impressed because Jeff was the first man who had ever told her, "You look great."

Her father would look at her and nod, as if to say, "Not beautiful but good," and Saul thought that the obsession with beauty in American culture was a sign of decadence. He always thought Ellen looked "fine," because all that mattered to him was her mind and political philosophy. She had long since realized that she'd never be any great beauty, but she had an enormous hunger to be attractive and longed to turn even one man's head when she entered a room. Now, here was this gorgeous man with his own car, telling her she looked great.

"Whom does she remind you of, Mimi?" Jeff asked as he drove. Mimi, a pleasant girl who shared none of Jeff's beauty, studied Ellen's face for a few seconds then said, "You're right, Jeff."

30

"Well," Ellen laughed, a little embarrassed, "who?"

"Our mother," Mimi said, looking sad, "she died of pneumonia last winter. You really do resemble her."

Ellen felt simultaneously pleased and embarrassed. For want of conversation she said, "You and Jeff don't resemble each other very much."

"It's his gorgeous new nose," Mimi giggled, while Jeff glared at her. "I'll have mine fixed, too, when I have some money."

They drove into Woodstock and stopped at a rustic-looking restaurant called L'Auberge. Jeff had made a reservation and he addressed the maitre d' in perfect, lilting French. Ellen was impressed again. They were shown to a table and Jeff ushered her protectively, a hand resting lightly on her back as he pulled out a chair for her and held it, making her feel fragile, special, precious.

"You speak French so beautifully," Ellen said, admiringly.

"Flatterer." Jeff smiled.

"He speaks six languages," his sister said proudly. "He majored in languages at college with a minor in French and Italian and he learned Japanese, Russian, and German in officers' language school. His French was so good they couldn't believe he had never been to France."

"I'd never been anywhere outside of New York City until the war," Jeff said. "My father was a post office worker."

Ellen sat there digesting this. She felt great admiration for Jeff, who seemed so Ivy League despite his poor background.

"Say something in French," Mimi said.

"Come on, Mimi," he chided gently, "stop embarrassing me."

"Oh, don't be embarrassed," Ellen said quickly, completely at ease now that she knew about his humble beginnings. "I think it's wonderful to have a sister who's so proud of you. I've always been sorry I didn't have any sisters or brothers."

"I guess you've needed an ally for defense against your formidable mother." Jeff grinned, and Ellen really liked him for understanding what she had to put up with.

"I've only taken one year of high school French," Ellen told him, "then I switched to Spanish. I don't seem to have much talent for languages but I adore the sound of French. I love Jean Gabin movies."

"I do, too." He smiled at her. "The best thing about French is that you can say anything, even the most pedestrian things, and they sound romantic. For example, I could say to you, *'J'ai envie d'avoir un cireuse électrique pour la cuisine,'* and it would sound swell."

"It does sound swell." She smiled, feeling inexplicably gay. "But what does it mean?"

"I wish I had an electric waxer for my kitchen," he said. The three of them burst into laughter. So this is happiness, Ellen thought.

"Say something else," she said.

"J'ai faim, et si je ne vois pas la carte, ma petite soeur va mordre le garçon," Jeff said flawlessly.

"What does that mean?" Ellen giggled.

"It means, 'I'm hungry, and if I don't see the menu, my little sister is going to bite the waiter.' "

"Jeff," Mimi squealed. "You're terrible but I am starving."

Jeff signaled to the waiter, who brought the menu. When Ellen stared at it, she felt completely out of her depth. She didn't want him to know how unsophisticated she was, that she had never been to a French restaurant. She had no idea what most of the items were. *Poulet* she knew was chicken and *fromage* meant cheese. But after that, she was lost.

"There's so much to choose from," she faltered.

"How about letting me do the ordering?" Jeff asked, and the two girls readily agreed. Ellen was happy again, enjoying a delicious sense of being taken care of. How wonderful it was to be out with a man of the world.

Jeff looked at the menu for a moment and the waiter hovered at his elbow respectfully. "How are the *escargots?*" Jeff asked.

"Excellent, monsieur."

"All right then," Jeff said. "*Escargots* for three, quenelles with the sorrel sauce, and the endive salad.

"And bring us," he said, studying the wine list, "the *Pouilly Fuissé.*"

The waiter bobbed his head in approval, gathered the menus, and glided away. He was back in a moment with the wine, which he opened with a flourish. He poured a little for Jeff, who picked up the glass by the stem, sloshed the wine around, took a mouthful, held the wine in his mouth, sloshed that around, then swallowed it, aware that the waiter and diners at the tables around him were watching him in fascination. He looked thoughtful for a moment while the waiter watched his face anxiously. Then, at last, Jeff smiled and the waiter, relieved, echoed his smile.

"An excellent year," Jeff said loudly to his audience; "you may pour for the ladies."

Ellen melted with pleasure. It was just like in the movies and it was what she had always dreamed of; not Chock full o'Nuts with Saul, not Ratner's Kosher East Side restaurant with her parents, but a French restaurant with someone who knew what he was doing. Even if she didn't like the wine. Her experience was limited to Manischewitz's wine, one step from grape juice, which her mother served for Passover. Tonight's wine wasn't sweet, was nothing like grape juice, but if you just sipped it, taking little sips, it didn't taste too bad.

"What did you order for dinner?" Mimi asked.

"Don't you trust me?" Jeff asked disarmingly, looking deep into Ellen's eyes as he answered his sister.

"Oh, yes," Ellen breathed.

"First tell me what you ordered," Mimi joked, "then I'll tell you if I trust you."

"*Escargots* are snails served in garlic butter."

33

"Ycch," Mimi said.

"Snails?" Ellen repeated.

"Please trust me," Jeff said affably. "If you don't like them, I'll send them back and order anything your little heart desires. Tonight, the sky's the limit. I want to make you happy. Can I make you happy?"

"Oh, yes," Ellen breathed, feeling as if she were floating in the air like the bride in a Chagall painting she had seen. His beauty made her dizzy.

While they waited for the food Ellen stole a sideways glance at Jeff's sister. Now she could see the resemblance but it was amazing how a changed nose had made such a difference. Ellen had worried about intruding but Mimi acted as if she were the outsider on Jeff and Ellen's date. She didn't seem to mind at all and there was no doubt but that it felt like a date, a lovely, glamorous, storybook date.

When they finished the first bottle of wine, Jeff ordered a second, and all three of them found that they were increasingly clever, amusing, good company, and happy. The *escargots* were as delicious as Jeff had promised, a little rubbery and garlicky but amazingly tasty. "A toast," Jeff announced loudly, holding up his glass, "to the lucky man who is surrounded by two lovely women, fine food, and the world that's waiting for him."

"Amen," Ellen said, gladly toasting him. She was in a trance, enchanted by this suave and elegant prince.

"Next," Jeff announced, "we have quenelles, which is the French word for very light fish dumplings." Then, putting on a French accent, he said, "Eet ees ze French equivalent of zee gefilte fish."

The three of them almost collapsed under the table at that one. Other diners looked with indulgence at the young people who were having such a fine time.

So this is what it feels like to drink, Ellen thought. How lovely, how light, like bubbles, like flying. Oh, please God, let him like me, let him like me.

34

When the quenelles came, Ellen said, "If I were French, I'd have these all the time. They're nothing like gefilte fish. These melt in your mouth."

"You look like you could be French," Jeff said, "doesn't she, Mimi?"

Mimi looked up from stuffing and nodded. It was obvious that she adored her sophisticated brother. She probably would have nodded to anything he said at that point.

"When you travel in Europe," Jeff continued, "you'll get good treatment because you won't look like the typical American tourist. Even though they're grateful to us for winning the war for them, they're still a little wary of folks in their Bermuda shorts with their cameras, popping out of every church and fountain. The gratitude of the Europeans doesn't stop them from trying to cheat us, I've found."

How thrilling. He knew Europe and, as he talked, the dream of travel also became a reality. Jeff was a spinner of dreams and he could easily convince you that the dreams would come true. If only she could travel with him, be with him forever. With a man like Jeff at her side, she would both belong to the world and be protected from it. But suppose she never saw him again after tonight? How could she lapse back to her former dull, drab existence after seeing how pleasant life could be? Well, he seemed to like her, toasting her each time he refilled the wineglasses, occasionally placing his hand on her own with a light, warm touch, assuming correctly that she welcomed his touch. She warned herself not to hope. This was probably the way men of the world acted with every woman. What a charmer he was. She'd often heard people described as "charmers" but Jeff was the first person she'd met who fitted that description. Also, she'd always thought it was a pejorative word, but you couldn't think so with Jeff. He was making her feel important. Of course, that was what charmers did, but maybe he really did like her. She continued to smile while her mind, despite the wine, kept racing around, tumbling over itself, worrying and hoping.

"I hoped I'd see you again," he murmured to her. "I liked you right away, Ellen, because you were so spunky. And my first impression was right. You're the most comfortable girl I've ever been out with. You're a great listener." Ellen beamed.

The waiter brought chocolate mousse and espresso and then the meal was over, the first sophisticated meal of her life. Full of good feelings, they drove back to the camp. Mimi said goodnight and went off to her bunk and Jeff and Ellen sat together in the car, talking, not wanting to say goodbye. The wine was wearing off and Ellen felt a vague sense of depression, but she knew there was a question she would have to ask Jeff before she became further involved with him. It was now or never.

"Jeff," she said, faltering as she drew his attention.

"Ma'am," he said with a mock southern accent, putting his arm around her shoulder.

"Jeff, I have to ask you a question."

"The answer, my love," he said, "is no. I am not engaged and I do not have another girl friend."

"That's not the question," she insisted, but she was glad to hear the answer.

"Okay," he said pleasantly, "what is it?"

"Jeff, I just want to know. I have to know. How could you work for the FBI? I mean, all that stuff, spying on innocent people, sending people to jail, ruining their lives?"

"Why shouldn't I have worked for the FBI?" he answered, not unkindly, genuinely surprised. "I fought for this country, didn't I?"

"But the FBI is different," she said. "They do terrible things."

"The Communists are doing worse things," he said. "Haven't you heard about their persecution of the Jews? Haven't you heard about the Jewish doctors being railroaded with phony trials? The Communists are a menace to the entire world and every one of us should devote all of our energies to stopping them right now, or they'll take over the world. People like you just don't see the larger picture. We should have dropped the atom bomb on Russia or Germany, not on Japan. Honestly, Ellen, do you think your outspoken friend Saul would be running around free in the Soviet Union? Not in a pig's ear. If you want a really good picture of what's going on in that country, read *1984*."

"Jeff," she said, not wanting to offend him, "I understand what you're saying but an awful lot of innocent people have been getting hurt."

"Where there's smoke, there's fire," he said. "But why should we talk about that now, Ellen? That's the past. From now on I'm strictly a businessman. Forget these silly ideological differences. The Japanese have a saying, 'There are many different flowers in the garden but each of them is beautiful.' You and I are two different kinds of flowers but tonight we found each other beautiful. Let's not spoil a beautiful beginning. You don't want to do that, do you?"

"Oh, no, no, no," she said, "of course I don't."

"I'm going to level with you, Ellen," he said, "the truth of the matter is I don't give a damn about politics for two reasons. The first reason is that an individual can never make much of a difference in a society as vast as ours, and the second reason is that I want to get ahead."

"Of course you'll get ahead," Ellen said. "Everything about you is just right. You exude success. You're the kind of person who is successful."

"That's what I figure, too," Jeff said. "I want to get rich and lead the good life with a wife and a couple of kids. And I can do it in public relations by concentrating on foreign markets. Where else can the Latin Americans get American know-how with a fine Spanish accent? I'm moving in big circles now. From that I've developed German accounts. It's good business. That's really all that matters. And I think I can get what I want. When I really want something, I go after it and don't stop until it's mine. But Ellen, politics is a trap. Those left-wing Commie friends of yours live poor and die poor. You don't learn how to survive in America by reading the *Daily Worker*. You learn to survive by reading the *Wall Street Journal*. And maybe even once in a while, *Fortune* magazine. Now, have I answered your question?"

Well, he really hadn't, but what the hell. She looked at him, nodded, smiled, and the next thing she knew she was in his arms. He really likes me, she thought as he kissed her passionately. She could hardly believe her luck.

"God, I'm comfortable with you," he said when he finally released her. "I love the way you look at me and listen and seem to think that everything I say is important."

"Everything you say is important," she said. "You're the most interesting person I've ever met. I feel as if I'm learning, every minute with you."

He looked at her and beamed with pride. She realized that she had said exactly the right thing, had felt exactly the right way.

"I have to go," he said. "It's a long drive back to the city. Keep your dance card open for next weekend."

Another long, lingering kiss. Then, with his arms around her, almost swooning with bliss, she kissed him again and said goodnight. All night she lay awake thinking about him. If you forgot about the FBI, he was exactly what she wanted. He was Jewish, smart, cultured, handsome, charming, suave, affectionate, and he had read Keats and Orwell. This was the man of her dreams. Jeff would be her very own knight, her handsome stranger who would tuck her away in a velvet-lined nest and keep her safe forever.

She had to admit that she felt guilt about Saul, but why should she? She hadn't promised him anything. Well, maybe there are promises people make to each other without words, but she had always told Saul about the kind of husband she needed. Saul would get over it. She was really doing him a favor. He could never be happy with someone whose needs were so different from his own.

She lay there thinking about Jeff's kisses. He was the first man ever to kiss her so passionately but she had felt nothing but a desire to please, to attract, to make him hers. She couldn't tell if her lack of passion was based on Jeff or on the rape. But what difference did it make anyway? How important was sex? Gail, the married counselor with whom she had become friendly, had told her that her wedding night was sheer agony but the passion she now had for her husband made it very difficult for her to be on the girls' side of the camp and to see him only at meals. And this passion, Gail had added, had not flowered until months after the marriage. Maybe that's how it would be with her and Jeff. Gail had also told Ellen that when she got married she wasn't a virgin but her husband hadn't even noticed. "If they get steamed up enough," Gail had said, "they don't notice a little thing like that." Ellen had been especially glad to receive this bit of information.

All right. So she hadn't felt any passion for Jeff tonight when he'd kissed her. That didn't mean anything. She was sure that, once married, her recurring nightmares of the rape would finally stop and she would become normal. And she was sure of another thing, too. If she were lucky enough to marry Jeff, she would do her best to make him happy for the rest of his life. She would be the best listener, the most supportive friend, the wisest and most discreet confidante. If things didn't work out for them sexually, she would never let him know. No, if she got him, she would treat him like a king for the rest of his life.

He came up the next weekend and took her to a local performance of *Madame Butterfly*. She had never before been to an opera and when the curtain went down and the lights went up, she and Jeff sat in their seats for a while, until she had stopped crying. Poor Madame Butterfly. It was so unfair. She had given her best to this man who felt no responsibility to her. It was a universal problem. That's what made the story so powerful.

"Oh, Jeff," she snuffled afterward when they were alone, "that was one of the great experiences of my life. I wasn't just weeping about the story. I was weeping because human beings can reach such heights through art. It kind of makes you proud to be a human being. I'd like to know so much more about opera."

"You can go with me," he said tenderly; "we'll get subscriptions to the Met."

Her heart turned over. She sipped her drink, a whiskey sour on the rocks, which she liked as much as she had the wine, and beamed at him. How happy it made her just to be with him. Whatever happened in the future, nothing would ever obliterate these golden days of courtship.

The next day, her day off, they took a picnic lunch and a boat far off to the other side of the lake. After lunch he stretched himself on the ground, lit a cigarette, and turned to her, "Oh, Ellen," he said:

> *"A Book of Verses underneath the Bough,*
> *A jug of Wine, a Loaf of Bread—and Thou*
> *Beside me singing in the Wilderness—*
> *Oh, Wilderness were Paradise enow!"*

"I love *The Rubaiyat* also," she said in a tender voice.

"Ellen," he asked, "Ellen, will you marry me?"

Her heart turned over and a great blaze of glorious light exploded in her head. There it was. It was done. That easily had she attained her heart's desire.

"Oh, Jeff," she said, the tears raining down.

"Why are you crying?" he asked.

"This is the happiest day of my life," she said.

"All the rest of your life is going to be happy, too," he said.

"People will say we're crazy, after only two weeks."

"How long did it take Romeo and Juliet?" he asked her. "Well," he teased, "you haven't really answered me."

Ellen suddenly knew there was a God and that if there was a heaven, this was it. "Oh, Jeff," she said, "I would feel . . . blessed." Then she began to weep again, joyfully, thankfully, while Jeff stroked her hair and made her promises for the future that not even a God could keep.

The wedding was set for the last weekend in August, so they could have the Labor Day weekend to move her into Jeff's New York City apartment. Each day, she could not believe her luck. It was everything she had dreamed of, this handsome white knight come to carry her across the water from Brooklyn to the world.

Jeff, traditional and conventional, approved of waiting until their wedding night before they slept together. Throughout the rest of the summer, he would visit her at camp and they would neck and pet and Jeff's face would grow hot and he would breathe heavily and moan and tell her he could hardly wait until their wedding night. She was pleased that she aroused him and although she continued to feel nothing, he seemed to think she was as passionate as he.

She had decided that she would never let him know her secret, never let him know of the rape, as much to protect him as to protect herself. She wanted him to feel proud of her, to see her as something special, something worth attaining, not in the way she perceived herself, as damaged goods.

Her mother had made all of the arrangements for their simple wedding but Ellen left camp ten days before the end, in order to have time to shop for her mother wanted her to get married in a long white wedding dress. "After all, you are our only child." Ellen also bought a going-away suit and a few skirts and blouses. For the first time in her life, she bought new panties, girdles, bras, and stockings all at one time. She and her mother even picked out a beautiful nightgown and peignoir for the wedding night.

Everything seemed easy, everything was falling into line. There was only one problem she still had not confronted: what to do about Saul. "I don't owe him anything," she kept telling herself, feeling anger at him because she felt guilty. But she had to see him; at the very least she owed him a goodbye.

They met at their old haunt, Chock full o'Nuts, at Washington Square. She blurted out her news immediately. She couldn't tell which part of her story shocked him the most, the rapidity of her engagement, losing her, or the fact that it was Jeff she was marrying.

"You can't be marrying a guy who worked for the FBI," was the first thing he said, looking dazed.

"He's not that way," Ellen protested. "He's different from the stereotype. He's even Jewish."

"Big deal," Saul said, "Hitler was part Jewish too."

"Hitler wasn't Jewish," Ellen said, "that's the craziest idea I've heard from you yet."

"He was so part Jewish," Saul insisted, "and he hated himself for it. That's why he wanted to wipe out all Jews; to wipe out the Jewish part of himself."

"I'm not interested in discussing Hitler," Ellen said with annoyance, "we're discussing Jeff and my impending marriage and I'm telling you that he's sensitive, cultured. He likes opera and he quotes poetry."

"The Nazis liked Mozart."

"If you say one more word about the Nazis," she warned, "I'm going to walk away. I came here because I wanted to tell you about my marriage and you're upsetting me. Would you like to come? It's a very small wedding, only twenty people, but I'd like you to be there."

"No, thanks," Saul said. "I'm a poor loser."

Silence fell between them for a moment. She looked at his face and realized that he was trying not to cry. She wanted to put her arms around him to comfort him for her defection.

"Please tell me you're joking, Ellen," he said, with one last burst of hope. "Tell me it's not true. You wouldn't sell out for a Arrow-collar ad, would you?"

"I'm not selling out," she snapped. "I'm in love and I'm marrying the man I love."

"I thought you loved me," he said sadly. "Don't you love me?"

"I'll always love you, as a platonic friend, as a brother. But I told you a long time ago, Saul, what kind of man I wanted to marry. I never lied to you. I always told you the truth."

"I never thought you meant it," he said in that same dejected tone. "I always thought you'd grow out of it."

"I meant it. I'm crazy about him and I'm marrying him."

"You're making a big mistake, Ellen," he said. "You will never be happy with the kind of guy who could work for the FBI."

"I don't want to discuss it anymore," she said. "I have to go now. Call me if you change your mind and want to come to my wedding."

"I won't change my mind," he said. "I guess I overestimated you."

He got up and walked out after flinging some change on the counter. Ellen could see that he was crying. Whenever she thought of him for a long time afterward she would get a hollow aching feeling in her chest. But now, she would have to push him out of her thoughts.

Ellen and Jeff were married the following week at the temple in Borough Park. It was a simple, inexpensive wedding but her father and mother looked so happy, so pleased with Jeff, so proud of him as they introduced him to their friends and relatives, that she knew she had chosen correctly. The only thing that marred the wedding for Ellen was that Jeff had forbidden Mimi, of whom Ellen had become very fond, from attending because he didn't like the left-wing crowd she had become involved with in Greenwich Village. Ellen felt sad that Jeff had no relatives there but he didn't seem to mind at all. He refused to discuss the subject of Mimi. After the wedding they piled her few possessions into Jeff's car and drove to his apartment. A honeymoon would come later, during Jeff's Christmas vacation. And then, there they were on their wedding night, Mr. and Mrs. Jeff Sheldon. Standing close together, they looked out of the bay window over New York City. A soft breeze blew in and ruffled her hair.

"Come to bed, my love," Jeff said.

Oh, God, Ellen thought, this was it. She hoped that Gail was right and that Jeff wouldn't notice that she was not a virgin. She had read several books about sex and they dispelled for her the myth that every woman has a strong hymen. In many women, the hymen gets broken just by normal activities. But it wasn't her concern over the hymen that was bothering her. It was the feelings of nausea that kept sweeping through her, up and down, as if she were on a boat. She kept warning herself sternly not to make a mess of this, to be rational and forget the past, but the very thought of sexual intercourse filled her with horror.

They undressed separately, shyly, then faced each other and went to bed. Jeff was rapturous, so involved in his own passion that he was unaware, fortunately, of her reactions. But Ellen kept seeing the faces of those ravaging monsters leaning over her, hurting her, humiliating her. She clenched her fists and closed her eyes and willed herself to give and have pleasure . . . but to no avail. All she could feel was an intense desire to have it over with so she could take a bath, wash the traces away, go to sleep, and wake the next morning as a young wife.

"Move, honey, move a little," Jeff moaned. She tried to move back and forth. "Yes, yes, that's the way," he said, close to orgasm.

From a distance she watched Jeff moving over her, loving her, making love to her, feeling, sighing, moaning, and then, with a joyous shout coming and coming and coming, filling her with horrible fluid. She couldn't decide, as he lay on her, exhausted, if she wanted to throw up or take a bath first.

"That was wonderful, love," Jeff said. "Don't worry, you'll loosen up eventually."

He rolled off her and was instantly asleep. Ellen got up and went into the bathroom. While the tub filled, she retched into the toilet. Then she threw in a large amount of bath crystals and the perfumed steam reassured her as she entered the loving embrace of the scented water. She washed and washed and washed, hating the moisture so deep inside her. Eventually, the water tranquilized her and she began to feel happy again. Well, sex was pretty unappealing, but so what? She would never show her distaste to Jeff, never cease to be grateful to him. Jeff was exactly everything she had wanted. He would protect her against all other men. The only thing, she asked herself as she stepped out of the tub, was the ironic question, "But who would protect her against Jeff?"

Jeff rolled over as she got back into bed. Then he reached for her, took her hand, and she felt his hard, hot penis.

"I want you again," he murmured. She could have screamed with grief.

In the four years that had passed since then, sex had remained a horrible act to be endured. She had actually welcomed her immediate pregnancy because it had, eventually, saved her from six months of sex. The pregnancy had also meant she couldn't finish her last year of college but she supposed she could always go back if she wanted to. Actually, now that she was supported by an up-and-coming young man, both Jeff and her mother assured her she had no need to work and so it didn't matter about the degree.

Her distaste for sex continued to plague her. It was even worse for her than for Victorian women, Ellen told herself, because they were taught it was correct to feel distaste but she felt guilty about it. In the twentieth century people were supposed to enjoy sex. But four years after marriage, the strongest inducement to liking sex had gone. To her utter amazement, she realized one day that she no longer liked Jeff. In addition, when the baby was two, she'd had a bad miscarriage.

Okay, okay, she had told herself, you can't have everything. It's a trade-off. Mephistopheles says you can have the American dream if you give up sex and repress your critical faculties. Would you take the deal? Of course she still would and without hesitation. So there they were, the all-American successful young suburban couple.

She had to admit that Jeff had fulfilled his part of the bargain. He had bought them their house, helped to produce a child, and was still affectionate. After four years, she was still grateful to him. How could she not be grateful for this beautiful house? The truth was however that she would have preferred to stay in Manhattan, close to movies, museums, shops, and her old Greenwich Village haunts. But that was not what young married couples were doing in the early fifties. Jeff's clients and colleagues had all followed the identical pattern: pregnancy and suburbs. "Who would want to bring up a child in Manhattan?" was the clichéd query of young wives, and Ellen had to repress the desire to say, "Me, me, me." She lacked the courage to express her seemingly selfish desires. She hadn't even really wanted a child this early but she went along with the pattern, thinking she must be wrong and all the others right.

Jeff worked such long hours that it would have been far better for him if they had remained in the city, but he said it was worth the hour commute to have a backyard for little Jennifer. He left home at 8:00 A.M. and rarely returned before midnight. Ellen would have preferred to work those long hours rather than to endure the boredom and isolation of the suburbs. After a while Jeff began to stay in the city for two or three nights during the week and Ellen found herself alone a great deal, but since he was only doing it for her and Jennifer, she tried to accept it all. "Don't worry about me," she had told him, "I have Jennifer and Pat for company."

Pat was the English au pair girl they had hired when Jennifer was born, and Ellen was genuinely fond of the cheerful young woman whose seeming contentment and lack of complexity she envied. After Pat arrived, Ellen was even more agreeable about Jeff's absences.

"No sex tonight," she would think with pleasure as she piled books on Jeff's half of the bed. Well, she had what she wanted. She was protected and secure and Jeff had begun to make a lot of money from the day they were married. But she kept feeling she had lost herself.

When she'd found herself pregnant immediately after marriage, she had wanted an abortion. Jeff had looked at her as if she were a murderer. "You'd have to go to Cuba for it," he had told her, "and God only knows if the operation would be sanitary. You might never be able to have kids after that and I want kids, Ellen. Lots of them. The rest of the world is like Versailles . . . especially in my racket. You can't trust anyone but your family. Please, Ellen. You have the kids and I'll pay for them. If you have this one, I'll buy you your first mink coat."

So along came Jennifer, the mink coat, and the suburbs where she knew nobody and had nothing to do with herself but go to the supermarket and brood about her mistake in marrying Jeff. She could have written a catalog of things she disliked about him. She had married so quickly, in such desperate haste, that there hadn't been time to examine and understand the character and personality of her husband. In her need for safety, she had pushed aside certain clues, been willingly blind to them.

She had since discovered that he was only interested in business. He read nothing except for the financial page of the *New York Times,* over which he would sweat and groan each morning. He had no hobbies, hated the movies (which she loved), despised the theater and art and had only a superficial interest in opera, mainly because it was so fashionable. The poems he had quoted to her exhausted his entire repertoire and she now had the feeling that he had used the same lines with other women. Jeff's only attitude toward culture was to use it for a few tag lines that would give a good impression. He had no real interest in anything but business success.

Even that meal in the restaurant had been designed only to impress her and his sister. Actually, cooking and haute cuisine lacked interest for him. He would patronize the best restaurants on Diner's Club just to be seen there and to be able to refer familiarly to them, but he didn't really care what he ate. Jeff would just as soon eat cornflakes as steak and his favorite foods were those of childhood: fruit Jell-O, chocolate pudding, rice pudding, mashed potatoes, hamburgers, chocolate cake, and milk.

47

She also disapproved of Jeff's attitude toward people. He was a user, a consumer, a spoiler, a person who took from the world but gave nothing back unless there was a payoff. He really cared about no one but himself. He believed that the poor, the maimed, the unfortunate, the unsuccessful were that way because they deserved it. "Fuck 'em if they can't make it. I'm all right, Jack," just about summed up his attitude.

Jeff's contempt for people extended everywhere. He regarded the masses as consumers whose value to him lay only in the extent to which they supported the firms he represented. When a PR campaign bombed, he would shake his handsome head and moan, "What are you going to do when people are so stupid they don't know what's good for them?" But if the public responded to his publicity, he would feel an equal contempt for their gullibility. "Stupid broads," he would say, referring to housewives. "They'll believe anything." He could relate to people only in terms of his business.

Through his business, they now had a busy social life. Ellen knew she never would have been invited to so many elegant cocktail parties were she not married to Jeff, and each time she entered one of them on his arm she felt lucky again. She mingled little at these parties but just stood beside him unobtrusively as he socialized. She would stand and smile and listen but would often feel a tumult of embarrassment within. For Jeff did not know how to converse with people. He did not talk and listen. In a conversation he would attempt either to solicit or impress, brag about how much money his firm was making, talk about new accounts, bad-mouth competitors, and describe future PR campaigns in boring detail.

Because Jeff was so handsome, many women tried to connect with him at parties and, seeing how desirable he seemed to be, Ellen would momentarily feel fortunate again. To his credit, he seemed oblivious to the invitations of other women. Business, money, power were his goals, not women. The unmarried ones would approach him, listen for a while to his reverence for the "PR racket," and then their eyes would glaze over and they would drift away when it became evident that no overtures for future meetings were being made. The married women, already bored with listening to their own husbands, would drift away even sooner. If you cranked him up he would discuss the PR business like the second coming but if the corporate button weren't pressed, he would sit off in a corner and make little notes in the black notebook he always carried. The only way to Jeff's heart was through a new account.

Once a woman at one of these parties had asked Ellen what Jeff was like at home. "Exactly the way he is here," Ellen had said, "his overriding interest in life is his business."

It was impossible to discuss personal problems or feelings with him. She had tried many times to discuss her distaste for sex and each time he would interrupt to tell her she was perfectly fine, then change the subject quickly to describe his latest campaign. She never responded enthusiastically but he never noticed.

"Don't worry," he would say, "I enjoy making love to you." He was already making notes for the next campaign. He was, at that time, never blue, moody, or depressed and so he couldn't understand her shifts of mood. His usual solution when she told him she was depressed was to tell her to go buy something, take a Miltown, take a drink. He was a great believer in the theories of Dale Carnegie. "You can't allow yourself to have negative feelings," he told her. "Try to control them the way I do. Negative feelings slow you up, they're bad for business."

Sex remained the major arena of her unhappiness. She remembered wistfully the time she had gone to the Margaret Sanger clinic for a diaphragm, shortly after their marriage, and had struck up a conversation with a pretty and friendly young woman who sat beside her. The woman had confided that she could not work in her new husband's store because she couldn't keep her hands off him. "I keep wanting to drag him in back to make love," the woman had told her. Ellen had listened in wonder and sorrow. It seemed that she alone was to be permanently barred from sexual pleasure.

To begin with, Jeff always hurt her. When his hand rubbed

49

across her clitoris (on the rare occasions that he could find it), it felt like sandpaper. His touch felt hostile and unpleasant. When his hands moved across her back, instead of stroking her, his fingers would dig deeply in, leaving finger-shaped black-and-blue marks wherever he touched her. She loved to have her nipples bitten but whenever he did, they were sore for days afterward. All of his insensitivities to people showed in the way he made love.

Jennifer's birth did not change her frigidity. When she started to have vaginal infections after Jennifer was born and she learned the names of a whole new family of germs, she actually welcomed the infections because each time she would legitimately be unable to have sex for a certain period of time to which she could always add a week or so.

Once the doctor had pointed out that she did seem to get an inordinate amount of infections. "Do you think your husband has sexual contact with anyone else?" he had asked, to which she had honestly and indignantly retorted that Jeff was above suspicion, just as she was. It was just something wrong with her body chemistry and poor Jeff was unfailingly patient about the long sexless periods.

Now here she was, after four years of marriage, with one child, one lovely house, one successful husband, a fine future, and she was frigid. When they made love she remained so tight, so constricted, that even after Jennifer's birth he still hurt her. The diaphragm jelly didn't help; it couldn't lubricate what didn't want to yield. Maybe nobody could have erased the scars of the rape, maybe nobody could have made her more responsive, she thought, but with Jeff there was still another problem. She didn't like the way he smelled. He was clean, of course, lots of deodorant and after-shave with interchangeable, masculine names; an endless stream of gifts and samples from his clients, so that wasn't the cause. It was the natural human body smell under all of the gook he sampled and wore and publicized and believed in, which repelled her.

50

At night, no matter how cold it was, he'd sweat and his sweat smelled rancid and unpleasant. After a while she had a name for it: Madison Avenue jitters sweat and she was always afraid the smell would cling to her. In the mornings, she would pick up his pajamas with the tips of her fingers and drop them down the laundry chute along with the sheets, pillow cases, and her nightgown. She bought two different colored pillows for them so that he would not accidentally use hers. Jeff thought she was irrationally neat, but he saw it as her problem, not as his, and they never discussed it. Who would ever think that under that magnificent exterior lurked a bad smell; a castle with decayed plumbing.

But of all Jeff's characteristics, the one that upset her the most, the one that drove her wild, was his chronic lateness. It was in regard to time that his contempt for people became most apparent. He was never less than an hour late for an appointment, and had been known to extend this to as much as three hours. The most irritating thing about him was that he never called to announce the delay. Lesser mortals were just supposed to understand his foibles, find them charming, and wait for him indefinitely, and with patience.

If a frustrated person-in-waiting left the meeting place, Jeff would eventually phone and rant and rave in an aggrieved tone: "You knew I'd show. You could have waited. Here I am killing myself for you and you're making a federal case out of this. All right, all right, string me up by my thumbs. Honestly, do you think I like to be late? I'm a nervous wreck because I was so worried about getting to you on time. Listen, I tried to call. I tried over and over again. Honest! The goddamned telephone company is falling apart. My operator sounded like she just got off the plane from Puerto Rico. But listen, let's forget about all that. The reason I was late was because I was doing something a little special, a little extra for you. I was late because I was working for you and honest to God when I get through telling you about it, you're going to get down on your knees and thank me for keeping you waiting. Listen, baby, would I snow you? You gotta have faith. Let's get together tomorrow and try this on for size. And 'cause I love you, just tell me what brand perfume your wife wears and by the end of the week, I'll get some to her. I know I don't have to. I want to. Honest, baby, I love you and all I want is for you to be happy. Do you think I'd deliberately keep my favorite client waiting?"

Ellen had waited outside restaurants and outside theaters for him, missing entire first acts, trying not to get upset. She attempted, whenever possible, to get her own ticket but this was sometimes difficult because his secretary would get them that very same day. On the few occasions she had obtained hers in advance, she was as nervous waiting inside for him as waiting outside. Even when she was in a seat, his lateness made it impossible for her to concentrate on whatever she was seeing. She kept having terrible fears, whenever he was late, that something dreadful had happened to him, even though she knew intellectually that he was only dawdling over dinner with a client. But the thought of life without him was so frightening to her that reason could not control her anxiety when he was so late. Unfortunately, people continued to forgive him for his lateness, and if the world accepted it, what could she do?

Weekends they had a fairly active social life through Jeff's business contacts, but the women Ellen met were the wives of clients and it never occurred to her to confide in any of them. Sometimes she heard one or another of them complaining about her husband but she never joined in with them. There was something dishonorable to her about maligning the person who clothed and fed you. So she steamed and stewed but confided in no one.

Once, even though she knew she would get no satisfaction, she tried discussing her problems with her mother, not because she expected her mother to understand but because she felt an irresistible need to articulate her discontents. Her mother listened to her list of complaints and then Mrs. Graetz's homely, lined face turned red and the screaming began.

"Sometimes," her mother shrilled, "I can't believe you had three years of college and stayed so stupid. Even I, uneducated as I am, a nothing, a poor immigrant who never had your opportunities, even I, who worked from the time I was twelve and thank God you will never know from my life, even I, even I am smarter than you. My God, my God, the way I've always worried about you. Always with your nose in a book, not so good-looking, no money, where would you find a decent husband? Who would want you? Why would anybody good want you? All my life, everything was on my shoulders. Even when your father was alive, everything was on my shoulders. Thank God, he lived to see you married so you gave him a little pleasure, not that you care about that. No, not you, why should you care about making your parents happy?

"All my life I worked for you. I could have gone out and gotten a job and been selfish like those working mothers. But I didn't want you to come home from school to an empty house. So every pleasure I denied myself for you. And when you got married, my fine lady, I knew that everything I did was right. Even though you were not so good-looking, you found yourself a wonderful husband. God was watching over you. You found yourself a man who would kill himself for you. And let me tell you this, my fine lady, there are millions of women out there who would die to get a man like Jeff. You should have seen them at the Concord last summer; rich women, pretty women, friendly women, cheerful women, women who would never say a word about a husband's being late if he was killing himself to make money for them.

"Ellen, you got to be smart. Stop thinking only about yourself. You have a good man there. The whole world admires him and he thinks only about you and the baby. Who else, younger even than thirty, has done so well? He loves you, he loves the baby, he knocks himself out for you. And you think it's a crime if he's late for the theater. What does a play mean? Without theaters and movies you can live but without clients you can't. There's a lot more to life than theater and it's time you realized it and started to act like a mother, like a wife, not like a spoiled child."

"But I don't like Jeff anymore," Ellen said, "and I don't know what to do about it."

Her mother turned red again, clutched at her heart, and fell into a chair. "You won't be satisfied until you give me a heart attack," she moaned, fanning herself with a magazine.

"You don't like Jeff. That's a joke, a big joke. You don't like Jeff? You, a little nothing, no money, no looks, a rotten disposition. God only knows what would have happened to you, you with your Communist Party, the Rosenbergs, the Teachers' Union, all that crazy stuff. What would have happened if you hadn't married him? Right down the drain with that crazy Communist boyfriend who will never make a living. I used to shiver every time you went out with that Saul. Him, I suppose you would have liked. Him, in some cold-water flat on the East Side, living next to pushcarts. I can just see you now, my fine lady, on the Lower East Side, from where your father and I escaped, thank God, I can see you there, dressed in thrift shop clothes with furniture from the Salvation Army, instead of in this beautiful house with your first mink coat already. All my life, did I ever have a mink coat?

"My God, Jeff could have gotten anybody. Let me tell you, my fine lady, you should wash his shirts by hand to show your gratitude. And don't ever come to me again with, 'I don't like my husband.' Like has nothing to do with anything. You just live with him and be nice to him and behave yourself and have another child. That's what you should be doing now. It's no good to have one child. Ask me, I know. Just look at you. Jennifer is three years old. Get pregnant again. It's your duty to provide a sister or brother for her.

"You don't like Jeff," she continued to mutter. "Who did you like? That Communist boy and his divorced mother. The big mistake is I should have sent you to Brooklyn College instead of to that college right in the middle of Greenwich Village. But I wanted the best for you. I didn't know any better then and who knew you'd turn out to be the Queen of Greenwich Village but anyway that's water under the bridge and there's no point in crying over spilt milk so you'd just better start to like your husband.''

Ellen sat down exhausted and tuned out the rest of the raving. But her mother's crazy harangue made her think. What exactly did she mean when she said she didn't like Jeff? Was she any better than he? It wasn't honest to criticize his business methods and his value system while she was benefiting from them. People were beginning to refer to Jeff as a publicity genius. Suppose he really was some species of genius, a pop Michelangelo. What right did she have, really, to be so critical? He was never cruel to her, never yelled at her, was generous with money, was far more loving to her than her own mother. And actually, what did she give to Jeff in return? She was a poor bedmate, she did not want the large family of children Jeff wanted, and if Jeff contributed ninety percent to the marriage, she contributed only ten percent and that same amount could be contributed by many other women, by any other woman. No marriage was perfect and if she wanted to stay married she had better make up her mind to accept everything. Jeff was imperfect, but so was she imperfect. The world was imperfect. But with this imperfect man she could have a wonderful rich life and without him, there was nothing. She would try to be as cooperative as possible in bed and she would force herself to think positively, to like him, to even try to love him. This was the only future path that made sense. She knew what she had to do. And besides, this way she was safe.

Filled with remorse at her lack of gratitude, Ellen devoted herself to the house, polishing each piece of new furniture as if it were a religious object. New material possessions came with each new account. Jeff's agency continued to flourish. As he had predicted, he was lucky that he'd been sent to language school during the war for it had made him the first Madison Avenue PR man to corner the exploding international markets with the aid of American know-how. Each weekend, Jeff came home with exciting stories about new accounts.

And while Jeff continued to woo new clients, Ellen continued to clean her house. She dusted and vacuumed and vacuumed and dusted. Her house was clean enough even to satisfy her mother and Ellen's boredom increased in direct proportion to the cleanliness. Finally, unable to stand her life any longer, she applied for a position as assistant teacher at a nursery school and, to her delight, was hired. Nursery schools had become so popular that this one, La Petite Ferme, had two sessions a day and Ellen was able to enroll Jennifer in the same session in which she taught. She worked with the four-year-olds and Jennifer was in the three-year-old group. The head teacher under whom Ellen worked was only twenty-two, two years younger than Ellen, but she had completed her college work and student teaching. Every day, as Ellen performed the menial tasks to which she had been assigned, she regretted not having finished school. She should have become engaged, finished her senior year, then married. But she had been so terrified of losing Jeff. She decided that she would return to college and get her degree as soon as Jennifer was in school all day. She'd been afraid that Jeff would object to her working but he had been pleased by it.

"It's better for me," he said, "because I won't have to worry about being away from you so much. But frankly, babes, what I really think is that you should get pregnant again. Jennifer's three. It's time."

"Sure. I'll put away the diaphragm," she said, but she didn't really mean it. She couldn't quite articulate it but another pregnancy seemed like entrapment to her. She knew that was foolish. She had Pat, they would get a sleep-in maid, and she adored Jennifer. So why didn't she want more children? Lots of people had miscarriages and went right ahead with breeding. But the thought caused her such uneasiness that she didn't even want to examine her motivations.

Her mother, of course, was highly critical of her failure to

56

give Jennifer a sister or brother. She couldn't understand why Ellen needed a job. "I don't know why Jeff lets you do it," she said. "You don't even make enough money to pay Pat. It's an insult to Jeff. I know lots of women whose daughters are married to men who are a lot less successful than Jeff and their daughters don't work. You can't work and run your house right."

"Oh, Mother, that's what I have a maid for."

"You can't trust maids. Thieves, all of them. Believe me, I know from maids."

Ellen suppressed her grin. Her mother had never in her life employed a maid.

"There are things," Mrs. Graetz continued in a voice of doom, "that no maid can do. Your drawers are messy, your sterling is tarnished, your glasses have spots on them. Good Waterford with spots. All my life I drank from old jelly glasses but at least they were clean and your Waterford has spots. My jelly glasses were spotless."

Ellen burst out laughing.

"Laugh, laugh," her mother said, going into her indignant stance, "but if I had Waterford I'd be home to take care of it. Someday you'll come home from those germy kids and find some of your Waterford broken. And what, may I ask, will you do then?"

"Why, then—" Ellen whooped with laughter—"I'll drink from jelly glasses."

For weeks after that, whenever she felt gloomy, all she had to say to cheer up was "jelly glasses." The following week she went to Altman's and sent her mother a complete set of Waterford, for which extravagance her mother scolded her for weeks.

Now that she was working, Ellen was more content, but Jeff was going through a rough period. The cause was Amos Landor, Jeff's biggest client and, according to Jeff, the worst son of a bitch in all New York.

"He's demanding all my time," Jeff told her, "and the guy's crazy. Every day he makes a scene about something. He'll scream and rant about a release, I'll change it according to his specifications, and then he'll scream and rant some more and want the original one back. There's no dealing with him, Ellen. He's certifiably crazy but I need the bastard."

She was sorry to see him so upset, sweating, showing his Madison Avenue jitters. "Why don't you just drop his account," she said, "if he makes you so nervous?"

"Don't be stupid," Jeff snapped. "You don't give up a client of Landor's size. I'm afraid that he might drop me and without any notice. One of these mornings I'll open the *Times* and the lead story on the business page will be that Landor has transferred his account."

"Would your business be in financial trouble if he did drop you?" Ellen asked. Jeff kept all business details from her so it was hard to judge the necessity for Jeff's panic.

"Are you kidding?" he boasted. "I could lose ten clients and still not be in trouble. I'm the hottest small agency in town."

"Then why don't you let him go?" she asked. "There are more important things in life than holding on to ulcer accounts."

"Such as what?"

"Such as peace of mind," she said.

"Working in that nursery school has addled your brains," he said. "It's easy enough to have peace of mind with four-year-olds, especially when you have me running interference. In my business, when you have peace of mind, you're no longer in the running. The reason I let Amos give me ulcers is because I want to give you and Jennifer peace of mind."

She sighed. He caught it. "Listen, babes," he said, "I don't notice you turning down any of the things Amos's account buys."

"I work," she said. "I make enough money for my personal needs."

"Your pay is a joke," he said. "You might just as well stay home."

"Oh, for heaven's sake," she snapped back. "I was only try-

58

ing to be encouraging to you. Do you want me to just listen and say nothing?"

"That's the ticket." He grinned. But he wasn't joking.

Amos Landor was head of a conglomerate that had dotted the approach to New Jersey with lower-middle-class housing developments which promised, on omnipresent billboards, thanks to Jeff's inventiveness, that you could live a lot better if you moved into one of Landor's future slums. Actually, Landor had done a great deal to alleviate the postwar apartment shortage.

"I think it's ironic," Ellen had once said, "that you can earnestly publicize the kind of housing you wouldn't be caught dead in."

"What's ironic about it?" Jeff asked, aggrieved. "I also publicize milk I don't drink."

He has no conscience, Ellen thought. He would promote anyone for the right fee. But Landor was getting under his skin. Landor was short and wiry, had a pale, freckled nutcracker face, and was thin and brittle from the nervous tension he generated in himself and others.

"I don't get ulcers," he was fond of saying, "I give them."

Landor's office, high atop the Landor fiefdom, featured a rosewood engraved desk with eight phones in a line. Standing there, he would hop from foot to foot and from phone to phone like a demented, tap-dancing juggler. His father, a shriveled old furrier from Europe, sat in a straight-backed chair in a corner of the office and watched his son all day; just watched—sitting with wrinkled hands folded atop his cane, his back straight, watching expressionlessly while his *boychik* multiplied the empire.

Landor's favorite time of night to call Jeff was 3:00 A.M. because he was a bad sleeper and Jeff was unfailingly courteous. One night he called Jeff in hysteria to report that someone had climbed up on one of his largest billboards under cover of darkness, crossed out the word *City,* and substituted *Shitty.*

"Landor Shitty," Amos screamed so loudly that Ellen could hear him. "Landor Shitty. Is that what I pay you for? Landor

Shitty? With all I spend on advertising and PR the people should love me. Landor Shitty! I could get that without your services."

Ellen repressed an impulse to laugh because poor Jeff was sweating. Listening to him soothe and humor the humorless monster, Ellen was filled with unexpected love and tenderness. God, what a job. What a lousy field publicity was. You really had to have nerves of steel to deal with all the lunatics. Each time Ellen heard what Jeff had to go through she reproached herself for not loving him and tried all the harder to make few demands on him and to make him happy.

2

Jeff's problems with Landor were endless. They seemed to dominate his life. Ellen tried to stay out of Jeff's way when he came home but one Friday night he looked so drained and exhausted that she was really worried about him.

"Give me a drink," Jeff said, staggering toward the bar.

"Since when do you drink?" Ellen asked, surprised.

"Since Landor. After Landor. In response to Landor. The only response to Landor is alcoholism or death."

He took a drink and sank down on a couch. Hearing his voice, Jennifer came tumbling into the room, carrying her artwork from nursery school.

"Daddy, do you want to see what I made?"

"Not now, baby. Later. Daddy is too tired."

"I want you to look at them now," she insisted.

"Out," he stormed. "Go watch TV. I'll see them later. Okay?"

"Not okay," Jennifer said, her little body trembling. She went out sobbing.

"She never sees you," Ellen said, "and she adores you."

61

"Now don't start," he threatened. "I've had about all I can take today." Gloomily he finished his drink.

"Do you want to tell me about it?" she asked.

"Why not," he said. "I tell you, Landor is crazy, certifiably crazy. But nobody dares to mention it because the son of a bitch is so successful. I mean, today was outright lunacy."

Landor had spent hundreds of thousands of dollars with Sheldon Public Relations but that day, "out of left field," he decided he'd been overcharged four hundred dollars. The minute Jeff reached his office Amos had begun to complain about the overcharge.

"I said to him," Jeff said, his voice still shocked with disbelief, "you can't be seriously making such a fuss over four hundred dollars. I'll take you to Pavillon a couple of times. At that point, he let out such a high-pitched scream I thought he'd flipped. I stood there in absolute terror, watching the guy. He ran to the window and butted his head against it several times. I was afraid the lunatic would break it. Then, howling in pain from the butting, he grabbed his head and went down on his hands and knees on that gorgeous white carpet. He started to bang his head on it, screaming at me all the while, 'You're trying to kill me. Thieves. All of you are thieves, robbers, bloodsuckers. You're all trying to ruin me but you won't get away with it. It's not for nothing they call me Cheap Amos. I'll die before I let you cheat me out of a dollar.' "

"My God," Ellen said. "Then what happened?"

"He rolled into a fetal position and began to weep. Right through this, his father, who's there all the time, just sat watching without changing expression. Maybe the guy is dead. Looks like a wooden cigar-store Indian. Honest, Ellen, I didn't know what to do. I finally figured I'd just leave so I started to walk and his secretary intercepted me.

" 'Where are you going, Mr. Sheldon?' she asked me.

" 'I can't take any more of this,' I said.

"The woman looked positively terrified. 'Please don't leave him this way,' she whispered to me.

" 'I'm going,' I said. 'I can't believe that with all the dough he spends he's going crazy over four hundred dollars.'

" 'He's so good,' the secretary whispered, 'he has a fear of being taken.'

"Well, Amos continued to weep and whine and I couldn't decide what to do. If I walked out, it was goodbye to the account. I figured the hell with it. I'd give him back the four hundred and tack it on to his account somewhere else."

Ellen could visualize the scene as Jeff told her the rest of the story. Sweating in his three-hundred-dollar suit, Jeff had wiped the perspiration off his face with his sleeve, and sat down on the rug beside Amos.

"Amos, Amos, baby, listen to me," Jeff had pleaded. "Please stop carrying on. I'll reduce the bill four hundred. You were right. Honest, Amos, you were right. My bookkeeper must have made a mistake. So stop crying and as soon as I get back to my office I'll see to it that the bill is changed."

Amos sat up on the carpet, hugging his knees, and said, "I don't want to think you're just doing this to make me happy, Jeff. I couldn't stand that."

"Of course I'm not just doing it to make you happy." Jeff had sweated. "I'm doing it because you're right. Honest, pal, you've got me licked. Right is right."

Finally Amos smiled. He stood up, wiped his eyes, smoothed his silk shirt and satin tie, and sank down again into his desk chair.

"Jeff," he said, "I love you. You just proved that my faith in your intelligence hasn't been misplaced. You're one smart boy to cooperate and in return I'm going to do something for you. To show my appreciation, I'm going to recommend you for EL."

"EL?" Jeff asked. "What's that?"

"You must be kidding. I can't believe any smart, successful businessman doesn't know what EL is."

"Well, maybe I once knew and forgot," Jeff said weakly.

"It's okay, it's okay, baby," Amos said. "I'm happy to contribute to your education. I like to do nice things for guys who do nice things for me. EL stands for Executive Leaders. It's an organization of men under forty who are heads of corporations that do at least two million dollars' worth of business a year or employ more than fifty people. You qualify on both counts. Not that meeting qualifications is enough. You have to be recommended by a member, and lots of people get turned down. But you won't be turned down, Jeff, baby. Not with me recommending you, you won't. Nobody I ever recommended has been blackballed. If you know me, you're in. So you made a wise decision today, Jeff, a plenty wise decision. You returned my four hundred dollars to me but the contacts you'll make in EL will return that to you a hundred times this year. Jeff, baby, you're going to be grateful to me for the rest of your life. I'm going to make your life because, let me tell you, baby, there's no more exclusive club than EL."

Jeff had finished the story and he poured himself another drink. "So what do you think of that?" he asked Ellen.

"You're right," she said, "he really is crazy. I'm sorry you have to put up with that sort of thing, Jeff." She walked over to him and put her arms around him to comfort him but he didn't want her comforting.

"It's okay," he said, "it really worked out for the best. I spent this afternoon asking around about EL and Amos was right. Getting me in is like giving me an expensive lifetime gift. You have to retire at forty so I have nine good years ahead of me, the best years of my life, and the accounts I get during those years and the friends I make in EL will stay with me for the rest of my life. So it all worked out for the best."

"Then how come you've had two stiff drinks and look like a nervous wreck?"

"It will pass," he said. "The next big account will make it only a distant memory."

"Well, I think Landor is crazy," she said indignantly. "I'm amazed that anyone so crazy can be so successful."

"Maybe it helps." Jeff laughed. "So what if he's crazy. I won the round."

"You?" she asked in a surprised voice. "You didn't win. Landor did."

"What are you talking about?" Jeff asked roughly.

"He won," Ellen persisted, knowing she was foolish to do so, "because you didn't tell him to take his account and stuff it. He had you sweating, pleading, kneeling on the floor, cajoling and, finally, thanking him for throwing you a bone. Why should you thank him for getting you into an organization when to do so meant submitting a false bill. Your bill was fair, wasn't it?"

"Well, to tell you the truth—" he grinned sheepishly—"we overcharged him a lot more than four hundred. We always pad our bills. What the hell. With the way he wastes money . . ."

"Jeff, that's terrible."

"Do me a favor, Ellen, and stick to your four-year-olds. You don't know anything about the way the business world works. You can't even balance your own goddamned checkbook. So just buzz off and let me handle the business affairs of this family. Save your ridiculous morality for the nursery school classroom. Speaking of which, I'd better spend a few minutes with Jennifer now."

"Come on down now, Jennifer, honey," he called up the stairs. "Daddy isn't tired anymore."

Jennifer walked down the stairs warily, holding on to Pat's hand.

"Don't you have a kiss for me?" Jeff asked.

"Not anymore," she said. "I gave all my kisses to Pat."

Later at dinner, as they ate their dessert, Pat dropped her bombshell. "I'm going back to England. Actually, I've been here too long already. I have a boyfriend waiting at home and I want to get on with the business of my own life before my looks have flown."

Ellen looked at her with love. What a fine friend she'd been to her and Jen. Ellen felt she could more easily dispense with Jeff than with Pat. Even though Jen was only three, she understood what was happening.

"You can't go," she wept, flinging her little arms

around Pat's neck. "Take me with you, Pat."

Pat pushed her chair back from the table and took the sobbing child onto her lap. "Soon you'll be going to kindergarten, love," she said, "and you'll have so many friends that you'll forget all about me. And you're growing up so fast you don't need a nurse anymore. You can even tie your own shoelaces. But don't cry, love. I'll send you a box of wonderful presents from England; your very own bunny bowl and a matching egg coddler. And I promise to see you again. You can come and visit me in England."

"Do you really promise?" Jennifer asked, trying to stop her tears.

"Yes, my little love," Pat said, smoothing back the child's hair.

"And you can't take me with you now in your suitcase?"

"No, my little love. How would your parents feel?"

"He wouldn't care at all," Jennifer said. "He wouldn't let me show him my pictures before." At the memory, she began to sob loudly again.

"Oh, for God's sake," Jeff exploded. "I've gone through enough today. Take her upstairs, Pat. She's giving me a headache."

"What's the matter with you, Jeff?" Ellen protested. "Take her in your arms and give her a kiss. Tell her you love her." Jeff stomped out of the dining room and slammed the door of his study.

"Come on, love," Pat said. "Let's play horsie." Jennifer got up on the back of the kind, rawboned English country girl and Pat galloped upstairs, snorting and neighing, while Jennifer screamed in delight.

Angry at Jeff, Ellen sat there brooding over her coffee. She understood how Jennifer felt. She, too, could have wept in sorrow at her feeling of abandonment. She had grown so dependent on the sensible, rational, au pair girl. Now, with Jeff away so much during the week, she would have no one to talk to. Jeff was thrilled about the prospect of EL but that meant nothing to her. It was Jeff's world.

The truth of the matter was that the very idea of joining an organization of the rich scared her. She'd be out of her depth with the "beautiful people." She remembered a Mary McCarthy short story she had read, "The Man in the Brooks Brothers Shirt," in which the heroine had met an upper-class man on a train and been painfully reminded of her personal and social class deficiencies. Although the story's heroine felt confident about competing in intellectual circles, she knew she'd be a flop on the beaches of Southampton, competing with debutantes. That was how Ellen felt. Well, there was no point in worrying about it now. Perhaps Jeff would not get in.

But it took only a few weeks for him to be offered membership in EL. There was no doubt but that Amos was a powerful advocate. Too many men in the club did business with Amos and he was too dangerous to cross for anyone to blackball Jeff. Amos had a reputation for strength because he didn't give a damn what anyone thought of him.

"The guy's incredible," Jeff exulted when he told Ellen about his admission. "He's like a goddamned chameleon. I learn from him whenever I'm with him. When he talks to the laborers he sounds like a hard hat and when he's talking to someone from EL he sounds like a Harvard graduate. Today we had lunch with his very good friend from college. Know who that friend is? It's the governor of Delaware. Can you imagine. Just that simple. 'Jeff, I want you to meet my old roommate, his honor, the governor of Delaware.' At first I thought he was kidding, but he wasn't.

"Listen to this story he told me, Ellen. He said his friend, the governor, had once asked him, 'Amos, which one of us do you think is more important?' And you know what Amos said? Honestly, Ellen, this will kill you. Amos said, 'I'm more important because I can buy lots of governors but there's only one of me.' And you know what, the bastard's right. He's unique and he can buy governors. So what do you think of that?"

"I think it's disgusting," Ellen said.

"There we go again," Jeff said, "little Miss Holier-than-thou. You think you're better than anyone else because everyone else does the dirty work for you."

Ellen sighed. "Please, Jeff, let's not get into that again. All right. I think it's a funny story and I think Amos is an admirable robber baron."

"His wife joined us for lunch today, too," Jeff said.

"Ooh, what's she like?" Ellen asked.

"Gorgeous," Jeff said, "and a real lady. She was wearing an emerald necklace that Amos said he bought at Van Cleef and he showed me the lining of her sable coat. He really is something. Know what he had embroidered on the lining? One of my PR slogans. Can you imagine, one of my slogans on the lining of a sixty-thousand-dollar coat. There it was, 'Live it up a little with Amos.' I tell you, I was really flattered. She looked gorgeous."

"She wore that to lunch?" Ellen said. "What does she wear when she gets dressed up?"

"Very funny," Jeff said. "It wasn't just that she looked gorgeous. She's some classy lady. She's soft and quiet and she smiles all the time. She sits and waits pleasantly for Amos and she never looks bored or moody like you."

"From your description," Ellen said, "I'd say there's a lot less to her than her clothes."

"Oh, very funny, very funny," Jeff said. "Always ready with the nasty wisecrack, aren't you? It's the mark of a small, jealous mind. The best thing that could happen to you would be for you to model yourself on someone like Marilyn Landor."

"I like myself just the way I am now," she said angrily.

"Yeah, well," he said, "that's part of what's wrong with you. When I married you you were enthusiastic, cheerful. But you certainly dropped that pose as soon as you started to lap up the gravy."

She started to answer him, then stopped. What was the

point. It didn't surprise her that Jeff was increasingly critical of her. Nothing could surpass her growing distaste for him. Oh, well, she thought, maybe this was just the nature of marriage. It would be good for them to become involved with EL. It would make Jeff happy and she might make some women friends.

Their initiation into EL was to be held the following month at the exclusive Westchester Country Club. EL didn't have a clubhouse of its own but used fine hotels and country clubs for its meetings, dinners, seminars, and installations. Jeff was more excited and cheerful than she could remember. Boxes of new suits, monogrammed shirts, and old school ties began to arrive daily from Brooks Brothers. Ellen alternated between anticipation and fear.

The sight of the boxes and increasing insomnia made Ellen finally realize how she felt about the EL installation.

"Jeff," she said, "you'll have to become a member of EL without me. I don't want to go."

"You must be crazy," Jeff said, "here we are, about to have the biggest honor of my life, and you don't want to come. It's an honor for you, too."

"All I would be is an appendage. Why do you need me at all?"

"Listen, Amos tells me that EL is big on wives and families. Wives are expected to come. It's a very straight organization in regard to that. Amos said nobody even plays around in EL and an unmarried guy can't get in."

"I wouldn't expect such people to play around," Ellen said, "so why is it such a big deal that they don't? And why don't they, anyway?"

"Too much money at stake," Jeff said. "Some of those guys have made the big mistake of joint ownership of everything with their wives."

Ellen wondered why that was a mistake. It had to be better than being in her position and knowing nothing about her husband's finances. It had to be better than having everything doled out to her, even though Jeff was a generous dispenser of largess. It still made her feel like a child, having to ask for everything. She knew better than to raise this with Jeff again now. It always made him angry.

"We're getting off the subject," Ellen said. "They're still going to admit you, with or without me. Just say I have a headache."

"You're going and that's all there is to it," Jeff said. "I would think you'd want to go, want to see me honored."

"I would like to go for that," she said, "but, honestly, I'm scared because I don't know what to wear. You have me nervous because of your description of Marilyn. What do you think would be appropriate?"

"How should I know? Women are supposed to know things like that. Why don't you pick up copies of *Vogue* and *Harper's Bazaar?* They might help you. But honestly, Ellen, it isn't that complicated. It's just a summer afternoon going on into the evening. I suppose you should get a cotton or a linen dress . . . not low-cut, not loud, quiet, conservative, expensive. Just go to Bonwit's and tell them you want an expensive understated dress with perfect lines, that won't stand out. And then, for God's sake, go and get a decent haircut and manicure. Go to a place like Elizabeth Arden or Revlon and get a good makeup job, refined, not too flashy, a haircut, your nails, maybe even your toenails."

"Jeff, this is ridiculous. You're being installed. You get *your* toenails done. Why should I have to start tying myself into knots for complete strangers? I'd rather spend my time reading or with Jen. They're installing you, not me. Leave me home."

Jeff grabbed her upper arm hard, whirled her about, and for the first time in their marriage looked as if he were about to hit her. He was so angry his face turned red and his hazel eyes looked at her with hate.

"Now listen, you stupid broad," he shouted. "I'm getting sick and tired of living with a deadbeat. I'm also sick and tired of your peculiar sense of humor. Once and for all, get it through

70

your head that EL is business and that if you want to keep eating, you had better not screw it up. You're going. You're going to look great and when we get there, you're going to smile and keep your mouth shut. You are not going to discuss ideas. You are not going to express your political philosophy. Stay off the subjects of Korea, Negroes, American Indians, and the State of Israel. Watch Marilyn and try to be a normal wife, like her. Try to remember that you're not in business for yourself. You can't go through life like some goddamned parasite while I do all the work. I need you as part of my team. I need you to be charming to prospective accounts, to smile, to chat, to be an asset to me. You're going to start to act like a team member or you can just ship out. You can't go through life just pleasing yourself. Either shape up or ship out. . . ."

Ellen listened in terror. My God! Ship out? To where? How? With what? If Jeff dumped her, her life would be ruined.

"All right, all right," she said. "I'll get myself fixed up. You don't have to worry. Everything will be fine."

"That's better," he said. His rage subsided immediately. Had it all been an act? It didn't matter if it was. It was quite evident that Jeff had given her her warning.

Dispiritedly Ellen examined herself in the mirror and was convinced again that there was no way she could compete or fit in with the beautiful people. Her natural equipment wasn't that good. Her legs were too hefty and even now, just past twenty-four, varicose veins were beginning to appear. Her breasts were too large and her skin was spotted. Her hair held a set for exactly five minutes after she left a beauty parlor and she couldn't seem to stop biting her nails. She was no beauty, never had been a beauty, and never would be. Moving into a world in which she believed she was destined to feel inferior terrified her. It seemed an act of deliberate self-destruction but she felt there was nothing she could do but go forward with Jeff.

She bought a simple linen dress with a scooped neckline and wore her high school charm bracelet and her $5.95 gold hoop earrings. She had spent a day at Elizabeth Arden and her skin glowed, her new haircut promised to hold, and the way they had taught her to apply makeup made her look surprisingly pretty. The manicurist had cut and pushed her cuticles until they were smoother than ever before and she had bought a chemical to put on them which had such a terrible taste that it made her instantly pull her hand away from her mouth whenever she forgot that she must not bite her nails.

Jeff was thrilled by her appearance. "You look great, Ellen," he said, "thanks."

She could have cried at his approval and felt an unfamiliar rush of affection. She really did want to please him. He looked perfect, of course, except for a line of perspiration on his upper lip and the nervous smell. So he was anxious, too. Of course. Why did she always think he was exempt from the fears and insecurities that plagued her? It was just that he was forced to cover, to hide, to play the strong, secure role required of the president of a large business. She gave him a little hug, wordlessly trying to give him encouragement.

"We're moving into the big time, babes," he said as they drove into the club's impressive circular driveway. A uniformed attendant took the car from them at the door and moved it in position behind a line of other cars waiting to be parked.

"Oh, Jeff, isn't it beautiful," Ellen said, looking at the white clubhouse that looked like an antebellum mansion. At one end she could see the magnificent, Olympic-sized pool and from the back of the other end stretched the perfect, green golf course. He didn't answer and she looked at his face. He was close to tears.

"Damn it," he said, "ours is the only station wagon. How could I have been so dumb? Why wasn't I smart enough to rent a Caddie or a Lincoln? Well, I won't make this mistake again."

"Please, Jeff," she said, trying to console him, "don't get so upset. It doesn't matter. You'll still get into EL."

"Of course it matters," he snapped.

"Once we get inside," she said, "nobody will connect us with it."

72

"You're home most of the time," he said, "you drive the car. Why can't you ever think of this kind of thing?"

Ellen sighed. So it was her fault again. The car really was a mess and she never remembered to get it washed. Each Monday she drove him to the train, each Monday he commented on how messy it was, and then she went off to her job and promptly forgot his complaints. He had reminded her many times about getting it washed but she never had time. She preferred to leave it out whenever it rained. But the car was dirty outside and messy inside as well. The back was a jumble of dirty shirts, schoolbooks, Jennifer's toys, shoes that needed mending, and deposit bottles. She would have to make up her mind to go through the car-wash procedure or to remind Jeff to have it washed on the weekends. But it was a shame to spoil the evening now with this problem.

"Tomorrow," Jeff said angrily, "I rent a car for me. There's no point in getting you a good car. You'd just have it looking like a shithouse in a week. I want a clean, undented car that isn't all crapped up. I won't let you get near it."

"All right, all right," she whispered, "please don't make a scene. Somebody will hear you. Nobody saw us arrive in the wagon and we can leave when it's dark so nobody will see us get into it."

"The boy who parks cars saw me get out of it," he said.

"Oh, for heaven's sake," she said with mild irritation, "the boy who parks the cars probably would love our station wagon. You don't have to impress him, too."

Grudgingly he moved with her into the club. "You can just bet it won't happen again," he grumbled. She said nothing. The familiar guilt and depression were creeping over her and the momentary confidence she had felt when he liked her appearance had evaporated. She faced the evening with dread.

Amos was waiting for Jeff and he greeted them warmly, pleased that his protégé had been admitted so easily. "I've been waiting for you, old buddy," he said, putting his arm around Jeff's shoulders.

"Damned nice of you, Amos," Jeff said, and Ellen realized

he had been anxious about the possibility of having to make his way without a guide. Again, she felt the rush of affection that occurred whenever he showed his vulnerability.

"Not at all, not at all," Amos said, exuding the charm that always made his enemies trust him one more time, "it's the way we do things in EL. Customary to wait for new members one sponsors."

Jeff introduced him to Ellen and Amos's eyes flicked briefly over her and dismissed her. "Quite a husband you have here," he said, "star quality. A meteoric rise, everyone can feel it, I'm not the only one. And he did it all by himself. I always tell myself that the thing most responsible for my success was Marilyn's daddy's money. But your husband's a real winner. I tell you, I love the guy. He's made my name a household word. Come over here, I want you to meet my wife Marilyn."

I want to cry, Ellen thought. That's all I want, to go off and cry someplace. Now, in addition to looking lousy, it's Marilyn's daddy's money. I knew it would be like this.

But Amos had each of them by one arm and was propelling them across the floor to where Marilyn stood waiting impassively, a quiet, reserved, elegant blond lady, dressed in a simple white summer suit and wearing diamond earrings, a tremendous solitaire, and a diamond and emerald necklace filling the scoop in her blouse. She looked quiet, poised, serene, classy. Ellen couldn't hope to compete with such assurance. How did someone get to look like that, everything quietly shrieking money and good taste, the good taste canceling out the ostentation? No wonder Amos dismissed her with a glance. He probably felt sorry for Jeff when he saw her.

"Would you like to go to the powder room?" Marilyn whispered in perfect, modulated tones. Ellen automatically lowered her own voice to a whisper and said, "I'd love to." She couldn't wait to escape from Amos's contempt. Now she understood why Jeff wanted to keep that account. Amos was intimidating. His eccentricity was the eccentricity of royalty, and it was just what would appeal to Jeff.

Marilyn walked in front of her, leading the way, and Ellen admired her erectness, fine posture, and regal bearing. Ellen straightened her shoulders and willed herself to look poised, but she felt like a total fraud. What was she doing here and whom was she kidding? The wall of mirrors in the elegant ladies' room reinforced her new understanding. Mirror, mirror on the wall, please don't tell me. She took off her junk jewelry and dropped it into her purse. New toys for Jennifer. She thought she looked better without the jewelry and was pleased that her hair and makeup still looked fine. She was starting to calm down when the door opened and a girl who looked like a cross between Susan Hayward and Paulette Goddard swept in on the most beautiful legs Ellen had ever seen off the screen. The ladies' room attendant practically genuflected before the newcomer.

"How was your trip to Europe, Mrs. Wein?" the woman asked.

"Absolutely divine" was the answer in a voice made of husky honey, a voice low and beautiful and rich. Oh, those voices. Ellen could have wept again. Only someone from the right family and the right school and the right social circle could ever speak like that. It was a voice that resonated with the triumph of nature and nurture. Ellen felt like a Cockney, by comparison.

"Who's that?" she whispered to Marilyn, her curiosity overwhelming her desire to seem cool and poised.

"Kimberly Clare Wein," Marilyn whispered. "She and her sister come from a famous old family. Doesn't her face look familiar to you? The year each came out, the newspapers and magazines were full of them. They were each the deb of the year. Her sister married an Italian count and lives in Rome, but Kimberly married Jonathan Wein. Surely you've heard of him?"

"No, I haven't," Ellen confessed.

"You should start to read *Town and Country,*" Marilyn said. "That's the only way you can find your way around. He comes from the Wein family, the most famous Jewish philanthropists in the United States. They're related to the Rothschilds."

"The Rothschilds," Ellen exclaimed. "I know that name.

Everyone does, of course. I'm really impressed."

"So is everyone else," Marilyn said, permitting herself a little smile, "except for Kimberly. She married him as a last resort. After all, those girls had scarcely been bred to marry Jews. The amusing thing is that he could buy and sell her sister's count. The sister and brother-in-law gamble and more than once Jonathan has paid off their gambling debts. He's really a fool. Kimberly only married him for his money and the brother-in-law is an anti-Semite."

Ellen was a little surprised at Marilyn's vehemence but she happily listened to the gossip. This way nothing was expected of her. "They've been married for ten years," Marilyn continued, "but they have no children and rumor has it that they never will have any. With his illustrious name and family, he could scarcely be expected to bring his child up as a Catholic. And she certainly could not bring up a nobleman's niece or nephew as a Jew. The brother-in-law is first cousin to the Pope. Jonathan is better than Kimberly deserves and someday I just hope he wakes up and sees her for what she is."

"Do you see them outside of EL?" Ellen asked.

"We do not," Marilyn said. "We used to invite them all the time. Sometimes they would show up, other times they would cancel at the last minute, ruining the seating arrangements, and they never invited us back. We're good enough to visit but not good enough to invite back."

What a joke, Ellen thought to herself. Apparently she wasn't the only insecure wife in EL. It was really funny to find that this paragon Jeff so admired had feelings similar to her own.

"I have to admit that she's beautiful," Marilyn continued, "and doesn't she know it. Of course, she isn't as beautiful as the countess. And she feels inferior because her sister has a title."

Marilyn sprayed herself with perfume before they left. Ellen had never thought to carry a purse-sized perfume with her. It wouldn't hurt to pick up some tips from the other women. How else could she learn?

"What kind of perfume is that?" she asked.

"Cabouchard." Marilyn named the magnificent fragrance and Ellen made another mental note.

Jeff and Amos were waiting in the hallway with a tall, imposing-looking woman, who looked about Jeff's age.

"Ellen, meet Kate Evans," Jeff said. "She's EL's first woman member and president of her own knitwear company. We handle her publicity."

"How do you do," Kate said with a warm smile, graciously bowing her head, a perfect Park Avenue chignon with a startling, elegant white streak at one temple. Kate radiated so much friendliness and goodwill that Ellen liked her at once. She felt so comfortable that she said the first thing on her mind.

"What a beautiful necklace."

"I'm so glad you like it," Kate beamed, seeming genuinely pleased by what Ellen had said, "it belonged to Marie Antoinette."

"*The* Marie Antoinette?" Ellen asked.

"So they say." Kate laughed. "Everything winds up at Parke Bernet if you wait long enough."

"I've never been to that store," Ellen said.

"Of course you've been to the Parke Bernet auction gallery," Jeff burst in with a hearty laugh, squeezing her arm. Kate watched them speculatively.

Ellen ignored him, fascinated by the necklace. It was part of history. Amazing to think that the neck that had worn them wound up on the guillotine.

"It makes history seem so close," she said to Kate, and Kate rewarded her perception with another friendly glance. Here was a woman she could talk to, maybe even be friends with someday. Kate didn't make her feel inferior.

"That's what I thought, too," Kate said, "when we bought it."

The necklace sparkled and glittered as Kate talked. It didn't seem possible to Ellen that they could be real diamonds. What were they? There were so many stones and even the one-carat ring Jeff had given her for their engagement had cost almost a thousand dollars.

"Are they real diamonds?" she asked Kate.

"Of course they are," Jeff muttered through his teeth, keeping the smile plastered on his face, "Kate would only wear real diamonds." Ellen could feel his hand tighten around her arm again at this faux pas.

But Kate continued to be nice. She wanted to rescue Ellen.

"I asked the same question the first time I saw the necklace," she said, and Jeff looked mollified.

I like her, Ellen thought again.

Kate was wearing a floor-length dress, although Kimberly, Marilyn, and Ellen all wore equally appropriate street-length dresses.

"How do you like this dress?" Kate asked. "We just bought an Italian knitwear concern and we're experimenting with lightweight knits for summer. I think it's absolutely marvelous, completely uncrushable. It's so sheer and lightweight that I'm not too warm at all."

"I love it," Ellen said, "I'd like to own one just like it."

"Come up to my showroom any time and I'll give you one," Kate said. "Wear it for a time and let me know how it stands up."

"You don't have to give her one," Jeff said. "Ellen didn't mean that."

"Relax, Jeff," Kate said, slightly steely. "I know exactly what Ellen meant. I'm not in the habit of misreading people. Call me, Ellen, and we might find time for lunch together."

Jeff beamed and Ellen looked at Kate with gratitude. Kate saw Ellen's eager face and looked pained.

"And I would really be pleased to have you try a dress for us. You'd be doing us a favor."

"The dress won't look as good on her as it does on you," Jeff said. Ellen couldn't help cringing.

"Really," Kate said lightly, "we're not competing." Her blue eyes were cold and steely.

She doesn't like him, Ellen thought, but she probably lets him do her publicity because he's so good. What a smart lady; no wonder she's so successful.

A white-haired, ruddy-faced man came up to them and greeted Jeff warmly. "Glad to have you aboard, fella," the man said, pumping Jeff's hand. Then he twinkled at Ellen.

"This is my husband, Will Sweet," Kate said to Ellen. Kate and Will smiled at each other affectionately. Ellen couldn't help noticing how comfortable they were together. Will greeted Ellen warmly and then he and Kate led the way toward the dining room. Ellen watched her in admiration. What a woman! How wonderful to become a member of EL on your own. It was evident after only their brief meeting that Kate was her own woman. She hadn't had to marry a financier, she didn't have to whisper, she didn't have to worry about saying or doing the wrong thing. She was a queen, tall, secure, erect, the equal of the men in EL. She was exactly the kind of woman Ellen would like to be: free, rich, independent, unafraid.

Their progress to the main dining room was impeded by a small crowd surrounding a tiny man with a protruding paunch, with a homely, but magnificently bejeweled little wife at his side.

"Who's that?" Jeff asked Amos.

"Samson Plari," Amos said, "you must have read about him last week. He just bought the Octagon, Ltd., network of stores. Each year he buys up more companies. A real coup, this time. Came here ten years ago from Czechoslovakia, a penniless math teacher, and now he's a tycoon. Come on, Jeff, I'll introduce you."

"I'd like to meet him," Jeff said.

Don't look so hungry, Ellen thought. It makes you look like the wolf licking his chops in "Red Riding Hood."

Amos elbowed the group aside with his usual finesse and introduced Samson to Jeff. Samson looked up at handsome Jeff and quipped, "I wish I could be so tall." Jeff looked down, struggled for a riposte, then said, "And I wish I could be so rich."

Everyone roared with merriment. Jeff had said exactly the right thing. He had defused, relaxed, and made everyone kin with his smart, snappy response. Two successful men had shown their vulnerability and everyone else now felt free to be human for a little while. People repeated the two remarks for years afterward. With Samson still chuckling, he and Jeff walked toward the hors d'oeuvres table. Jeff was a conquering hero and Samson did not leave his side until dinner was served.

Jeff and Ellen sat at the head table with five other new EL couples. To Jeff's right were seated Tina and Harry Chase. Jeff whispered to her that Harry had made his fortune by installing and maintaining beauty parlors in hotels and department stores across the country. He was a tall, quiet, plain-looking, balding man who seemed to act as foil for his wife, an attractive, slender, red-haired young woman who immediately began to chatter without inhibition to Ellen, across Jeff. Then she asked Jeff if he would change seats with her, which he was glad to do so that he could start to pitch Harry's account.

Artlessly and guilelessly babbling away, Tina started to speak to Ellen like an old friend as soon as they changed seats. She told Ellen that she had been born in Indochina to missionary parents and that they had returned to the United States as refugees when the war had broken out. She had been working as a receptionist in one of Harry's salons when Harry, a bachelor, had come in and fallen instantly in love with her. They had been married for six years. He was ten years older than she and she was twenty-eight, only four years older than Ellen. Ellen was grateful for Tina's unself-conscious talk which took the burden of conversation away from her.

"Isn't this exciting, isn't it absolutely marvelous," Tina exulted to Ellen. "It's taken five years for those damned snobs to admit us. Honestly, they all think they're so special and forget that once they were newcomers, just like us. Lots of times I told Harry to just forget about it but he was determined. Harry is like

80

that. That's the way he was with me. When he wants something, you can bet your life he gets it. Say no to him and he gets determined. That's what makes him impossible but, let's face it, that's what makes him sexy, too."

Ellen looked over at the placid man shoveling big chunks of a roll into his mouth, chewing away placidly while Jeff talked business to him, and she wondered. You certainly couldn't tell what was sexy from the outside.

"I always say for a man to be sexy he's got to be a business success. Don't you agree?"

Ellen nodded, amused and fascinated by the unusual topic of conversation.

"Of course," Tina continued, not missing a beat, "I have known sexy men who weren't wealthy. I think jocks are sexy, too. What do you think?"

Ellen nodded again, not saying anything, just transfixed by Tina's openness.

"Anyway," Tina continued, "Harry found the perfect way to get into EL when he met Kate. She's one of our best customers and one day she mentioned to him that she belonged to EL. It was simple after that. She commands a lot of respect, let me tell you, and has a kind of cachet because of being the first woman so they don't like to turn her down. Actually, she's the only kind of woman who could have been admitted to EL, although I suppose others will be admitted in the future. But Kate has the right looks for these guys. I mean, just look at her; she's completely nonsexy, like a tall, rectangular box. I think she kind of looks like a man. So she's their token woman. Anyway, they didn't turn her down and so here we are."

"I think she's attractive," Ellen said, feeling it would be disloyal not to say anything.

"Well, who said she isn't attractive? Everything that Christopher can do to her, she gets done. Attractive but definitely zero in the sex-appeal category. Screwing her or even thinking of her that way would be like screwing the Queen Mother."

"Who's Christopher?" Ellen asked.

"You must be kidding," Tina said. Ellen shook her head.

"My God," Tina said, "you really are out of it, aren't you? Christopher's is our very best salon. In fact, Christopher's is absolutely the best salon in all of New York City. Our only close competitor is Mr. Kenneth. Most of our places are in department stores but Christopher has his own brownstone on East Sixty-eighth and I helped to pick out the wallpaper. I have quite a flair for that kind of thing. Why don't you come there with me, one day? I spend one day a week getting everything done, even mustache waxing. I spend half my life there, sometimes. I want to tell you, it's no joke getting this shade of red. Do come with me." She looked Ellen over. "It would be good for you," she added, not unkindly.

Ellen flushed but she didn't mind the remark. Tina was a run-on speaker but she didn't seem malicious.

"Did you have a hard time getting into EL?" Tina asked.

"I don't think so," Ellen answered. She didn't want to tell Tina how easy it had been for Jeff.

"Well, we have lots of wives of EL'ers at Christopher's and let me tell you, I don't know what EL has to be so superior about. Just last year there were two suicide attempts and ten nervous breakdowns. Not to mention the ten divorces. Suicide and divorces I'd expect, but nervous breakdowns? Why so many of those?"

"I guess business pressures push these men over the edge," Ellen said. She visualized hospital wards permeated with Jeff's familiar fear stench.

"It's not the men," Tina said, "it's the women who break down. They're the ones who can't take the pressure. You should hear the things they tell Christopher and then he tells me. But, breakdowns or not, it's better to belong than not to belong. The contacts are invaluable and EL'ers have lots of fun."

"If they have so much fun," Ellen asked, "why the breakdowns?"

"It's because of the circles," Tina said.

"What do you mean?" Ellen asked.

"Well, inside this organization," Tina said, "at least according to what Christopher has told me, there are circles and circles. You can tell how people are doing financially by the table they're sitting at. When you see a couple sitting next to empty seats, you know his business is on the skids."

"I can't believe that people won't sit with members who aren't doing well," Ellen said, genuinely shocked.

"Why should they?" Tina asked, equally surprised.

"It's immoral," Ellen said. "A human being is more than his financial rating."

"Not here, he isn't." Tina laughed. "Listen, the only sin in EL is business failure and that's the only kind of morality anyone cares about."

"Well, I think it's wrong," Ellen said. "Don't you feel it's wrong?"

"Of course not," Tina said. "I agree with it one hundred percent. Why should we pay a high initiation fee to sit with deadbeats? If we wanted to associate with failures, why would we bother to join EL in the first place? There are plenty of failures floating around outside. People join EL for business reasons and they're entitled to get what they pay for."

"But suppose you were friendly with a couple," Ellen persisted, "and they started to have business reverses. Would you just stop being friendly with them?"

"Probably," Tina said. "Listen, all of us who get into EL have joined a charmed circle, a solid gold circle. People who get in aren't expected to break that solid gold circle. The only way you're supposed to go is up, up, up into the high and mighty platinum circle. And the people in the platinum circle don't associate with those in the gold circle, any more than those in the gold circle associate with business failures."

"Who's in the platinum circle?" Ellen asked. Tina nodded her head toward a table close to the dais and told Ellen who the people at the table were. First there was Kimberly and next to her was a large, red-headed, pasty-faced, freckled man, who Ellen assumed was her husband. Tina also pointed out Enid Taylor, a minor actress who was heiress to a major automobile fortune. Her husband, Ronald, an exceptionally handsome man, pure Ivy League, was heir to an oil well fortune. The third couple were Sheila and John Fernwood, owners of the renowned Fernwood Leather Company, and the fourth couple were Donald and Beryl Surrey of the Surrey Publishing Company.

"What makes them platinum?" Ellen asked.

"Old money, mucho old money." Tina laughed. "They sit together and we sit together, and that's the way it is and it's the normal way to do things."

Ellen looked out from the head table at the assembled, beautiful people. Circles within circles. It was incredible. EL. Executive Leaders. Some brave new world!

Tina was drinking quite a bit and getting increasingly open and friendly. Ellen wondered how so slender a woman could drink so much wine. But Tina was happy and cheerful and friendly and Ellen could see that even if she was a bit of a fool, she was having a better, more relaxed time than Ellen was. Ellen dug into the first course, a seafood cocktail with huge shrimps and chunks of lobster. She had to remind herself to eat slowly. This was the kind of food she loved but even when Jeff took her out to dinner with clients she did not feel comfortable ordering so expensive a first course.

"I like you," Tina said, after her next glass of wine. "You're such a good listener. Listen, I'm going to Christopher's on Friday. How about joining me? Your first visit will be complimentary. If you come with me in the morning you'll bump into Milton Berle's wife. She's a regular on Fridays."

"I'd love to," Ellen said, "but I can't. I have a job."

"I haven't worked since I married Harry. What do you do?"

"I work at a nursery school."

"A nursery school," Tina said, wrinkling her lovely nose, "of all the ycchy things to do. All those little kids with running noses. How absolutely disgusting. Why do you do it?"

"I like it."

"Impossible," Tina said. "I remember, with horror, my parents' little school at the mission. All the kids had lice and impetigo. Well, my parents were old-fashioned and they didn't know better, but why should you work in a nursery school? It's like being an au pair girl. Really, nobody works in nursery schools."

"Maybe nobody else does it." Ellen laughed. "But I do."

"Every day?"

Ellen nodded.

"Well," Tina said, her voice starting to sound a little husky drunk, "you must be either a saint or an absolute masochist. I think it's terribly brave of you to get up every day. Some mornings I can't get up at all. The only thing that keeps me going is my analyst, Dr. Bloom. I see him five days a week and the appointments get me out of bed. Otherwise, I'd be a basket case. I really admire your energy, Ellen. I'm too neurotic to ever hold down a job."

Tina kept amazing her. She could not believe that anyone could be so cheerful about being neurotic and unable to function. Ellen had always thought that seeing an analyst was something a little disgraceful, shameful, something you hid from people like an idiot child, but Tina didn't seem to care at all if people knew.

"Well, if you can't come to Christopher's with me," Tina said, "perhaps we could meet for dinner one evening when Harry works late. Where do you live?"

"Freeport."

"Where's that?"

"It's on the south shore of Long Island."

"The south shore," Tina wailed, "but nobody lives there. Why on earth do you live there?"

"I like our house," Ellen said stoutly, "and it's near Jones Beach."

"Jones Beach," Tina exclaimed, "but nobody goes to public beaches. I'd rather die. We have a house in St. Thomas and you can visit us there. Kate goes to the Vineyard and sometimes we go with her. Her plane picks us up on the East River on Friday afternoons. Maybe you could come, too. But Jones Beach! Yccch!"

The band began to play and people rose to dance. "Isn't that the squarest music?" Tina grimaced. "It's straight out of Guy Lombardo. Listen, do you think Jeff would dance with me? I never get to dance and I'm afraid nobody else will ask me. Harry won't dance and Christopher warned me that it's an unwritten rule that men dance only with their wives at these functions."

"Why is it a rule?" Ellen asked. To her, it seemed perfectly logical that men would dance mainly with their wives.

"According to Christopher," Tina said, "men dance primarily with their wives because they see so little of them outside of EL. Honestly, some of these couples see each other *only* at EL affairs. A lot of these guys fool around but they don't fool around where it can hurt them. The wife of another EL'er is not to be taken lightly. Not to be taken, period. These guys fool around with secretaries, bachelor girls, salesgirls, women who won't ask marriage, girls who will lick their hands if they take them out to dinner and buy them a bottle of perfume. These guys are too smart to do anything to jeopardize their careers or their finances."

"I'll ask Jeff to dance with you as soon as he comes back," Ellen said. Jeff had left the table and was wooing Samson Plari, squatting down, almost kneeling at his feet. "He's a good dancer."

Companionably, she and Tina watched the dancing couples. Brooks Brothers doing the fox-trot with Dior. No flash. No fancy steps.

"God, notice how carefully they dance," Tina said.

"You make it sound as if all these men were cut out of a mold," Ellen said.

"They might as well be," Tina said cheerfully.

"But they're not all the same," Ellen protested. "For example, we're Jewish."

"So what?" Tina answered. "Just look at the people out

86

there. Nobody practices religion. Nobody cares about religion. Nobody looks Jewish or non-Jewish and nobody looks low-class. The hair's all straight or straightened, courtesy of God or Christopher, and the noses are also all straight, courtesy of good breeding or Dr. Saphire. Nobody is obese. Being Jewish doesn't really matter here. Money matters ... money and looks. But mainly money. And mostly it's new money and the men are all hustlers. That's why I say they're all cut out of a mold.

"Sure, sure, there's old money in the platinum circle, like our auto heiress, but the reason she and her husband associate with the solid gold circle is that it's a little livelier than in her usual circles. It's a diversion for them. Besides, she's an actress and I suppose that makes her a little more democratic. To be frank, even the platinum circle isn't where she really belongs. She's right up there in the diamond circle. But maybe there aren't enough interesting young people in the diamond circle for her. When the diamond circle gets boring they join EL or get active in the arts. Who knows. She's an exception. Most of us run true to type."

"Are there any colored members that you know of?" Ellen asked.

"I don't think so," Tina said. "But anyway, why would EL admit them if they did apply? Who needs them? They don't control any big money or have any influence politically. But in ten years, I'll bet one light-skinned enough and rich enough will apply and maybe he'll be accepted. And then you'll see that he looks just like the white men in EL ... only a little more sunburned. I think there are a couple of Oriental members out west."

Many of the couples were still dancing but Jeff hadn't returned to his seat. Ellen was glad that Harry didn't dance so that she could have Tina's company. Otherwise, she would have felt foolish sitting there alone for so long. Wryly, she watched Jeff doing his ritual wooing. He was floating about, talking to present and future clients, smiling, flattering, currying favor. His handsome face gleamed with perspiration and his smile seemed slashed on.

Well, there was nothing to do but eat. The waiters had brought the chateaubriand and Ellen attacked hers lustily. Tina lit a cigarette and left hers untouched.

"How can you ignore such marvelous food?" Ellen asked.

"I took a Preludin before I came," Tina said. Ellen looked at her blankly.

"Diet pills," Tina elaborated. "I live on them. I have a doctor who prescribes them by the hundred and when they stop working, he gives me a shot. I have a tendency to be fat and frankly I'd rather be dead. That's why I smoke so much. Actually, I hate smoking but it helps me to keep from eating.

"There's a little side effect to Preludin," she giggled. "They give you the world's greatest orgasms. You hardly need a man to go with them."

Ellen stopped eating for a moment and looked at Tina in amazement. This was the most eccentric person she had ever encountered. And Tina blithely continued.

"Some of his patients have swallowed tapeworms," she said, "but that kind of disgusts me. How do you feel about tapeworms? I don't like to think of something alive inside me, feeding off me. But it's a foolproof way of staying thin. I just take Preludin and smoke like a fiend. Sometimes nothing cuts my appetite and then I take a couple of sleeping pills and go to sleep until my hunger passes."

Feeling like a disgusting glutton, the edge taken off her pleasure at the food, Ellen, nevertheless, proceeded to demolish her steak. She was beginning to feel rather depressed at being stuck in her seat rather than dancing with Jeff even once. The lights dimmed and a row of waiters marched in bearing flaming baked Alaskas. Ellen felt like a child watching fireworks. She had never had baked Alaska before and, ignoring Tina's disapproving glances, she proceeded to finish every drop on her plate.

"You'd better meet my doctor," Tina said, "or you will be very very very sorry." Ellen ignored her and ate a few petits fours to still her depression. She felt even more depressed after eating them. Despite Tina's unusual conversation, she was a little bored. She had now been sitting in this seat for three hours and she found herself wondering if anyone ever before had listened to Tina for that length of time. She tried to signal to Jeff with her eyes that the waiter was taking away his food but he didn't seem to care. He was a hunter, tracking his prey, and food seemed extraneous for the moment.

"Are you going to join the women's investment club?" Tina asked.

"I don't know anything about it," Ellen said.

"Well, most of Christopher's customers belong to it. The EL women meet once a month with a stock market expert who helps them to invest their money. They meet on Thursday mornings."

Ellen shook her head. Perhaps her job *would* eventually get in the way.

Finally Jeff asked her to dance and she began to enjoy herself. He was a superb dancer, probably could have danced professionally if he hadn't considered dance the province of gigolos and homosexuals. Ellen didn't dance as well, but it was easy to follow him and she enjoyed his expertise and the esthetics of moving well to music. He made her feel secure and protected on the dance floor. Without him, she would never have dared such intricacies.

"Tina wants you to dance with her," Ellen told him.

"Sorry, babes," he said, "I don't have time. I'm here for business, not for fun. Come on, I want to introduce you to a couple of my clients."

He led her to a table off in a corner and introduced her to Michael and Davida Stewart. Stewart, president of a chain of record stores, was a short, stocky, black-haired man, whose speech showed Ellen immediately that he was not one of the elite. She was amused that his reaction to her was identical to Amos's. His eyes flicked over her, then dismissed her. "Pretty terrific husband you've got," he said.

"How do you do," Davida uttered. She seemed in a different

social class from her husband, was pencil-thin, quiet, repressed, and terribly nervous. Apart from the requisite diamond earrings and solitaire ring, she was totally plain. Her straight brown hair was drawn back into a bun, her chest was flat, and her dress managed to look terribly expensive and terribly commonplace at the same time. She wore no makeup, not even lipstick, and seemed about ten years older than her husband. She looked so unhappy that Ellen's heart went out to her. The woman seemed even more insecure than Ellen. There was no chance to make conversation now so Ellen merely smiled and filed the name away for future dinner parties.

"A smart guy," Jeff said as he danced her away, "up from the streets but he married the boss's daughter. I mean, look at the guy, a grease monkey who married real class. He could retire right now."

"Didn't she look very unhappy to you?" Ellen asked.

"Yeah, well, I think Michael plays around a little. But that suffering Joan Fontaine look is typical for that kind of Long Island society broad with the pencil between the teeth speech. She's damned lucky to have Michael. I mean, without her old man's dough, she would have been an old maid."

At the end of the set he introduced her to another client, Leonard Benson, heir to a large hotel fortune. Myra, his wife, was lissome, dark, charming, and petite, and Ellen envied her spunky self-confidence. She had read about the Bensons on the women's page of the *Times* when they were interviewed in the roof garden of their exclusive New York hotel. Myra had been quoted as saying that her favorite designers were Dior and Mollie Parnis. She had told the interviewer that she had no close women friends because her adored husband was her best friend. Ellen had remembered the interview because she had wistfully envied a woman who felt that way about her husband.

The Bensons were not the only hotel owners in EL. Jeff pointed out Rob Bright to Ellen. He was heir to another hotel chain who had recently married a starlet from Iceland. Mrs.

Bright was heartbreakingly beautiful, a statuesque Norse maiden whose looks threatened every woman there. But for once, her looks did not concern Ellen.

"Rob Bright," she gasped, "isn't he the guy who worked for the Un-American Activities Committee?"

"The very one," Jeff said. "He's a good man. I met him when I worked for the Bureau."

"Do you know how many careers he's wrecked?" Ellen whispered indignantly.

"They probably deserved to be wrecked," Jeff answered. "Where there's smoke, there's fire. Come on, let's say hello. I've done such a good job with Leonard's publicity, I might be able to convince Rob to come with me. Their hotels are so different there wouldn't be any conflict and I'd really like a stable of hotel owners."

"I can't talk to such a man," Ellen said. "I don't want to meet him."

"Listen, stupid," Jeff snapped, the pasted-on smile never leaving his face, "if you're so worried about career wrecking, how about starting to worry right here, at home. Do you want to wreck a potential client? Come on, Ellen. Don't be such a tight-ass all the time. What do you care? It's ancient history. It has nothing to do with you."

Without giving her time to deliberate further, Jeff waltzed her across the floor to where Rob and his wife stood.

"Jeff, baby," Rob said, clapping him across the shoulders, "welcome. I had no idea you'd even applied; was away during the voting. But you didn't need my vote, old buddy. I'm really glad to see you." He and Jeff shook hands warmly, then introduced the wives.

Rob was as tall as Jeff, about six feet two, and very thin. Everything about him was soft and shiny, like an Easter chick, with his soft blond hair, his watery smile, his white, frail hands. It was hard to picture him as a rabid anti-Communist, hard to see him as a destroyer and monster. Ellen found that she was incapable of being rude to so gentle a person in a social context of this kind. She could have publicly carried picket signs and demonstrated against him, but in this context, she was defused.

Jeff and Rob made a date for lunch at Christ Cella and the party started to break up. Tina ran over to her, hugged her warmly, took her phone number, and said she'd call her the next day. Jeff made the rounds saying goodnight to everyone. He was so exultant about his success that he didn't even complain when they got back into the dirty station wagon.

"It's goddamned fantastic," he rejoiced. "I got five new leads tonight."

He was unaware of Ellen's silence. She thought of how she had smiled at Rob Bright and she felt defiled. But what exactly could she have done? What should she have done? It would have been bad manners and bad for business to have spit in such beautiful, well-bred faces. And, after all, Rob hadn't done anything to hurt her personally. What would it have accomplished if she had been rude to him? She would have hurt Jeff and helped nobody. If she hurt Jeff, she hurt only herself, ultimately. She owed Jeff more than anyone else. So wasn't it her duty to help to advance his career? Besides, if most Americans not only accepted but even applauded the witchhunting of Rob Bright, shouldn't she go along with the rest? Wouldn't it have been foolish for her to jeopardize a potential client because of some abstract political principles that most Americans didn't agree with anyway? Why should she stand up and be counted if nobody gave a damn? Jeff was apolitical and probably she should be, too. When they were rich and successful enough and didn't have to worry about being associated with unpopular causes, she would snub people like Rob Bright. But until then, her first loyalty had to be to Jeff, not to society. If Jeff left her, she would be nothing. A strong, powerful, successful Jeff stood between her and a frightening, hostile world. Despite these past four years of marital security, she had never forgotten that rapists lurked and waited right outside the charmed gold circle of marriage.

But somewhere, deep inside her, the tingly glow from the

wine was turning to bile and a voice was rambling around within her screaming, "betrayer," and the voice was bitter and errant as a lonely bum in a subway at midnight. She pushed away her feelings of self-disgust.

Jeff was totally unaware of her mood. He kept reliving the triumphs of the night. "Kate Evans is going to increase her budget, Michael Stewart wants a whole new campaign, I'm having lunch Monday with Samson and Tuesday with Rob. My God. They loved me. Did you notice, Ellen? They loved me and I'm going to get every goddamned one of those accounts. I'm going to have to look for more space, enlarge the art department, train a few more men. I tell you, Ellen, the sky's the limit. You've found yourself a real winner, as if you didn't know. I tell you, there's no stopping me. I did it all myself. I didn't marry the boss's daughter and I didn't have a rich daddy. I did it all myself. One of the first things we have to do after I get a new car is to get you some decent jewelry. If you wear that costume crap, nobody will think I'm successful. Then we have to start thinking about moving. And Ellen, baby, we have to start thinking about the next kid. It's a waste for me to do so well without a son to hand it on to. We've got to have a son."

He put on the radio and started to sing along with the romantic tune that came on next. "I feel horny, I feel sexy," he crooned. "I feel happy and sexy and succsexful. Get it, Ellen, succsexful." His free hand moved over her breast but all she felt was depression.

"You like that, don't you?" he whispered heavily. "That always gets you hot, doesn't it? Unzip me, baby, and play with me."

"Don't be silly," she said, "it's dangerous. Just drive."

"It's not dangerous," he said, "lots of times I jerk myself off on long trips. Come on, Ellen, I want to feel that marvelous torture of *not* coming all the way home."

"But suppose you do come," she said, nervous as a rat in a maze, "why can't you wait until we get home?"

"I won't come. Over a suit this expensive? Not a chance."

"But I feel nauseous, Jeff. I ate too much."

"Bullshit," he said. "You always feel nauseous nowadays, if you don't have a headache. Come on, Ellen."

"But suppose somebody sees us."

"At this hour of night? Nobody's going to see us. Wait! I have a better idea. Lie down with your head in my lap and suck me all the way home."

"No, we'll get a ticket."

"Damn it, stop making excuses. Let me worry about the ticket."

"But, Jeff," she wailed, close to tears, "I don't want to. Not here."

"But I want you to," he said. She shook her head.

Suddenly he was in a rage, filled with fury. "I don't want to," he mimicked her, "not here. And too tired when we get home. Or Jennifer will conveniently wake up or you'll have a headache or you won't be able to find your diaphragm. Not here and not at home."

"I guess I'm just not very sexual," she murmured weakly.

"That's nothing new," he snarled, "but if you're not interested in sex, Ellen, the least you could do is try to make me happy. Damn it, I feel great, triumphant, and you're doing your best to spoil my evening. Is that what you want to do? Spoil my evening?"

"Of course I don't want to spoil your evening," she said. "I'm glad you were so successful."

"Really? It's hard to tell that from here. Listen, Ellen, it's time we got a few things on the table. I'm shooting straight up, like a rocket, and I'm prepared to take you along despite your frigidity, your lousy housekeeping, and, let's face it, strictly ordinary looks and background. I want to give you all the good things I'm going to get for myself. Now, why should I do everything for you, if you're prepared to do nothing for me?

"I loved you when we got married and I still love you, Ellen. But you've changed. At the beginning, you honestly seemed to worship me. I used to love the way you looked at me and listened to me and praised me. You used to make me feel absolutely perfect. Was that all some kind of goddamned game to make me marry you?"

"No," she said, "I honestly felt that way. But everything changes after marriage. You're not my knight on a white charger anymore. You're my husband. We live together, we know each other, we're older. It's normal for things to change after marriage. Surely you didn't marry me only because I praised you, did you, Jeff?"

"Of course not," he said. "I felt comfortable with you. I still do. I wouldn't have felt comfortable with a rich girl like Marilyn. Besides, money goes to money. A girl like that wouldn't have looked at me. I loved you and I felt comfortable with you and I still love you, Ellen, in spite of everything that's wrong with you. I don't think you would ever find anybody to love you as much as I do. And you should still be proud of me. Did you see the way people talked to me tonight? My God, I'm hot, I'm really hot. I was working away, getting all those leads, making new friends and clients, but I didn't see anybody going into raptures over you except for that crazy broad who kept yapping away at you while you stuffed your face. You weren't even smiling up there."

"I can't eat and smile at the same time," she said.

"Very funny, very funny. Then stop eating. The truth is, Ellen, I want a little appreciation. You're damned lucky to have me. There are a million ordinary little nursery school helpers who would give their eyeteeth to suddenly be elevated into the cafe society. There are dozens of women who would give me a blow job for a bottle of perfume and I want to give you the world. Do you want me to start cheating?"

"But, Jeff," she said, feeling guilty, confused, and close to tears. "I'm not in the mood. Do I have to be in the mood just because you're in the mood?"

"In the first place, babes, you're never in the mood. In the second place, the answer is yes. You do have to put yourself out and you do have to put out even when you don't feel like it if you want me to be strong and successful in business and keep bringing home the bacon. Tonight has been the high point of my life and you're like a fucking saboteur, trying to spoil it. Damn it, I give you everything and I'm only asking you to do what any normal, loving wife would do. Now are you going to do it or not?"

"All right, all right," she said, as she gingerly unzipped him.

"Damn it," he snarled, "it's not a snake. It's not going to bite you. Bend down and take it in your mouth."

She took it in her mouth and felt as if she would suffocate. Jeff's familiar, sickening smell filled her nostrils. She tried to make her mind blank as rhythmically he started to move back and forth in her mouth. Then, suddenly, just as they turned into their driveway he yelled, "Hold it," grabbed the back of her head with one firm hand and held it immobile while he spurted into her.

She thought she was choking, dying, drowning, suffocating, about to throw up. He pulled away from her and semen started to flow out of her mouth, over his pants, down her mouth and neck as she struggled up. She sat there in shock as they pulled into the garage.

"That was super, babes," Jeff said, quickly getting out. "Got to get this off my pants before it stains. Close the garage door, will you, babes?"

He dashed into the house and she sat there wearily, leaning her head against the door, gasping for air, wanting to vomit, befouled by the stench enveloping her. She grabbed a Kleenex tissue and wiped around her mouth, face, throat. "Tonight has been the high point of my life," she heard Jeff saying again in her mind. "Oh, you lousy bastard," she wept, "you'll pay for this. My God, you were supposed to be my protector and I need protection from you. You'll pay for this. Just you wait and see."

Weeping, she walked into the house.

3

During the time that followed their joining EL, despite the many dinner parties to which they had been invited, Jeff and Ellen had not reciprocated. The thought of a fancy dinner party seemed to Ellen beyond her capacity and Jeff fretted because their house was too small, the furniture too cheap, the dishes only inexpensive stoneware rather than china. Besides, Freeport was definitely not a classy address. They had already spent a few Sundays visiting real estate agents in more acceptable areas (by EL standards), such as Kings Point, Sands Point, Locust Valley, Scarsdale, and Greenwich. It was just a matter of time before they would move. Jeff had hoped that they could defer reciprocation until after moving but since that was still somewhat off, he decided they should go ahead with the party.

"We can call it a moving party," he said. "Then everyone will know we're going somewhere better."

Someone referred him to Mrs. Parry, a competent woman from Freeport who did a unique kind of catering with her sister. They cooked a gourmet dinner in their home, brought it to the client's house an hour or two before the dinner, set the table, arranged the flowers, warmed the food, and then served the dinner. Their brother served as bartender.

"You won't have to do anything but look pretty," Jeff told her, "and pleasant, too, if you don't mind."

Jeff insisted on selecting the menu himself: shrimp remoulade, filet mignon, Caesar salad, broccoli Hollandaise, and, for dessert, profiteroles, fruit, brie, and wafers. Regardless of his own preferences, he knew what would impress others.

During the year, Jeff had taken a course on wine tasting and he was more knowledgeable now than when he had first taken Ellen to that wonderful first dinner. He was starting to buy wines by the case at Sherry's, and even though she did not think she would ever really love wine, Ellen was beginning to be able to taste the differences between them.

To this first dinner party, they had invited Tina and Harry, Kate and Will, Michael and Davida, Amos and Marilyn, and Myra and Leonard Benson. Ellen's dining room table could be extended to seat twelve. At the last minute, Myra came down with a cold so they substituted their next-door neighbors, the Mozers, for the Bensons. The Mozers had been very friendly to Jennifer and Ellen liked and felt comfortable with them. He was a City College graduate with a blossoming practice as a tax lawyer. Susie Mozer had been a secretary but now she was eight months pregnant and was anxiously awaiting their first child.

Susie had put on so much weight that she lumbered like a dinosaur when she walked but she didn't care. She and her husband were totally indifferent to prevailing winds of fashion and even the kindest friend could not describe them as good-looking. But despite their lack of attractiveness to others, they seemed wonderfully attractive to each other. Irving Mozer obviously adored his wife, looked at her as if she were the most gorgeous woman around, and Susie walked, despite her ponderous weight, as if she believed that she was beautiful. They were a complete mystery to Ellen.

They were a mystery to Jeff, too. Part of his self-centeredness was his desire always to look perfect. And he couldn't understand how other people would not care about appearance.

"They'd never get into EL," Jeff said, "and the others might think we're crazy to be inviting them so be sure you explain to everyone that we invited them because they live next door. Otherwise, they might think the Mozers are our friends."

"They are our friends," Ellen said.

"You know exactly what I mean," Jeff snapped. "We're planning this party to enhance our image, not to sabotage it."

She was glad they were having the Mozers. She would seat them near Kate and Will because they were the only ones capable of seeing beneath the Mozers' exterior. The two couples would like each other.

The evening turned out to be surprisingly pleasant. Kate and Will were not the only ones who liked the Mozers. The relaxed behavior of the couple was so noncompetitive that everyone, even Jeff, relaxed for a little while. The Mozers ate without worrying about weight, praised everything lavishly without concern about seeming unsophisticated, and were genuinely but disinterestedly pleased to learn about the successes and triumphs of the other guests. Ellen could tell, watching Irving in action, that the last thing he would do would be to pitch someone's account at a small, informal party like this one.

Irving Mozer won Ellen completely with "this week's favorite joke."

"There's two guys," said Irving, "two guys who've been friends for thirty years; Joe and Harry. One day Joe says, 'Harry, I gotta tell you something. I've never liked you.' And Harry can't believe it. 'What do you mean? We've been friends for thirty years. We opened our businesses together. We raised our kids together. We all play bridge together.'

" 'I know,' says Joe, 'but I've never liked you. You want to know why? It's because you're pretentious.'

"And Harry looks at Joe in complete shock and he says, 'Pretentious? Moi?' "

They all howled with laughter. It was the perfect joke to describe most of EL, and for the moment they were willing to let down their guard and admit it. The happy atmosphere put Ellen in such high spirits that she decided to tell a little story about her teaching.

"I get so tired of standing," she told the group, "that I bought these perfectly awful-looking space shoes and when I get into school, I change and put my street shoes away and put on the space shoes and then I change back to my street shoes before leaving. One day one of the children said to me, 'Why do you change your shoes before you go home?' and I answered, 'I don't like people to see me in these ugly shoes.' Well, he just stood there and looked at me and then he said, 'But we're people, too.' "

But nobody laughed at her story and she felt like an idiot. Why had she thought that story would amuse the guests?

"What a charming story," Kate said with her usual kindness and support.

"Those shoes really are the ugliest," Tina murmured lazily. "It's a wonder you don't scare the children."

"Do they really mold them to your feet?" Davida asked timidly, and Susie Mozer added, "God, if I had a pair, I'd wear them all the time."

"I wouldn't work with children," Tina said, "if they gave me an entire space suit. It's hard enough to have one monstrous son like mine."

Ellen looked up and saw Jeff regarding her with chilling hostility, observing her as if she were a stranger. My God, had she said something wrong? Was Space Shoes one of his clients? Did Amos wear space shoes? Damn it, what had she done? She dreaded the time after everyone had gone, at the end of the evening, when Jeff would tell her succinctly but in cutting detail of all of her errors. She stumbled through the rest of the evening with a smile that was sheer grimace. What had she done?

Kate lingered last to thank her and kiss her goodnight.

"If you ever think of changing jobs," Kate said lightly, "you might try working for me. I have a very hard time getting honest, sincere people."

"Why, that's very kind of you, Kate," Ellen said, her eyes watering. She wished she could keep Kate and Will there to protect her from Jeff's wrath.

Ellen fled up to the bedroom while Jeff paid Mrs. Parry. As soon as she was alone, she couldn't stop the tears she had been holding back. Why did things have to be this way? Why couldn't she expect that Jeff would take her in his arms after the guests left, showing friendship and affection because they'd achieved a successful evening together? Why did she always have to be so frightened?

She heard him come in and pretending nonchalance, sat in front of her mirror brushing her hair while he regarded her with that same detached, frozen glance she had seen earlier that evening. Finally, she could stand it no longer.

"All right," she snapped, turning around and facing him, "what went wrong this time? What did I do wrong?"

"It's not that you did something wrong," he said, "it's that you are something wrong."

"And what the hell is that supposed to mean?" she asked angrily.

"Have you ever realized," he asked, "that you speak badly?"

"No," she said ironically, "that's one of the things you haven't pointed out to me before."

"Sharp as I am," he said, "I somehow never noticed until tonight. But suddenly I realized that your speech was not like that of our friends. Your speech is the same as those two deadbeats next door. You sound like them."

"And what's wrong with that?"

"Pure New Yorkese."

"Well, I am a New Yorker. You wouldn't expect me to have a southern accent. Nobody ever complained about my speech before. *You* never even noticed it before."

"But we never moved in EL circles before either," he said, "and I don't want people to be able to peg my wife as coming from Brooklyn. You can instantly tell that the Mozers have no class. Strictly Rego Park. I don't want people to meet you and peg you that way."

"Well, nobody else has ever complained about my speech," she said.

"Amos commented on it," he said quietly.

"Amos? Why would he be interested in my speech?"

"He said Marilyn mentioned it to him."

"Marilyn?" Ellen felt betrayed. She had thought, despite the essential superficiality of their relationship during this past year, since they encountered each other mainly at parties, that Marilyn liked her and that she could be herself with Marilyn. Apparently that was not so.

"I suppose I should be flattered that such important people," she said with heavy irony, "would take time to be concerned with my speech, but I don't care what they think. What makes them so special? Marilyn is too terrified of Amos to speak above a whisper and Cheap Amos is a boor. What right does he have to criticize anybody? Cheap Amos rolling on the floor!"

"If you keep throwing up every little business thing I tell you," Jeff said, "I'll stop telling you anything at all. But anyway, what Amos does has nothing to do with you. He can afford to do anything he wants and you can't."

Ellen sat there, demoralized and confused. She had tried her best, wanted Jeff to be proud of her, even forgiven him that awful scene in the car a year ago, but nothing she did seemed to be enough for him. When she improved in one way, he was criticizing another part of her. It didn't seem right that he was discussing her inadequacies behind her back with his new friends.

"I don't want to discuss this anymore," she said. "I want to go to sleep."

"Let's get back to your speech," Jeff insisted; "we have to do something about it."

"What would you like me to do? Cut out my tongue? There's no way I can ever talk like Kimberly Clare Wein. You can't erase my background. You're not Professor Higgins and I'm not as eager as Eliza to change. I'll never be able to talk as if I have a pencil between my teeth. I can't change my speech without seeming ridiculous and phony. I don't hear what seems to offend you, so how can I change it? Besides, Jeff, I think that *what* I say should be as important as how I say it. Marilyn may speak beautifully in your estimation, but I've never heard her say anything the least bit intelligent."

"I'm only trying to help you," he said, "to help us. Listen, if Carmine De Sapio could learn to speak beautifully, so can you. And Marilyn and Amos like you and want to help you. Why do you always act as if people who criticize you are your enemies? They're really your friends but you're too thin-skinned to realize it."

"I don't want to be criticized," she said.

"Who does? Nobody likes to be criticized but I have to take criticism and all kinds of other shit from clients every day and I take it with a smile because it's in my best interests. And this is in your best interests.

"Marilyn knows of a speech teacher," he continued, "named Helen Fern who works with singers at the Met, Congressmen's wives, people like you who are moving up and need help with their speech. I don't know why you have to act so tragic about it. Would you be sitting there crying if you needed braces on your teeth? All I want to do is to help you. You can pretend that you're an actress. They're always working on speech improvement. Helen Fern used to be an actress and now she works on diction and pronunciation and helps people with poor speech to get rid of dialect, regionalisms, pronunciations that peg them and she makes them more socially acceptable."

"Socially acceptable to who?" she snapped. "Oh, pardon me, I mean, to whom? I told you, I'm not Eliza Doolittle. I'm not some little flower girl. I had three years of college and I'm a nursery school assistant teacher and my speech is perfectly good enough for that."

"Well, your job's nothing to brag about. You never heard of anyone with social position or money who taught in a nursery school. That job's strictly for losers. Which brings me to something else. I'd appreciate it if you wouldn't go around volunteering the information that you work in a nursery school. And you don't have to tell people that you went to NYU. That's practically as bad as going to a city college. If anybody asks you, you can't tell them you went to a Seven Sisters school because all the other women in EL went to them and they might trip you up on that. Tell people you went to Cornell. Cornell's acceptable and it's so big that nobody will ever be able to catch you out on that."

"Oh, Jeff," she said, "I'm not going to lie about where I went to school. I don't care if people know I went to NYU. I tell you what, I won't lie. I just won't say anything."

"All right," he said, "that will have to do."

"Can we go to sleep now?"

"I'm still not finished. I want you to call Helen Fern. At your first appointment, she'll tell you how often you have to come. Marilyn said probably three times a week would do it."

"Three times a week? What does she charge?"

"Thirty-five dollars."

"A week?"

"An hour!"

"Over a hundred dollars a week? My God, Jeff, that's sinful. I could never spend money that way."

"Don't worry about the money, babes. I'll have her bill it to the business."

"But, Jeff," she said weakly, knowing she was already defeated, "how can I go to New York three times a week with my job? And now that Pat's gone, I like to spend as much time as possible with Jen."

"Give up the job. You know you're working for peanuts. I don't think there's another wife in all of EL who teaches in a nursery school and public school teaching has no class. But if you were teaching in a college, that would be impressive. Why don't you go back to school, finish your B.A. and work toward your M.A. and eventually your doctorate? A doctorate really impresses people. You should hear Amos talk about his cousin, the college professor. It's one of the few things that really impresses that *schmuck.*"

"Well, I'll think about it," she said, grudgingly.

"At's a ma girl," he said, and instantly fell asleep.

She climbed into bed and stared at him. How beautiful he looked, even asleep. He always delighted her esthetic sense but he was showing some signs of the struggle. He was thinner and there were new lines on his forehead even when he slept.

Why did she battle with him over everything? Why couldn't she just give in? The things he asked of her weren't really so bad. What was the battling about? All he wanted was to be as good to her as possible. Self-improvement was a mass movement. Hadn't she heard that self-improvement books were big sellers? So why couldn't she just accede gracefully to this opportunity to feel comfortable with the beautiful people. She decided to talk things over with Susie Mozer. She liked Kate and Tina but felt most comfortable with Susie.

"Please don't mention in front of Jeff that I've discussed any of these things with you," she begged Susie, when she visited her the next day.

"I wouldn't tell Jeff the right time," Susie said.

"Why not?"

"There are lots of things I could say," Susie said, "but I won't. After all, he's your husband and I guess you love him. But it depresses me to see you being treated like a doormat. You're so nervous your hands shake whenever he talks to you."

"That's not so," Ellen said defensively, regretting that she had confided in her neighbor. "He's a good husband and father and he loves Jenny and me."

"Maybe he does," Susie said, "in his fashion. Maybe my observations are all wrong. Maybe I should just mind my own business. Irving and I had a long talk about you and Jeff last night and he said if I told you how I felt, you might end our friendship. I hope you don't. But it makes me sad to see someone as young as you look so unhappy. Can I express myself or will you be angry?"

"You can say what you think," Ellen mumbled. "I don't have to agree with you and you may not be right."

"Okay," Susie said, "fair enough. It's just my opinion and I may be wrong. But, Ellen, I don't think Jeff's a good kind of person. And I don't think he's a good person for you."

"I don't know why you would think that," Ellen said hotly. "He was perfectly courteous to you and Irving last night and most of the world admires and adores him."

"Admires, maybe," Susie said, "adores, probably not. I knew you'd get angry but anyway, here I go. Listen, Ellen, did you read the book, *The Caine Mutiny?* Yeah, I figured. Almost everybody has. Well, remember that character Keefer in the book? He gets everyone stirred up and then he retires to his cabin and he isn't blamed for anything at the end. He's the only one who comes out lily-white. Well, that's the way I see Jeff. He's the kind of person who can cause an awful lot of misery and guilt but would never take the responsibility for what he's done."

"I don't know why you say that," Ellen said.

"I've been living next door to you for over a year," Susie answered. "I can see how unhappy you are."

"I'm as happy as you," Ellen said firmly, whistling in the wind.

"Listen, Ellen, I really like you. I'm not trying to be mean. But you're *not* happy. Forget about me. This isn't some kind of happiness competition. I look at your face, your mouth, your eyes, and I can see that the only times you're happy are when you're with Jennifer or going to work. But your marriage doesn't seem to nourish you. I don't think it could nourish anybody. Jeff isn't evil, as far as I can see. But he's so damned self-centered, so

106

egoistic that he can't see anybody but himself. The guy's in conflict, too. I really think he loves you and needs you in his own way. You're all the family he has. Everybody needs some kind of attachment. But he doesn't want to need that attachment. That's why he's angry so much of the time. I don't dislike the guy, Ellen. I feel sorry for him. There's a feeling of sadness and desperation underneath all the charm. He acts as if he feels lost and disappointed that all of his success leaves him feeling empty. At least that's the way I see it. I don't think he'll ever make you happy and I don't think anybody could ever make Jeff happy."

Popular psychology, Ellen thought as she left, vowing never again to discuss anything personal with Susie or anybody else. If all she could have in life would be a façade of happiness and success, she would do everything she could to achieve that. But during the days that followed she found herself filled with almost unbearable nostalgia and regret. "Maybe I should have married Saul," she told herself. During the last five years, from time to time, she had heard of Saul. He had become a teacher, was working on his doctorate, had married a girl from Borough Park, and already had two children. The last she had heard, he still lived in Brooklyn. Brooklyn! She shuddered. No, she had to be honest with herself. If she still lived in Brooklyn she would be longing for her present life. But at least I should have slept with Saul, she thought. The truth is that I'll never know if there's something wrong with me, with Jeff, or with us, until I do sleep with someone else. She had messed up her life and she could do nothing but go forward with the life she had chosen.

She turned her thoughts from Saul to her present situation.

Everything seemed to be pushing her to give up her job. She was missing the EL events held for women, the fashion shows, investment club, charity luncheons. Hardly a day passed that Jeff did not urge her to take speech lessons and she found herself growing increasingly insecure about the way she sounded.

But she finally made her decision because of Jennifer. The child had been unhappy, weepy, complaining constantly of stomachaches, since Pat's departure. She now spent mornings at the public school, but every day she had a temper tantrum about getting on the bus and many times Ellen was forced to drive her and to be late for her job at the nursery school. The half-day work that had seemed so satisfactory when Pat was there now meant that she was away from Jennifer most of every day.

Every morning Jennifer would weep, "I don't want to go to school, I want to stay home with you, Mommy," and every afternoon there was a scene outside the house when she refused to come inside with the housekeeper. She would shriek and scream until finally the housekeeper would pick her up and carry her, kicking, spitting, and scratching into the house. Finally the housekeeper's ultimatum: either Mrs. Sheldon was home by two or she was leaving. Ellen had to leave home too early for the morning session and arrived home too late to be on the afternoon session. She would have to resign; it would make life much less complicated.

She really would not mind being home with Jennifer because she adored the child. Although she felt it was essential for Jennifer to play with other children, to avoid the loneliness of being an only child, if Jennifer wanted her mother there when she came home from school, it was Ellen's responsibility to be there.

When she went to the school's director to give notice, Mrs. Stark was annoyed as well as disappointed that she would have to look for a replacement in the middle of the year. "The children love you," Mrs. Stark said regretfully.

"I know," Ellen said, "and I'm really conflicted about it. But I just can't keep working and give Jennifer her due and give Jeff his. Besides, he keeps talking about having another child and I suppose it would be better for Jennifer if I did."

"What about your due?" Mrs. Stark asked gently.

"Yes, well, there's nothing I can do about that. But I will miss getting my own paycheck, small as it is. Somehow, getting paid gives me a feeling of dignity."

"Keeping you home will be a powerful responsibility for

Jeff," Mrs. Stark said, her kind face creased with genuine concern. "It can't really be good either for Jeff or Jennifer to separate you from work you find so fulfilling. You should be doing more work, not less."

"Oh, well," Ellen sighed. "The die is cast. Maybe someday I could come back."

"I would always have room for you. There are plenty of jobs like this one. You can always find a job. That's not the problem. The question is if you will ever be able to return emotionally. It seems to me that you're turning your back on something that gives you great pleasure in order just to be another supported housewife."

"Most of the women I know don't work," Ellen said. "In fact, only one of my friends does work and she's president of her own knitwear concern."

"Just because they don't work," Mrs. Stark said, "doesn't mean that's right for you. I think you're more like me. I've worked all my life. Marriage was never enough for me either."

Mrs. Stark hugged Ellen and seemed close to tears and Ellen shared her sadness. Why had she done this? She had made another wrong choice, another wrong turn, but she seemed unable to choose correctly. At least now she would have plenty of time for all of the responsibilities involved in Jeff's career. That should be enough for her. And Jeff was so pleased about her decision that she started to feel better about it. "At's a ma girl," he said.

"The children will miss me," she said. "I feel bad about quitting in the middle of the year."

"Forget it. They'll get over it in a day. Kids have short memories. Why don't you go out and buy yourself a new raincoat. Get a Burberry. The crummy one you wear makes you look like a refugee. I want you to look like a glamorous spy."

Her mother was also delighted. "Who needs that nothing little job," Mrs. Graetz contributed with her usual wisdom when Ellen called to tell her. "Maybe now you'll have another child."

But it was Jennifer's reaction that made Ellen feel she had

made the right decision. "You mean you'll be home all the time now?" Jennifer squealed. She threw her arms around Ellen and hugged her tightly.

Well, Ellen thought, everyone was pleased and that was that, but she would miss going to a job each day. "I really was very good with children," she told herself, "calm, loving, efficient. I hope that Jennifer has lots of teachers like me. Well, I suppose I can always go back someday."

Jeff's approval was short-lived. He continued to nag her about her speech and finally she made an appointment with Helen Fern.

"Get ready for the big time," Jeff told her. "By the end of next year we'll be ready to move into our mansion, the house where we can spend the rest of our lives. And by then, I want you looking and sounding like a queen."

Helen Fern lived on Fifth Avenue and Ellen felt intimidated the minute she walked into the mirrored lobby. The doorman's eyes traveled over her in quick appraisal. The snob's snob. She was wearing her expensive new Burberry and Delman shoes. Did she pass? Apparently so, for the doorman tipped his cap. She felt a perverse surge of triumph at having passed the Cerberus of the building.

The elevator operator also looked her over carefully, then humbly kept his eyes on the floor as he brought Ellen up to the penthouse. His timidity and respect again reassured her about her appearance.

He looks at me, she thought, the way Jeff and I look at the members of the platinum circle. The very idea of the platinum circle drove Jeff crazy. "We may be in the solid gold circle for now," he said, "but we're moving. We're gonna be right up there in the platinum circle someday. There's no stopping me."

The elevator door opened on a polished wood hallway and she started to ask, "Which apartment," but quickly saw, before making the faux pas, that there was only one apartment on the

110

floor. She again felt intimidated and the intimidation increased as soon as the uniformed maid, looking like a Mary Petty illustration, opened the door.

The maid looked at her suspiciously. She wasn't fooled by Ellen's new clothes, or so it seemed to Ellen. The maid showed her into a lavishly furnished living room, filled with Art Deco mirrors and furniture, and informed her that Madame Fern would be in shortly. Ellen walked to the window and looked out over Sheep Meadow in Central Park. A view of Central Park, like the uniformed maid, was another of the possessions she had always associated with the very rich. She wondered if she would ever be comfortable and casual about these things and thought how extraordinary it was for a single woman to have such an apartment for herself, not to get everything through a man.

When Helen Fern made her entrance she found herself speechless. Helen was straight, slender, carved of white marble, with hair like a helmet of blazing white, and eyes a powerful blue. What extraordinary presence. She wore an embroidered blue caftan, darker than her eyes, and the clinging fabric revealed a body that even a thirty-year-old would be proud of. She had to be at least fifty, Ellen thought, although her face was unlined. Ellen stood there shyly, certain that Helen, as well as her maid, could see right past the raincoat and shoes to the insecure little nursery schoolteacher she was in her own mind.

"Come in, dahrling," Helen said in a deep, cavernous, melodic voice, "and do stand up straight."

Her voice was a work of art. Mutely, Ellen trailed after her into the workroom, feeling like a hulking immigrant behind that magnificent posture and carriage. In the hallway, her eyes lingered on a piece of sculpture.

"Lipchitz," Helen said and Ellen made a mental note to find out who that was.

Helen sat down at an antique table with rosewood inlays and magnificent patina, switched on a tape recorder, and said in that impressive voice, "Tell me about yourself."

Ellen was terrified of the tape recorder. "I don't know what to say," she faltered.

"Why don't you begin with your reasons for coming here."

"I came because, because, Jeff wanted me to improve my speech."

"Jeff, I assume, is your husband. Really, I'm not interested in what he wants. You're not a child. I'm interested in what you want. Do *you* want to improve your speech?"

"I guess so."

"What do you mean, you guess so? You must be more positive, more affirmative. Have you ever listened to yourself on a tape recorder?"

Ellen shook her head abjectly.

"Do you have any idea of how you sound, Mrs. Sheldon?"

"No, I really don't," Ellen said, "but I'm aware of how other people sound and a lot of them sound better to me than I do."

Helen asked her a few more questions, just to get something on tape, then told her to sit back, relax, and listen. Ellen blanched as she did. As bad as her voice was, it sounded particularly so in juxtaposition with Helen's magnificent deep contralto.

"My God," Ellen said, "I can't believe that that tiny, whiny, breathless, childish voice is mine."

"But there it is," Helen said, "incontrovertibly. Most people are shocked when they first hear themselves," she added, not unkindly. "Actually, your voice is not quite as high-pitched as it sounds. The tape recorder does that to everyone."

"I sound like a frightened little girl."

"You sound like what you seem to be," Helen said. "If you change the way you sound, it may help you to change the way you feel. You tell me you've been working in a nursery school as an assistant teacher. You must have been particularly good with children if you were able to overcome the handicap of that voice. Usually, such voices cause discipline problems in the classroom."

Ellen cringed. How could she have been so unaware all her life! No wonder poor Jeff had been embarrassed.

"Your voice also pegs your class," Helen continued. "It announces to the world that you are a lower-middle-class New York who has attended public schools. It tells the listener that you are insecure, childish, and unsure of yourself . . . certainly not a person who merits listening to."

"How can you tell all of this from my voice?"

"I was an actress," Helen said, "and an actress has to understand different regions, dialects, social levels, and emotional shadings. In addition, I am aware of pace, and you rattle on like a child. Your feelings float right to the surface. You are not self-contained, not poised. You're emotionally disorganized, on a see-saw, and your continual mood shifts are accurately reflected in your voice. We must work with that as well as with your actual speech production. Your speech is a manifestation of your total personality. Is that clear?"

Ellen nodded and her eyes filled with tears.

"For heaven's sake, don't cry," Helen said impatiently. "You must stop being so childish. You're here to be helped and I can't help you by lying to you about what I see. Think of me as a doctor. The truth may hurt, undoubtedly it does, but you will thank me when we have finished with each other.

"You are only twenty-five, half my age, and you have an entire lifetime before you. Women are beginning to come into their own and will have increasing responsibility and leadership in this society. I can make you sound like a leader, give you the poise to do with the rest of your life whatever you want to do. I can help you to sound like a woman, not like a naughty child."

Ellen wiped her eyes and waited.

"Now for the next point," Helen continued. "Your posture is abominable. A lady stands as if she's proud of herself, but your posture constricts your voice. I want you to stand over there at the lectern and read this first passage from Genesis. You must practice daily at home and listen to yourself on the tape recorder.

"We have to bring your voice up here to the roof of your mouth. At the moment, it's way back in your throat. Then we have to lower the pitch so you sound like an assured woman, not like a petulant twelve-year-old."

Ellen stood at the lectern and started to read.

"Stand up straight," Helen prodded. "You cannot produce beautiful sounds if your posture is so bad. Your chest cavity must be open, free, in order to resonate. You will have to get in touch with Alain LeFleur. I cannot do this all by myself."

"Who is he?" Ellen asked.

"I give ladies rich voices." Helen smiled. "And he gives them rich bodies. He lives with his boyfriend of thirty-five years in a fabulous old carriage house on East Seventy-seventh Street. The exercise room is sumptuous and he works with only one client at a time so there's no lack of privacy and none of that usual, horrid gymnasium odor. It's the most pleasant environment possible for firming up. Alain is usually all booked up because his clients buy hours by the year, at a cost of five thousand dollars for one hour, each week, per year. Then, whether they use the hour or not, the time is theirs and is kept for them, in case they fly into town unexpectedly. He has no time for new clients unless a regular leaves and that rarely happens. I've been visiting Alain now for twenty-five years."

So that accounts for her magnificent body, Ellen thought.

"However," Helen continued, "you may be in luck if you call him immediately. Our young Senator's wife used to be a steady client. She owned three hours a week but she can hardly commute now from Washington to New York City. So, if you hurry, you might be able to get all three hours."

"Fifteen thousand dollars a year?" Ellen exclaimed in horror.

"Well, of course that's up to you," Helen said. "If you do not wish to spend more than five thousand, he will give you exercises to do at home between sessions and you will still improve."

"I'd have to ask my husband."

"But do take care of it today," Helen urged; "you may never have the opportunity again."

"Did you mean the wife of Senator Dunstan?" Ellen asked.

"Yes, indeed," Helen answered, "you're in good company at Alain's."

It was all impossible, Ellen thought. Five thousand for Alain and seventy-five hundred for Helen. That would be twelve thousand, five hundred dollars a year, a fortune, four times what she had made in the nursery school. It's ridiculous, decadent, narcissistic, and I won't do it, she thought.

"Since we are being frank with each other," Helen said, "there is one more thing I'd like to mention to you. You should do something about your hair."

"My hair?"

"I'm afraid it's all wrong."

"What's wrong with it?"

"It's curly. Verging on kinky, actually. It looks low class; Puerto Rican, Italian. You'll notice that nobody well dressed has curly hair. You'll have to straighten it or get a wig. I prefer straightening. Even the Senator's wife straightens her hair. But a wig is acceptable if it's made of human hair. Above all, no synthetics." She shuddered. "Nobody wears synthetics except manicurists and ladies of the night."

Ellen felt so mortified that she was again close to tears. It took all of her will to hold them back, but hold them back she did. She had thought she looked so nice, had even thought the doorman and elevator operator looked at her in admiration, but instead, everything about her was all wrong.

Helen picked a card off her desk and handed it to Ellen. "If you don't get it straightened," she said, "go to Dick Delaney. You'll have to call for an appointment, you can't just wander in. He does all of the wigs for television and the movies."

"How much is a wig?" Ellen asked.

"You certainly are concerned about money," Helen said with some asperity. "It's unbecoming, Ellen, to be always asking how much things cost. When you go into a restaurant do you examine the menu and weigh what you want against how much it costs?"

"Of course," Ellen said. "I never order lobster."

"You must stop that at once," Helen cautioned her. "It's terribly gauche. It's best if you don't even look at the menu. Either ask the maitre d' to recommend the specialties or else simply ask for what you want. I am always dieting so when I go out for dinner I usually ask for broiled fish, a salad without dressing, and some club soda. And I always force myself to leave half of everything on my plate.

"Nevertheless, to answer your question about the wig, a good human hair wig starts at about four hundred."

Ellen felt as if she were floundering in whipped cream. Each subject she and Helen touched on caused a little ping, a light went on, a bell rang, and the money total rose. And she was the pinball, staggering from point to point.

"Four hundred dollars is a lot of money," she said. "I've always kind of liked my hair. I never have to do anything with it. I just shampoo it, let it dry, and it stays in curl."

"But it's not fashionable," Helen said, "and you cannot effect your transformation in parts. What good would a beautiful voice be if your hair were *outré*? And what does it mean if you end up spending fifteen thousand dollars on yourself this year if you spend an extra four hundred for a wig? It's a far better expenditure than a new fur coat. So wear your old fur coat for another year. The total transformation I'm talking about will last for the rest of your life. You won't have to do anything until you're ready for a face lift."

Ellen was beginning to feel amused. Each frame of reference was so different from her own that there was no point in further discussion. How could she explain to Helen that she regarded a fur coat as a lifetime investment.

"I'll ask Jeff about everything," Ellen said, "and if he says we can afford the things you suggest, I'll go along with you."

"There's a dear girl. And there's a smart girl. Many people are born rich, Ellen, but hardly anyone is born looking or sounding beautiful. Those qualities are acquired and that's the purpose of money. You can acquire visual and auditory beauty if you are willing to invest enough time and money."

Feeling somewhat dazed by her experience, Ellen slouched out into the foyer where the next client stood waiting. Ellen gazed at him in awe. He was an absolutely gorgeous man, clad in immaculate tennis shorts, about six feet tall, with a head of thick, wavy, lustrous black hair, worn a bit longer than was fashionable. This hair framed a magnificent, bronzed face, green eyes, and flashing white teeth which now shone when he smiled enthusiastically at the two of them. He stood there almost preening. Everything about his appearance was an esthetic delight. Ellen was sure Helen approved completely of him. He looked like a Renaissance prince or a Donatello statue. He continued to flash his blinding smile at her and shyly, self-consciously, she smiled back. A cat can look at a king!

"This is Giovanni Lampedusa," Helen told her. "He is here working with *La Stampa,* the Italian newspaper, and I am helping him with his English."

"Dear, beautiful lady," he said, kissing Helen's exquisitely manicured fingers, "you are not only helping me with my England, you are helping me with my life."

Ellen hid her ragged nails in her coat pocket.

"English," Helen corrected.

"My English—" he twinkled at Ellen—"she is very poor. I needa the lesson every day but today, forgive, I miss. I have-a the special tennis match. You will forgive, Helen? Ah, beautiful Helen. Helen of Troy."

"Who can refuse you anything, you cherub," Helen said, the frost melting before his radiance.

Oh, God, Ellen thought, another phony charmer like Jeff.

"I'll see you tomorrow at our usual time," Helen said, shaking her head disapprovingly, but enchanted.

Giovanni again kissed her hand. "I thank you, my bellissima teacher. You are the saint."

He walked out of the apartment with Ellen and they waited for the elevator together.

"You play the tennis?" he asked.

"No," Ellen said shyly, not daring to look into his eyes.

"I am very good," he said. "Number one with the tennis. You come watch sometime and I win for you."

117

When they got into the elevator Ellen kept her eyes on the floor, self-conscious before his exuberance and beauty. She felt as unpoised as a schoolgirl sighing over Elvis Presley. He put his hand under her chin and turned her eyes up toward his.

"Why do you hide so pretty a face?" he asked.

She was completely tongue-tied before this gorgeous creature. They stood for a moment in the lobby.

"Is yes?" he asked.

"Is what yes?" Ellen gasped.

"Is yes you come sometime and watch me? And then we have espresso and you tell me how I am so wonderful?"

Ellen burst out laughing. He was so delicious, so guileless in his arrogance.

"And then what do you tell me?" she asked. She was flirting for the first time in her life.

Giovanni took one of her hands in his. "*Amica mia,* I don't talk with you. I look at you."

He raised her hand to his lips and lightly kissed her fingers. "I must see you again, my dahrling," he said in a perfect imitation of Helen.

Abruptly then, he looked at his watch and prepared to hurry off. "I must go, my dahrling. I cannot be late for the tennis. Quick, quick, tell me when we can meet?"

Scenes from movies and fragments of Italian melodies ran through Ellen's mind. Rossano Brazzi, Vittorio Gassman, Ezio Pinza, Enzo Stuarti, Marcello Mastroianni, all those magnificent Italians and now, and now, Giovanni Lampedusa and Ellen Graetz Sheldon, late of Brooklyn. She felt like a flower suddenly hit by a ray of sun. Of course his act was not to be believed, but oh, how she liked and needed it. Maybe because he was foreign he really did find her attractive and it wasn't all a clichéd Italian ritual. How wonderful if he found her attractive before she had her hair, her voice, or her figure straightened out.

"Quick, quick, my dahrling," he pressed. "I will be late for the tennis."

Her heart was pounding wildly. "I'm married," she said tragically.

"But of course," he said, "everyone is married. I, too, am married. I am not asking you for marriage."

He sighed, pressed his hand against his tortured heart, looked again at his watch, and gracefully turned to leave. He stopped a few feet away, looked back at her with dramatic passion, said, "I weel call. From Helen I weel find the number." He blew her a histrionic kiss, again pressed his heart, and was off.

What a delightful interlude. It had picked her up to be thought attractive after Helen's negative assessment. She went off to meet Tina for lunch at the Plaza, feeling surprisingly cheerful.

Tina was there already, looking as magnificent as usual in a brocade dress and matching coat trimmed with mink. They ordered a bottle of good wine, the Plaza's famous tossed chef's salad, and raced to talk.

"Remember when you didn't like wine?" Tina asked, and they laughed together.

"You really look great today," Tina said. "I've never seen you look so cheerful. Don't tell me. I know. There's only one thing that makes an old married woman look that optimistic, and that's a little affair. Come on, Ellen, who's the man?"

"You know I'd never have an affair," Ellen said.

"You'll change," Tina said airily.

Then Ellen told her about Giovanni.

"He sounds divine," Tina said. "If you don't want him I'll take him."

"He's not mine to give." Ellen laughed. "I'll probably never see him again."

"How did you get to Helen Fern?" Tina asked.

"Marilyn recommended her to Jeff."

"Oh, yes, I think she worked with both Marilyn and Amos."

"Well, I don't see that she did such a great job with Amos," Ellen said, "he speaks like a stevedore."

"Rough speech is his stock in trade," Tina said. "He does it

119

to *épater le bourgeois*. His construction workers feel comfortable with it and it disarms his competitors by giving them a false sense of superiority. Listen, with the way Jeff has Amos's name plastered all over New York, he could afford to speak any way he likes. But actually, he's quite canny and he could speak perfectly if he chose. That's why he went to Helen. But I think she worked a lot more with Marilyn."

"That doesn't show either," Ellen said; "she whispers."

"But such cultured whispers." Tina laughed. "It's kind of hard for her to speak up with that monster of a husband but you know that when he's not around she speaks quite beautifully. She told me that when she first went to see Helen, armored in diamonds like some kind of insect, she was practically mute. That's what ten years of marriage to Amos had done to her. The reason I know is that she used to go to Helen's right after Dr. Bloom."

"Dr. Bloom? You mean Marilyn uses your analyst? Why does she see an analyst?"

"Wouldn't you need one if you were married to Amos?" Tina asked, and they laughed in agreement together. "As far as Alain is concerned, many of Christopher's customers go to him and they swear by him. I would go myself but instead Harry is building me an entire gym in our house. That way, I can exercise whenever I like. You can come and use it, too, but first I think you should go to Alain to learn what to do."

After lunch, Tina left her to go home and Ellen walked over to Jeff's office to tell him about her adventures. As usual, he was irritable and absorbed in his work and she felt as if she were intruding. He listened with half an ear, then said, "Don't worry about the money. I keep telling you we can afford any of these things. So just do it and tell them to bill the office."

"Do you want to have dinner tonight and go to a movie?" she asked.

"Can't, babes, have an important appointment with a client."

"All right," she said, "I'll go home. I don't like to miss dinner with Jennifer anyway."

120

"Fine, fine," he said.

"Jeff, I'm really grateful to you for spending all this money on me," she said.

"It's a good investment," he answered. She waved goodbye and disconsolately drove home. Why did she feel let down? Why did she always want something of Jeff that he couldn't give?

She went to see Alain LeFleur the next day. His street was one of the most beautiful in the city, radiating a quiet, luxurious gentility with its townhouses, expensive antique shops, and neatly manicured trees. Ellen noted that there was a townhouse for sale next door and she wondered if they were rich enough to afford it. She had no idea because she still didn't know how much money Jeff made. None of their expenses seemed to bother him and she knew that he was putting away large chunks for their future house, so she assumed that all was well. It was a strange, infantilizing feeling for her to know as little about her husband's finances as she had about her father's. Whenever she asked Jeff for information, he dismissed her with a glib command not to worry her pretty little head. She really would like to know, to be treated like an adult, to have a joint checking account instead of having to go to Jeff for everything now that she no longer had her little salary. Little as it had been, she missed her own paycheck and the feeling of independence it had given her.

Alain occupied two floors of the carriage house. At the top of the stairs she was met by Alain, a man with a body so slim and supple in his leotard that it was hard to believe he was over sixty.

"No, no, my dear," he exclaimed by way of introduction, "do not make so much noise. Put your foot down softly. Lift your weight up toward heaven as you climb. Each time you come here, from now on, practice a graceful climb up the stairs until you can do it without making a sound."

More suggestions, but from him she didn't mind. He was pleasant, kind, warm, but impersonal, a living paradox, a man who despised the female flesh he shaped and molded. He had been a dancer in his youth and like Helen Fern had sensibly channeled his expertise into a modest gold mine when he'd grown too old to perform. He and Bruce, his housemate, were constantly showered with gifts from grateful clients. Bruce kept the books for Alain and it seemed a comfortable relationship. They didn't own the carriage house but had the loan of it for as long as they wished.

"I'm just a poor artist," Alain told Ellen, "I could never afford a house like this one. Did you notice the one next door? They're asking four hundred thou and it will probably be snapped up right away. Perhaps your husband would be interested. A terrible chore to traipse here from Freeport. Why do you live there? I don't know anybody else who does."

She was beginning to feel paranoid about her address. Jeff had been right about that, too.

The dressing room where she changed into her leotard was lovely and filled with delicious fragrance from the soap—heavy, beige, grainy, English oatmeal soap. Timidly she came out of the dressing room but her self-consciousness was immediately minimized by his clinical impersonality. He looked her over carefully, measured her, and uttered an occasional hum. When he had finished he said, "Mrs. Sheldon, there's a great deal I can do with your body and posture, but I'm not a miracle worker. You'll have to get rid of those breasts. You might as well have a fifty-pound rucksack strapped to your middle. Thank God breast reduction operations exist and they're absolutely safe. You'll have to have one. After that, we'll be able to get the rest of your body in shape. But you must have the breast operation because no amount of dieting will reduce them. Once they're off, we'll be able to achieve almost perfect measurements."

"A breast operation?" She had never heard of such a thing. Bobbed noses, yes, but never breast reduction.

"Cup of tea," he said. "Quite ordinary, really. I know several ballerinas who reduced themselves to little more than nipples. Large breasts are impossible, my dear, make the entire body look fat. They inhibit athletic prowess, prevent graceful dancing, prevent you from wearing clothes without a bra. It makes you look matronly and you're too young to have a matron's body. Have you ever noticed that all leading models are flat-chested? Now I'm not advocating anything as extreme for you as what ballerinas do. They don't have to totally come off.

"What exactly is your bra size? Thirty-four-DD?" He shuddered. "A terrible size. I want you to be reduced to a thirty-two-B. I'm not greedy. Some people might push for the A but I would accept the B. But a B is the maximum. Anything bigger than a B looks cowlike.

"I'll give you the name of my clients' favorite plastic surgeon. After your recovery, you will need two hours a week with me. I'll hold the two hours for you if your husband will send me a deposit. I'll use them for someone else until you're ready. Would that be all right?"

"I'll ask my husband," she said, depressed.

"Nothing to be sad about, my dear," he said, "and you needn't be afraid. It's just a routine sort of operation and afterward you'll thank me."

She dressed quickly, filled with self-disgust. What a visit. She had found someone who despised her body even more than she did. She left and made straight for Rumplemayer's, where she ordered a hot fudge sundae with all the trimmings. The hell with all of them.

But when she called Tina, Tina agreed with Alain completely.

"I never wanted to say anything," Tina said, "but your breasts do spoil your figure. I'm lucky that I'm built like my mother and you know that missionary types were required to be flat as boards."

"So you think I should do it?" Ellen asked.

"I know you should do it. Let's do it right away. I'll go with you next week. I could ask the doctor for referral to a face lift specialist."

"Tina, you're kidding. You're much too young for a face lift."

"Just getting ready," Tina said. "At the sight of the first wrinkle I willingly go under the knife."

The plastic surgeon's office was on Central Park West and also had a view of the park.

"You're nobody in New York," Tina said seriously, "unless you can see the park."

Ellen was glad today that she had Tina cheerfully babbling away at her side. What am I doing here? Ellen asked herself. It's insane to let someone take a knife to my perfectly serviceable, functional, healthy breasts. Jeff had always said he liked large breasts but when she told him about Alain's advice he had told her to at least investigate it. The initial visit to the plastic surgeon was a hundred dollars. Another waste of money. But if the surgeon was honorable, maybe he would say that Alain was wrong. It was worth a hundred dollars to prove it.

In the center of the waiting room, on a polished pie-crust table, stood an antique silver service with coffee and tea, and Wedgwood platters of miniature Danish pastries. Despite Tina's horrified looks, Ellen proceeded to enjoy herself with the delicate cakes, thick with nuts and raisins. She could smell the real butter. "From Dumas's," the receptionist told her, when she inquired.

The couches were filled with women, each one more beautiful than the next. None of them were stuffing themselves with pastry, Tina reminded her. Ellen looked at each in turn and wondered what had been done to them. They all looked practically perfect. She and Tina flipped through copies of *Vogue, Harper's Bazaar, Town and Country,* and *Elle.* Alain was right, now that she was noticing. Not a single model had breasts. Well, so what if they didn't. Who was it that had the right to set a standard that went contrary to nature? There should be room for diversity in shapes and sizes. Damn it. It was the fault of all those homosexual men, like Alain.

Suppose women set a standard that men's penises had to conform to a certain length or be amputated or stretched. Ha! Fat chance any man would ever agree to that. Why were women such sheep? Why was she being railroaded into something she didn't want?

"The whole thing's ridiculous," she told Tina. "I won't do it."

"Be reasonable, Ellen," Tina said. "Accept reality. No woman who wants to model, get into movies, move with the cafe society, or get into the platinum circle, has big breasts. Even in the movies, big breasts are always considered low class. People like Jayne Mansfield and Marilyn Monroe are jokes and all because they have big tits. You know that the real ladies, the ones who are respected, like Grace Kelly and Audrey Hepburn, are all as flat as I am. Flatter!"

"The surgeons are all men," Ellen brooded. Were there any female plastic surgeons? If there were, how did *they* feel about chopping off perfectly good breasts? What did they do with the parts they chopped off? Down the drain? She shuddered.

My body is no longer me, she thought. I'm no longer me. Now my body is other, the enemy, something to control, to master, a separate object to be pawed, handled, manipulated, examined by strangers. Why am I letting myself do something I don't want?

She was getting restless and complained to the receptionist.

"Doctor is the best in New York," the receptionist reproved her. "Most people are delighted to wait. You are free to leave if you wish, without charge."

She slunk back to the couch, intimidated. Tina had curled up on one end and was fast asleep. Finally it was Ellen's time and she was ushered into the doctor's office. The doctor immediately reminded her of Alain because of his way of talking about her body as an inanimate object. Shivering, she took off her bra, wondering if she smelled of perspiration. She sat on the examining table, naked and nervous. He carefully looked at her, touched her, prodded her, made some unintelligible remarks to the nurse, then finally spoke.

"Now this is the situation," he said at last. "You need *not* only a breast reduction, you need new nipples as well. Your nipples are misplaced and too large."

He took out a felt-tipped pen with which he began to draw on her breasts. The nurse brought a mirror. "This is where your nipples should go," he said, with a flourish of his pen.

"You really think it would be a good idea for me to have this?" she asked tremulously.

"It would make an extraordinary difference," he said.

"Is there any danger of cancer from this operation?"

"Breast reductions have no known link to breast cancer," he quickly reeled off. "Of course, we do not know what causes breast cancer. What we do know is that very few women who develop breast cancer have ever had breast reduction operations. The only known drawbacks to such an operation are the following. First, you will not be able to breast-feed any future babies."

"That's all right," she said, "I didn't breast-feed the first one."

"The other drawback," he said, "that might matter is that your nipples will no longer be subject to erotic sensation."

"What do you mean, will no longer be subject to?" she asked anxiously.

"To put it more precisely, the nipples will be numb."

She was so horrified that she could not speak for a few minutes. All she wanted to do was to get out of there. If there was one part of her body that was unquestionably an erogenous zone, it was her nipples. The only way Jeff had ever aroused her at all was to squeeze and bite on her nipples. Sometimes swimming, or standing in the shower, just feeling water flowing over her nipples, would result in a contented feeling of sensuality.

It seemed impossible to imagine enjoying sex without her nipples. Every little squeeze would cause a spasm, an erotic contraction of her vagina. Sometimes she had felt as if she could have orgasms merely from the touching of her nipples. And now, the doctor was calmly proposing that she let this go, that for the sake of her appearance, she give up her erotic potential. The little pleasure she had sexually would now completely disappear.

"This is our photographer," the doctor said, interrupting her frantic thoughts. "She will take photographs of your breasts. Then you may get dressed and we'll set a date for the operation."

She set it for her twenty-sixth birthday, certain that she would somehow get out of it, but now she found she was obsessed with breasts. When she was dressed they looked too big, when she was naked she could see the misplaced nipples, when she touched them, enjoying the lovely erotic sensation, she wanted to cry. She even initiated sex with Jeff, attempting to store up memories of the feeling in her nipples.

She tried discussing it with Tina but Tina couldn't understand why she was making such a big fuss. "So what if you lose sensation in your nipples," Tina said, "you can pretend your breasts still excite you afterward and Jeff probably won't even notice the difference."

"I'm not worried about Jeff's not noticing the difference," Ellen wailed, "I'm worried about my loss of sensation."

"But the truth is," Tina said, "nobody has big breasts."

"*I* have big breasts," Ellen said.

"That's what I'm saying," Tina answered. "That's why you have to have the operation. Look, sweetie, who cares what happens in bed. Looking beautiful is better than an orgasm. In fact, looking beautiful is its own orgasm. The best kind."

"Oh, sure, it's easy enough for you to talk because it's not you facing loss of feeling in your breasts."

"Listen, Ellen, I have loss of feeling all over. That's one of my problems. You're lucky if you have loss of feeling in only one place. But don't worry. If you lose it in your breasts, you'll get it back somewhere else. Like blind people. Their hearing becomes very sharp. Listen, you're worried about your nipples but I'm worried about survival during the next two months. Dr. Bloom is going to Europe for the summer and I expect to have a nervous breakdown the minute he leaves the city. You'd think that after all the money I've spent on him, he'd consider me a little bit. *I'm* not allowed to miss a session but when he goes on vacation, there's no stopping him. What does he care if I turn into a basket case. What do you care? All you're worried about are your nipples."

Talking to Jeff about it was fruitless, no help at all, and finally one night she told him she was going to cancel the operation.

"Ellen, for God's sake, I've heard nothing else from you these past few weeks but your worries about the operation. Make up your mind what you want and stop carrying on about it."

"Do you want me to have it?"

"What I want has nothing to do with this. It's up to you."

That wasn't the answer she wanted. She wanted him to say, "No, no, my darling, you're beautiful just the way you are and I love you. Don't change a thing."

"I'm really afraid to have it," she said. "I think it will be very painful."

"Then don't have it," he said in the abstracted way in which he usually talked to her nowadays.

"It might be dangerous," she said. "You might lose me."

"I spoke to the doctor. He said it's a simple operation. It's done every day and you'll be completely anesthetized. I don't think you have to worry."

"But the doctor said my nipples will be numb forever after."

"So what if they are?" He really didn't understand the significance of what she was about to lose.

"Suppose your penis were to be numbed," she said.

"I'd get a hell of a lot more work done," he said. "But I've had the equivalent of your breast operation. I was circumcised at birth and my cock isn't numb. So maybe your breasts won't be either. You'd better make up your mind right away, Ellen, and be done with it. I don't want you throwing it up to me later that I made you do it. It's your decision alone."

But events had been set in motion. It was all a chain. For Alain she needed the breast operation, for Helen she needed Alain, for Jeff she needed Helen. Her mind filled with lovely images of not needing a bra, of being able to wear all of the halter-top swimsuits she had always turned down, of the freedom to run

128

and jump and bound without those annoying appendages flopping up and down. Why, it would be wonderful; a new kind of freedom. How foolish she had been to hesitate.

"All right," she said, "I'm going to do it."

He was pleased. She could see that right away. "I think you made the right decision." He smiled.

Now she was beginning to look forward to it as much as she dreaded it. The day before she was due at the hospital, Ellen dropped in to see Susie Mozer, now pregnant with her second child. She wanted to tell her she'd be away and when she told Susie where she was going, Susie expressed herself clearly. "I think the operation is sick," she said.

"It's no sicker than a nose bob," Ellen said defensively.

"A nose bob is equally sick if the person doesn't need it. You don't need this breast operation. You look just fine to me. Why should you go through hell to conform to some kind of ridiculous EL norm? Suppose tomorrow the cafe society decides that big breasts are in fashion. What will you do then?"

"No chance of that happening." Ellen grinned.

"I have big breasts," Susie said, "but I accept myself the way I am. I don't want to look like anybody else. I want to look like me."

"But suppose your husband didn't like the way you looked," Ellen said.

"Then he wouldn't be my husband for long. Long ago I realized that I could never be a beauty queen. But I wasn't going to let that ruin my life and I married a man who liked the way I looked. We may not be beautiful enough for the EL but we couldn't care less. We look great to each other. What a person is inside is more important than what he is outside. You should know that, Ellen."

"You're probably right," Ellen sighed, "but how can you find out what a person is like inside unless you're attracted by the outside?"

"There's appearance and appearance," Susie said. "Anyone in his right mind would say you're a nice-looking woman, far better looking than the average. So why are you doing this?"

"I just don't want to look like a freak in our circles." She laughed uneasily.

"There are freaks and freaks," Susie said. "Some people might think a woman who chops off her breasts is a freak *after* she does it, not before."

Well, she had heard the other side of the argument from Susie but it didn't change her mind. The date was set; the day after her twenty-sixth birthday. Mrs. Graetz was coming to stay with Jennifer, an event that caused Jennifer no pleasure.

"I don't like Grandma," Jennifer said, "because sometimes she says mean things about you."

"Oh, my loyal little love," Ellen said, pulling the child to her and covering her with kisses. Her heart was filled with love for her daughter, her loyal little friend, probably her only real friend. "Just spend a few days with Grandma and then you and I will have the whole summer to spend together," she told Jennifer.

Ellen found herself thinking about Saul constantly during the days before the operation. If only she could talk to him. He would understand her ambivalence immediately, would tell her to drop the operation, that narcissism was the enemy of social conscience. He would urge her to turn her mind to important things; to picket, march, demonstrate, petition, persuade, or console with him. He had been her only true friend and during almost five years of marriage she had not found another like him. Perhaps if she called him that very minute, he would comfort her. But to what purpose? They were both married and since Saul tended to make the best of everything, he was probably as happily married as she was not.

During the next days she alternated between exhilaration and despair but she realized there was no way of going back. The operation had to be done. But her terror never left her and she was glad she would have Jeff's big, strong frame to lean on when she went to the hospital. She never dreamed she might have to go to the hospital alone.

130

"We have to leave here for the hospital at about eleven," she said to him, the day before the operation.

"Christ, Ellen," Jeff wailed, "you can't spring these things on me at the last minute."

"What do you mean, last minute? You paid for the operation. You knew the date. I told you it was the day after my birthday."

"I see. Somehow you're making this my fault. Do you think I have nothing to think about but your operation? Haven't I done enough? After all, I paid for it. The least you could have done was to remind me of the date. You have little enough to do."

"Whose fault is that?" she snapped. "I had plenty to do when I was working but you wouldn't rest until I gave that up."

"Christ, Ellen, you do have a way of twisting everything I say. Most women would be grateful to a husband who got them out of an underpaid little job like that. But you're never grateful for anything, are you? No matter how I bust my balls. In any event, you're reminding me too late. I have a new account to pitch tomorrow. But even if I didn't, I can't figure out why you need anybody to drive you to the hospital. It's not as if you're sick or something. You're in perfect health. If you weren't they wouldn't be doing plastic surgery on you. And if you weren't in perfect health, you can bet your life I'd be there at your side.

"Oh, come on, Ellen. Don't curl your lip at me that way. Haven't I always been around when you needed me? Didn't I drive you to the hospital for Jennifer? And I'll be right there to take you when you have another kid. When you can't drive, you can bet your life I'll be there. When you need me, nothing's going to get in the way. But, damn it, Ellen, all they're going to do to-morrow is admit you. I'm not going to let you make me feel guilty about this. I've got clients."

"But, Jeff," she said, "I'm scared. The doctor said they do more than just admit me. He scratches the operating lines into my breasts with a needle and without anesthetic."

"If you needed anesthetic, he'd give it to you. For Christ's sake, this is the twentieth century. Doctors don't stay in business by torturing patients."

She struggled to find something to say, caught as usual between what seemed perfectly sensible to Jeff and her own emotional needs.

"Come on, babes," he said, putting his arm around her, "just relax. You know the doctor said this initial procedure is a big nothing, that it only takes five minutes. Then all you have to do is go to your private room, watch TV, and read. Christ, I wish I could have a vacation like that. Come on, Ellen, be a good girl. You're always so goddamned emotional about everything. Everything's going to be fine. You'll be an absolute knockout. Okay?"

"No, it's not okay. I don't want to go to the hospital alone."

"That does it," he said. "Get off my back. I have clients. Where do you think the money for all your self-improvement comes from?"

"Jeff, I need *you* tomorrow, not money."

"I simply can't, Ellen. I'll be there with you in the evening to get the car. Just put it in the hospital parking lot and I'll take the train from New York. Then I'll drive home from the hospital. Come on, Ellen, be sensible. Be grateful. I've given you a three-thousand-dollar operation for your twenty-sixth birthday. Doesn't that count for something?"

"I guess you're right," she said, "but promise me you'll be there when I come up from the operation. Okay?"

"Would I disappoint you? Wasn't I there when you had Jennifer?"

"All right," she said. It was sensible, it was logical. So why did she feel so abandoned?

"At's a ma girl," he said playfully. He always got playful when he'd gotten exactly what he wanted.

She held Jennifer tightly in her arms before the child left for school the next day. "I'll call you tonight, honey," she said. "I'll call you every day until I come home. I love you."

"I love you, too," the child said.

"Five years old," Ellen's mother scolded, "and not a brother or sister in sight. That's what you should be going to the hospital for. It's not right to have an only child."

"You did," Ellen said.

"See!"

"Please don't start on that, Mother. I'm nervous enough."

"So when were you ever not nervous? Go, go, go to your operation. Don't worry about your only child. She'll be fine with her grandma."

Gritting her teeth, Ellen took off. What a lousy life. Here she was, going to an operation she dreaded and could have lived without, disliking the people closest to her, her husband and her mother.

She had been told that the usual hospital admittance procedure was different in her case. She would meet the doctor, he would take her to a small operating room to scratch the lines in her breasts, and then she would go to her own room. Because the doctor had asked her to be there at one, she was there at twelve-thirty. Jeff had often jeered at her punctuality but she was always compulsively early, as if to compensate for his compulsive lateness. She waited and waited but the doctor didn't appear. She tried to read but couldn't concentrate. Despite her growing hunger, she was afraid to leave, should the doctor appear at any moment. She felt an irrational fear of angering him because she was so completely in his power.

Her desire to leave was at war with her despondency and lassitude and she sat there in the sterile waiting room, listening to the bland music, riffling through out-of-date magazines, growing more depressed by the moment. All about her were the truly unfortunate people who had come for help with terrible diseases, not for self-indulgent cosmetic purposes. The whole procedure was mad. Today she was healthy, independent, ambulatory, and tomorrow she would be bedridden, pain-racked, and dependent. And for what? Would smaller breasts improve her relationship with Jeff? Not a chance!

She seemed to be the only person sitting alone. Four generations of one family came in together—a sparrowlike great-grandmother, her daughter, granddaughter, and the granddaughter's baby. Apparently, it was the mother who was ill. She sat there, yellow, in terrible pain, with her aged mother comforting her on one side and her daughter comforting her on the other. The baby cooed in the young mother's arms. They were obviously poor. The daughter, Ellen noticed ironically, had large breasts. But it was evident that they cared about each other.

At three o'clock the doctor swept in, flanked by two interns, not the slightest bit apologetic about having kept her waiting. He was in a foul mood, snapping at the interns, carrying on a running complaint about the inefficiency of the hospital, acting annoyed with Ellen, as if she had interrupted something important. If I had my husband here with me, Ellen thought, he'd be behaving better.

He led her to a small examining room and told her to take off her blouse and bra and lie down on the examining table. She lay there while the surgeon and interns impersonally examined her breasts as if they were melons on a fruit stand. The doctor poked and pointed, giving an anatomy lesson, as if she had left the room and only the detached breasts remained.

Then he began the scratching process. It was not simple, but was instead the most painful experience of her life. Inexorably, he scratched deep agonizing lines with a needle to provide a guide for his scalpel the next day. Ellen started to moan and cry.

"Stop that at once," he snapped.

Then he turned to the intern. "All right, now, you do the other and I want no mistakes."

"Mistakes?" she wanted to scream. "I'm not doing this so an intern can get experience. This is my body."

But the pain was so intense that it wiped all other thoughts out of her mind. The intern was far less deft than the doctor and she started to writhe and scream. The doctor and other intern grabbed her shoulders with fingers of cruel steel and held her still. "Just relax," the doctor said with no feeling whatsoever. Ellen tried to repress her hysteria. Then the doctor was hissing at the intern, "You are the clumsiest worker I've ever come across. Get out of here. I'll clean up your mess."

Even in her pain, Ellen was amused at his unprofessional behavior. It reminded her of the old Mike Nichols-Elaine May nurse and doctor skit in which they're having a lovers' quarrel and ignoring the dying patient. "I don't care if the patient does die," Nichols says stoutly, "I'm not going on with the operation until you say you love me."

Finally the agony was over and she was left with dull aching in her breasts, like the ache that remains in a tooth for a few hours after it's filled.

"There now," the doctor said, "that wasn't too bad, was it? You really make our work more difficult when you move around so much. Most of our patients don't find this painful."

"How would you know, you son of a bitch," she wanted to say.

"See you tomorrow," he said airily; "the worst is over." A hospital aide came and took her to her room, helped her to undress and get into bed.

Now she was alone, but restless. She couldn't sleep. The nurse brought her a painkiller and she tried to read but couldn't concentrate. She called Jeff's office but he was out. She called home and spoke to Jennifer. There was nothing interesting to watch on television. Again, unsuccessfully, she tried to read. Her breasts hurt, she had a knot of despair in her stomach, and loneliness cut through her like the surgeon's knife. She turned on the television again, and after the painkiller began to work, she dozed fitfully until dinner came. She called Jeff's office again to remind the secretary that visiting hours at the hospital ended at eight.

"Please ask him to bring me *The New Yorker, Vogue,* and *The Nation,*" she said, "and some good fruit. I can't eat this hospital food."

She lay there waiting for Jeff. Six o'clock, seven o'clock,

eight o'clock, nine o'clock. She was suddenly filled with anxiety. Jeff had been killed in an accident on his way to see her and she would be left alone. She called home. No, her mother hadn't heard from Jeff. There was no answer from his office at this hour. Where was he? Anxiety and depression kept alternating. It was impossible to think that he wouldn't show up. He had to get the car, even if seeing her didn't matter. A devastating feeling of abandonment swept over her. She was a prisoner in a hospital, the victim of mad scientists, the hapless heroine of a melodrama.

At ten o'clock, the door to her room opened and shut softly and there he was, handsome, magnificently dressed and groomed, carrying the biggest bunch of red roses she had ever received. He dropped them on the bed and spitefully she kicked them off. They landed on the floor with a sigh.

"Are you crazy?" he asked.

"Where the hell were you," she hissed, barely controlling a desire to shriek.

"There you go again," he said, "trying to make me feel guilty." The iron screens came down in his eyes and he started working himself up to the defensive anger that he always used to shut out dialogue, to evade his own responsibility. Where had he learned that offense was the best defense? Probably back in the FBI.

"You should feel guilty," she said. "Where were you?"

"You know, Ellen, I'm an adult. You're not my mother. I don't have to account to you for every moment. Where was I? I was working, that's where I was. First I had my brush-up Italian lesson. Then I told you I had to take some clients to dinner. They are new clients—an Italian furniture manufacturer who's trying to break into the American market. I can't believe that after the kind of day I put in, you're screaming at me. I was working. I couldn't wait to get here but you know my clients. Now tell me, babes, how's a ma girl?"

"Jeff, did you ever think that you might say to clients, 'Gentlemen, excuse me, my wife needs me'?"

"Absolutely," he said, "and when you need me, I'll be at your side. You wanted me here. I'm here now and all you're doing is screaming at me." He picked up the flowers and smiled at her. Then he bent over to drop a kiss on her cheek.

"I smell liquor."

"Yeah, well, clients drink."

"I'm not smelling the liquor on your clients."

"Damn it," he exploded. "I bust my ass to get here, spend thirty dollars on your flowers, and this is your gratitude. Liquor! You're complaining about liquor! You know *I* don't drink. All day long I wanted to get here. Now you're complaining because I had a drink with clients. What should I do? Tell them to drink alone? I knew that no matter what I did, no matter how hard I tried, you'd be right in there, zapping me with criticism. It's impossible to satisfy you. I give and give and what do I ask? All I ask is a little sympathy, a drop of gratitude. I kill myself for you and Jennifer and all I get in return is abuse."

"Please, Jeff, I've heard all that a hundred times before. Let's try to talk rationally. Can't you understand at all why I would be upset?"

"You're upset because you're high-strung and neurotic. A normal person *wouldn't* be upset under these circumstances but you always make such big issues out of nothing. You should feel happy about these roses. I had to go to three florists to get the right color."

"Please don't con me, Jeff. Your secretary probably got them."

His guilty, sheepish look gave him away. How well she knew him!

"So what? I told her to get them. Doesn't that count for anything?"

"I wish it did. Where are the magazines and fruit?"

"Oops, I forgot. Now don't give me that accusatory look. Didn't I bring the flowers? What the hell, Ellen. You're not going to be reading much or eating much for the next few days. I promise you, I swear to you, that I'll remember next time. Who knew you wanted them that much?"

Ellen said nothing. This was what always happened. She got upset, then confused, then guilty. She realized that she preferred to be alone.

"You'd better go," she said, "you're not supposed to be here this late."

"Screw their hospital rules, those rules are made for other people."

But a passing nurse rescued her. "Sir," she said firmly, when she saw Jeff sitting there, "you're not allowed in here this late." She was starched, prim, shocked at the breaking of the visiting rules.

"It's okay," he said, flashing her his dazzling smile, "I'm her husband. It's pretty lonely at home without her."

Instantly, the nurse succumbed to his charm. "Still," she said more kindly, "you must go."

"Well, if I have to, I have to." He smiled. "You're only doing your duty and I have the greatest respect for that." He ostentatiously took out a twenty-dollar bill. "I want you to take special care of my wife. She's a little scared. You know how women are about operations. I keep telling her that it's nothing but she's terrified. And will you do something with these flowers?"

He moved closer to the nurse, trying to dazzle her with his beauty, trying to make her his accomplice. Ellen watched in embarrassment. He was hitting the wrong note with that twenty-dollar bill. That was how his generosity often made Ellen feel. As if it were a payoff. The nurse made no move to take the money. Cheers for her, Ellen thought.

"That will not be necessary, sir," the nurse said. "I try to take good care of everyone on the floor."

Her reproof was wasted on Jeff. He had no natural sense of embarrassment. Ellen wanted to pull the covers over her head.

"I'm leaving it right here on this shelf," he told the nurse, "and there will be a lot more where that came from, if you treat her right. She's pretty special to me, you know."

With elaborate charm, Jeff bent over to kiss her and she turned her back to him. "Sleep well, babes," he said. "See you tomorrow, gorgeous."

Ellen started to cry as soon as he had gone. "Now," the nurse said, "don't you be making yourself upset. You know these men. They don't understand our pain. Just take your sleeping pill and you won't do any more worrying tonight. Nothing to worry about. Lots of women save for years for this operation. So take your pill, sleep well, and just keep remembering that you're going to turn out beautiful."

She rearranged the pillows, poured a glass of water from the carafe, and held out the small paper cup with the pill. Ellen took the pill, then took the nurse's hand and held it for a moment, trying to use its warmth to warm her heart.

"I'll fix the flowers now," the nurse said, "and you'll see them tomorrow."

"Please take some home," Ellen said, "I'd like to share them with you."

"Thank you, no," the nurse said kindly. "I'll just enjoy them here with you. They'll be making the room smell lovely for both of us."

"You've been so kind," Ellen said, drifting off to sleep. "Thank you very much."

"Just part of my job," the nurse said, as she carried the flowers off to find a suitable vase. Ellen fell into blissful unconsciousness.

She was again tranquilized the next morning so that although she felt some anxiety, some moments of loneliness, these passed quickly. The operation took five hours and Ellen spent an additional three in the recovery room. When they wheeled her back into her room, she dimly noted that Jeff was not there, then fell back to unconsciousness again. She slept through the night and it was not until midmorning of the next day that she finally recovered full consciousness and awoke to excruciating pain.

She lay flat on her back, unable to move. Minutes passed, seeming like hours, but no nurse came. The doctor had told her before the operation that she must lie perfectly flat for forty-eight hours, but she would not have been able to move, regardless of his instructions. Her breasts were on fire, the unrelenting pain interrupted only by her realization that she had to urinate. She had to summon a nurse. Slowly, she moved her hand toward the buzzer, the flames licking at her every inch of the way. Her arms felt as though they had been wrenched from the sockets, then sewn back on again. It seemed to take fifteen minutes before she reached the buzzer. At last, sobbing, she was there. Thank God! With her remaining strength she pushed the button down, finally heard it click, and sank back into her agony.

She lay there waiting. Nobody came. She must have dozed, then waited some more. How long had she been waiting? Minutes, hours, days? So dopey that it was hard to determine the passage of time, she thought she dozed off again, then awakened, then slept and awakened again. Still nobody came. Unable to wait any longer, she felt herself urinating in bed, the wet warmth spreading beneath her, returning her instantly to infancy. Still she waited. Then she fell off to sleep again.

She was awakened by a hard, impatient, "For Christ's sake. Look what you've done."

This was not the gentle, compassionate nurse of last night. This one was angry. "An adult like you," she snapped, "unable to hold your water. Why didn't you buzz?"

Ellen was confused. She had buzzed. Hadn't she? Maybe she'd never reached the buzzer. Perhaps she hadn't pushed hard enough. She was too sleepy to tell.

Another nurse came in, equally disapproving. Controlling their annoyance to some extent, they roughly changed the bed, washed, powdered, changed her, and sternly warned her not to let it happen again. She lay there on her back, a powerless, beached turtle, a reproved, wounded orphan.

"Next time," the nurse said, shoving the buzzer closer to Ellen's hand, "ring when you've got to go."

She jabbed Ellen with a needle and Ellen blissfully floated off again, carried on a cloud. She dreamed.

140

Jeff was driving a taxi and she was the passenger in back. She kept tapping on the glass partition, asking him to stop, but he couldn't or wouldn't hear her. She began to bang, frantic to escape. With a squeal of brakes, he pulled over to the side, slid back the divider, and turned to her in fury. His entire face was marked with white paint, like an aboriginal mask, and in his hand he held a gun, pointed at her. A shriek froze in her throat.

"Get out," he snapped. "Get out of my car. I warned you but you wouldn't listen."

He came around and tried to pull her out while she screamed and screamed, trying to catch on to something to prevent herself from being ejected. She knew exactly where they were. It was 135th Street and Twelfth Avenue, a desolate stretch they passed when they got on the West Side Highway at 125th Street. It was a wholesale meat section, alive during the day but totally deserted at night. All around them, on tremendous hooks, were hanging carcasses of meat and she knew that if she let go of the jump seat, the only thing she had found to cling to while he pulled on her feet, that she would be hung up there on a hook, along with the other carcasses. She was screaming and screaming and screaming but nobody heard her. The world was deserted and there was nobody to come to her aid.

"Time for dinner," she heard a male voice say and she looked up to see an orderly putting her dinner tray on the eating table that went across the bed.

"What time is it?" she whispered.

"Five o'clock." He raised her bed slightly but the gravity on her breasts was so painful that she asked him to put her down again. She didn't want to eat anyway.

She had slept all day and she had to go to the bathroom again. Moving her hand she pressed the buzzer, saw the light go on outside the room, and waited. Damn it, not again. Nobody came. She saw her food congealing as she struggled to keep from urinating. The orderly returned to collect her tray and clicked his teeth in disapproval. "A waste of good food," he said.

"Please," Ellen whispered, "you must get the nurse for me."

"Nothing I can do," he said. "The light is on outside your room. This is a busy time for us. Just hang on. She'll be here soon."

Finally she came, the sidekick of the grim one. She was pleased that Ellen had controlled herself and helped her onto a bedpan, another terrible, excruciating experience that seemed to take forever. When they were through, with her remaining strength, Ellen whispered, "Please, in my purse. Get my address book. I'd like you to reach a friend for me."

The nurse dialed and at last Tina was on the phone. The nurse propped the receiver next to Ellen's face. As soon as Tina said, "Hello," Ellen began to cry weakly.

"Don't you have a private nurse?" Tina asked, shocked. "I was going to visit you tomorrow. The truth is, I hate hospitals so much I've been putting it off. Hang on, Ellen. Stop crying, your nose will get stuffed and you won't be able to blow it. I'll be there in an hour."

Ellen drifted off again into that painful, aching, half-sleep. When she awakened, Tina was sitting there, looking magnificent in her gray Chanel suit and flaming red hair.

"You poor baby," Tina said, "you look the way I feel. Dr. Bloom has a Freudian convention this week in Aspen and I may not pull through. How do you like the shade of my nail polish? It's a new one. Come on, tell me, you can be honest."

Ellen started to laugh, felt the extraordinary pain of her stitches, and repressed it.

"What day is it?" she asked Tina.

"Saturday."

Saturday? She'd been operated on Thursday morning. A day and a half had passed since then. Where the hell was Jeff? He didn't work on Saturdays. She had promised to call Jennifer each day and she'd missed two days. She would have Tina dial for her in a little while.

"Where's Jeff?" Ellen asked. "Is Jennifer all right?"

"Everything is super," Tina said; "you don't have to think about anything except recovering. Jennifer and your mother are

142

overeating together and Jeff had dinner with us last night. He looked in on you but you were out for the night so he came over to us. He took Jennifer to the Bronx Zoo today. He'll probably be here around dinner time. Poor dear. He's been terribly concerned about you. But the doctor told him everything was fine and said you weren't having too much pain."

"How would that quack know?" Ellen said. "He hasn't even been in to see me."

"He was probably in while you were unconscious," Tina said. "Why were you so upset when you called me before?"

Ellen told Tina all that had happened and Tina listened sympathetically.

"I know just how you feel," she said. "Dr. Bloom doesn't really understand my suffering either. But what can you do about them. Doctors! They treat us like cattle. Oh, yes, Ellen, Jeff got the new Italian furniture account, and he's very excited about it. I called him before I came over here and he said I should tell you about the account and the zoo. I told you should have a private nurse and he said, 'By all means.' Apparently, your doctor hadn't told him it was necessary. Anyway, one is on her way here and now you won't have any more trouble getting tender loving care. I'm not surprised Jeff didn't think of it on his own. That's the way men are. But a private nurse is essential. Remember this for your next plastics op."

"You'll never get me into a hospital again," Ellen said. "Never, never, never."

"That's what we all say," Tina said. "I've had my nose fixed three times. The second time, they forgot to remove some of the packing. I breathed through my mouth for two weeks because my doctor picked that time to go on vacation. Honestly, I just despise doctors. They're always on vacation, just when you need them most. Last night I had an absolutely spectacular dream and by the time Bloom decides to return to New York I'll have forgotten it. So what can we do? We just have to endure our suffering."

Ellen remembered her terrible dream and shuddered. "It's

good to have you here, Tina," she said. "I've been feeling so abandoned."

"Well, what did you expect?" Tina asked.

"What do you mean?"

"I'm used to it by now," Tina said. "Sweetie, once they join the solid gold circle, we never see them. They all see themselves in a race after that and they're always busy running. The only problem is that the finish line keeps moving away from them. The best thing we can do is get out of the way so that they don't trip over us as they run. Do you think Harry's any different from Jeff? Either he's working or he's shacking up. I mean, what do you think I'm doing with Dr. Bloom? I'm trying to get used to being alone."

"Shacking up?" Ellen exclaimed. "You don't mean that."

"The hell I don't," Tina said.

"Don't you mind?" Ellen asked.

"I used to, a little, at the beginning," Tina answered, "but now, I could care less. Whenever he shacks up with someone he brings me a present. The bigger the infidelity, the bigger the present. The last one must have been positively volcanic because I got a chinchilla jacket out of it. Face it, Ellen. They're all such bastards. They tell us they're killing themselves in business for us but it's really all for their teentsy little egos. I mean, they keep running even after they have as much money as they need. So the only thing we can do to survive, other than Dr. Bloom, and a bit of cheating ourselves on the side, is to protect ourselves. Do you?"

"Protect myself how?"

"Money, dodo. How much money do you have in your bank account?"

"I don't even have a bank account," Ellen said sheepishly. "Jeff keeps track of finances and gives me an allowance at the beginning of each month. I use that plus my charge accounts."

Tina looked white, shocked, horrified. "No bank account?" she shrilled. "I can't believe it. I mean, that's absolutely the worst

144

thing I've ever heard. I can't get over it. What a terrible way to live."

Ellen would have giggled if that didn't hurt so much. Having no bank account shocked Tina but not Harry's philanderings.

"It is positively terrible that you have no protection," Tina continued. "Sweetie, you've got to start building your own little fallout shelter the minute you get out of here. First, open a savings account in a different bank from the one Jeff uses. And don't tell him anything about it. Then start socking away money as fast as possible. For every dollar you spend, put another dollar in the savings account. Start padding your housekeeping bills.

"Another thing you should do is to start buying things and giving Jeff the bill. Ask him for the money to pay it. Tell him you have to go to the department store anyway. Then return the merchandise and keep the money. No problem with that at any decent store.

"In addition, there's Bonnie Rose. She's got a very classy resale shop and she'll give you cash for designer clothes as long as they've only been worn once or twice. Of course, she only pays about half of what the stuff costs but at least she pays cash."

Tina sat there grinning like a very clever little girl.

"That's a pretty terrible way to live with someone," Ellen said.

"You can't cheat someone you're not close to," Tina joked. "Sweetie, it's just about the only way to survive marriage. You may have thought you were vulnerable when you were single, that you'd be safe when you got that solid gold circle on your left hand. Ha! That's a myth. You just exchanged one kind of vulnerability for another kind."

Tina rolled her perfectly shadowed eyes heavenward and continued to rattle on while Ellen dozed off again. She awakened briefly to see Tina still sitting there reading, and her presence made Ellen feel better.

Jeff finally arrived around dinner time and told her he could only spend fifteen minutes because Jennifer was waiting in the car. Tina had gone but the private nurse was there.

"That's all right," Ellen said, "I don't want Jennifer to be alone. Please give her a kiss for me and tell her I love her. Are you coming back later?"

"You don't need me now that you have a private nurse," he said. "Tina's having a little party because she didn't want me to be alone on a Saturday night."

He could have spent Saturday night here with me, Ellen thought. She fell asleep again, before she could brood about it.

The next day the doctor pronounced her fit for minimal elevation. Her private nurse, a placid, middle-aged Irishwoman, took care of her every need. The day before she was discharged, Helen Fern called her.

"How are you, dahrling," came that low, beautiful voice. "Does it look marvelous?"

"I have no idea yet," Ellen said. "I'm still swathed in bandages. I look even bigger than before because of the bandages."

"I'm proud of you for being so brave and dynamic," Helen said. "It's absolutely thrilling, like that Joan Crawford film about the woman who has the face operation. We're really lucky to be living in this era of plastic surgery. Just think how it would have helped poor Cyrano. It's positively thrilling."

"Not so thrilling for the victim," Ellen said. "If I had known the extent of the pain, I assure you I never would have gone through with it."

"Well, it's over now," Helen said, "and a certain Italian has been asking me for your phone number. You made quite an impression on the divine Giovanni. He was tragically disappointed when he did not run into you again here."

"I hope you didn't tell him about this operation."

"Certainly not. It's not the most romantic image to project to him. Besides, if I had, you'd be up to your neck in the most indiscreet floral displays outside of a gangland funeral. You'd have some difficulty in explaining it to your husband."

"*He* hasn't been here long enough to notice anything," Ellen said, "but even if he did, he'd never worry. Whatever Giovanni

146

saw in me, assuming he doesn't automatically respond this way to women, Jeff certainly doesn't see. Of course I don't believe in this sudden infatuation, Helen. He probably comes on this way to everyone."

"Don't underestimate yourself, my dear. I didn't give him your number but here is his, in case you ever want to contact him."

"I'm really flattered out of my mind, Helen, but honestly I couldn't."

"Why not?" Helen asked. "It's theater, drahma. Besides, an occasional fling is good for the skin, hair, and nails."

"I'll think about it." Ellen couldn't help laughing at Helen's prescription. But first things first. It was time to go home. She called Jeff's office to tell him what time to pick her up, and she was met with the familiar wall of irritability.

"Damn it, babes, I can't," he said. "It's that new Italian account. I'll call Tina and ask her to come for you. Between her and a nurse you'll have no difficulty in managing."

He was right, of course, but she felt terribly disappointed again.

"I'll fill the bedroom with flowers for you, babes," he said. "I don't know if I'll get home tonight but your mother and Jennifer are waiting for you."

"I'd like you to be waiting, too," she said.

"Have to run now, babes," he said. "I'll call you later."

She hung up furiously, then called Helen back. "I've been thinking, Helen, and I would like to talk to Giovanni. Could you ask him to call me at home tonight. It's all right. Jeff won't be home."

"You naughty girl," Helen said, with a low, throaty chuckle. "To think I expected you to merely be a stodgy little *nouveau riche*. What great fun to put you two delightful children together."

She and Helen agreed that her speech lessons would begin in the fall and she said goodbye.

Tina and the nurse took her home and, as Jeff had promised,

their bedroom was filled with flowers. At first, Jennifer hung back in horror at the sight of her mother in thick bandages and evident pain, but after her dinner she came and sat next to Ellen on the bed, watching television with her and holding her hand.

"I'm glad you're home," she told Ellen. "Grandma has stinky breath and she's always trying to kiss me." She cuddled next to Ellen and Ellen rejoiced in the girl's warmth, reaching her through the covers.

A few minutes after Jennifer went off to bed Giovanni called.

"All these many weeks," he said, "I look for you but you no come. I suffer. When will I see her again? The tennis is not so good. My heart she is not so good. And now, thanks to God, our dear teacher, she give me your number. Everything now is number one again." He breathed feverishly into the telephone. "*Cara mia,* when you will meet me?"

"July first," Ellen said firmly. No coyness now.

"But that is perfect, *cara.* My wife and the *bambinos* go then to Elba for the summer but my maid, she does not go with them. Has boyfriend in New York. Was cook for Fellini. Made the special fettucini for Mastroianni. To my apartment then you will come for dinner. She is number one with the cooking. And then I give her the evening for to go see the cinema. Is good?"

"Fine," Ellen said coolly. "I'll be there. I'll call you the week before to confirm."

She wrote down his address, Ninetieth Street and East End Avenue, right near Gracie Mansion. He gave one last passionate exhalation into the phone.

"I do not make the smile until I see you again, *cara mia.*" Oh, God, what was she getting herself into?

Ellen awakened at 2:00 A.M. when Jeff finally rambled in.

"How's a ma girl?" he asked jovially. "I'm proud of you for making it home without me. I can't wait until you knock them dead in EL. Ready for that?"

"Sure thing," she said, "today EL, tomorrow the world."

"That's the way I love ya," he said, "upbeat. Did Tina tell you I got the Italian account?"

She nodded.

"But that's only part of the good news. That was the account I was waiting for. We're going house hunting as soon as you're up. We're going to get a house in Mamaroneck, Green Haven! Right on the water. Near Rob Bright."

"Are you sure you want to move?" Ellen asked. "There's really nothing wrong with this house and Jennifer likes her school. I hate to take her away from her friends."

"She'll survive," he said. "We should have been out of this dump years ago. We're going to get rid of everything. Japanese modern is out and early American is in. This time we'll get a good decorator."

"I really wish we didn't have to move," she said. "I'm used to it here. Let's think about it for a little while."

"Nothing doing," he said. "Face it. Nobody lives in Freeport."

"Somebody's been talking to Tina," she teased.

"Don't buck me on this, babes," Jeff said in his most winning manner. "We'll really be happy in a new house. I'll be able to relax a little then. This is what I want for you and Jennifer and me. And when we get to Mamaroneck, then we'll finally have a son for me. This is what I've wanted all this time. Admit that you want it as much as I do. Then we'll be able to entertain in style. You know that not another EL member lives in Freeport. When I'm with new clients, I'm ashamed to tell them where I live. We'll get a house that will last for the rest of our lives, the kind of house Jennifer will be proud to be married from. We won't ever have to move again."

"What if I said no," she said playfully.

"If you don't go with me," he said turning ugly in one of those mood shifts that always terrified her, "I go without you." His face reminded her of the war mask in the dream.

"All right, Jeff," she said quickly, "if the new house is

what you want, of course I'll go with you."

"Good girl," he said, instantly switching back, "maybe this operation is just the beginning of the new you."

"I wouldn't be a bit surprised," she said, thinking of her future tryst with Giovanni. She lay back, took her sleeping pill and painkiller, and waited to drift into sleep. Things really were fine. She, the little nursery schoolteacher from Brooklyn, was going to have a house in Green Haven, try to build a bank account, and, on top of that, have a magnificent Italian lover just like in the movies.

Moi, she thought to herself in amusement, and then she fell asleep.

PART TWO

4

The weeks that followed Ellen's discharge from the hospital passed uneventfully. She marked the passage of time by the fading of the scars around her breasts. Most of her days were a limbo in which she floated: reading, watching TV, trying exotic new recipes, playing with Jennifer during long, happy afternoons.

Jennifer was a pretty child, a docile one, described by her first-grade teacher as well behaved at all times. She was the same at home: grave, well behaved, self-contained, reserved, and unusually orderly about her possessions. She never expressed her feelings to Ellen or anyone else. Ellen felt she was "going through a stage," and devoted time to bring her out of her shell.

"Maybe she isn't in a shell," Tina said. "You keep thinking there's something under the surface to bring out. What you see might be what she is." Ellen didn't believe it and she found it both amusing and surprising that after all her exposure to Dr. Bloom Tina could still perceive people so superficially.

Jeff continued to come home very late so Ellen found herself skipping dinners. She'd sip a glass of wine as she sat with Jennifer, who still insisted on eating from her Beatrix Potter bunny bowl. Then after Jennifer was tucked in, Ellen would sip another glass while she read or watched TV. The results were amazing. Daily, the pounds slipped off. She realized happily that she might need Alain in the future for posture and carriage but she wouldn't need him for weight.

Six weeks after the operation, she went to Bergdorf's for an entire new summer wardrobe. Reveling in her new thin body, she found herself buying things she could never have worn before . . . marvelous low-cut clothes made for flat-chested ladies by men who didn't seem to like women. She bought sheer blouses, a strapless gown, her first two-piece bikini. The bill came to fifteen hundred dollars, more than she had spent cumulatively on clothes during the almost six years of marriage. And she loved every minute of it.

She had only been in Bergdorf's once before, with Tina, when she had bought the pair of shoes at Delman's. It had been one of those stores she had been afraid to enter, afraid even to browse in, fearful of and intimidated by the salespeople who seemed able to judge on sight which customers could really afford to buy, and equally intimidated by the wealth and chic of the other customers.

Now she went there like a conqueor. Since other El wives shopped there and since she was a EL wife, she could now shop there, too. She was not only a EL wife because of Jeff's membership, she was beginning to look like one and she enjoyed every moment . . . the deference of the floor receptionists, the politeness of the salespeople, the private dressing rooms, the efficiency and beautiful speech of the saleswomen who seemed like royalty in exile.

She remembered with amusement the days when she had shopped in discount stores like Loehmann's or Ohrbach's, where you tried on clothes in communal dressing rooms along with dozens of other women. ("No more than three items per customer allowed in at any one time.") The suspiciousness of the salesgirls was matched by the paranoia of the customers who had simultaneously to try on clothes and hang on to their purses. Close your eyes for one minute and you'd have nothing left to shop *with*.

You bought clothes at places like Loehmann's and Ohrbach's because you needed clothes. You shopped at Bergdorf's because you didn't need clothes. You shopped for elegance, for a massage for the psyche.

Despite Jeff's obvious approval of her appearance, they had not made love at all since the operation. Both of them pretended that they were waiting for the scars to heal, but the truth of the matter was that nearly six years of indifferent sex had left them devoid of urgency. Her new appearance and seeming docility seemed to give both Jeff and herself as much satisfaction as they needed. He was busier than ever between his business and the hunt for the perfect house, and their weekend encounters were now pleasant and impersonal, friends instead of lovers. Ellen found herself thinking increasingly of Giovanni, and to her delight the scars of her operation had faded by the time she called him the week before their arranged appointment.

"*Cara*," he crooned, "I have suffered so much the insomnia waiting for this moment."

Ellen wondered wryly if he really remembered which elevator conquest she was.

"I have thought of nothing but you, only you, day and night," he continued. She grinned to herself in some embarrassment but repressed her disbelief and tried to deal with this extreme, almost comic flattery. But even if he was honest, if he really was so attracted to her, she really couldn't go through with infidelity, could she? Despite Tina's lightness about the matter, it still seemed to Ellen a taboo that she could not transgress casually.

"You will come to my apartment for dinner?" he breathed urgently. "My cook will make the special pasta . . . home-make. You will love."

Food? Well, maybe that's how these things went. Food first!

Or maybe he was really only asking her for dinner and that would be fine. It would give her a chance to get to know him, to flirt, to feel some excitement, and to escape without breaking that taboo. Well, why not? She had never had "home-make pasta."

She felt feverish after hanging up. J. P. Morgan's big hit song, "Danger, Heartbreak Ahead" was blaring on the radio and Ellen felt as if it were a symbolic warning to her. What would Jeff do if he found out she had seen another man, even if they never got beyond the "home-make pasta" stage. A likely story. Who would ever believe that? But the danger, itself, was a kind of aphrodisiac. When she thought of the meeting her breath went short and she felt a turbulent churning inside. The idea of Signor Lampedusa filled her simultaneously with terror and hope. His unfamiliarity, the exoticism of another culture, excited her. What would it be like to be married to such a man? What did he eat for breakfast, talk about in bed, how did his life-style differ from theirs? She could hardly wait for the moment of seeing him and yet she dreaded it, too. What would they talk about? Her fevered speculation thrilled her, troubled her, made her feel alive and renewed.

The meeting came at a particularly opportune time. They had planned no summer vacation so they could house hunt. Jeff was busy every day but none of her lessons would begin until fall and Jennifer spent her days at a fine day camp near them. Ellen had nothing to do with this new lovely self other than to plan for her first affair. Look, she told herself, if you don't want to go to bed, you don't have to. You don't even know this man. You'll simply say no and plan for another meeting. He isn't going to rape you. Up until the day of their meeting, she wasn't sure she'd go through with it.

And then the day was there and half in a dream she bathed, oiled, made up, tweezed, arranged, teased and combed her hair, smoothed and matched, and finally, after changing clothes three times, she was ready for the drive into the city. The drive was excruciating, her heart pounded violently, and she found herself perspiring despite the car's air conditioning. She parked, as Giovanni had instructed her, in the garage under his building, feeling as nervous as if the attendant would someday reveal her visit to a private detective. You've been seeing too many movies, she reminded herself.

Giovanni's apartment house stood at East End Avenue and Ninetieth Street. The beautifully tended grounds of Gracie Mansion stretched beyond the wall on the opposite side of the street. She rang for the elevator and when it came she sank onto the velvet-covered bench inside, suddenly weak, almost nauseated. What the hell was she doing here, preparing to meet an absolute stranger. The romance of the idea had departed, leaving her only with a feeling of how ridiculous her behavior was. If she was getting back at Jeff, this was a dumb way to do it. She was doing something she didn't want to do, because he did things she didn't like. Since he would never know of her revenge, it was doubly foolish. Besides, she thought, filled with guilt, this was a hell of a way to reward Jeff's generosity to her. After all, he had paid for the new image which she was about to make a present of to a stranger. She made up her mind that all she would do would be to chat, have dinner, and leave. She had promised Giovanni nothing. She breathed a little easier at her decision that no matter what, she would not be unfaithful to Jeff.

When she left the elevator, she caught sight of her reflection in a hall mirror and the sight revived her. That's a damned attractive woman, she thought, smiling gleefully at the slender, chic woman wearing a clinging blue dress she could never have worn in the old days. She rang the bell and the maid answered, jabbering away warmly in Italian. She padded away to get Giovanni while Ellen admired the expanse of East River immediately visible through the eastward wall of glass. It was a magnificent, romantic setting, a setting out of a movie, a fantasy about owning New York. So many beautiful places in her own city and only now was she getting to see them.

Then Giovanni came rushing in, exquisitely attired in a silk shirt with flowing sleeves, like a costume out of *The Three Mus-keteers*. Curtain going up, she thought. He obviously did remember her for he was wildly enthusiastic about her new appearance. "But what have you done to yourself?" he asked. "Before you were beautiful but now you are divine." She smiled demurely. She wasn't telling.

The maid served them a dry white wine in chilled heavy Baccarat goblets. Just holding one made her feel aristocratic. As they sipped and looked out at the East River, Giovanni dramatically courted her. When he would forget the grand gestures, the clichéd Italian male attitudes, she actually found that he was interesting and quite intelligent. *La Stampa* had a permanent office in New York and his job was to do articles and special features about outstanding Italian-Americans. He had just completed one about John Ciardi, a poet she had not heard of before but planned to find out more about immediately.

But no sooner did he begin to speak to her as a thinking human being than he would suddenly remember that she was a woman and he would revert to his operatic attitudes. Two minutes on an intellectual topic and he would return to the hand kissing and the heart pressing.

Dinner and the maid's hovering presence provided another diversion. Course after course arrived. It was the first homemade gourmet Italian cooking she had tasted and she sampled it all: veal with gigantic black mushrooms, homemade pasta with delicate clam sauce, *osso buco,* Italian salad with feta cheese and little shiny black olives, a veal loaf with hard-boiled eggs embedded in the center, and antipasto. After she had finished with homemade spumoni and Italian cheesecake, she could think of nothing she would rather do than to throw up and go to sleep. Everything felt too tight, her girdle, new bra, new clothes. Irritably she worried that she had undone all the slimming-down aftereffects of the operation.

They lingered over their espresso, cognac, and amaretto and then the maid got her coat, nodded to Ellen, and went into temporary exile. He explained, "She goes to find the long movie with her friend."

Now what, Ellen wondered. If he had reached for her at that point, she would have instantly fled. But to her surprise, he said, "Listen, my dahrling, I want you to hear something beautiful."

He put on a record and, sipping some amaretto, she sat back to listen. When the record began, she could scarcely believe what she was hearing. Music of overwhelming beauty, sweetness, romance, came from the phonograph. A sigh escaped her.

"How magnificent," she said, "what is it?"

" 'Songs of the Auvergne,' " he told her. "The most beautiful music in the world for the most beautiful woman I have met in New York. Is the music of love."

Enraptured, with his arm around her, she listened, her senses tingling, every emotion on fire. Too soon the beautiful voice faded away and he turned to her.

"Come, my dahrling," he said in a tremulous voice, and shaking with emotion she followed him into the bedroom. There, above the double bed, almost as wide as the bed, was an overpowering, tremendous statue of Christ in his final agony on the cross.

"You make love under this?" she asked.

"Do not worry. It will not fall down on us."

"But it makes me uncomfortable."

"You can shut your eyes, *cara mia*," he murmured, beginning to kiss her neck and unzip her dress.

"Just a moment please," she said, pushing his hands away. She darted into the bathroom, took off her clothes, examined her new breasts to reassure herself that they looked normal enough for a stranger's eyes, washed herself, took her diaphragm out of her purse and inserted it, and wrapped herself in a luxurious bath towel. Feeling as if she were going off a high diving board, she made the plunge.

Unlike her, completely at ease, he lay naked in a romantic pose, draped across the bed. Dispassionately she realized that he had a beautiful body. She also realized, looking at him posed like

The Naked Maja, that she had absolutely no interest in this man. She was filled with regret. There was no point in her being here. It would give her as little pleasure as making love to Jeff.

"I think I should warn you," she said, somehow hoping to get out of it, "that I am not a responsive woman."

"I do not understand," he said.

"Frigid," she said. "I am not responsive to sex."

Apparently his command of English included this word. He tossed his handsome head and laughed with classic Italian self-confidence. "Frigid." He laughed. "That means, how you say, cold? That is the big joke. There are no frigid women, *cara mia,* only poor lovers. Come to me."

She went, desperately hoping he would prove her wrong, praying to herself that some man could finally wipe out the rape. But after half an hour of energetic pumping, profuse sweating, exclaiming in Italian, and rolling his eyes beseechingly to heaven, he had finally come but she hadn't managed to utter even a passionate squeak. She gazed morosely up at the crucifix as he shuddered to a halt. She felt a little guilty at her lack of response after all his work. It would have been polite to have pretended, she thought, but that wouldn't have been fair either. Maybe it was because her nipples were now numb, maybe it was all too soon after the operation.

To her amazement, he seemed to think that they had enjoyed a wonderful coming together. "That was mahrvelous, *cara,*" he said still playing the operatic tenor, "number one." He turned to her again but she deftly slipped out of bed and fled to the bathroom, mumbling explanations about how she must get home. She bathed quickly, dressed, and came out to the living room, where he sat sipping a brandy and gazing contentedly at the view. He really was rather a nice man.

"When will I see you again?" he asked. "Tomorrow? The day after? When?"

My God, Ellen thought, he isn't kidding. He really liked me. If he liked that performance, what must his wife be like? Or maybe Giovanni too had been entranced by the strangeness, the exoticism of a foreign lover. She was flattered and said she'd call him. Thanking him effusively, she said she thought he too was number one as she disengaged and moved toward the door. Finally, she was free and felt a heady, intoxicating sense of liberation. Well, she'd finally done it after listening to endless descriptions of Tina's escapades and it was no big deal. She had not been struck dead and she was not consumed with guilt. Nor did it mean she was starting a pattern.

As she drove she tried to examine her feelings. She had felt boredom and difficulty in finding a common conversational ground. She also had intense remorse for having overeaten. That was about all. She had been unfaithful and it didn't seem to make any difference. Her only guilt was over the food.

But as she drove, her momentary exhilaration at escaping unscathed left her and she realized she did not feel good about the evening. It had been purposeless, a waste. What did other people get out of affairs? She had hoped that with this stranger she might find the spark, the passion that she and Jeff lacked, but she had been wrong. Perhaps their poor relationship was not Jeff's fault and he and she were still paying the price for that terrible rape nine years ago. Bitterly disappointed, she could have wept at the thought that she might never know the sexual joy that came so easily to people like Tina.

Her heart started to pound as she drove into the garage but her housekeeper had left a note to inform her that Jeff was staying overnight in the city again. He had left no phone number. Where was he, she wondered. Was he too somewhere under a giant crucifix, trying to make some other woman happy because he thought that he had failed with Ellen? Perhaps her evening with Giovanni had served some purpose for it had shown her that Tina's way was not her way. She swore to herself that this would never happen again and vowed to try even harder than before to make Jeff happy.

The rest of the summer passed uneventfully and in the fall

she filled her time with lessons and the continued search for the perfect house. They had seen many that looked fine to her but Jeff had a particular image in his mind and he was determined to find that image or else to build one himself. Ellen was secretly pleased at the delay, so that Jennifer could begin second grade with her friends.

One morning, shortly after Labor Day, Jeff called her from the city. "Meet me this afternoon at Miller's. We have to be outfitted for English horseback riding."

"We don't ride."

"But we're going to learn how. There's a EL seminar in October at Redridge Ranch and I'm going to begin daily lessons so I look good when we get there."

Redridge was the best place in Connecticut for classic English riding. She had seen ads for it in *The New Yorker.*

"Listen, Jeff," she said, "there are lots of things in life I have always wanted to do, but riding is not one of them. I don't want to ride. I don't even like to pet horses. I want to go back to school and get a job."

He ignored her. "You'll love riding," he said. "You can try at least, and if you still don't want to, you can just walk around looking gorgeous in the correct clothes. Okay?"

She had learned not to buck him. When Jeff wanted something, he got it. In order to live pleasantly together, she had decided, she would give in on everything. That was the price for her protection, her security.

"Be there at three o'clock," he said. "You'll adore yourself in boots and breeches; very slim, very sexy, very British."

"Who could resist that?" she murmured with irony that was, as always, lost on him.

She met him at Miller's, a charming old-world riding emporium filled with the pleasant, sporty fragrance of leather and saddle soap. Jeff's promptness was evidence of his belief that riding was going to be a business asset. They each bought high black leather boots (Jeff ordered a pair made to his measurements in addition to the pair he took), smooth silver spurs, fringed, feathered crops, British tweed riding jackets, sweaters, stock-tie blouses, stretch leather gloves, and several pair of stretch breeches in canary and beige. Last, they fitted the hard black velvet hats. Finally, they stood together, decked out in their finery, seeing their images reflected in the large, three-way mirror. Ellen let out a gasp of pleasure. The horsey set!

"Jeff, we're gorgeous," she exulted, hugging him. "If only my poor murdered *shtetl* relatives could have seen this."

"We certainly don't look Jewish," he said with quiet pride.

"I don't like that," she said, but she understood what he meant. In the old country, it was Cossacks who wore boots and rode horses. Still, it bothered her that not looking Jewish, whatever that was, was considered a value. It was the EL homogenization Tina had mentioned to her long ago.

The bill came to over a thousand dollars. "An expensive weekend, Jeff," she couldn't help commenting as they loaded the car with their packages.

"Not to worry," he answered. "I keep telling you not to worry. I'll write it off as a business expense and get new clients through this. I'm taking my first lesson today. It's about time I did some sports regularly."

He was always so eager, so optimistic, so willing to try new things. If only she really cared about him. "Don't put too much pressure on yourself," she said, feeling guilty for her thoughts.

Despite her apprehensions, Ellen immediately liked Redridge Ranch. The central building had a two-story vaulted cathedral living room with a huge fieldstone fireplace stretched across one wide wall, a long mahogany bar across the other end, large bearskin rugs thrown everywhere, wonderfully comfortable leather chairs and couches, a game-playing center for cards, a Ping-Pong table, a pool table, and a pinball alcove. Up on the loft level was a television room and library. Off one wing was the dining hall and the other wing led to an attractive indoor pool. The luxurious bedroom units were located across from the main structure but attached to it by an indoor, sheltered corridor, forming a U-shape, in the center of which was the outdoor pool.

Down the road, past the pool, she could see the stables and outdoor ring where a few riders were practicing. Ellen stood beside the new Cadillac while Jeff went to check in, and she sniffed with delight, for the first time, the unique blended smell of hay and horses. The country smells reminded her of the summer camp where Jeff had first enchanted her, and she instantly loved Redridge.

A boy came out with Jeff to take their luggage, and after finding their room, she followed Jeff to the bar for a cocktail. Amos was already there, raving loudly about a lawsuit against him. Tenants were charging that his buildings were turning into slums, replete with rats and uncollected garbage, and the charges had been given much coverage in *Newsweek* and the *New York Post.*

"Those ungrateful sons of bitches," he was fulminating. "Can you imagine taking me to court because the apartments are too noisy! Who's making the noise? Am I making the noise? No apartments have better soundproofing than mine."

"But . . ." Ellen started to say, saw a warning glance from Jeff, and stopped. She'd almost dropped the mask. What bullshit Amos was spewing. She'd read the newspaper charges. Soundproofed! The lack of soundproofing was one of a long list of charges. The famous development was falling apart. All of Jeff's publicity couldn't change that.

"Pearls before swine," Amos raged, chomping on a cigar while Marilyn stood there silently, pained and tense.

"The problem with those tenants is that they never had a decent place to live before so they're letting it get run down. You take the guy who says he leaned against the wall and fell through to the next apartment. How can anyone fall into another apartment? That's plain crazy. He probably sees flying saucers, also.

"I'm wise to him," Amos said, his voice getting tearful and emotional, "I'm wise to all of them. It's all part of a tenant plan to

164

undermine me and get me to lower the rents. Over my dead body. 'Improvements or no rent.' Well, we'll see about that. You know how much that creep weighed who said he fell into another apartment? One hundred and twenty-five pounds. Could someone that light fall through a wall? You know damned well it never happened. He probably deliberately made a hole to discredit me. If he thinks I'll take the blame for holes he knocks in walls, he's crazier than I think he is. I wasn't born yesterday. Holes don't just happen. Somebody has to make them."

His face was red and his eyes were bulging. Marilyn stood there, Jeff stood there, assorted other people stood there, and they all were listening to him seriously and sympathetically as if he were rational. Ellen wondered if she was the only person there who thought Amos was crazy. Oh, well, she stood there toadying like the others, so who knew what was going on behind their sympathetic façades.

"I swear, Jeff," Amos continued, "I'll get something on that weirdo if it's the last thing I do. I have detectives checking him out already and let me tell you his past is mighty mighty suspicious. Might be a case for the FBI, eh, Jeff, baby?"

"It might be indeed," Jeff said gravely.

They wouldn't use the FBI to check on a dissident tenant, Ellen thought. Why, that was ridiculous. She shuddered involuntarily. It wasn't ridiculous. She felt herself getting depressed.

"Jeff, baby," Amos was crying, his ready tears almost brimming over, "why are they attacking me? All I've done is help them. I've built beautiful apartments for them, tried to expose them to the finer things of life, and they hate me for it. They should see the living conditions in Russia. That would change their tune."

"There, there," Jeff said, patting him on the back.

"They're just jealous," Marilyn whispered dutifully.

Amos's eyes focused on Ellen's deliberately impassive face. He had never trusted her. Now, he waited. Jeff nudged her.

"Societies rarely appreciate their great men," Ellen said, keeping her voice neutral. Amos smiled. A breakthrough.

"What a wife," Amos beamed, and Jeff nodded approvingly.

She was getting restless but Amos hadn't finished. Mopping his eyes, he told them, "Listen, I love this country. It's been good to me and I've been good to it. Do you have any idea of the taxes I pay? Do you know how many men are employed because of me? Before Amos there was no low-cost housing, only slums and developments. And the niggers got the developments. But I showed this country that poor whites also have rights, that they're entitled to decent housing also. I gave my tenants goddamned wading pools for their lousy kids and now they hate me for it.

"Jeff, baby, this is your area. We gotta show the public what a real philanthropist is. I'm giving, not taking like those robber barons, but the public forgets how those bums made their money. The public loves the Rockefellers, the Vanderbilts, the Guggenheims. The thing is we gotta do something about my image. Maybe I should try to buy an ambassadorship. Whadya think? Some place like Luxembourg. Where the hell is Luxembourg, Marilyn?"

"I don't know, exactly," she whispered.

"The only thing," he continued, "is I don't want to go and *live* in some goddamned foreign country. If I'm an ambassador, I have to live there. If I build housing there, I don't have to stay. No, an ambassadorship isn't for me. It might even interfere with building contracts. But it wouldn't be so bad if Marilyn was with me. I could build and we could buy the ambassadorship for Marilyn."

Marilyn shivered and Ellen repressed a grin. If Marilyn were ambassadress, all ceremonies would have to be conducted in whispers.

"It's really too bad," Amos rambled, "that my kids aren't old enough yet for an ambassadorship, but that will come. Maybe I could be offered one, Jeff, and then modestly refuse. Think that would improve the image?"

"Not bad, not bad," Jeff said. "Let me think on that one." Jeff kept acting as if Amos were sane. What an act, Ellen thought.

"I've got another idea, Jeff," Amos continued. All of the listeners except for Jeff, Marilyn, and Ellen had drifted away. "How about an honorary degree. Can you get me one of those?"

"In what field?" Jeff asked seriously.

Ellen watched them in disbelief. Jeff isn't acting, she thought. He really seems to think Amos is sane. He must have brainwashed himself.

"What kind of honorary degree?" Jeff repeated.

"Something like the Nobel Peace Prize," Amos said, striking a Napoleonic pose. Ellen, unable to control herself, let out a sudden guffaw. Jeff covered for her.

"It's too soon to try for that," Jeff said. "I think our best bet would be your friend, the governor of Delaware. For a sizable campaign contribution he might be able to influence graduation exercises at the university."

"For a campaign contribution I could probably have the university," Amos said.

"I'll take care of it," Jeff said.

Amos threw his arms around Jeff, hugged him, called him old buddy, and wiped his tears away with a cocktail napkin. Then he scooped up a handful of potato chips with his tear-drenched fingers, popped them into his mouth, and rubbed his hands on his pants.

"I thought you were trying to lose weight," Marilyn said, venturing forth on the one safe topic.

"Women, women," Amos said to Jeff, rolling his eyes heavenward in pain, "always trying to dominate you."

Ellen looked at Marilyn standing there smiling. No sense of irony there, no answering glance to meet her own. That woman has a Fabergé egg for a brain, Ellen thought, or she's lobotomized or drugged.

As usual Tina saved the evening when she came bustling in, shrieking with pleasure when she saw Ellen. "My God," she said, "you're absolutely gorgeous. I'm positively jealous. I'll have to tell Dr. Bloom about this. You're bringing out my worst competitive instincts."

They smiled at each other, friends. Tina had looked gorgeous for a long time, and nobody could compete with that glorious red hair. She dragged Ellen over to the bar where they smiled at their reflected images. Ellen was endlessly pleased with the new, lovely self reflected back from the bar mirror, her hair a sleek, straight pageboy and her body lithe, slim, and erect. Marilyn came and eased herself down beside them, her face showing her fatigue for a moment.

"Do either of you ride?" Tina asked.

"Yes, of course," Marilyn said, "but I don't like to."

"I don't ride at all," Ellen said, "do you?"

"If I hadn't learned to ride a horse as a child," Tina said, "I'd still be in China. But honestly, Ellen, everyone rides. You'll have to learn how."

Ellen was about to answer when Kimberly Clare Wein walked into the room. She'd obviously been one of the riders Ellen had seen in the ring, and she was dusty, flushed, and magnificent.

I could buy everything sold in Miller's, Ellen thought, but I will never look like that. Her momentary pleasure at her new beauty lessened.

Kimberly leaned against the bar and motioned to the bartender. "Two Scotches," she said in that unmistakable, husky, upper-class voice. Kimberly's poise was regal. She turned to the little group at the bar and introduced the man at her side.

"This is Lenny Unger," she said, "the riding master here."

The riding master? Poor typecasting. He was a square, chunky, swarthy man, wearing horn-rimmed glasses. Not the slightest bit athletic looking, he was overweight, wore faded breeches, and a T-shirt.

"Strictly non-U," Tina whispered to her. "What do you think of him?"

"I don't know. I expected a British, stiff-upper-lip kind of person, but honestly, all that matters to me now is that he gets me on a horse and protects me from falling off."

"Kimberly's having an affair with him," Tina whispered again.

"Oh, Tina, don't be ridiculous. You've been reading *Lady Chatterley's Lover.* Why, somebody like Kimberly couldn't even have a conversation with him."

"So maybe they don't talk. Honestly, Ellen, everybody knows about them. It's the Stanley Kowalski syndrome."

"Behind Kowalski is Marlon Brando," Ellen said, "but you can't tell me there's anything that special behind that man there. I mean, what would she see in him?"

"He's madly sexy," Tina giggled, "and if you weren't so repressed you'd feel his sexuality. He just emanates it. Every woman who comes here lusts for him. We've been coming here for years, and I've seen it with my own eyes. Riding is a very sexy sport. And jocks are very sexy men.

"I've seen dozens of women fawn over him. They like him and they trust him. They don't worry about getting hurt when they ride with him. If he says, 'Go over a jump,' they know they can do it, that the horse can do it. He knows his horses and he knows his customers. Do you know how important that is? Besides being a father figure, he's smart enough to be a hundred percent discreet. Even if he's screwing half his clientele, you never hear it from him. *They* talk, but he doesn't. He's part of an army of jocks who service rich ladies, but most of the others talk. Actually, he's more decent than most."

Ellen sat there listening, like a servant at the keyhole. Whenever she thought she was getting a hold on sophistication, Tina came along with more of her Christopher gossip and Ellen realized again how essentially naïve she was.

"I know a woman in Bev Hills," Tina continued, "who was having an affair with her tennis instructor. Then she found out that he was also involved with her teenage daughter and her teenage son. Lenny's not like that. One affair per family . . . and he's definitely not gay."

"But aren't women afraid to have affairs with a man who's so talked about?"

"The thing is," Tina said, "nobody's ever really sure who is and who isn't having an affair with him. Except for Kimberly, of course. That's not new gossip. The only time things get sticky is when someone gets serious about Lenny. Like if she starts to think a Saturday night roll in the hay means love."

"What does it mean?"

"Nothing," Tina said, "absolutely nothing. Lenny's here Wednesday through Sunday screwing Kimberly or someone else but on Sunday nights, it's back to the little apartment in Brooklyn with the dowdy wife and the kids who need braces. Kimberly and the others have no part of his real world and you certainly won't find him on the guest list for her Fifth Avenue world. When they leave here, there's no connection at all. To paraphrase dear old Harry Truman, 'The fuck stops here.' "

"Have you ever, you know, with him?" Ellen asked, daring for the first time in her life to ask a woman a question like that.

"I don't remember," Tina said. "I think maybe once, but so long ago, I'm not sure. I'll have to ask him one of these days."

What incredible insouciance. But why was it so incredible? After all, she had almost forgotten that night with Giovanni. And that night with him had no relation to the rest of her life. Sexual compartmentalization, that's what it was.

"Just tell me one thing, Ellen," Tina said in exasperation, "haven't you ever fooled around?"

Ellen didn't answer. She found it so difficult to lie.

"You sly thing," Tina said, "I'll get it out of you someday." The dinner bell rang and they all trooped in to the dining room.

Dinner was served early that night so there could be formation riding in the outdoor ring under floodlights after dinner. During the meal, Amos continued his running conversation, shoveling two portions of everything into his mouth, never bothering to swallow before continuing his discussion with Jeff about the purchase of new honors for himself and family. Now he was talking about getting an honorary doctorate or LL.D. Ellen resented having to sit with him for dinner but it would never occur to Jeff not to sit with his main client. Once a client was his, he never stopped servicing.

She was worried about the next day's riding lesson. Jeff said the lessons he had taken in the city had given him enough security to get through the weekend but she was terrified at the prospect of riding. It seemed terribly late to be starting. Even in the realm of sports, she realized, there were circles within circles. It was maddening, particularly since riding was a barometer of class. She wouldn't be able to make the mercury budge. What's more, these people had ridden since childhood and were part of the horse show circuit. Enid Taylor, the auto heiress, and her oil well husband, rode with something called Golden's Bridge, Kimberly rode in a Virginia hunt, and Donald and Beryl Surrey did their hunting in Ireland, where they had just purchased a castle.

The Surreys were new clients of Jeff's and they thought everyone rode. "You're joking," Beryl had said when Ellen confessed that she'd never attended either the Dublin or Madison Square Garden shows. "Well, which shows do you attend then?" she had asked. "Next season you must join us."

After dinner, Ellen and Tina sat in the bleachers watching the formation riding. Marilyn had gone to bed, pleading a headache, and Tina, who had dressed for riding, decided she was too sloshed from dinner to bother. Jeff was riding in formation next to Enid Taylor. He really had guts, Ellen thought admiringly. Sitting on the horse calmly, looking handsome and aristocratic in his new riding clothes, one would have assumed he'd had far more than one month's lessons. But there he sat, with blithe savoir faire, seemingly without fear. He seemed to be a natural rider and he looked so majestic that again she knew she was right to rely on him to make her world secure.

The formation riders began in a single file, first walk, then trot, then canter. Jeff had probably spoken to Lenny before the ride and slipped him a tip for a well-schooled horse, for his horse followed very well. Next they rode two abreast, then three, then four. Riding four abreast they rotated around a center axis, forming a rotating star.

Lenny rode beside Jeff, occasionally saying something to him, and Jeff continued to manage well. At least he stayed on, although Ellen could see a great difference between his riding and that of experienced riders. After the formation ride they played pass-the-crop, a kind of tag on horseback that was gay and exciting. Jeff was able to stay on, to get the crop when it was passed to him, and to pass it on again quickly. It was a pleasure to see the EL'ers turn into laughing children in this version of a childhood game. Ellen enjoyed seeing them all act so human.

Lenny rode with the group, directing, organizing, soothing, reassuring with his solid calm. Ellen watched him with interest. His competence did, as Tina had said, make him seem sexy and dynamic up there. Well, horses did that for men. Conquistadores! She watched the muscles in his firm brown arms and a little shiver ran down her spine. How different he was from Kimberly's white-skinned, pale-haired, frail-looking philanthropist husband. It was the difference between milk and meat.

The game seemed to go on forever and Tina staggered off to bed. Alone, Ellen became bored so she too left to go back to the main house. Since all of the other watchers had long since departed, she didn't think Jeff would be upset by this. When she entered the bar, she looked around for someone to sit with and she saw Michael Stewart's wife, Davida, a sad, depressed little thing, sitting hunched over at the bar.

Ever since the EL installation, two years ago, Ellen had felt a particular sympathy each time she'd seen Davida. Although Michael Stewart, with his chain of record stores, was Jeff's client, the two couples did not socialize outside of EL, and Michael came to many EL functions without Davida, always making an excuse such as illness or the necessity to stay with the children. On those occasions when they had both attended an EL function, there had always been so many people around that Ellen and Davida had not been able to speak on a personal level.

Davida still wore no makeup. When they had first met, Ellen had thought she looked ten years older than Michael. Tonight, she looked even more aged.

"Didn't you want to ride," Ellen asked, just to say something to make conversation, "or watch?"

Davida shook her head. The diamond earrings glittered. "I've

172

seen lots of riding," she said. She picked up her drink with shaking hands. Then big tears began to fall down her cheeks.

"Why, what's the matter?" Ellen asked sympathetically. She had never seen anybody look more unhappy.

"Michael wants a divorce," Davida said in a hopeless voice.

"Why?" Ellen asked, truly horrified. Divorce had always seemed a disgrace to her, a public admission of failure.

"He only married me for my father's money," Davida said, "but now he can manage on his own."

"What are you going to do?" Ellen asked.

"I won't give the divorce to him," Davida said. "If I hold on long enough, maybe he'll change his mind."

"Did he say why he wants the divorce?" Ellen asked compassionately.

"He wants to marry a girl named Candace. She's young, beautiful, a debutante. She's me, twenty years ago, only prettier. Apparently he's been pursuing her for months and he wants to marry her. Can you imagine, her mother is only five years older than I. Isn't that funny?"

"It's not funny," Ellen said gently.

"He's only doing it because he wants to go up the social ladder," Davida cried, "and she would only do it for money. My money! She's a socialite, young, beautiful, from a good family. A real trophy for a poor Greek boy who started out with nothing. She wouldn't have looked at him when I married him. But I married him, took him into my father's business, made him everything he is today, and now he wants to trade me in for a new model. I was with him all the way, every step of the way, and now he's forgotten all he owes me."

Ellen couldn't help asking, "Do you still love him?"

For a moment, Davida looked surprised. "Oh, no," she said, "he's not very lovable. In fact, he's not nice at all, he's a street fighter, an opportunist. I loved him at the beginning before I saw that he didn't care anything for me. No, I don't love him but I'm used to him. We've been married for fifteen years. I don't love him, but I do love my way of life."

Ellen knew that they lived in Larchmont, west of Mamaroneck, where Jeff wanted to live.

"I love Larchmont," Davida continued. "I love my life there." She kept mopping at her eyes with the little bar napkins, not wanting anyone but Ellen to notice that she was crying. "I belong to the garden club and the church social club. I love having dinner at the Larchmont Yacht Club, where we keep our boat. I love decorating my house and working in my garden. I love everything about my life. I'm the only happy housewife I know, and now he wants to take this away from me."

"Oh, Davida, maybe it will all blow over."

"I doubt it. He says he's going to file for divorce or fly someplace for it."

"Doesn't he need your consent for that?" Ellen asked.

"I don't know," Davida said, "it's my first divorce. I have to get a good lawyer, then I'll know what to do. I guess I could stay in our house with the children. They like the school and have loads of friends, so they wouldn't be too disrupted."

"Do you still have a lot of money of your own?" Ellen asked.

"I have nothing," Davida said, "except what Michael gives me. I guess he'll provide adequately, but not lavishly, for the kids and me."

"Well, then, you would be able to continue the life you love, wouldn't you?" Ellen asked, trying to encourage her.

"The suburbs are no place for women without husbands," Davida said. "I've seen what happens to such women. All social invitations end, the women live in isolation in their own houses. It won't even be the same at the garden club. The women will continue to be polite but all social relations outside of the club will cease. Divorced women are pariahs in the suburbs."

"Maybe it will be good for you ultimately," Ellen said, not believing her own words. "I mean, maybe it will push you into new hobbies, maybe a career."

"I don't think there will be anything good about it," Davida

174

said soberly. "I won't last more than two years. Both of my parents were alcoholics. I'm afraid that as soon as I find myself alone, I'll start drinking."

"Listen," Ellen said, patting her hand, "I don't want to seem out of line, but maybe you should see Dr. Bloom. Tina sees him all the time and she says he's great for making you feel better about yourself."

"I don't need Dr. Bloom," Davida said, "Michael does. And what good can Dr. Bloom do? He can't change the circumstances."

"I'll try to help," Ellen said. "I'll call you and maybe we can go to a museum together. I'll help you make it through this period. Maybe it will all blow over."

"You're being very kind," Davida said.

"It could happen to any of us," Ellen answered.

"It does happen to an awful lot of us," Davida said. "The reason you don't hear more about it is that women like me feel so defeated that we go quietly, just fade away like old soldiers are supposed to do. They trade us in, like cars, for new models. I'm old and I'm finished."

"How old are you?" Ellen asked.

"I'm forty-five," Davida said, "and Michael is thirty-five. According to statistics, in my social class, I'll probably live past seventy. Thirty years of loneliness lie ahead of me if he goes through with this divorce. It really makes one question society's focus on extending the life span. For what? Thirty years of boredom lie ahead of me." She looked at Ellen bleakly, horrified by her own vision of the future.

"But you'll find something to do," Ellen said.

"Yes," Davida answered, signaling to the bartender, "drink."

Ellen felt such mingled pity and contempt for Davida's defeatism that she wanted to shake her. But she also identified with her and was compassionate. If Jeff ever turned his back on her, she'd be in a similar position. With a rich, successful husband, she had power and without him she had nothing and she was nothing. She couldn't even make enough teaching nursery school to feed herself and Jennifer. Once you lost the "king," you were stripped of the trappings that went with him, you turned in his credit cards, and were turned out in the world, defenseless, alone, and without a way of making a living. Money and the man. The man and money. Davida's plight was a warning to Ellen to behave herself or she would be out on the streets again, as vulnerable to spoilage and rape as when she'd been a girl.

After Davida left, Ellen saw Kate sitting alone at a table and she went over to sit with her.

"I thought you loved riding," Ellen said.

"I wanted to ride, but I'm not feeling as well as usual. Indigestion, I think.

"How lovely you look, Ellen," Kate said, "you're completely different from the shy girl you were two years ago. Now tell me, what are your future plans? Are you going back to school to finish your degree? I wish I could interest you in working with me."

"I'd love to work with you, Kate, but I don't have any skills that would interest you. What could I do for you?"

"Let me think about it," Kate said, "and just come to me when you're ready. I look for general intelligence and a certain integrity, rather than for specific skills. You can always learn skills on the job."

"First, I think I must go back and finish my B.A.," Ellen said. "It might sound silly to you and I know nobody really cares, but I feel embarrassed about not having finished college. As soon as I have, I'll come to you for a job."

Then they talked for a while about Davida. "Isn't it tragic?" Ellen asked.

"No," Kate said, "it isn't. Davida will have a home, her children, herself. The best thing that could happen to her would be for her to be forced to get a job."

"Perhaps you could give her a job," Ellen ventured.

"Not I," Kate said, "she's too self-indulgent. All she wants is a reason to drink."

People began to file into the bar from the formation ride. Jeff was ruddy with triumph. "Never thought I could stay on," he said, flushed and happy, "and I aced it. What do you think of that?"

"I was proud of you," Ellen said, "that month of lessons certainly paid off. Nobody would have guessed you were almost a beginner."

"Right," he said, "and we're going to keep that little secret. Lenny's giving me my private lesson at six-thirty tomorrow morning, out in the fields, so no one can see I'm not an experienced rider. Bad for the image. He'll give you your lesson right after mine."

"Also out in the fields?"

"I don't know. Does it matter?"

"Don't you want to give the impression that I, too, grew up like National Velvet?" Ellen asked impishly.

"It's enough for *me* to ride well," he said. "It's more important for you to keep quiet or say the right things than to ride. I liked what you said to Amos but that laugh you let out almost messed things up. You have to watch those reactions."

"Yes, sir."

"You're not funny, Ellen. It's not worth losing an account for you to have the pleasure of laughing whenever you please."

They walked to the bar, Jeff ordered a drink, and she told him about Davida.

"I know all about it from Michael," he said. "Some of these guys think their PR agencies are their psychiatrists. He really intends to go through with the divorce so I suggest you don't waste any time with Davida. You never saw much of her, anyway. We've never even been to that precious house of hers. But we'll be seeing a lot of him socially in the future. He should have dumped Davida years ago. She's done nothing but drag him down. Wait till you see the dish he wants to marry."

"Don't you feel sorry for Davida?" Ellen asked.

"That's like asking me if I feel sorry for the agencies that don't get the account. That's the way the ball bounces. Somebody wins and somebody loses. Just the way I do with accounts. Be honest, Ellen. Who could be proud of being married to Davida? If she wanted to hang on to her husband, she should have taken better care of herself."

"She took good care of him," Ellen said, but Jeff had turned to greet Kimberly's husband, Jonathan, who had just arrived, looking alien in his suit and tie, his paleness accentuated in its contrast with the healthy flush of the riders. Kimberly ran to him with a great show of rapture.

"You made it after all, darling," her deep, husky voice trilled. She hooked her arm through his and led him to their suite.

Ellen watched Lenny, left standing alone at the bar. He stood there smoking a cigarette, holding a drink, deflated, a large man who seemed suddenly fragile, vulnerable, disappointed.

Tina sidled up to Ellen and whispered conspiratorially, "He looks as if he's beginning to take the lady seriously."

"Well, she's so gorgeous," Ellen answered.

"He's seen loads of gorgeous women."

"I'm sure he has," Ellen said, "but did you see the way he looked after her when she left? Gave me gooseflesh. Reminded me of the way Montgomery Clift looked at Elizabeth Taylor in *A Place in the Sun*. The poignance of the unattainable."

"You really are a nutty romantic," Tina said, "that's one of the things I love about you. He's been screwing her for over a year, from time to time. So what's so unattainable?"

"He may sleep with her, but he can't possess her soul," Ellen persisted.

Tina burst into laughter. "She hasn't any! Honest, Ellen, you can't go around thinking people are like you. You remind me of those dopey people who think their animals have the same feelings they have. Or that their plants do. Lenny's incapable of feeling the things you're projecting on to him. He's stupid. All people who work with horses are stupid. They're only one step higher than the horses. The only time I've ever seen Lenny worrying about something unattainable was about bigger tips. The loss of Kimberly's tips would bother him more than the loss of Kimberly."

With that, Tina went off to dance the Twist. Ellen looked over to see Jeff playing cards with Samson. Ever since that first night at the EL installation, Jeff had been the agency for Samson's business, and each year the sprawling conglomerate of Octagon, Ltd., grew. With Samson, as with Amos, Jeff played the court flatterer, soothing his clients, doing extra little jobs that went far beyond what would and should have been expected of him by other accounts, trying always to walk the tightrope of servility without seeming to be on a tightrope at all. However, Samson, though demanding and sometimes difficult, was not crazy as Amos was and Ellen had never seen Jeff drenched with perspiration because of him. Their first words to each other, "I wish I could be so tall" and "I wish I could be so rich" had become EL legends. Valerie, as magnificently bejeweled as always, sat beside Samson doing needlework. Yes, that was what a good EL wife was like, Ellen thought: silent, docile, her head bent over an acceptable hobby. Valerie, like Jeff, was always in attendance at Samson's side. Twentieth-century courtiers.

Lenny still stood at the bar alone. Restless, a little anxious about the prospect of riding the next day, Ellen decided to talk to him. She walked over to where he stood, said hello, and asked for a cigarette. Rudely, not looking up, he handed her one. She waited, then lit it herself. She sat down on the empty bar stool next to him, ordered a whiskey sour on the rocks, and introduced herself.

"I know who you are," he said grumpily, still not looking at her.

"I thought you might not remember me," she said, embarrassed by his lack of friendliness. "I guess you know that I have a lesson with you tomorrow morning. I wanted to talk to you because I'm a beginner and I'm terribly frightened."

"So what else is new?"

"I hope you'll give me a quiet horse."

"Don't worry. We never lost a guest yet. We have to worry about the horses, not the guests. You should see the way some of these *schmucks* bring the horses in; dripping, foaming. It's the horses I worry about."

Damn his rudeness. She'd make one more attempt, then move away. She'd feel a lot better about riding if she could establish some kind of relationship with him. If he still refused to be friendly, she'd go to bed. Once Jeff got involved in a card game he could play all night.

"I'm a complete beginner," she repeated. "I don't know if I've made that clear. I've never been on a horse, not even once. Is there anything you can tell me to make it easier?"

"Sure," he said, "it's like fucking, just like fucking. Now if you don't mind, I don't feel like talking."

"You're a rude child," she said, taking her drink and getting off the stool.

"Wrong," he said, "a rude adult. Listen, wasn't there ever a time you didn't feel like talking?"

"Right now," she snapped.

He looked up at her like a battered bull. "All right, all right," he said. "I'm sorry. Want to dance?"

"You don't have to be polite to me just because I'm a guest," she said. "It's my husband who does the tipping. You can just go right back to being off duty."

He reached over, took the drink from her hand, threw her cigarette on the floor and stepped on it, and pulled her on to the dance floor. They danced. She held herself at arm's length and made a tight, disapproving line of her mouth. He ignored her reactions and started to tell her a joke.

"Three people go to a psychiatrist," he said, "who has perfected a new technique for therapy. The first patient goes into his office and the doctor holds out a handkerchief and says, 'What does this remind you of?' "

Lenny pulled her off the floor. "You're a lousy dancer," he said sternly. "I hope you do better on a horse." Effortlessly, he picked her up and set her back on the bar stool, ceremoniously handed her her drink, and gave her another cigarette. This time he lit it for her.

"The patient looks at the handkerchief, moans, and says, 'Diapers. It reminds me of diapers. They were always tight, my

180

mother made them too tight. All my life I've been chokin' because of those damned diapers.'

" 'Okay,' the doctor says, 'you're cured. Next patient.'

"The next patient comes in and the doctor does the same thing. The patient looks at the handkerchief, starts to cry and says, 'The handkerchief reminds me of poverty. Endless poverty. Clothes hanging on lines, my mother always washing, always being poor. Now I know why I'm always so depressed.'

" 'Wonderful,' the doctor says, 'send in the third.'

"The third patient comes in and the doctor goes through the same routine. The patient looks at the handkerchief, thinks for a minute, then says, 'It makes me think of fucking.'

" 'Really,' says the doctor, 'how very interesting. Why does it make you think of fucking?'

" 'It's because everything makes me think of fucking,' the patient says."

Lenny leaned back and looked at Ellen, like a naughty boy, waiting for her response.

"Not really funny," Ellen said, "but I get your point."

"I'd like you to get my point," he said. He grabbed a toothpick from the bar and proceeded to clean his teeth. When he was finished he led her on to the dance floor again.

They were friendlier toward each other this time, and Ellen found herself intrigued by him. When a gigantic burp escaped, he seemed totally undisturbed. He was a primitive, natural, untamed; no wonder the ladies enjoyed him. He probably made love with the same uninhibited fervor with which he drank, smoked, and rode. He enjoyed himself artlessly, like a child.

Finally she excused herself, surprised that she wanted to stay and dance with him, afraid that it might not look quite right. She was reading in bed when Jeff came in.

"Listen to this," he said, excited, "Samson wants to sell his house in Green Haven. He's bought a house on Beekman Place in New York City. He told me about it and sounds exactly like what I want. It overlooks the Sound, has a swimming pool, tennis court, a greenhouse, good entertaining space, lots of kids' rooms, each with its own bathroom, two maids' rooms and a guest room. He'll be ready to move in January or June. My God, Ellen, can you imagine? I was a poor boy and now I'm going to buy Samson Plari's house. And after this, people will talk about it as Jeff Sheldon's house. I'm not going to bother to look anymore. Samson said we can come over any time and look at it."

She had never seen him happier. He whirled about the room in a fever of joy. "I'll be thirty-three," he said, "and I'll have one of the finest houses in Westchester. I did it, I did it, Ellen." His eyes were full of tears and he reached for her. They made love quickly. "Got to be up early for my lesson, babes," he said, rolling over and going to sleep. "This is the happiest night of my life."

Ellen felt stirred up and restless. Quietly she got up, pulled on her T-shirt and shorts, and tiptoed out of their room. The moon was full, and the soft Indian summer air was filled with that wonderful perfume of horses and hay that she had instantly loved. The full moon illuminated everything. She walked down the caked dirt road to the stable, listening to the crickets and the rattle of loose pebbles as she moved. She was beginning to feel better. As she approached the stable she heard voices and instinctively she stopped and flattened herself into the shadows. The voices were unmistakable: Lenny and Kimberly.

They were making love. At first, she couldn't believe it. They were making love standing up, leaning against the side of the barn. Ellen stood there hypnotized, paralyzed, an unwilling voyeur. Their encounter could not have lasted more than ten minutes. Then Kimberly smoothed her short skirt down and he zipped his jeans up. She heard Kimberly say, "This is the last time."

"Why?" he asked harshly.

"Just so. I'm getting bored. That's the way it is."

A moment of silence. "It's your loss, baby."

"Mine?" A low, throaty laugh.

"Sure, lots of dames around like you. Only one of me. Lots of good fish in the sea."

Again, that cool, insulting laugh. "Then I hope you catch

them. Hold out your hand. Here's a hundred-dollar bill. That should help us to part friends. I hope you're not too proud to take it."

"Hell, no," he said. "I've rendered services far beyond the line of duty."

"Friends," she asked lightly, obviously not giving a damn.

"Sure," he answered. "I won't even remember you next week. You'll be just another cunt to me."

Kimberly reached out and slapped him and then, wallop, he slapped her back. She let out a gasp, then a contemptuous laugh. Poised, not hurrying, she turned her back to him and casually walked off toward her sleeping husband. Lenny lit a cigarette and leaned against the fence, exhaling smoke at the moon. Then Ellen heard a low, jagged sound. He had put his head down in the cradle of his arms and his broad muscled shoulders were heaving up and down. Could he be crying? Maybe he had really cared about her. But he had taken the money. A hell of a way to make a living! Ellen waited until he'd begun to walk away to the servants' quarters before she made her escape. She slipped into bed feeling profoundly disturbed by what she'd seen.

Before leaving for his early morning lesson the next day, Jeff awakened her so she would have time to dress and get some coffee. Waves of nausea swept over her, but she was determined to master her fear. The regal formality of her new riding clothes gave her some faint confidence. At least she looked like a rider. She went to the dining room, swallowed a mouthful of coffee, then walked the path to the barn as if she were walking the plank. Lenny and Jeff were talking and both looked pleased.

"I'm a natural," Jeff told her, "I can't wait to get back in the saddle again."

"I'm frightened," she whispered to him.

He hugged her ostentatiously, then handed a twenty-dollar bill to Lenny. "Take good care of my wife," he said, "she's the only one I have."

"We take good care of all our guests," Lenny said, pocketing the money. Ellen winced, embarrassed at both of them.

"Give me a gentle horse," she pleaded.

"This one's dead," Lenny quipped, leading one out of the stable for her, "only we haven't told him yet."

She smiled, gratified at his attempt to make her laugh, and she let him help her to mount from the mounting block. The horse moved an inch and she let out a cry and slipped back. Lenny gently patted her and told her to try again.

"Just take it easy," he said, "try to relax. The horse isn't going anywhere and I won't let anything happen to you. You're a hundred percent safe with me. But please don't scream again. It makes the horse nervous and it makes me nervous. Don't worry. I'll have you on a lead line. All we're going to do today is walk in the fields, enjoy the horses, enjoy nature, and you can enjoy the privilege of being with me. Please believe me. Nothing will go wrong."

Relaxation spread through her. She was grateful that this gruff creature was so compassionate. Finally she was mounted. Holding her horse on the lead, he led her out into the nearby meadow. They went at a slow but steady walk. The fresh warm morning, the moist grass, the magnificence of colors of the changing leaves gave Ellen an unusual feeling of exhilaration and well-being.

"Nothing like nature, is there?" he asked, sensing her mood. "Today we walk. If you like, this afternoon you can try posting. If not, we can leave that for tomorrow."

They walked companionably, breathing, looking, not talking.

"Early mornings are always best," he said, "while the air is fresh."

She nodded in agreement and again there was a period of silence.

"How long you been married?" he asked gruffly, apropos of nothing tangible.

"Over six years."

"Happy?"

"Of course," she said. "Why do you ask?"

"Because I think your husband's a *schmuck,*" he said, in his customary, rude delivery.

She wanted to say, "How dare you?" but a certain innate honesty and curiosity prevented her from acting indignant. But she was curious.

"Why do you think that?" she asked. "Because he tipped you to take care of me?"

"Hell, no. That's what I'm here for. I have no pride. I can't afford that luxury."

"Then why do you say that?"

"I know that type of guy," Lenny said. "I see guys like him all the time in my business; the smart-ass, short-cut guys, the Madison Avenue Brooks Brothers types."

"I didn't know that you worked elsewhere," Ellen said. "What kind of work do you do?"

"When I'm not here," he said, "I'm a wholesale stockings salesman."

"Stockings?"

"Yeah, stockings. Your face looks like I said 'condoms.' Why do you look so surprised? Not fancy enough? The president of the company I sell for belongs to EL. So don't look down your nose that way."

"I'm not looking down my nose," she said. "Don't be so defensive. I come from a poor family myself. I was only surprised because that seems like such a tame activity after the ruggedness of riding. I can't think of any job more different from riding."

"Both jobs have one thing in common," he said. "You're dealing in both places with the same self-impressed *schmucks.* Which brings me back to your husband. He's one of those guys who thinks short cuts are meant for him and rules are made for other people. He wanted to go into meadows that had 'No Trespassing' signs posted and he was really pissed-off that I wouldn't let him. He thinks he's so special that no bullet could mow him down.

"But that's not the only thing. Take riding. I've devoted my entire life to it. You can study for fifty years and ride every day

185

and think you know everything about horses, and you still don't. But your *schmuck* husband thinks that after a month's lessons, and just because he can stay on, he's a rider. He doesn't want to understand horses or riding. All he wants to do is impress people. He kept saying to me, 'Make me look good,' and I kept telling him that there are no short cuts, no way to make him look good without a couple of years of lessons and practice. Then he tells you he's a natural like he didn't hear a word I said to him. He's a natural *schmuck,* but not a natural rider."

Ellen felt a sudden flash of liking for Lenny because he was the first person, other than the Mozers, who seemed to share some of her feelings about Jeff. This flash of liking was immediately followed by feelings of guilt. Where was her loyalty? How could she permit him even to say such things? And who was he to judge? A stockings salesman on horseback who routinely serviced the women customers! A vulgar gigolo devoid of pride. How could she give credence to any of *his* ideas. Guilt made her cold.

"Really," she said, "I'd rather not discuss this subject anymore. The whole world raves about my husband. They say he's a go-getter, a dynamo, that he'll be a multimillionaire before he's forty."

"Oh, sure, sure," Lenny said. "I know that type. They're so selfish you can't even describe them as selfish, any more than you can call a steamroller selfish. I know his type is successful. That's why I hate them. They're like blind forces moving ahead and smashing anything that gets in their way. Better make sure you don't get in your husband's way, lady."

Ellen didn't answer. She was thinking. All right, so Jeff was a seriously flawed human being. Who was better? That Casanova Giovanni? This vulgar jock beside her? Amos, whose wife was afraid to speak above a whisper? Michael Stewart, who was going to dump his old wife, the way an old horse is put out to pasture? Samson, whose wife had to sit beside him while he played cards? Harry, who was openly and unrepentently unfaithful? Maybe there were better men in the world but she hadn't met them. And then she thought of Saul. Was he better now? She didn't even know if that reality would live up to the memory.

"Hey, pay attention," Lenny said. "Are you comfortable?"

"I'm fine," she said, "I like it. Could we go just a little bit faster?"

"Sure, tiger," he grinned. Then he showed her how to trot. "Up, down, up, down," he chanted. He slipped his hand under her elbow and lifted her in rhythm. "Up, down, up, down." Despite her terror, she could feel the warmth of his hand through her jacket. And she liked it.

Finally she was able to struggle up and bounce down in a weak imitation of the correct way. She was strained and perspiring but enjoying herself.

"I'm not afraid," she said like an exultant child and Lenny nodded and smiled in approval. She cared what he thought of her and beamed at his nod, as pleased as a child getting a gold star in school.

Just then, the air was filled with the sudden thunder of galloping horses. Both she and Lenny were completely surprised. She looked at him for a quick, panicked moment as two horses flashed by and her horse jerked the lead line out of Lenny's hand and dashed after the other two. Paralyzed with fear, on the verge of hysteria, she grabbed ineffectually at the slight mound in front of her English saddle but it was not enough to hold onto.

She reached down, trying to wrap her arms around the horse's neck and she found herself slipping . . . going . . . going . . . gone. She hit the ground and instinctively rolled over away from the pounding hooves. She could hear Lenny's horse galloping after hers. She lay on the grass for a few dazed moments, then sat up gingerly and began testing to see if she was injured. No pain anywhere. Not hurt, she stood up, carefully brushed off her new breeches, and sat down under a tree to wait for Lenny's return. In a few minutes he came galloping back over the hill, holding her horse on the lead line, and she waved to him. A look of real concern and relief spread over his face. He didn't look the slightest bit tough.

"Good girl." He smiled at her while dismounting. "I'll give you a leg up. Don't worry about the horse's taking off. I have him securely. Now, stand close to the horse, bend your leg, grab the saddle with both hands, one, two, three, lift."

He pushed her up effortlessly, she was back in the saddle, and the horse had not moved. He remounted his own horse in one swift, upward leap, took her lead line, and turned back toward the stables.

"I'm going to kill your husband," he snarled.

"My husband?"

"Him and Amos Landor, galloping out that way without regard for nobody else! You're not supposed to gallop unless you can stop your horse. I've seen *schmucks* like that on the ski slopes, the same kind of guys. Without taking a single lesson they come schussing down the slopes and God help the guys who didn't get out of the way. They were the ones that got hurt, never the schussing bastards. Let me tell you, if I owned this place, those two guys would never get on another horse."

"Would you like to own a place like this?" she asked, to change the subject and calm him down.

"Don't make stupid conversation. I'm lucky if I get to own a car before it breathes its last. People like me do all the work and we never get to own a goddamned thing. Sure I'd like to own this place. Why do you ask? Would you like to buy it for me?"

"You don't have to be so unpleasant," she said.

"Oh, yeah? If I'm pleasant it's good for you but it doesn't do a damned thing for me."

They said nothing more until they reached the barn. Jeff and Amos were leaning against the edge of the barn, Jeff smoking a cigarette and Amos chomping, as usual, on a cigar.

"Put those out," Lenny snapped. "Don't you see the 'No Smoking' sign? I assume you two big-shots can read."

He got off his horse, helped Ellen to dismount, gave the horses to a stableboy, then walked over to them.

188

"Mr. Sheldon," he said, making it sound insolent, "you and your friend over here almost killed your wife. She should sue you both. If she wasn't related, I'd advise her to. One more little stunt like that and I'll make sure neither of you ever gets a horse again at this place."

Amos got red and looked on the verge of a heart attack. Jeff held out a crisp twenty-dollar bill, said, "Sorry about that" in a contemptuous tone, and then tried to smooth it all over with his Arrow-collar smile.

"I don't want a tip, you *schmuck,*" Lenny said. "I want you to understand the seriousness of what you did. I want an apology to me and your wife."

"My wife is my business," Jeff said, "but as for you, I don't apologize to the hired help."

Like a reflex action, Lenny's fists shot out, one, two, in the stomach, and Jeff was down.

"Don't you dare hit me," Amos shrieked in terror. "I have connections. You'll never work again. Don't you dare touch me."

He went fleeing toward the main house, Lenny strode angrily into the barn, and Ellen bent over Jeff, crying.

"Get your hands off me," Jeff said, close to tears. He had never before in his charmed life been struck. "This is all your fault."

He struggled to his feet and limped off, trying not to show his pain.

"Do you want to lean on me?" Ellen asked.

"Just leave me alone," he said, pushing her arm away. She followed him into their room, where he dropped onto the bed.

"Should I get a doctor?" she asked.

He didn't answer her. After a while he fell asleep, then he awakened, took a shower, plastered on his success smile, and they went to lunch as if nothing had happened. She never heard either Jeff or Amos refer to it again.

That afternoon, Lenny had one of his assistants take the trail ride out so he and Jeff were spared further confrontation. After the trail ride had gone, Lenny took her out again for another lesson into the magnificent countryside and by the end of the lesson she was able to do a weak imitation of posting. She was exultant, never having been an athlete and never having thought she had any athletic ability.

"May I try to canter tomorrow?" she asked Lenny in a cold and businesslike voice. After all, no matter what Jeff had said, it was barbaric to hit him.

"You can try to canter when you feel ready," he said.

"Could we go out for two hours instead of one?" she asked. "Of course, we would pay for two lessons."

"You can have whatever you pay for," he answered. She didn't answer.

"Mad at me?" Lenny asked.

"Only an animal uses his fists," she reproved him.

"Okay," he said, "so I'm low class and I'm an animal. I don't care what you think of me just as long as you pay my fee." They did not say another word to each other all the way back to the stable.

Early the next morning she wandered down to the stable and found Lenny in the tack room.

"No breakfast?" he asked.

"I want to see how you saddle up," she said.

"That's the right attitude," he said. "Listen, I know you're angry with me about hitting your husband yesterday but I'm not about to apologize. I said he was a self-impressed *schmuck* and I still think so. Guys like me do all the work and guys like him get all the gravy."

"I don't want to discuss my husband with you," she said, annoyed. "You don't know anything about him. He works ten times harder than you do and he puts up with just as much shit from clients. He's a self-made man. He didn't take his success away from anybody and whatever he is or does is none of your business anyway."

"Okay, okay," Lenny said in mock penitence, "I'm outta line. I apologize. I won't ever talk about that *schmuck* again."

The morning was so beautiful that it was hard to stay angry.

190

It was a moment of epiphany, perfect weather, a wonderful new figure, fine clothes, plenty of money, and the beginning of a new hobby she loved. They rode companionably, walking, trotting (God, she was stiff), and finally, after an hour, cantering in a peaceful little meadow. She had never felt more triumphant in her life.

"It's easier than trotting," she said. She loved the rhythm of cantering, the smooth, circular, moving back and forth in the saddle. And then, it came, as she had really known it would since yesterday.

"We have a little cabin near here," he said. "We can dismount and give the horses some water and you can rest there for a few minutes. Two hours is a long ride for a beginner. I only agreed to it because the cabin is here."

She followed him, saying nothing. She could hardly breathe. They walked their horses, single file, along a hidden forest path. She was an Indian maiden in an old Western romance. The sights, smells, and atmosphere of the woods heightened her sudden euphoria. The horse moved solidly and steadily, warm between her thighs.

They reached the cabin and Lenny tied up his horse while she waited. Oh, God, he was going to make love to her. She suddenly knew that he would try. Wasn't that what he did? Wasn't he a jock who serviced women for tips? Would she? How could she? No, she couldn't. A glass of water, back on the horses, and that was all. After all, he wasn't going to rape her. Nothing to be afraid of. He walked over to her, placed his hand on her thigh, and smiled up at her. She felt as though she were going to faint. She could feel the warmth of his hand through her breeches. Then he reached up for her and she slid down into his waiting arms. She could feel the warm body of the horse behind her as Lenny kissed her for the first time. And suddenly nothing mattered but the pure warmth and sensuality of the man. Instinctively she knew this was a man with whom she could be herself completely.

Then taking her by the hand he led her inside. The large

room with its slate floor and Indian scatter rugs looked romantic and charming. At one end was a wall-width stone fireplace and there were several large couches about the room. The only other furniture was a small bar and refrigerator. He handed her a cold beer and she shivered suddenly, despite the heat outside. Then he lit a cigarette and offered her one. Sitting close to each other, feeling each other's warmth, savoring every minute, they smoked companionably and sipped their drinks. She felt in a dream, relaxed, comfortable, waiting for him to lead the way.

He ground out the butt of his cigarette, reached for a boot jack from a shelf, and pulled off his boots. Then she reached out for the jack.

"No," he murmured, "let me." Slowly he tugged on each of her boots, slowly, slowly, and they slipped off her legs with sensuous little hisses. In a dream she felt him open her stock and unbutton her shirt. He pulled the shirt from her shoulders then buried his face in her breasts. Then he kissed her neck, her arms, her back. And finally, when she thought she would go wild with unfamiliar desire, he pulled off her breeches and she stood there naked before him. He looked at her, smiled, and let out a low whistle. "Wow," he said.

Gently he eased her back on the couch and then, starting at her lips, he proceeded to gently kiss her, moving his lips downward slowly, covering every inch of her bare skin with kisses. Then, spreading her legs, he proceeded to gently lick her clitoris. Jeff had never done this and the excitement of breaking this taboo was almost enough to bring her to orgasm. It didn't matter at all that her nipples were numb.

"Hold back, baby, just hold back," he said. "Hold back, don't come yet."

Don't come, he said, because he had no doubt that she would and could come and she was filled with a wild lightness of spirit at the thought that she need no longer worry about orgasms. She was in his hands. He was calmly sure that orgasms would happen . . . and so was she. The sure knowledge that she would achieve it freed her to enjoy getting there. He would take care of her the same way he did in riding. He would not leave her aching, edgy, unsatisfied, as Jeff did. He was not making love to himself, floating in his own cocoon as Giovanni had. He was aware of her. He was aware of her and he cared about her reactions and would bring her to orgasms.

Then suddenly the rush was upon her and she felt herself coming, coming, coming, coming, don't stop, coming, coming, and then, joyously surprised, so this is what it's like and before she had finished coming he was inside her and she was joyously thrusting herself against him, meeting the rhythm of his movements, and like a scream of lightning he came and she came. Then she came again and again, making up for all the years of not coming, opening wider and wider to him, melting and dying around his hard cock. Great waves of warmth shot through her and her entire body convulsed in an ultimate orgasm, the most wonderful complete feeling she had ever known.

"I told you riding was like fucking." He smiled down at her. She cuddled against him, feeling better than ever before in her life. And then, he reached for her again.

On the ride home she waited for him to say something about the future to her but he didn't. She felt she had to say something. "When can we meet again?" she asked him.

"Never."

"Never," she said, surprised and hurt.

"You're a lovely woman, Ellen, and don't think I wouldn't like to see you again. But there's no point to it. I have my life to live in Brooklyn and you have your life with EL and those two points are on different planets. I might get to like you and then what? Sooner or later you'd get tired of me, then you'd tip me and tell me to get lost. We haven't anything in common, so there's no point in getting involved."

Her moment of hurt evaporated. He was absolutely right. The very word Brooklyn made her shudder. And she could understand why he feared to be hurt again the way Kimberly had hurt him. But she would always be grateful to him for making her normal. He had given her a priceless gift.

"Thank you," she said when they reached the barn.

"Any time you're here." He grinned.

They smiled at each other and said goodbye.

5

While Ellen was trying to forget what sex had been like with Lenny, she was grateful that Jeff had found his dream house. It occupied her time in the months that followed and eventually the house was in perfect order and ready for them. Green Haven is at the tip of Mamaroneck and extends into Long Island Sound. It is gold country, quite beautiful, and the house was as magnificent as Samson had described it. Five master bedrooms with fireplaces, five baths, a large study for Jeff, a game room with built-in audio equipment, front stairs and back stairs going from the maids' rooms to the kitchen (and ultimately two maids in those rooms up the back stairs), and an Olympic-sized swimming pool in the exquisitely landscaped back lawn. The front of the lawn sloped down to the Sound and had a dock for boating although the water was too polluted for swimming.

Jennifer, despite her sadness at leaving her friends, delighted in the pool and in the buzzer system which ran from each room to a register in the kitchen, so the maids would know to which room they were being summoned.

Jeff was positively beatific. "We'll fill the house with kids now, right, babes?"

Ellen nodded assent but realized she probably would never go through with it. She knew that if she did have another child or two the responsibility for the rearing would rest completely on her shoulders. Jeff had never seen much of Jennifer and now that she was going through a homely, toothless stage, he seemed increasingly distant. Jeff wanted only beauty and perfection about him that reflected his own. Jennifer never complained about it now but Ellen could see how badly Jeff's lack of interest had hurt her. So what was the purpose of producing more children for him to ignore?

She had to admit to herself, however, in regard to the house, that Jeff had been completely right in buying it. It was so beautiful, so correct, so symmetrical, that everyone who entered it admired it, felt comfortable and elegant in it. She thought about Lenny and was grateful for escaping enriched but unscathed. She could have lost everything she cared about, like poor Davida.

The completion of the house, of her work with the decorator, left her at loose ends but she managed to fill her days at Alain's, at Helen's, meeting Tina or Kate for lunch, shopping and planning activities for Jennifer. Whenever she started to feel bored or think that she was wasting her life she'd read a book or do more exercise. She never questioned her life again until Michael Stewart's wedding. When the invitation arrived, it upset Ellen more than she would have expected.

"He's such a louse," Ellen said to Jeff, "that if we had any kind of moral fiber we wouldn't go to the wedding."

"There are lots of paupers with that kind of moral fiber," Jeff quipped.

"But still, what he did to Davida is so terrible. It's so insulting. Would you ever do that to me . . . trade me in for a new, younger number?"

"I made you into a new number," he joked. "I've invested too much money in you to trade you in. Besides, never underestimate the extent of my apathy. I don't have time to look for a replacement. Business comes first." He was joking, maybe.

"Thanks a lot," she joked back.

She was getting along well with him now that she had learned how to dissemble, but Jennifer continued to invite his rages. Jeff came into their bedroom on the night of Michael Stewart's wedding and found the girl playing in Ellen's new mink-lined brocade cape, while Ellen dressed.

"Get the hell out of that," he yelled brutally at her; "it's not some kind of Halloween costume. It's not a toy."

"She's not hurting it," Ellen said, quickly coming to her defense.

"I'm not hurting it," Jennifer echoed. "I was pretending to be a princess."

"Then go pretend in something that costs less," he said. "Besides, you're not clean. Your nose is running and you have chocolate pudding smeared around your mouth."

"I don't have anybody to play with since you made me move here," Jennifer said.

"Maybe if you looked better, you would have friends," he answered her.

Then he turned to Ellen, ignoring Jennifer's presence. "The kid's too fat," he said. "Stop stuffing her and tell that to your mother and the maids. She looks like something out of *el barrio*. Rich kids are supposed to be thin."

"I have nobody to play with," Jennifer mourned.

"You should have a brother. Then you'd have somebody to play with. That's what we need around here."

"Would you like me better if I was a boy, Daddy?" Jennifer mourned, her eyes filling with tears.

"I'd like you better if you'd get cleaned up and lost some weight."

"Jeff, how can you say such things to her?"

"I'll wait for you downstairs," he said, slamming his way out of the room.

"Must you go out tonight, Mommy?" Jennifer asked. "I hardly see you anymore. I'm at school all day and you're at those dumb parties so many nights. I'll forget what you and Daddy look like."

"Tonight's a must, my love," Ellen said, "and I'm sorry I have to go. I'd much rather be home with you. But I promise I'll bring home a piece of wedding cake for you."

"Will you wake me up to kiss you and see the cake?" Jennifer asked. "Sometimes I get so lonesome. Those two maids spend all their time with each other, not with me."

"Yes, I'll wake you up, my darling," Ellen said, holding the girl close to her. She felt depressed. She had already been depressed at the thought of granting implicit approval to what Michael had done, by attending the wedding, but now, suddenly, she felt a gnawing concern about Jennifer. There she was, alone much of the time in the house with two maids who were interested in her only for a salary. She was not doing as well in school as in the past and had still been unable to break into a social circle. Poor Jennifer. Her parents were going round and round in a gold circle but she was alone. Well, Ellen vowed, no matter what enticing EL functions came up in the next month she would stay at home with Jennifer instead. The only problem was that when she stayed at home rather than going into the city to meet Jeff or their friends, she felt as bored and lonesome as Jennifer. But she vowed to get to work on the problem the next day. A boarding school in which Jennifer was surrounded by other children might be the solution but Ellen would miss her terribly. She would have to discuss the matter further with Jennifer tomorrow.

It was time to go. Ellen walked to the top of their majestic, carved mahogany staircase and looked down. Jeff stood at the bottom in his dinner jacket, looking heartbreakingly handsome, even more so now with the few gray hairs flecking the blond. She floated down to meet him, her brocade dress, weighted at the bottom, moving gracefully as she swept down the stairs. She held out the mink-lined brocade cape, which matched, and he draped it over her shoulders. Ellen saw them reflected in the Chippendale mirror; frozen in time, the all-American lie.

"Seven years," Jeff exulted at their reflection, "seven years and we have it all. And you're only twenty-seven. Well, looks like I'm getting gray."

"It's distinguished," Ellen said, "makes you look even more handsome."

"So what," he said gloomily, "only six more years in EL. But I'm not giving up hope. I'm trying to push through an amendment to our constitution to extend the age to forty-five."

"What difference would it make if you had to leave at forty?"

"I love it, that's what difference it would make."

"But you'd still keep the friends you've made, still keep the clients, wouldn't you?"

"In this business," he said, "you can't bank on anything. You can never stop hustling. Let's go. No point in worrying about that tonight. If I get that amendment through that problem will be solved."

In the car, both Jeff and Ellen were quiet. Ellen was dreading the evening and couldn't help wondering what Davida was doing tonight.

Davida had called Ellen several times before the wedding, anxious to talk to anyone who seemed like a friend. She wanted Ellen to meet her for lunch but since Ellen felt her loyalty had to be to Michael and his new wife, Candace, there didn't seem to be any point in encouraging Davida. That seemed like little enough to do for Jeff.

The most recent call had come about a week ago. Tearfully, Davida had told Ellen that Michael wanted her to attend the wedding and was resentful that she wouldn't. He had told her that it would be best for their children, who were attending, if they could see their mother in a friendly rather than a rancorous position.

"He's unbelievable," Davida said. "He asked if I were angry and said that after all these years the least I could do for him would be to not make him feel guilty."

God, these men, Ellen thought. They were always saying "the least you could do for me" and that always turned out to be the most that any one person could ask of another.

"What nerve," Ellen said, "doesn't he have any sensitivity to your feelings?"

"No," Davida said, "his sensitivities are all reserved for his own feelings. He thought he was being generous when he said that if I wished, he would be glad to arrange for an escort for me. He kept saying it would be better for the children if I attended."

"What a bastard," Ellen said. "What he really means is that it would soothe his conscience if you attended. I feel bad about going, Davida, honestly I do. I tried to get out of it. But Jeff would be furious if I didn't."

"He's right, I suppose," Davida said. "Business is business. None of these men can afford sentiment. You're the nicest person I met in EL, and if I'd stayed married, I know we could have been friends."

"We can still be friends," Ellen said, feeling penitent and thinking she would meet Davida one day for lunch and hope Jeff wouldn't find out. Of course, if Davida mentioned it to Michael and he told Jeff, Jeff would storm for a week.

"I'll call you the day after the wedding to tell you about it if you like," Ellen said.

"We'll see," Davida answered.

Everyone from EL had turned out for Michael's wedding, adding to the bride's own contingent of beautiful people. The women glittered in their tans and diamonds. Angry as she was at Michael, Ellen could see why he had been overwhelmed by Candace. The bride was blond and willowy with that magnificent healthy American look; straight, heavy blond hair, flawless tawny skin, large innocent blue eyes, small but well-formed breasts, flat hips and boundless self-confidence, which Ellen was to later find protected her from the realization that she was dumb. Everyone called her Candy and she looked like a precious sweet.

The bride's mother was also prototypical. A lifetime of enforced thinness had resulted in a tough, taut body which had managed to become completely unerotic, despite the carefully maintained weight. Her face was tanned and leathery from golf and tennis; the regulation blue eyes had faded and were red and watery from the cocktails that were as habitual as the exercise. She stood beside her daughter in the receiving line; a picture of before and after.

Ellen shivered. Time bankrupted the ideal, no matter how much money and effort were expended on the body. Ultimately, what was the meaning of the days she herself spent at Christopher's, Alain's, and Helen's. Everybody got old, everybody was betrayed, everybody died. The sadness that had resulted from the hostile interchange between Jeff and Jennifer stayed with her, despite the gaiety of the other guests.

Tina had told her that most of Candy's guests were listed in the *Social Register* and even the minister, tall, distinguished, with graying temples and bright blue eyes, seemed to have been plucked from some Main Line tree. A triumph for central casting!

The guests smiled approvingly as the brief ceremony was concluded. Ellen was amused at the upper-class absence of emotion. Even the sealing kiss was a little peck, a business transaction, the concluding action of a marriage made in Dun and Bradstreet. All pleasant smiles, the guests had just toasted the couple with champagne when the policeman appeared. He moved purposefully toward the bride and groom.

"Probably parked next to a hydrant," Tina joked.

All movement ceased and everyone watched while the policeman stopped in front of Candy and Michael. The children stood beside their father. Ellen felt gooseflesh rise on her arms as the bride let out a childish wail of displeasure. The guests stood there frozen.

"Davida has killed herself," Candy shrieked. "How could she do such a thing? She's ruined my very first wedding."

"Oh, God, that poor woman," Kate murmured, moving

over to Ellen. "We should have done something. I feel terrible about that. Somehow I sensed disaster but I did nothing."

"It's outrageous," the bride's mother snapped. "That woman had no sense of proportion. Imagine such poor taste!"

Michael stood there deeply shocked. The children had put their arms around each other and were trembling with grief.

"Jesus Christ," he finally muttered to the cop, "she warned me but I didn't believe her. I mean, she was out of her mind. How could anyone believe she'd do something so spiteful just to ruin my wedding."

The bride continued with her temper tantrum while the dazed and embarrassed Michael struggled for self-control before the watchful gaze of his EL associates.

"I knew she was a troublemaker," Candy wailed. "It's all your fault. We could have been married in Paris. We didn't have to be married here just so you could have all your friends."

Michael turned to the policeman again. "This was a hell of a time to barge in. How did you know to come here?"

"She called us just before she shot herself," the policeman said, "and told us to notify the bride and groom. How the hell were we to know you were the ex-husband and that she was doing this to get even? We just thought you were the next of kin. Listen, I'm going. I done my job. The body's at the morgue."

Michael's children, a boy of fourteen and a girl of fifteen, their faces contorted with grief and horror, walked over to the policeman.

"Where the hell are you two going?" Michael bellowed.

"We're going to the morgue," the boy said manfully, trying not to cry.

"The hell you are," Michael yelled. "You're not going anywhere. You're not spoiling my wedding. Come on, kids. There's nothing you can do now. What's the point? Don't spoil this for me. I'll call Campbell's right away and they'll take care of everything. I tell you there's no point in going to the morgue. I promise you I'll take care of everything. I'll even defer my honeymoon for a day. What do you say, kids?"

Ignoring him, the children followed the policeman out. Michael stalked after them dementedly and positioned himself in front of the policeman. "I'm going to make a complaint about you," he stormed. Impassively, the officer put one arm around each of the children and they left that way. Michael gritted his teeth, agonized his face into a smile, and stomped back to the bride. Candace still looked stormily petulant and her mother looked on the verge of a heart attack.

"They'd call *her* heart attack a case of Cartier arrest," Tina said.

"Poor Davida," Kate said. "If she couldn't get her revenge from living well, she certainly got it from dying well. I should have listened to you, Ellen, when you suggested I give her a job. I feel very bad about this. I should have felt more compassion. Well, after this, I vow that for the rest of my life I'll never again turn my back on a friend."

"It wasn't your responsibility," Tina said. "It's a rough world and there's no place for losers." Kate ignored her.

"I feel guilty, too," Ellen said. "She called me several times. I should have seen her."

"You certainly should not have seen her," Jeff said, hearing her. "The woman was obviously a psycho. This just gives you an idea of how she always made Michael's life hell. I've heard of lots of ex-wives pulling dirty tricks but this is the worst yet." Ellen snatched her hand from his arm.

The orchestra began to play "The Most Beautiful Girl in the World." Waiters dashed about pouring French champagne and Michael swept his debutante onto the floor. Her handsome, well-preserved father followed with Candace's mother. In five minutes everything was back to normal. The dance floor filled, gay laughter floated throughout, and Davida became old news.

"Good old Anglo-Saxon insouciance," Kate murmured to Ellen.

"Five minutes," Ellen mourned to Kate. "My God, five minutes. Poor Davida. A useless gesture."

Poor Davida, undemanding, pathetic, used up then exiled

from paradise. Not fair, Ellen thought, not right and not fair for a husband to dismiss a used-up wife. Men kept doing it and getting away with it, making the country into a vast junkyard of discarded women.

Tina dragged Ellen off to the ladies' room. "What a night," she said, "I keep thinking there are no new experiences but this is certainly a first. I can't wait to tell Dr. Bloom."

"Michael is a disgusting monster," Ellen said. "He cares more about pleasing Candy than about being with his kids at a time like this."

"Who can blame him?" Tina said. "Children are a pain in the neck. I don't know when they ever start to pay off. I dislike Jacques more each year. I'm glad I never succumbed to a second child. I should have stopped before one."

"I don't care what you say," Ellen said, "he's a monster and he's disgusting. No heart."

"There you go again with those romantic ideas," Tina said. "It isn't Michael's fault. Everybody gets divorced. But Davida was a fool and this only proves it. What could be more stupid than to kill yourself to get even. She didn't realize that he'll be ecstatic at saving years of alimony payments. You know my friend, Monica, the chanteuse? Well, she told her lover that if he left her, she'd kill herself by taking sleeping pills. He asked her if he could hang around to watch because he'd never seen anyone die before. He wanted to photograph it. Then she did what Davida should have done. Monica took off after him with the kitchen knife, he tripped over her hassock, and had to spend nine months in a cast that reached up to his dick. Monica laughed like crazy, then went and found someone else. She was smart but Davida was stupid."

"But Davida told me she wasn't getting enough money from Michael to manage."

"That's what I'm saying," Tina repeated, "she was stupid and naïve to give him all of her money in the first place. I hope you're putting away money."

Ellen was embarrassed to tell Tina that she wasn't. She

would think her as naïve and stupid as Davida. But there really hadn't been any need to all these years. Whatever was wrong with Jeff, no one could deny that he was generous. Still, perhaps she should start to put some away. Strange that it was easier to think that what had happened to Davida could never happen to her than it was to plan intelligently for future change.

"Davida wasn't stupid," she protested to Tina. "The only thing wrong with her was that she was a decent woman. She was a Holyoke graduate."

"So what?" Tina said. "I never even went to college but I can understand the world. They didn't teach her the right things at college. She didn't learn the rules of war. Little Candy may be young, but did you see her mother? You can bet your life those ladies know the score, learned it in the cradle. When Candy's finished sucking Michael dry, *he'll* be the one wanting to kill himself. What a sucker! Thinks he got a bargain! That's a joke. Christopher tells me Michael's also laying the mother."

"I don't believe it," Ellen gasped. "It's impossible. Why would she? Why would he?"

"Michael would do it just because it was offered to him. He's a sucker for flattery. He'd be dazzled at getting two at one blow. But Candy's mom, Barbara, is probably doing it to stay close to Michael's money. It's evident that she isn't doing it because of any grand passion. Mom's the type who gets her kicks from winning at tennis, and five'll get you ten she hasn't touched her husband in fifteen years. They're the kind who substitute liquor for sex. But she probably puts on a pretty good act for Michael and it's for money. Michael thinks Candy's family is so aristocratic, but actually Davida came from a much finer background. Candy's family are decayed aristocracy and they desperately need Michael's new money. What a joke. Michael took everything from Davida, tossed her aside, now is giving everything to Candy who will do the same to him. Candy hates her mother so Mom is just covering herself in case Candy decides not to share."

"Terrible people," Ellen said, shuddering.

"It's life," Tina said cheerfully. "It's kind of fun if you don't care too much."

Myra Benson swept into the ladies' room and greeted them. Because Leonard Benson's hotel chain was a client of Jeff's, Ellen sometimes sat with Myra at EL events but since Leonard's chain spanned the world ("Someday he'll have the Ho Chi Minh Benson Hotel," Tina had joked), they traveled a great deal and she and Ellen were on the same impersonal terms they had been at when they first met. In her heart, Ellen continued to be jealous of the woman who had been quoted in the *Times* as saying that her husband was her best friend. The three women greeted each other cordially.

"We are positively horrified that this should have happened in our hotel," Myra said. "The place is already swarming with reporters but Leonard has put on extra security guards to keep them out. We'll have to figure how to get Michael and Candy past them later on. If Leonard had any premonition of this, he would have asked them to get married somewhere else. I can't think this will improve our image."

"For heaven's sake," Ellen said, "how can Davida's death only mean a hotel's image to you?"

"What's wrong with her?" Myra asked Tina.

"She gets like that," Tina joked, "ignore her. But honestly, Myra, this won't hurt the hotel's image at all. It will only make the image more romantic. I don't think you have to worry."

"We do hate sensationalism," Myra said.

"Are you putting on weight?" Tina asked Myra.

Myra grinned. "I'm pregnant again. This will be number three. My house is like Grand Central Station. I have one au pair girl for each child. I've only put on a few pounds but you notice because I'm so short. Dr. Dorban has me on a special diet to *lose* weight during pregnancy. His theory is 'figures first, fetuses second.' I've never used him before but my old obstetrician moved to Palm Springs and I can't go there to have this baby. But now

I'm delighted that I was forced to change. It's a pleasure to have an obstetrician who understands the necessity of a good figure. After my second baby I was so stretched that I almost had a nervous breakdown when we opened the Puerto Rico Benson and I saw my figure in the paper. I swore then that I would never get that stretched again. I could go through life without a third child, but I can't go through life fat. Fortunately, with Dr. Dorban, you can have your figure and your baby too."

The conversation triggered Ellen's guilt about not having another child. On the infrequent times they had sex, she kept her diaphragm safely in place. Idly she listened as Tina and Myra gossiped.

Enid Taylor was divorcing Ronald, Jr., and marrying Tim Scott, the actor. "Twelve years married to old oil wells," Tina said, "and she leaves him for a guy born in the East End of London. Tim Scott's father was a ragman. Everybody knows that. To his family, Cockney is high class."

"She's probably doing it for her career," Myra said, "and besides, Ronald is bisexual. You know who his new boyfriend is? Peter Theodore, you know, the man who owns the chain of telephone answering services. Enid's probably doing it mainly for help in becoming an actress, not that Tim isn't quite a catch for anyone."

After a few minutes of gossip, the three women made their way back to the ballroom. The guests were chatting at their assigned tables for dinner as if Davida had never existed. Ellen grabbed Tina's arm in excitement.

"Look," she said, "over there, sitting near Harry, at our table, isn't that Benjamin Dalway?"

It had to be Dalway. She'd seen his Giacometti-like body and gaunt face on the back of his book, *Middle Class,* which had been on the best-seller list for over a year, and had made the quiet sociologist a media star. Always referred to by his last name, he was now an adviser and close personal friend of the young Senator Dunstan and was universally acclaimed for his dry, New England wit and his democratic philosophy, which was all the more admired because of his Boston Brahmin background.

"You're right," Tina said. "I've seen him on television. What a bore. I hope I'm not stuck with him."

"I think he's sitting next to my chair," Ellen said, "because Jeff is on the other side. How exciting. I'm thrilled."

"That's probably why you got him," Tina said. "Practically everybody here is a Republican and Candy told Christopher that her mother was searching wildly for someone to seat him next to. They must have heard some of your ideas."

Delighted, Ellen walked to her seat and Dalway, who had been talking, sprang up to hold her chair, twinkled at her, then sat down and picked up his story. He held the center of the stage and the others at the table, even Jeff, hung on his every word as he told anecdotes about his celebrity tours across the United States, clever anecdotes designed to simultaneously impress the listeners with how modest he was while at the same time reminding them of his worldwide acclaim.

Dalway's wife, Linda, was another matter entirely. She was a small, anemic-looking, indifferently dressed woman, who reminded Ellen vaguely of Davida. There was the same feeling of almost pathological repression in Linda as there had been in Davida. The disparity in the sizes of Dalway and Linda was as noticeable as the difference in their personalities.

Neither Dalway nor the other man at their table, Murray Morano, was a member of EL. Dalway's wife was related to the bride and Morano, a business friend of Michael's, had clearly been seated with Jeff because he had an account and he wanted to get into EL. If anybody could take care of both, it was Jeff. Bunny Morano, a plump blond bubbler, whose baby-doll dress alone would be enough to keep them out of EL forever, shrieked with joy when she learned that the Sheldons were Green Haven neighbors.

"We'll have to see each other all the time," she fawned and Ellen smiled coldly, finding herself disapproving of these people as "low class." Three years in EL and she had gradually assimi-

208

lated the EL point of view. Jeff noticed her coldness to Bunny and dragged her onto the dance floor.

"Be extra friendly," he warned, "because Murray's president of Bestway Transit and if we get that account you can have sable."

"I already have mink," Ellen said.

"I'll do my part and propose him for EL," Jeff continued, "but you've got to do your part and romance his wife."

When they returned to the table, the others were all dancing, except for Dalway and Linda.

"My wife read your book," Jeff said. "Next September she's going to go back and finally finish her college degree. Then she wants to get her master's and her doctorate. What are her chances of getting a college teaching job as soon as she has her B.A.?"

"Doubtful," Dalway said.

"Do you have any connections?" Jeff asked.

"In what regard?"

"I mean," Jeff continued, blundering on, clearly out of his depth, "could you help her to get a college job after she gets her B.A.?"

"What college would you like?" Dalway asked ironically, but the irony went right past Jeff.

"Normally," Jeff continued, "I'd say Radcliffe but that would be difficult to get to. How about Barnard?"

"How soon would you want this?" Dalway teased.

"The minute she finishes her degree."

"You do understand that it's very difficult to get a college teaching job with only a B.A., don't you?" Dalway asked.

"For most people," Jeff said, "but not for everyone. I would be willing to make a sizable contribution to Columbia, if they would hire her. All she would want would be a little part-time job. So if you could tell me how to go about this, I'd really appreciate it. You're the only person I've met recently in the academic racket."

Humiliated and angry, Ellen pushed her chair away from

the table, excused herself, and left the dining room. She couldn't believe that Jeff would embarrass her so. What a fool Dalway would think she was and she had been so anxious to talk to him. She stood looking out the window, down to Fifth Avenue, while she struggled to regain her composure.

"Perhaps some fresh air might help," Dalway's voice said behind her.

She flushed and turned to look at him. "Please accept my apologies," she said, "I'm so embarrassed."

"It's all right," he answered. "Businessmen always think they can buy academe. Besides that, people ask me to do things for them all the time. That's what happens when you achieve a certain modicum of fame. It's a little cold out, but would you like to go for a brisk walk?"

"I'd love to," she said.

He got her cape and draped it appreciatively over her shoulders. "There is nothing more beautiful," he said, "than an expensive young woman.

"Don't be embarrassed, my dear, by what your husband said," he continued. "If you really do want to teach at a college, go back to school and contact me after you have your master's. Perhaps I can help you to get an assistantship while you work toward your doctorate. How does that sound?"

"It sounds fine," she said. "I have to do something or I'll go mad. It's either go back to school or get some kind of job with my friend Kate."

"The important thing," he said, "is to do something. In my book, *Middle Class,* I mention the terrible inertia of upper-middle-class women who have nothing to do except to consume. What should, theoretically, seem enviable, instead turns out to be destructive to the psyche."

Ellen knew what he meant. Shopping and amassing had become boring to her. Why did she need sable after mink? After a few minutes they walked back. Ellen felt much better.

"I do hope our paths will cross again, my dear," he told her

210

before they returned to the table. "Be sure to call me if you're ever near our campus. I'm in the phone book; never liked the idea of an unlisted phone."

Nobody had missed them. Jeff was dancing an amorous fox-trot with Bunny Morano, Tina and Harry were dancing, and Murray, too, was somewhere else. Only Linda sat at the table, waiting for Dalway. All he did was give her a curt nod, and then he went off to dance with the bride. As soon as he was gone, Linda flowered, and she began to talk animatedly to Ellen about her visit to Bernard Berenson's Italian estate, I Tatti. She spoke rhapsodically about the beauty of the art, the magnificence of the locale, of the variety of birds and flowers, of the perfection of the weather, and of the tiny jewellike insects. She spoke like a blind person remembering the last sights before the darkness.

But as soon as Dalway rejoined them, her animation spluttered and died out and she returned to total silence, a wind-up doll that had run down. Silently she sat there and silently she drank. Looking at Dalway's mute mate, Ellen felt great compassion. Linda, wife of the famous liberal, was terrified into total silence by his presence and Ellen, wife of the great huckster, had to curb her tongue even more rigidly than her appetite.

A hush descended on the room, the orchestra played a fanfare, and the announcer informed the guests that the bride and groom would now cut the cake, an enormous, five-tiered one which was centered on a round table at the edge of the dance floor. Hearing the announcement, and as if to get a better view, Linda stood up and unsteadily wove her way across the room toward the round table, where Michael and Candy were posing for the photographers before making the first cut.

Nobody's eyes were on Linda, who, drunk and enraptured by the beauty of the cake, leaned on the edge of the table to get a closer look at the bride and groom on top. From across the floor, Ellen gasped in horror. In a slow-motion movie, Ellen could see Linda's feet going out from under her as all of her weight pressed on one side of the round table and the back tipped up as she fell.

211

A cry of horror went up from the powerless assemblage as they saw the enormous cake toppling forward, splattering Michael and Candy, and landing with a sickening crash on top of Linda. For a few seconds, the guests sat in their seats, paralyzed with horror.

Tina was one of the first to recover. "I'll bet she's the first person ever killed by a wedding cake," Tina said, while she and Ellen watched Dalway dash to the site of the debacle. They could see Linda's arms waving weakly from the floor.

"That's one way to prove your baking is light," Tina joked. "This wedding is absolutely jinxed. Do you think Davida's ghost did it? No, probably not. Davida's ghost wouldn't have a sense of humor."

"That is one damned silly broad," Jeff said. "She ought to be put away."

Kate came walking over to their table and dropped into Dalway's empty seat. "My God," she said, "I can't believe what I've seen. That poor woman. I never realized she had a drinking problem."

They could see Linda sitting on the floor now, licking icing off her fingers, seemingly not hurt at all.

Candace was completely out of control. "It's Davida," Candy shrieked, "she's put a curse on this wedding. She's cursing us from the grave."

Photographers had suddenly materialized and they were wildly snapping away while Michael alternated between trying to calm Candy and begging the photographers to "give us a break, fellas."

Leonard Benson went running for security guards while Candy continued to scream. Seeing the bride's very real hysteria, Ellen began to feel some compassion for her. Why, she's really just a very young girl, Ellen thought, she can't possibly be the barracuda Tina described. At that moment, Michael helped his bride out of the room while her mother attempted to fend off the photographers who refused to stop photographing the melee.

Linda was the only calm one, a happy drunk, smearing patterns of icing on the floor and occasionally popping a candy decoration into her mouth. The bride and groom dolls, perched atop the wreckage, suddenly attracted her attention and she crawled over to them, squashing cake under her as she crawled, until she had grasped the dolls firmly in her hands.

Dalway was now kneeling beside Linda, trying to get her up, but instead of getting up, she now stretched to full length, rolling back and forth in the cake. The guests started to leave, not wanting to watch poor Dalway in the midst of his humiliation.

Kate turned to the group at the table. "How about everybody coming to our house?" Kate asked. "This will give you all a chance to see it."

Tina told Ellen she had been dying to see the house. "It's on Fifth and Seventieth; forty-five rooms, two elevators, used to belong to that department store heiress. You know, the one who ran off with her gardener."

"It doesn't seem right for us to leave this way," Ellen said. "Shouldn't we offer Dalway some help?"

"We should not," Jeff said in annoyance. "The hotel has employees to take care of that."

As if on cue, Leonard Benson returned with an army of cleaning men who immediately began to set things right. Ellen wanted to say goodbye to Dalway but decided he would only be further embarrassed by expressions of sympathy. Poor man. How awful to be married to an alcoholic. She glanced over at him compassionately.

"Just keep walking," Jeff said. "This is not our business."

Ellen joined the group that was walking out, but she still felt somehow disloyal. Dalway had been so kind to her. Perhaps she could send him a note, just to express her sympathy and concern. No, why bother. He probably wouldn't even remember her after the unbelievable incidents of the night.

What an incredible wedding it had been. Perhaps Davida had been revenged after all. When Ellen took her last backward glance before leaving the ballroom, Linda still sat there playing with the cake, happily clutching the dolls, and giggling uncontrollably.

"It's off to the funny farm for that one, you can be sure," Tina said as they stepped into her Rolls-Royce.

Since Kate had dashed ahead of them, she now stood in the cavernous marble-floored reception hall to greet her guests. To Ellen, Kate suddenly looked thin and tired and the white streak in her hair no longer looked chic. It made her look old. And for once, Jeff agreed. "She looks as if she might be having business problems," he whispered to Ellen. "I'll have to make a few calls tomorrow to check it out."

Ellen repressed an ironic smile. How typical of Jeff to see business as the sun around which the whole world revolved. Over the years, members of EL had incestuously acquired bits of one anothers' businesses, so that trouble for one often meant anxiety for many. It fostered a mutual concern that on the surface resembled friendship.

When Will offered to give a tour of the residence, as he referred to it, everyone wanted to see the legendary house. Even Tina was awed into silence as he showed them around the miniature Fontainebleau. The only sounds were the click-click of the women's heels across the marble floors and Will's modest, casual words of explanation as he guided them. The walls and ceilings were ornately carved and covered in gold leaf. Each Louis XIV piece was of museum quality.

"Now I'll show y'all where we really live," Will said in his soft, Tidewater cadence. He led the group to the elevator and they went up two floors to the kitchen, a magnificence of wood, copper, brass, and old brick, which took up an entire floor.

Kate had kicked off her shoes and the guests, feeling comfortable, followed her lead. While a maid arranged the shoes in a neat row, a delivery man arrived bearing endless white boxes of Chinese food from Ruby Foo's. The barefoot EL'ers, in their perfect dinner jackets and designer dresses, sat around spooning lobster Cantonese out of cardboard cartons, like ordinary mortals. How strange it was, Ellen thought, that informality should become a gay game to these people . . . like Marie Antoinette playing at shepherdess.

Kate sat off to one side, talking to Ellen about Davida.

"I'm still so terribly shaken by it," she told Ellen, "but everybody else seems to have already forgotten. That poor lonely woman. And those poor kids. What a legacy for them; a father who's a fool and a mother who's a suicide."

"Tina thinks that Davida was also a fool for not anticipating betrayal and preparing for it."

"You know that Tina's view of life is somewhat simplistic." Kate smiled at her and Ellen grinned back affectionately.

"You're so lucky," Ellen said. "You're the only woman I know who has her life in control."

"Nobody ever really is in control," Kate said, half-joking, half-serious. "You just think people are in control if you happen to meet them between crises. I was a three-time loser before Will. But even so, I never learned to protect myself the way Tina would. Husband number one was a crook, used to write bad checks and sign my name, had endless business problems, and was basically a con man and a crook. He was so flamboyant that I decided I wanted just the opposite with husband number two. Oh, by the way, husband number one kicked me in the stomach one day when I refused to cover his bouncing checks any longer, and that caused a miscarriage.

"Husband number two was just the opposite of number one, I thought. He was a schoolteacher and I loved him because he wasn't a crook. But that reason ran out after about a year. I wanted to divorce him because he was pathological about money. He kept stashing his own away and sponging on me. When I told him I wanted to end it, he came in while I slept and took out every single item in the house, except for the bed I was sleeping in. He plundered me. I had nothing left; a zero bank account, no friends, no family in New York. The only thing that kept me

215

from killing myself was my hatred for him. I went to work in the knitwear business and met husband number three. He was very rich, and twenty years older than I. He was good to me and I cared for him, but we had only five good years together before he died. And then, Will came to work for me and changed my life. Since then, he's been my right hand, my staff, and my support. We've had a good life together.

"So, as you can see, things haven't always been good for me, but even so, I don't agree with Tina that Davida was a fool for not anticipating betrayal. I don't think you can live that way. I think a woman should work, should have interests and some money of her own but when she has to start padding housekeeping bills and cheating her husband to sock away money, the marriage is over. The best protection, really the only protection for a woman, is a career. Which leads me to you. When are you going back to school?"

"I've definitely made up my mind," Ellen answered. "I'm finally going back this coming September. After the EL group goes to Japan in July, I'll be ready. Are you coming to Japan with us?"

"I certainly hope I can," Kate said, but the expression on her face belied the enthusiasm in her voice. Again, Ellen was conscious of the fact that Kate did not look well. But before she could ask her what the matter was, Kate went on speaking. "I understand," she said, "that Myra Benson is coming even though it will be her eighth month. Leonard's opening a new hotel in Tokyo and Myra has never yet missed a hotel opening. Well, I guess she knows what she's doing."

"I hope you'll come," Ellen said. "It wouldn't be the same without you."

"I really want to," Kate said. "Everybody's really grateful to Jeff for making these arrangements. It makes us feel especially comfortable to be with an American who studied Japanese. His talent for languages is amazing—and he's been able to get some very good accounts from that, hasn't he?"

"Yes. He started with Spanish accounts, and now he has Italian, German, French, and of course Japanese accounts. He's even been invited to lecture on public relations," Ellen said proudly.

"That's quite an honor," Kate said. She suddenly winced in pain.

"What's wrong?" Ellen asked anxiously.

"Oh, it's nothing," Kate said, "just a little muscle spasm that comes and goes." Then, changing the subject she said, "Remember, Ellen, if you ever decide that you want to work with me instead of going back to teaching, be sure to let me know."

"I have to finish what I started," Ellen said. "And I'm really rather shy. I don't have the personality for business."

"You never know until you try," Kate answered.

Jeff was very quiet on the way home. It was unusual for him not to discuss an evening out with her. As they approached their driveway, Ellen remembered her promise to Jennifer. She would just have to tell her the story the next day and Jennifer would understand why she didn't bring her any cake. She'd also promised to wake her up but it was too late. Besides, she wanted to know what was bothering Jeff. She dropped a kiss on the cheek of the sleeping girl, then went into their bedroom and closed the door behind her.

"All right," she said aggressively, "now I'd like to know what's bothering you. What faux pas did I make? I didn't tip over the cake and I didn't ask Kate if her diamonds were real. So what is it?"

"It's the house," he said gloomily.

"The house? Which house?"

"Our house. It can't compare with theirs. That's the way to live. Fifth Avenue. No commuting to the suburbs. There are many mansions out here but that house is one of a kind. That's the place to be. A Fifth Avenue address."

"Oh, Jeff," she said, feeling sorry for him. "Six months ago Green Haven was the place to be. Why don't you stop worrying about trading up and start enjoying what we have. You know this house is far beyond our dreams."

"Yeah, well, maybe I wasn't dreaming big enough."

"I'm not moving again," she said, "and I certainly wouldn't uproot Jennifer again. You said this would be our lifetime house."

"What do you know about anything," he said angrily. "If it were up to you, we'd still be in Freeport."

"Probably," she said cheerfully, determined not to let him upset her.

He lit a cigarette and gazed gloomily out the windows and across the lawn to Long Island Sound, which he had adored as recently as that morning. Poor Jeff! He reminded her of D. H. Lawrence's story, "The Rocking-Horse Winner," in which a house keeps whispering, "More money." The little boy in that story is killed by his mother's greed. She shivered and put it out of her mind.

Ellen's favorite room in the new house was her study, her very own room, and she was getting it organized in preparation for her return to college. It was the only room in the house in which she felt comfortable. It looked like a college dorm room and she had put an old couch and an old easy chair in it, furniture the decorator had banished from the rest of the house. Ellen liked to hear herself saying, "My study," as if she were really accomplishing something in there. Well, maybe not yet, but she would. The walls were covered with Jennifer's artwork which Ellen had saved since kindergarten: finger paintings, five-legged cows moving through purple fields, Christmas and Halloween decorations. It was Ellen's sanctuary.

But one Saturday morning, a few months after Michael's wedding, she picked Jennifer up at art class and returned home to find that she had lost her sanctuary.

"Look at my drawings, Daddy," Jennifer said, still trying.

"Later, baby," he told her. "Go watch television. I have a surprise for Mommy."

218

He led Ellen up the back stairs to her study, knocked on the door, and a ruddy, round-faced young woman in a maid's uniform came out and bowed formally to Ellen.

"Guten Tag," she said respectfully.

Ellen looked past her and saw two opened suitcases on the couch.

"Who are you?" Ellen asked. German accents made her wince . . . reminding her of the many relatives lost in concentration camps.

"Mein Nahm ist Ursula," the girl said. "I am ze au pair girl. *Dein Mann hast* . . . hired *mich.* I take care ze little girl."

"Why don't you get Jennifer and take her down to the kitchen," Jeff said cheerily. Ursula gazed at him adoringly, apparently understanding English better than she spoke it.

"As you wish, *mein Herr,"* she said, bowed, and went off to get Jennifer.

"How do you like your surprise?" Jeff asked.

Ellen stomped into her study. He followed her and closed the door behind them.

"How could you do such a thing without discussing it with me?" Ellen shrilled. "We don't need an au pair girl and I don't want a German one. How could you give away my study? In this whole house, that was the only place that was completely mine. Would I put someone in your study?"

"You can take one of the bigger rooms for your study," Jeff said, going into his crestfallen act that no client could resist. "Gee, Ellen, I thought you'd be pleased. It isn't as if you actually do any work in your study. By the time of fall semester, you can have another room fixed up. Ursula's the cousin of the girl working for the Moranos. When they told me she was coming to the U.S. I thought I'd surprise you. This way they can be together."

"I won't have a Nazi in this house and Jennifer doesn't need a nurse. I'm here and I don't have enough to do with myself as it is."

"But you'll have plenty to do when you return to school and then Ursula will be here to help you. Come on, Ellen, you know she's not a Nazi. The war's been over for almost fifteen years. She was a child; ten years old. She didn't kill any Jews."

"If she didn't, her relatives did. Where were her parents during the war?"

"Be reasonable, Ellen. When you go back to school you won't be able to supervise things here. As we entertain more and more, you'll find that you need more help. Ursula's an educated girl and she can teach Jennifer French and German. She also drives and as soon as she gets a license, she can do all of your shopping and errands for you. It's irrational to live in the past. Even Israelis buy Volkswagens. Besides, you should be amused by the reversal. She's working for us now. We're in the saddle; we're employing her."

"But we're not killing her or putting her in gas ovens."

Jeff looked at his watch. "Got a date to play tennis with Murray," he said. "The discussion is ended, Ellen. She stays. I want the Morano account and this is a chance for me to make them happy. Her cousin Marthe was so lonely here that she threatened to go back to Berlin unless she could have Ursula near here. So I agreed to bring Ursula over. Here she is and here she stays."

"You didn't do this for me at all," Ellen said. "You did it for the Morano account, pure and simple."

"Well, isn't that for you?" he asked.

"No," she said. "I've never bucked you on anything before, Jeff, but this time I won't give in. She goes."

"I hear she makes fabulous sauerbraten and red cabbage."

"No. I don't even speak German, Jeff, and you do. But you're never home."

Jeff was getting impatient. "All right, Ellen, I know when I'm licked. I have an appointment. You go down to the kitchen and tell her to pack. Then you drive her to Idlewild and buy her ticket home. Poor kid! She'll be pretty embarrassed when she gets off that plane. A real loss of face."

He ran down the front stairs, slammed the door behind him,

and walked off toward Murray's. Ellen walked down the back stairs to the kitchen. There they sat, Ursula and Jennifer, giggling and coloring away with Jennifer's pastels set.

"Hi, Mom," Jennifer said. She looked happy for a change. "Daddy told me Ursula's my new friend and she'll always be here with me so I won't be alone when you and Daddy are away."

Ursula sprang to attention, almost clicking her heels. She looked at Ellen with a frightened, craven look. Ellen looked back at her, noticed how pleased Jennifer seemed, and thought of how Jeff would blame her if he lost the Morano account.

"Sit," she said unsmilingly to Ursula. Then she went back to her lost sanctuary and started to remove her simple possessions. The next day was Sunday and she looked forward to Tina's company. She'd like to know what Tina thought of her new au pair girl.

Jennifer and Jacques were playing in the pool while the two women sipped cognac on the patio. Tina was dying to tell Ellen about her current affair with a tennis pro.

"Isn't it a little awkward," Ellen asked, "to pay him for your lessons and then to go to bed with him?"

"No, why should it be?"

"I don't know," Ellen said. "It would make me feel awkward."

"I don't pay him for making love to me," Tina giggled. Then she added, "But I would if he asked. I don't mind paying if I get fair exchange."

The two women sat quietly for a few minutes, not talking. Then Tina said, "I can't believe that you haven't cheated once in almost eight years," she said. "It's not normal. It's sick."

"I don't think spending your life on Dr. Bloom's couch is exactly healthy," Ellen answered.

"I never pretended to be healthy," Tina said. "What you see is what I am. But you go around pretending to be Pollyanna and it's not normal to be Pollyanna with no outlets."

"I'm going back to school in September," Ellen said. "That's my outlet."

"Oh, God, I've been hearing that for years. I don't think you really want to go back."

"Sure I do. It's just that I worry because I'll be so much older than the others. I don't like looking ridiculous."

"I don't think you should have those worries. So what if you look older. You're not there to please anybody but yourself. You'd be going for a purpose. It wouldn't matter at all what you looked like unless you wanted to make out with the students or professors. Do you?"

"Sometimes you have a one-track mind, my dear friend," Ellen said. "I wouldn't be going to school to meet men. I'd be going for some intellectual stimulation."

"Jeff's a bright guy," Tina said, "isn't that enough?"

"He's bright in a business way," Ellen said, "but not in my way. Know what he said when we went to see *Hamlet?* He said the play bored him. It's hard to believe that Jeff went to college. Hamlet bored him. He said, 'What makes Hamlet a hero? He's a thorough incompetent, a weakling, a failure, a dropout. I wouldn't have him in my office. And at the end of the play, because of his ineptitude, everyone is dead.' That's what Jeff said about Hamlet."

"He's right," Tina said. "I hate Shakespeare, too. Only airy-fairy English professors would make a hero out of Hamlet. Failure loves failure."

Ellen burst out laughing

"What's so funny?" Tina asked.

"Your unashamed, unabashed view of Shakespeare. You're not afraid of anything, are you?"

"I try not to be ashamed or abashed by anything," Tina said. "I don't have to be concerned about what anyone thinks. I don't have to answer to anyone. That's what I've been learning from Dr. Bloom."

"That's some marvelous philosophy," Ellen said. "The glorification of irresponsibility."

"You've always been hostile to Dr. Bloom," Tina said. "It's because you're really afraid of your own instincts. You're the kind of person who would benefit from an orgone box. And, speaking about instincts. You didn't answer my question. Haven't you cheated at all over the years?"

And so, against her better judgment, Ellen told her about the one-night stands with Giovanni and Lenny.

"Well," Tina said, "at least now I know you're human, even though you like to pretend you're better than the rest of us. How come you only saw those men once?"

"I don't know," Ellen said. "Maybe I would have seen them again if they had pursued it, but neither of them seemed interested in a second night either."

"You must be doing something wrong," Tina said. "Oh, by the way, I have an absolute gem for you. Guess who's next in line for el divorceo?"

"You?"

"Not a chance. Harry and I have complete freedom. We hardly see each other. So why should we divorce? We don't get on each other's nerves."

"How romantic." Ellen laughed. "Such good reasons to stay married. All right. I give up. Who is getting a divorce?"

"Samson Plari," Tina trumpeted, "multimillionaire midget owner of Octagon, Ltd."

"Samson? But he and Valerie seemed so happy. I remember at the ranch how Valerie sat at his arm doing crewelwork while he and Jeff played cards. I wonder why Jeff hasn't told me. After all, he's one of Jeff's biggest clients."

"Jeff probably doesn't know yet. Valerie only told it to Christopher yesterday."

"I'm sorry," Ellen said. "Divorce always makes me sad. It's hard to believe. He seemed so sober and serious and he and Valerie seemed so compatible and devoted. I thought they had one of the best relationships in EL."

"Nevertheless, it's trade-in time and the new model is a very racy little compact. Her name is Heidi, as in Heidi seek! Seventeen! Can you imagine? That makes Samson more than twenty years older. She weighs about ninety-five pounds and Valerie says Samson is in love.''

"How awful. Poor Valerie.''

"Poor Valerie nothing. Save your sympathy. Davida was a dope but Valerie is using Jim Anthony and since Samson makes over a million dollars a year, she'll do very well. And of course, when a woman has that much money, the men line up to become husband number two. She's by no means a charity case.''

"Who's Jim Anthony?'' Ellen asked.

Tina rolled her eyes heavenward at Ellen's continued ignorance of all those things that "everybody knows.''

"He's only the best divorce lawyer in the state, maybe in the country. Plays the market, too, and sometimes trades a fee for stock options. He's worth so much he could live fabulously and never handle another case, but they say he keeps on because he likes the ladies and enjoys the game. Of course, he handles cases for men, too, but he prefers the ladies. He strips the dumb husbands naked, unless they get to him first. But he finds it more interesting and more of a challenge to fight for the ladies.''

Some knight, Ellen thought. "The whole sordid business gives me the creeps,'' she said. "Doesn't it disgust you, Tina?''

"The only thing that disgusts me is when someone like Davida gets taken.''

"It's hard to believe,'' Ellen said. "It was just a month ago that I was at Elizabeth Arden's at the same time as Valerie. When I walked in, Samson was sitting there waiting, and he was still waiting patiently when I got through, an hour later. There he was, this tiny big tycoon, just sitting there patiently, reading back issues of *Vogue.* I said to him, 'So this is where tycoons spend their time,' and he smiled sweetly and said, 'Wives come first.' I felt a kind of jealousy because Jeff never waits for me. I wait for Jeff.''

"One of your big problems, sweetie,'' Tina said, "is that you believe what you see. Samson probably had some other reason for being there. If you didn't actually see Valerie, maybe he was waiting for his little Heidi. Or maybe he was looking for an acquisition. How can you be fooled by a sweet smile and manner after all this time? Samson wouldn't have gotten to where he is if he wasn't a barracuda. He's the same as all these short guys. He's only two feet tall so he has to keep proving that his cock is bigger than he is."

"Oh, Tina," Ellen said, "I love you because you make me laugh."

Tina looked up and noticed Ursula hovering at the side of the room, waiting to serve them, but obviously listening to their conversation.

"Listen, honey," she said to her in a way Ellen would never dare, "come back later. We have private things to talk about."

Like Uriah Heep, wearing what Ellen privately thought of as her shit-eating smile, Ursula bowed and backed out of the room.

"So that's the au pair girl?" Tina said. "No wonder you objected. I'll bet nothing about you or Jeff will be secret to her."

As soon as Ursula had gone, Tina continued to tell Ellen about Samson. "Some mutual friends of ours were at Pavillon and he came in with his teenybopper in tow. He told everybody, 'She's an actress.' Actually, she was a child actress turned adolescent hooker. Well, Samson, very naval, was wearing a shirt slashed open to the waist, a yachting cap, a little blue blazer, and sneakers. Nobody else could even get near Pavillon dressed that way so maybe he's bought the place. Nothing would surprise me.

"So after he introduces little Heidi, he gives her a slap on the rump in front of everybody, and sends her to follow the maitre d' to their table. Then he leans over to our mutual friends and says, 'Get a load of my actress. Seventeen years old.' So that's a second source besides Christopher."

"Incredible the way these men are turning to such young girls," Ellen said, shivering despite the warm day. "It makes me feel like our days are numbered."

"Oh, they are," Tina said, "I've been telling you that for years. Face it. The men who are the EL type are sharks, and Jeff and Harry are no exception. They'll use us up and trade us in for younger models when it suits them. And rich as they are, when it comes to divorce they'll plead poverty and try to screw us into garden apartments in Landor Shitty which is why you, just like the rest of us, should pay a preventive-medicine-type visit to Jim Anthony while you still have your looks. Once those guys dump us and we start crying—remember the way Davida looked, although she wasn't much to look at originally—we lose our looks mighty fast. Of course, Davida was a boozer, too. But everybody knows that no older woman can keep herself looking good without great gobs of money. Just file Anthony's number away with your doctor's, your dentist's, your analyst's."

"You know I don't have an analyst."

"You will." Tina grinned.

Ellen looked around at the magnificence of her home. The smooth green lawn sloped down to the dock and she could see how happily Jennifer and Jacques were playing together. The bulbs had come up and hundreds of crocuses, hyacinths, daffodils, and tulips dotted the grounds. Tina was wrong. Nothing could shake this tranquil loveliness.

"I won't need Jim Anthony," she said calmly.

"That's what they all say," Tina joked.

Ellen had never discussed personal things with a woman friend. Actually Tina was her first close woman friend, and now that she had admitted her indiscretions to Tina, she felt a little freer in talking about sex. She knew that she could ask Tina anything, without worrying about tactful preliminaries.

"Tina," she asked, "do you and Harry have a good sexual relationship?"

"It's super," Tina said.

"Even though you both fool around?"

"Because we both fool around."

"Well," Ellen asked, feeling like an idiot, "what makes it super?"

226

Tina reeled off her prescription without hesitation. "Harry doesn't come too fast, he's inventive, I'm always lubricated, he's always hard, and I have both kinds of orgasms without difficulty. He wants to make love when I'm in the mood and I always agree when he's in the mood."

"You're really lucky," Ellen said enviously, "to have a husband to whom you're so well suited sexually."

"I'm well suited to every man I sleep with," Tina answered. "That's one of my hidden talents. The men always think they're good. The truth is that they're good because I'm good but I let them have their little fantasies. What do I care? I get better sex by letting them feel good."

"And it hasn't become boring with Harry after twelve years?" Ellen asked.

"I never find sex boring," Tina said. "New things come up that revive Harry and me. For example, it really turns us on to make love in new places. I can't wait until we get to Japan, haven't been back to the Far East since my folks left. Of course, I was never in Japan at all. We're all so grateful that Jeff planned this trip for us, Ellen. None of us would have gone without him. It's so much better when someone speaks the language. One of the things that really turned me on was Jeff's scroll, you know, of all those positions. The one he brought back from Japan."

Ellen felt a shock run through her body. Jeff had shown her the scroll right after their marriage but she had long since forgotten about it. Why would Jeff have shown Tina his pornographic scroll? When would they have had the opportunity? When were they alone together? What an extraordinarily intimate thing to do. So intimate, the kind of pornographic experience that a man and woman would only have in bed. She felt so hurt that it took all of her willpower, all the control she had learned from Helen Fern, to hold back her tears. What should she do? Should she ignore it? No, if she did, she could never again feel free and open with Tina. Much as she hated to, she would have to bring it up.

How could they have been so disloyal. What a clichéd plot; my husband and my best friend! She had to ask.

227

"Tina, how come you saw Jeff's scroll?"

"He showed it to me when you were in the hospital."

Well, it had happened over two years ago. But that didn't mean that Tina had been deceiving her all this time, that Tina wasn't her friend. Perhaps her analyst had advised it. Or perhaps she'd had a free afternoon and called Jeff. Perhaps she had just been keeping him company while Ellen was in the hospital. She might have even bumped into him unexpectedly and cheerfully gone off to a motel room with him. She'd listened to Tina tell her endless stories about men. Why couldn't one of them have been Jeff?

"Did you sleep with Jeff then?" Ellen blurted out.

Tina wrinkled her forehead and tried to remember. "I think we came close to it while you were in the hospital," she said, furrowing her pretty forehead, "but to the best of my recollection, we stopped short. I mean I hardly remember, Ellen, so I guess that means we didn't do it. If you want me to, I'll ask Dr. Bloom. He probably has a record of it."

It may have been an act to cover guilt, but there was no malice in her. I really don't care after all, Ellen told herself, but she decided to ask Jeff about it the first chance they were alone.

"How come Tina saw your scroll?" she asked him that night as they were getting ready for bed.

"Did she?" he asked, going into his forgetful innocence routine.

"You know perfectly well that she did," Ellen said.

"Did she say that?"

"Yes."

"Then I guess she saw it."

"Is that all you have to say?"

"What would you like me to say?"

"I would like to know if you slept with Tina."

"Did she say I did?"

"She couldn't remember."

"Then I guess we didn't," he teased her. Then, in a mock

228

Humphrey Bogart accent, "I never knew a dame yet who could forget me."

To Ellen's surprise, she was crying. Jeff came and sat beside her on the bed. "What's the matter, honey?" he asked. "Honestly, Tina and I didn't sleep together. I like my women brighter than Tina. I don't remember how I happened to show her the scroll, but if I did, it was for purely artistic purposes.

"But to tell you the truth, Ellen, since you brought up the scroll, let's talk for a minute about sex. We've been making love, when we do, the same way we made love eight years ago. I want to try new positions. I like inventive sex, variety, change, experimentation. I'd like to try every one of the positions on the scroll but you know what I'd like to try most of all?"

"What?"

"Sodomy."

"Sodomy?"

"Yeah, sodomy! Why are you looking at me that way? It's quite common and nothing between man and wife is wrong."

"I don't think it's wrong," she said. "I just think it's disgusting."

"Yeah, but it's not healthy to think of it that way. Nothing in sex is disgusting."

"But I do think of it that way. Besides, doesn't it hurt?"

"They say not if you use Vaseline."

"Who's 'they'? You sound as if you've been having some pretty spicy lunch dates. I thought you told me you discuss business."

"Well, sure." He grinned sheepishly. "But you know how men talk."

"I still don't find it appealing," she said. "That's what homosexuals do, men in prison *have* to do it. I think it's wrong."

"Nothing's wrong if it gives you pleasure, Ellen. And if it didn't feel good, you wouldn't have so many people doing it."

"People do a lot of screwed-up things that don't feel good just to be perverse," she said.

"Come on, Ellen, let's try it. We can always stop if it hurts. I promise. A minute ago you were crying about Tina. Honestly, if you were a little more responsive, the way you used to be when we were first married, I'd never even look at another woman. Chasing takes too much time from business. But remember how you used to be, Ellen? I'll never forget that wonderful night we were driving back from the Westchester Country Club."

He really doesn't know anything about me at all, she thought, but he continued to insist and there seemed to be no choice but to give in. She could see that he was beginning to get angry and anything seemed better than facing that. "All right," she said, "I'll get the Vaseline. But remember, you promised to stop if it hurts."

"Sure, sure," he said.

And then it began. "Please do it slowly," she said, but he didn't. The minute he parted her buttocks and entered he was pushing hard and brutally and fast.

She had thought it would be somewhat uncomfortable but was totally unprepared for the extent of the searing pain. His body was pinning her down, her face was pushed into the sheets and she felt as if she were suffocating, drowning beneath his weight. She cried out in pain soon after he had started. "It hurts. Stop, Jeff. It hurts too much."

But Jeff was off on his own cloud of passion and he neither heard nor listened. He pushed and pushed and she stifled her moans so Jennifer couldn't possibly hear and in Ellen's mind she was back on that terrible street in Brooklyn again, once more being raped, and still unable to fight back. She thought she was drowning, dying, and she clawed the sheets in panic. Finally he was completely inside her and it didn't hurt as much as while he was getting in. But it still hurt and while he thrust and thrust again, oblivious of her, she thought she could actually feel something ripping within her. When he finally pulled out, the sheet was covered with blood.

Jeff was exultant. "It really does feel different," he said, "tighter. I've been wanting to try that all my life."

230

He was like an excited, triumphant little boy who had successfully raided the cookie jar. "Now we can try some of the other positions, too," he said as he turned over and fell asleep.

As soon as her pain had subsided to a dull ache, she covered the blood on the sheet with a towel, then sat in a warm, soothing, perfumed tub of water for an hour. Gradually, as she felt physically better, she started to feel somewhat detached. Jeff's comforting her for his possible affair with Tina with painful sodomy was no more than she should have expected.

6

*A*t the beginning of July, the EL'ers left for their convention in San Francisco. There were many West Coast people at the conference whom Ellen had not previously met but many of their old friends had come, too. Tina and Harry, Kate and Will, Michael and Candy, Amos and Marilyn, Samson and little Heidi, Leonard and Myra Benson, and a couple Ellen didn't know as well, Gabe and Laura Pine. Gabe Pine was president of Consolidated Fruit and as Jeff said, almost in warning to Ellen, "Very, very important." All of them were planning to go on to Japan with Ellen and Jeff. Some of them were staying across the street at the Fairmount Hotel but Jeff had chosen to stay at the Mark Hopkins, the Mark, as he fondly referred to it.

It had been at the Mark, looking out over San Francisco, that Jeff had enjoyed his last drink before leaving for the occupation in Japan. Since Jeff was usually a man with no time or respect for rituals, it fascinated Ellen to see his pleasure in his return in glory, and she enjoyed his success for him. Relaxed, happy, successful, charming, he was now at his best and, despite

232

all of their problems, Ellen felt comfortable with him. Good or bad, they were married and she was protected. He probably did his best and she could really see no possibilities for life without him. She felt grateful to him for bringing her here, for opening so many new worlds to her. Jeff, invited to lecture on PR, was a hero. There were scores of young Japanese men who wanted to learn marketing, public relations, and advertising arts from the country that had invented them. Haiku wants to learn how-to. What was more, it was the first vacation Jeff and Ellen had taken since their marriage.

They sat alone together in the bar at the top of the Mark, a romantic, soothing place. "You know," Jeff told her, his speech a little slurred from the champagne, "when I got to Japan, they thought I was a conqueror. But all I was was a poor boy with nothing going for me except for good looks and a certain facility with languages. I had nothing: no bank account, no connections, no family behind me. I didn't even have the self-confidence to think I could marry into money. I had nothing and I thought I was nothing. I came up here for a drink and I was half afraid they would turn me away despite my uniform. I was afraid the maitre d' could see right through me.

"And after the war, while I was working for the FBI, an army buddy took me sailing and he pointed out Green Haven; a legendary kingdom. I promised myself then that someday I would live there. And now we do and other people sailing by look at our house with envy. I came back in 1947 and was lucky enough to get a job with the FBI. They liked my looks, my height, my army record. I know you look down on that, Ellen, you think it's some form of prostitution. So what isn't prostitution. If it paid more, I'd a hell of a lot rather work for them than have to lick Amos's ass. I bought my agency in 1949 and still I had nothing. But I took the training I had from the army and from the FBI and built on that. A lot of guys tried it but I was good, right for the job, and overnight I was successful. It took eight years: eight years, babes, and now I have everything. You look just fine, classy, a credit to me and you speak beautifully. I have a daughter, friends, clients, respect. Everything except a son but what the hell, you're only twenty-eight, plenty of good years left. And I tell you, Ellen, it's just the beginning. I'm gonna make enough money to tell Amos to go fuck himself. I'm gonna make so much money they'll be giving *me* their honorary degrees, not Amos, and *I* won't have to buy them. Can you imagine? I mean, a Japanese trade association has invited *me* to speak to them. I didn't even have to solicit that account."

He was getting drunk and a little maudlin. "Do you love me, Ellen?"

"Of course I love you," she said.

"No, no," he said, "not that easy, glib way. Do you really love me?"

"I'm very grateful," she said, floundering for words that would be honest, "to you for giving me so much. I think I'm lucky to have found you. I think what you've told me so often is true. There are lots of people like me, but you're unique. I really believe that, even with the way we've fixed me up, and I'm grateful."

"Yeah, but," he said, more honest than usual because of the champagne, because he never drank more than one glass of anything, "sometimes I think you don't like me, don't like me at all. So much of you is closed off to me. I want to tell you something, Ellen. I know that I'm a hotshot right now and that people pretend to be friendly but they're really watching to see me fail. I need you to love me, Ellen. It's like Versailles out there. I need a friend in my corner. Are you my friend?"

"Sometimes," she said, carefully, "not all the time."

"Be my friend, Ellen, be my friend all the time. It's no good to conquer by yourself. Can't you be my friend all the time?"

"Oh, Jeff," she said, wanting to weep for them both, "I want to be. God knows I want to be. And I am grateful."

Sitting there, feeling rich, beautiful, healthy, with the lights of San Francisco twinkling beneath them, Ellen felt a surge of

234

hope, a renewal of optimism. All marriages had cracks, problems, ebbs and flows. Maybe the next ten years would be better.

While the men attended sessions the next day, the wives were flown to Disneyland in a private plane. Ridiculous, Ellen thought, like sending the children off to play. I wish I had Jen here, then going to Disneyland would make sense. She had wanted to bring Jen but nobody else was bringing a child and Jeff hadn't thought it would look right, so, kicking and protesting, Jennifer had been sent off to camp, a fine progressive one recommended by Susie Mozer.

I'll come back here with her someday, Ellen thought.

"Isn't it wonderful to be here?" Candy said as they entered the charming Main Street of Disneyland.

"I'm ambivalent," Ellen said, forgetting for a moment to wear the mask, "I think Disney is a real bigot. I don't like to spend a penny that will go to him."

"So who cares about that," Tina said.

"You sound like a Communist," Marilyn whispered. "Be careful. Remarks like that could hurt Jeff."

"It may surprise you to hear this," Ellen said nastily, "but I'm a person, too. My whole life doesn't revolve around Jeff."

"If you say mean things you'll spoil everybody's fun," Candy said. "You must have wrong information. You know the man responsible for Snow White and Bambi must be on the right side of things."

He is on the *right* side of things, Ellen thought. She still hadn't forgiven Candy for Davida's death, unfair as that probably was.

Ellen was bored and she missed Jennifer. Her little girl should be here with her, not these meaningless strangers. Why didn't these people ever do things with their children? Why didn't the solid gold circle include kids? Take Tina, for example, she actually hated her son, couldn't stand to be with him for five minutes. Ellen had been seeing all of these people for almost five years and had never met any of their children even at house parties, when the children seemed to have been spirited away. Well, what was the point in being nasty, in getting off cheap shots at Candy or Marilyn, who didn't seem to share her restlessness.

She did her best to join in and pretend pleasure, but the squeals of the other women seemed forced to her and, try as she might, she couldn't seem to enjoy herself. Even though she paid grudging homage to this antiseptic world of blond, blue-eyed guides, she didn't enjoy it. In this predictable, sanitary, well-ordered world, the smiling guides looked like robots and the robots looked like people.

She wished she could take a book out of her purse, sit down in a corner, and read, but she knew she'd be thought rude or strangely eccentric if she did. She remembered, with amusement, Tina's sympathetic question about the large size of Ellen's purses.

"Bottle?" Tina had asked.

"Books," Ellen had answered.

"Weird." Tina had shaken her head. "Really weird. Why do you need books when you're going to be with people?"

Ellen thought sympathetically of a story she had heard about Senator Dunstan's wife, who preferred a French novel to the cheering masses. "Get that woman pregnant and keep her home," politicos had warned the Senator. And like the Senator's wife, Ellen had no choice but to play the game, no choice but to go on wasting her life.

There was no one with whom she could discuss her growing obsession about wasting her life. Once when she'd mentioned this to her mother, she had sympathetically patted Ellen's hand and said, "It's hard when you can't get pregnant. Just keep trying. I heard about a doctor who . . ."

Tina, of course, didn't understand. "What do you mean, wasting your life? When I had menial jobs, I was wasting my life. Not now. Now I'm living my life."

Of course, Kate had understood. "You'll feel better as soon as you go back to school," Kate had said. The problem was that Ellen wasn't even sure if she did want to go back to school. For what? She could no longer visualize herself in an elementary classroom and the idea of more of those education classes at NYU that had bored her originally didn't seem like a source of renewal.

When Ellen thought about it, what she meant by "wasting her life" was that she seemed to be learning nothing new. She had stopped absorbing and was beginning to leak.

Tina's voice broke into her reverie. "Oh, my God, it's too awful."

"What's the matter?" Ellen gasped, shocked out of her thoughts.

"It's my best nail," Tina said, as close to tears as Ellen had ever seen her, "my best nail. Broken!"

Ellen burst into laughter.

"You don't even care," Tina said, aggrieved.

"Of course I care." Ellen laughed. "How could you possibly think I'm not involved with your nail."

I wish I drank, Ellen thought gloomily as she agonized through the rest of the day; eating southern fried chicken on the veranda of a movie-set plantation while grinning black musicians, dressed for a minstrel show, played synthetic Dixieland jazz.

They flew back to San Francisco that evening and the next day, without asking Jeff's permission, Ellen pleaded a headache when the women went shopping, used her copy of Jeff's Diner's Club card to rent a car, got a map from the car rental service, drove out to the Berkeley campus, and found the college library. Her spirits revived merely from being on a campus and this one had a particularly mad vitality and was overflowing with peddlers and tables, mixtures of posters and petitions, and arts and crafts booths.

She had a cup of coffee, then entered the library and stood there breathing in the atmosphere of books, the atmosphere in which she had always felt the most at home. She had abandoned her focus on books during the first years with Jeff without realizing that her reading had become desultory, but now she felt a

237

change again. Each day she was developing more awareness about herself, learning, for example, that she couldn't bear to be with groups of people day and night, couldn't stand the necessity to watch every word like a diplomat, couldn't stand to mingle only with people wrapped in a cocoon of wealth. And above all, she realized, it was up to her, not Jeff, to provide the kind of mental stimulation she needed.

The hushed voices and gently ruffling pages, the sounds that signaled tranquillity to her, began to flow through and soothe her. She sat and read *The Nation,* the *New Republic,* and the *National Guardian.* When she looked at her watch, it was five o'clock but she didn't feel ready to return to the hotel. She needed more time to be by herself. She called the Mark Hopkins and left a message for Jeff that she'd be home late and that he should attend the evening's festivities without her. She did not ask permission, she did not apologize, she did not explain where she was. My God, freedom is intoxicating, she thought, feeling joyous for the first time she could remember. Of course, Jeff would be furious about her individualistic sabotage of EL togetherness, but the hell with that.

Then she dared another first. She walked around and looked for a restaurant with a Diner's Club insignia in the window. Never before had she entered a good restaurant alone to eat dinner. When by herself, she would grab a cup of coffee at Chock full o'Nuts or some other bastion of on-the-run hostility, but on this night she sat down in a good restaurant, without a male escort, and she ordered a whiskey sour on the rocks and a steak. She was totally content. Traveling with EL had made solitude a priceless luxury. She lit a cigarette and refused to think about the inevitable scene that awaited her back in San Francisco. In her mind, she sang a little song. "I belong to myself, I belong to myself."

She finished her drink, ordered another, and fantasized about dropping out of sight, never going back, becoming a missing person, settling here in California, finishing school, getting a job, getting Jennifer, and living alone with Jennifer in a home without tension, a home filled with flowers and plants, a small, cozy home, just big enough for the two of them. She also fantasized that Saul, whom she had heard was teaching at Columbia, would get a divorce, come out to California, and that the three of them would live happily ever after.

"Are you expecting someone?" A man stood before her; about her age, dressed plainly in jeans, moccasins, homespun good looks; a straight, slim body. He smiled; completely nonthreatening.

"No," she answered, clear as a bell. "I'm not."

"May I join you?"

"If you like," she said, "but please understand that I don't need anyone to pay for my dinner."

"With that jewelry—" he laughed—"I wouldn't think so." White teeth, friendly, nice. Good company for dinner.

He ordered a drink from the waitress, who seemed relieved that the lone lady had turned into a couple. Ostentatiously, Ellen smoked her cigarette so he would notice her wedding ring. She looked at his hands. Good. He was married, too. She relaxed further.

They sipped their drinks, ordered others, and they began to talk on that extraordinarily intimate level people create on trains, planes, in unfamiliar bars. She started to tell him how she happened to be there, about her need to escape, about her boredom, loneliness, and guilt. His name was Todd Howard, and he, too, had escaped for the evening. He'd been standing at the bar, having a drink, when she'd entered and caught his attention. Like Ellen, he was going mad with boredom. He was an underpaid instructor at San Francisco State, had a wife, two babies, a zero bank account, and he was sick of everything. Living in two small rooms with babies crying and diapers everywhere was driving him nuts. Ellen's problems didn't seem at all bad to him.

"This is the first time I've ever done this," Ellen said, trying to be tactful, "but could I pay for your dinner? I have a charge card."

"Jesus." He laughed. "I didn't know where you were going with that 'first time' routine. I'd be delighted to have you pay for me, if that doesn't mean I have to sleep with you to pay for my supper."

They laughed uproariously about that, then continued to talk like old friends.

He was well built but painfully thin and Ellen experienced pleasure in watching him order filet mignon and shrimp cocktail, dishes he obviously wouldn't have picked had she not been paying. Like Oliver Twist, he asked for a second shrimp cocktail, wine, extra mushrooms and onion rings, and she was delighted. Between bites he told her that he taught in the Education Department. His only hope to get out of his present condition of poverty was to get a large government grant and he spent much of his free time writing up grant applications. But he didn't want to talk about education. That was what he did and thought about day and night. All he wanted to talk about was the legendary EL.

What did they do in EL? He wanted Ellen to describe their homes, their marriages, their divorces, their celebrities, their clothes, their parties. How had the EL men become rich? How much was new money, how much inherited? What was her house like, how much did she spend on clothes, where did she buy her clothes, how much did she pay her servants, did she have a gardener? They talked and talked. Where had she seen the expression with which he looked at her? Ah, yes, the way Lenny had looked at Kimberly.

"My wife," he said soberly, his eyes devouring her face, "is about your age and looks ten years older. And you look ten years younger than your age. My God, a twenty-year gap. She's overweight, her skin is blotchy, she has crow's-feet, and her hair manages to be simultaneously dull and greasy. You look as if you never have a hair out of place. Why can't my wife look like you? It can't all be money!"

But it is money, Ellen thought. She wished she could tell him the truth—that she was a great confection—that tens of thousands of dollars had been spent to create this fake, rich, discontented woman sitting across from him and that, furthermore, great sums of money had to be spent on maintenance. But she didn't want to see the admiration in his eyes dim, so she did not explain.

When the bill came, she signed it with a flourish, feeling secure and powerful with her charge card, even though it was in Jeff's name. It wasn't fair that this powerful pleasure of paying usually belonged only to men.

The waiter gave them another pot of espresso and they smoked a final cigarette. "What would you say if I asked you to go to bed?" he asked, a little cute so rejection wouldn't seem too bad.

"I think I'd like to," she said. It surprised her that she seemed so comfortable with him. Because he knew her field, education, he was her kind of person in a way no one had been since Saul.

"That's wonderful," he said, then sheepishly added, "but you'll have to pay for the motel room, and in cash."

She examined her wallet. "Five dollars," she said, "and a walletful of plastic power."

They looked at each other and grinned in amusement. Not enough cash between the two of them to pay for a motel room and she didn't dare to charge it to Jeff's account. No way of ever explaining that. He thought for a moment, then said, "They'll take my local check and I'll manage to cover it before it bounces."

But the moment had passed for her, destroyed by reality. "I'm getting nervous now about getting back to San Francisco," she said.

He sat beside her in the rented car, then leaned over and buried his nose in her neck. "How good you smell," he said, "what marvelous perfume. If I ever get to New York, would you be able to see me? Maybe I could go to some of your fancy parties with you and see how the other half lives."

"I thought you liked me," she teased. "Now I find you only want to meet my rich friends."

He was instantly upset. "Of course I like you. I don't know why I said that . . ."

"It's all right," she said, patting his hand. Why be cruel? She could see in him the same kind of self-interest that dominated the Jeffs and Amoses; the same hunger and ambition. The only difference really was that they had been successful, had chosen fields in which they could get rich. Saul had gone into education cheerfully accepting the fact that he would always be poor but Todd was obviously a different kind of man.

"Why did you go into education?" she asked.

"My father was a blue-collar worker," he said. "It seemed a step up. Now my father and brothers who stayed on the assembly line are making more money than I do. That doctorate sure seems like a hollow achievement to me."

"I'll be glad to see you if you get to New York," she said. Of course she would help him if she could. Why not? Everybody used everybody in EL, that's what connected the parts of the solid gold circle and made it a whole. She'd never been able to help Jeff in a business sense, but she might be able to help someone else trying to catch the ring. She doubted that she'd ever see him again but she wanted to leave him with optimism. It had been a lovely evening and she was grateful. They exchanged addresses and she left.

Her pleasant mood evaporated as she drove back to San Francisco. Jeff would be furious; no doubt about that. She knew his every mood by now. But really, what gave him the right to be? Wasn't a woman of twenty-eight a free adult, entitled to come and go as she pleased? And damn it, shouldn't a woman of twenty-eight carry more than five dollars in her purse? If Jeff paid for everything, it infantilized her. She really believed in her right to these things. So why was she in a cold sweat?

To her relief, their room was empty and she immediately took a hot, relaxing oil bath, turned on the television, and got into bed. But her peace was short-lived. When he entered and

242

saw her he slammed the door so hard that the entire room rattled.

"You did it deliberately, didn't you?" he screamed.

"Did what deliberately?" she asked, her voice shaking.

"You deliberately missed Samson's wedding party. I told you that he and Heidi were flying to Vegas to get married and that the reception was tonight."

"Honestly, I didn't remember," she said, pulling the covers tightly around her.

"Bullshit you didn't remember, you fucking saboteur. You know damned well I told you. Everyone was there, damn it, even people who don't owe Samson anything and you, the wife of his PR agency, you simply don't appear like some kind of fucking queen."

Like Vashti, she thought, and that's why she lost Ahasuerus to Queen Esther.

"How could it make a difference with so many people there?" she wailed. "Why should he even notice?"

"Are you some kind of fucking moron? You can bet your life he noticed. He asked about it. He asked about it because up until now he's liked you, and I assure you he's one of the few people who has. You're not the kind of person, Ellen, to go around winning popularity contests.

"He was trying to be tactful but I could tell he was goddamned hurt. 'Did she stay away, Jeff,' he asked me, 'because of respect for Valerie, because of friendship for my ex-wife? I'm only asking because I wouldn't want my little doll to have her feelings hurt. Did she stay away to show disapproval of my new marriage? I'm not saying it would change anything between us, Jeff, but I'd just like to know.' So what do you have to say to that, Ellen?"

"He's paranoid and I'm going to sleep."

"The hell you are," he said, ripping the covers off the bed. "I told him you had no feeling for Valerie and were delighted he'd found happiness with Heidi."

"Great. You always think of the right thing to say, Jeff.

That's why *you're* so popular. I'm going to sleep. I have no interest in Samson's child bride."

"I'm not interested either," he said, "but I am interested in his account and I can't afford to jeopardize it because of your stupidity. Get dressed."

"Dressed? You're kidding. I'm going to sleep."

"Dressed," he ordered in that FBI voice. "The party's still going on and you need to see Samson and apologize. Say anything you like. The car broke down, you got lost, anything you feel comfortable with."

"I feel most comfortable with not lying. I don't want to apologize. I don't have anything to apologize for. This is supposedly a free country. Why do you always act as if Samson is giving you his account as a present? You work hard and give fair measure for whatever he pays you. I don't belong to him and you shouldn't either. You do a job, he pays you, and your wife should be irrelevant. I don't want to get dressed. I took off my makeup and took a bath. Now I want to go to sleep."

In a second Jeff had yanked her from the bed and was shaking her. His voice sounded hysterical and he had tears in his eyes.

"I'm not asking you, Ellen, I'm ordering you. I need this account and I'm not going to lose it because of you. Do you hear me? I'm warning you, this is the last straw. Either you get dressed and cooperate or I'm ending the marriage."

Ending the marriage? Her heart skipped a beat and she felt faint. "Ending the marriage? Why?"

"I can't stand living with a fucking fifth column. I'm tired of squabbling around with you. I need a partner, not a deadweight enemy."

Without another word, she scurried into her clothes and brushed her hair with shaking hands. There was no time for makeup but it was so late that nobody would notice. As soon as she looked presentable she followed Jeff to the ballroom. There, in a big easy chair, Samson sat, a short, round roly-poly middle-aged man with little Heidi asleep on his lap. Beside him, she

244

looked thin and childlike. Around her slender neck hung the fabulous pear-shaped diamond Tina had told Ellen about. Heidi's eyes were closed and he was rocking her gently and humming to her.

Samson smiled as they approached. "Shussh," he cautioned, "she's asleep." He cradled his bride like the parent of a child and people started backing out of the ballroom, whispering, walking on tiptoe, facing forward toward this new royalty as they tried not to disturb Heidi. Samson continued to rock his little doll. If he had the slightest interest in Ellen's appearance, he gave no sign of it.

"See ya in the morning, Sammy," Jeff whispered, but Samson continued to rock, oblivious of them both. Ellen was furious.

"And on that appearance our marriage depended?" she asked Jeff with heavy sarcasm as they walked back to their room.

"Not taking any chances, babes," he said.

She had plans to meet Kate for breakfast the next morning and couldn't wait to tell her what had happened. To her surprise, Kate was not sympathetic.

"Sometimes you make me impatient, Ellen, dear," Kate said, but not unkindly. "Marriage implies some kind of deal and your part of the deal is that you be by Jeff's side. I think you made a mistake and that it was wrong for you to miss the party. I have racked my brains and I cannot figure out why you insist on living this way. You're unhappy with Jeff and he's probably not happy with you either. Neither one of you wants to or is able to give the other what he needs. Honestly, Ellen, there's no reason to live this way. That's what incompatible means. There's a world full of men out there. We're suffering from overpopulation and yet you insist on staying married to a man with whom you're not compatible. I tried three times before I found happiness."

Then, for the first time in her life, Ellen told somebody else about the rape. Kate listened impassively, then said, "You have to free yourself from the past, Ellen. That rape happened eleven years ago. It's wrong to let one such episode dictate the rest of your life. That may be the reason you married Jeff but it can't be the reason you stay married. Have you tried to figure that out?"

"Often," Ellen said, "and I think of poor Davida. Life is rich, varied, fun with Jeff. I wouldn't be here right now if not for him. I don't think I can live differently anymore."

"You have to make up your mind," Kate said, "and if you want to stay, you'll have to fulfill your part of the bargain better. If you don't, one day Jeff will surprise you unpleasantly. My personal opinion is that you should try to get out of the marriage while you can, that *you* should make the change. Try to learn from me."

"But you're a risk-taker," Ellen said, "and I'm a coward. I'm incapable of making a change."

"You'll change when you have to," Kate said. "Now let's make up our minds to have fun in Hawaii and not to worry about anything."

It was difficult not to feel wonderfully happy in Hawaii with such weather, the floral smells, the air scented with plumeria, the marvelous beaches, water she could lie in for hours, and, at dusk, the torches lit in the streets and the smell of teriyaki steak wafting to all corners of Waikiki. She even found the airport delightful. It was just a little building, set in a field, with native girls waiting outside, holding beautiful leis.

Many of the other EL'ers, of course, had already been here. In Waikiki, as usual, they stayed at the Royal Hawaiian, an elegant pink building, right on the beach, with lanais on which they could sit for hours sipping marvelous Mai-Tais and rum drinks out of coconut shells. And those pineapples, sweeter, richer, addictive, better than any she had ever tasted in New York! Then she discovered mangoes and began to devour several a day until Tina warned her that they were fattening, so she reverted to grapefruits without sugar, her staple in New York. What irony, she thought, to be surrounded by so much magnificent food and be unable to eat it.

246

All of the EL'ers seemed more relaxed and happy than she had ever seen them before, lying in the sun, trying to surf, or settling for rides on catamarans rowed by native boys. Days and nights drifted by in a haze of pleasure. They all went snorkeling and she felt dependent on Jeff as he bravely led the way, unafraid, through undulating sea plants, holding her hand, knowing she would be timid in this extraordinary undersea world of dizzying colors. Sometimes they sailed a little boat that Jeff handled perfectly. He was at his best in an environment that challenged him physically and he was as instantly competent here as he had been on a horse. His body had never looked more beautiful than when he strode the beach in a bathing suit. Women's eyes would still flick over him as they walked together, but now she too was lovely and she no longer saw that unspoken question in their eyes, "How did such a plain woman get such a gorgeous man?"

Days were filled with interesting events; a luau with a whole roast pig, a visit to the Dole Pineapple Factory, and a one-day cruise of Pearl Harbor where many wept as the guide pointed out the U.S.S. *Arizona,* overturned in the water, and serving as an eternal coffin for the men buried in it when it was hit by bombs. The guide told of the Japanese sneak attack with such drama and flair that indignation, which had grown dormant during the twelve years since VJ-Day, was stirred up again.

"The goddamned Japs," Amos said. "My brother died at Guadalcanal. Every time I hear someone start to criticize Truman for dropping the bomb, I could puke. Who started the war? Who forced them to attack us? Dirty sneaks. Smiling at Roosevelt in Washington, smiling and bowing, and all the time they were planning to destroy us. But does anybody remember the boys under the *Arizona?* No! All they talk about is how the Japs were innocent victims of the A-bomb because they were yellow. Bullshit. They were bombed because of what they did right here in Pearl Harbor and if the bomb had been dropped sooner, we would have saved a lot more American lives. It never would have been used against them if they didn't deserve it."

"It never would have been dropped on the Japanese if they weren't yellow-skinned," Ellen said, dropping her mask. She didn't know if she really believed that but she couldn't stop herself from baiting Amos. "It was pure and simple racism. How come it wasn't dropped against the Germans?"

"Because the war in Europe ended months earlier, stupid," he said. "I know your goddamned Party line. If the Russians had dropped the bomb on the Japanese, people like you would be calling them 'people's heroes!' "

Jeff gave her hand the usual warning squeeze and she said no more. Why should she bother? What difference did it make if she expressed her opinions or not? They couldn't change anyone. Jeff brought the subject up again later when they were alone.

"I like the Japanese," Jeff said. "I liked working with them and I had a Japanese girl friend there. I found them hard-working, decent people. They were as much the victims of their government as were the men killed at Pearl Harbor. But there's no point in antagonizing Amos. You know he's a little crazy. So there's no point in antagonizing him and rocking the account."

"What's worth rocking an account for, Jeff?" she asked.

"Only one thing," he grinned, "if they don't pay their bills."

When there were no activities, the group would sunbathe in its own little roped-off compound on the beach. All of the women had purchased Hawaiian clothes, loose muumuus and sarongs which made them feel more comfortable in the warm weather. The loss of EL formality increased the easiness between them.

They had all put their jewels in the hotel safe but Heidi wore the enormous diamond around her neck even on the beach. She ate little, dreamed into space, and collected stacks of baby orchids. Heidi was getting brown now, looking like a pagan goddess, her pale hair spilling over her shoulders above the pink sarong. She and Candy paired off together because they were a different generation from the other women.

"Don't you just wonder what Samson talks to her about?" Kate murmured.

Myra Benson ate ravenously now that she had escaped from Dr. Dorban. "I'll never forgive this child," she said, patting her eight-month stomach, "but I can't fight my appetite any longer. Well, I'll take it off as soon as the baby is born; maybe go to a reducing spa for the month."

Whenever Ellen looked at Gabe Pine her pleasant sun and rum haze was shattered by the same feeling of revulsion she had felt on meeting Senator McCarthy's sidekick. All of the best imperialist exploiters seemed to belong to EL, she thought to herself. Apparently, it was Gabe's company's influence, ties with the U.S. government, as well as Gabe's own personal fortune, that had contributed substantially to keeping Batista ruling in Cuba for as long as he had. She had heard about Gabe's company way back when she was still mingling with Saul and his friends. She still remembered what they had said, that American slaves were better off than island natives because at least the plantation owners felt some compulsion to feed them, if only to protect their investments.

Now Gabe had switched his base of operations to Central America. The situation there, he claimed with deadpan understatement, was "more stable." Translated, that meant that the military was in power and anyone who stepped out of line got shot. That did make things very stable. No trial, no lawyers, no long, drawn-out imprisonment. Shot! Clean and quick!

"A far more humane way of dealing with criminals," Gabe said, "than the way we torture criminals for years in our legal machinery."

"Don't you believe in trials?" Ellen asked, keeping her voice neutral. Kate grinned at her from her chair nearby.

"Not for criminals," Gabe's wife Laura broke in. "Why should the innocent taxpayer have to support a criminal for forty or fifty years?"

"Some taxpayers aren't so innocent," Kate joked.

"Off with their heads?" Ellen asked.

"Exactly," Gabe answered smugly. Jeff flashed her a warning look.

Criminals dealt with, Gabe began to complain of the American mistreatment of the banana. "Americans wreck them," he complained, "by putting them in the refrigerator."

"The red bananas here are positively orgasmic," Tina interjected.

"So why don't you let Jeff handle your account?" Samson asked. "He'll get people to put bananas where they belong."

Ellen let out a giggle. Jeff glared at her.

"Could you really do that, Jeff?" Gabe asked.

"Oh, baby, could I ever," Jeff said. "Give me six months and everyone who listens to TV or radio will stop putting bananas in the refrigerator.

"We'll do it discreetly," Jeff continued. "The public service image. 'This message is brought to the consumer as a public service by Consolidated Fruit.' We'll use a classy, serious voice, a doctor voice like Lionel Barrymore's, the voice of someone you can trust, someone who really cares about the public."

What a public service, Ellen thought.

"I have a neat idea, Jeffy," Heidi broke in. She was making a lei out of her baby orchids. "I think you should have a happy colored man, sort of like Harry Belafonte, and his shirt should be opened to his waist and he should speak in that kind of sexy, calypso voice and say, 'I pick the banan' for you. Never put in de refrig . . .' "

"What a girl," Samson boomed, "smart as well as beautiful."

"It stinks," Gabe said. "You think I want to end up with only niggers eating bananas?"

"I was only trying to help," Heidi said, aggrieved.

"Nobody asked you," Gabe answered. "We're trying to have a serious discussion."

A serious discussion! Ellen, Will, and Kate burst out into whoops of laughter.

"I wish the three of you would shut up, too," Gabe said.

"Why don't you two go and discuss business somewhere

else?" Kate said firmly. "None of us want to listen to you."

Good for Kate. When she spoke, people listened. Gabe and Jeff walked outside the solid gold circle enclosure and went off alone down the beach.

"I liked what you said before that dumb broad interrupted," Gabe said as they were walking away. "A classy voice to give a classy message. That's good. When we get back, how about spending a weekend with us in Honduras? You'd both love it there. Maybe we'll have a big party for everybody from EL. What do you think about that?"

"Super, Gabe baby," Jeff said, following him.

For the next few days they all continued to loll on the beach or drift near shore on rubber floats, reading novels that wouldn't be hurt by the loss of an occasional page, dubbing this sport, "aqua-reading." Gothic romances and pornography ranked high. Harry took a copy of *Tropic of Cancer* out on a float and he became so engrossed that he got a blisteringly severe sunburn. "It's wrecked our sex life here," Tina complained, "and you know what a turn-on a vacation is. I don't know why tragedies always happen to me."

It became a EL joke on that trip. If something were provocative or arousing or appetizing, they would ask themselves, "Is it worth the sunburn?"

Jeff and Ellen were lying on beach mats one day when Amos came and plunked himself down beside them. "Listen to this, Jeffy, and tell me if it isn't the funniest joke you've ever heard."

Jeff put on his subservient smile, nudged Ellen, and she banged her book shut in irritation.

"A guy came to Waikiki," Amos said, "and he didn't like the texture of the sand. So he had his own sand company fly in fine white sand. Then he wanted to sunbathe naked and the management forbid it. So he rented the entire hotel. He had to wait a day until they could clear out all the guests. Finally, after all the guests had gone, he came out of his room, walked down to the beach, took off all his clothes, lay back on the fine white sand, looked out at the empty water in front of him and exclaimed, 'This is the life. Who needs money?' "

Jeff laughed uproariously, dutifully, and Ellen squeezed out a small laugh. From nearby came Heidi's voice, "But he did need money, Amos, didn't he?"

"Listen to my little doll," Samson caroled.

Amos lowered his voice to talk to Jeff, not caring if Ellen heard, but not wanting anybody else to overhear.

"Jeff, baby," Amos said, "I want to give you a little advice about EL since I was the one sponsored you and I've been in a lot longer than you. I really know the ropes in EL."

"Don't you think I do?" Jeff asked anxiously. He sat up. "It's been about four years now, Amos."

"Well, old buddy," Amos said, "it may be four years but you still have lots of things to learn." The menace in his voice was not lost on either of them. Ellen reached over to take Jeff's hand but he pushed her away irritably.

"What's up?" Jeff asked.

"Well, it's about Murray Morano, you know, that creep from Michael's wedding. I heard you're sponsoring him for EL. You can't be serious."

"Why not?" Jeff asked. He was sweating but not from the sun.

"He'll never get in."

"So what?" Jeff asked. "I can sponsor and the board can reject."

"That's not the point. We never know. By some fluke he might get in and then it would be Jeff Sheldon who would be to blame. And everybody would remember that and it would kill your image. Listen, Jeff, it's no secret that Bestway Transit is Mafia-controlled. Morano is nothing but a union thug, except he happens to be in management. In any event, he's no gentleman and his wife looks like a Vegas hooker with those two-inch lashes. Look at it this way, Jeff, would Jon Wein sponsor a thug for membership? Would a Rockefeller sponsor a thug for mem-

252

bership in his exclusive club? Sure, he might not be turned down if a Rockefeller sponsored him, but a lot of people would wonder what the thug had over Rockefeller to get him to do it. And if you sponsor Morano there are only two things people will say. They'll say either that you have such a low opinion of yourself that you're willing to associate with anybody, or else that it's strictly a payoff for his account. I mean, anybody with any brains would know it wasn't because you thought he'd be an asset to EL."

Jeff was as annoyed as he ever permitted himself to be with clients. Caught with his hand in the cookie jar! "Come on, Amos," he said, "when you sponsored me did people think it was so I would do your PR?"

Or for a lousy four hundred dollars? Ellen thought.

"Of course not," Amos said. "You're reversing the situation. If you had sponsored me, people would have been certain you were doing it to get *my* account, because there are lots of PR agencies but there's only one of me. But even if that were the case, nobody would mind because I'm socially acceptable. Get the analogy? Everybody would automatically assume that I sponsored you for friendship, because there's really nothing you do for me that most other agencies couldn't do."

You ungrateful bastard, Ellen thought. Jeff was totally deflated now.

"Let me paint you a picture," Amos continued expansively. "You're at an EL dinner and at one table you see the Morano crew because once he gets in, he'll bring his whole Mafia family with him. Right away you would ask, 'Who let those creeps into EL?' Now if somebody said the sponsor was Jeff Sheldon, a lot of people might be sore enough to take their accounts away from Jeff Sheldon. So whatever you made from the Morano account wouldn't be worth it. Because I tell you, Jeff, those people multiply like rabbits. Instead of being EL, Executive Leaders, it would be changed to YLM, Young Leaders of the Mafia. But anyway, Jeff, the guy's going to be blackballed, so why not be smart and withdraw your sponsorship before you make everybody nervous?"

"You're absolutely right, Amos, as usual," Jeff said in his best sincere manner; "you're a good friend. Thank you for bringing this to my attention. I'm really grateful, fella. Consider it done."

"I knew you'd smarten up," Amos said. "Hey, that was some joke wasn't it? 'Who needs money?' Some joke." Still chortling, he walked away.

Jeff was furious. He whispered hotly about it to Ellen although the smile remained pasted on his face. It's like *1984*, Ellen thought, where the television even monitors the expressions on people's faces.

"I can't tell Murray," Jeff whispered, "that I'm withdrawing his application. It's not just his account. He's setting up five others for me. I'll lose millions of dollars and besides, it would be a loss of face. It would show him that I don't have much power."

"So you'll lose the accounts," Ellen said, wanting to comfort him. "You have plenty of accounts now, don't you?"

"With our overhead," he said, "I never have enough accounts. I'll figure out something. Maybe I'll tell Murray that I did submit his application but that it was blackballed."

"Why don't you go ahead and submit the application?" Ellen said. "After all, Amos doesn't own EL. If he gets in, it will mean that he's not as bad as Amos makes out."

"Yeah, but if he gets in, I'll lose Amos's account. I'll just have to lie to Murray and tell him I submitted his name, fought the good fight, but was defeated by someone who had it in for him. Someone who has a lot of unshakable power. I'll tell him it was defeated by Amos."

"Games like these have a way of backfiring," Ellen said.

"No, no—" he waved away her concerns—"the more I think about it the better it is. You see, in the back of my mind, I keep wondering why Amos is so down on Murray. Every day in his business he deals with thugs, and the Mafia, too. If he didn't, he'd be out of business. Why is Amos doing it? He says, to begin with, that he's concerned about my reputation. You know that's sheer bullshit. Cheap Amos is never concerned about anybody's reputation but his own. It's also crazy to think that after Murray comes the deluge. Murray wouldn't even have the right to sponsor anybody for three years and then everybody he sponsored would have to be passed on, same as he. If the board didn't like him, they wouldn't let any of his friends in. So far as his wife's appearance, that's bullshit, too. Every wife who joins EL gets smart and starts to look like the other EL wives. I mean, I'll never forget the difference between you and Marilyn that first night.

"No, there's something more to it. I'll bet he doesn't want Murray in EL because there's bad blood between the two of them. I'll bet that Murray's company once did some hauling for Amos and that Cheap Amos refused to pay union scale. He probably tried to shake Murray down the way he did me, with that four hundred, but Murray doesn't need Amos the way I did, so Murray wouldn't play ball. Murray never forgets or forgives that kind of dealing, so Amos is uneasy about having Murray in."

"So what are you going to do?"

"I'll withdraw my sponsorship first. That will take care of Amos. Then I'll get a little information to back up my assumptions. I'll make a few discreet calls to find out the connection between Amos and Bestway Transit. Shouldn't be hard, with a few bucks in the right places. If my hunch is right, I'll never have to tell Murray I withdrew my sponsorship. I'll tell him Amos blackballed him. Then he can blame Amos, I'll be a hero to both of them, and I'll keep all the accounts."

"Be careful," she said, "you may be getting out of your depth. Amos is a major shark and he's an old hand at dirty dealings. Maybe you should just do it Amos's way and tell Murray the truth about what happened. You can then be a friend to Murray but you won't get trapped in lies. Or maybe you shouldn't even identify Amos to him. What's the point of starting a war. After all, despite that four hundred dollars, Amos has been as good a friend to you as anyone in EL."

"There's no such thing as friendship in business," Jeff said. "To increase profits, I'd cut Amos's throat and he'd cut mine. He's no friend to me. I hate the guy. I'd love to have the opportunity to hold something over him. I have to take two Miltowns every time I meet with him. Sometimes I think that even if it meant losing the account, I'd cheer if Landor City caved in on him. I'm still of some use to him, but don't get the idea that's friendship. The truth is, Murray will probably be far more useful to me in the future."

"Oh, Jeff," she said, "it's a hell of a way to live."

He grinned a bittersweet smile for effect. "It's the nature of the beast," he said, "let me know when you come up with a better way."

When Jeff left to make phone calls, Will sat down beside her to chat. Ellen was glad to see him. He was a genuinely nice man, and Ellen loved his southern gentility. His silver hair and soothing voice always made her feel good.

"Why aren't you having a good time, honey?" he asked.

She looked at him appraisingly. They had never had a personal talk but from the way Kate talked about him, she knew he could be trusted.

"It's not that I'm having a bad time," she said. "After all, most people would give anything for this kind of vacation. The first week I was high, but after a while, Hawaii seems like too much whipped cream; kind of sickening. And lying around on a beach, even the most beautiful beach, becomes boring. All my life, Will, I've been intensely aware of time, and I always thought I'd use my time for something purposeful. To learn something more, to *be* something more. From some points of view, you might think I am a lot more, a lot better than when we joined EL, but in my heart, I really don't think so. Now, I don't use time, I just waste it. Nine-tenths of my life is devoted to being a consumer or to being with people I really don't care much about. I once read that Julius Caesar said, 'Time is the only thing that man is born with and yet he gives it away to the first pandar who comes his way.' "

"Most people would be pea-green with envy."

"People always envy what they don't know much about. I myself, at one point, would have envied this life, but I don't now, and I could kick myself sometimes for not being happy. At night, when I smell the plumeria and the torches are lit, I think of young lovers walking hand in hand along the beach and I feel arid and sterile, as if my life is over, that nothing wonderful is ever going to happen to me again, that it will always just be more of the same as what I have now. How is it possible to feel used up at the age of twenty-eight, at loose ends, futile somehow, uneasy with myself and with my life."

"That's called *Weltschmerz*," he said gently.

"What's that?"

"It's a kind of mental depression caused by comparing how the world is with how you wish it would be; a kind of romantic pessimism. However, my dear girl, the young fellow who most notably suffered from it in literature was a fellow called Werther, and I think he was a pup, somewhat younger than you. The state is considered more appropriate for teenagers."

"Are you criticizing me?" she asked. "Telling me I'm too old for *Weltschmerz?*"

"Heaven forbid. I wouldn't dream of criticizing you. You're a lovely, intelligent woman and I'm truly sorry that you don't feel useful and happy. We have such a way of complicating things that can be so easy. For example, do you know what the Polynesians call sex? The Blessing of the Islands. Isn't that beautiful? A blessing, rather than a curse. A blessing! Nothing to be ashamed of."

"That's lovely," she said. "Sometimes I think that's what I do, complicate simple things. I worry that maybe I'm unhappy because I'm neurotic. That nothing could make me happy. Isn't it neurotic to have everything and be unhappy?"

"Depends on your definitions of 'everything' and 'neurotic.'

257

If you're unhappy, then you don't have everything. And one definition of neurosis is that it's the gap between potential and achievement. That's why Kate's usually so happy. She has always utilized every bit of her potential."

"I don't know what I have potential for," Ellen said.

"Nobody does abstractly. It emerges from action, not from thinking about action."

"I'll think about that," she said. "Thank you, Will. How did you get to be so wise?"

"I'm not wise, honey," he said with a sad little laugh. "I'm anxious and troubled and besides, it's always easier to give advice to others. Since you've been kind enough to trust me with your confidences, Ellen, I will give you one of my own. You're the only person in EL who will know this. The secret will emerge eventually anyway, but I'm hoping to keep it quiet as long as possible.

"I'm telling you now, Ellen, dear, because I want to help you, to give you a gift, and the gift I'm going to give you now is the awareness of how precariously we are all perched and of how we must accept and enjoy, rather than suffer over every moment. Forgive my asking, but have I the assurance that for the moment you will tell no one, not even your husband or your friend Tina?"

"I wouldn't even tell them my rank and serial number."

He didn't smile at her rejoinder. Instead, his blue eyes reddened with unshed tears.

"Kate has cancer," he whispered.

"Cancer?" she whispered back in horror.

"One breast. We hope only one breast. More tests must be done."

"Will they have to remove it?"

"I'm afraid so. Soon after we return to New York. She insisted on this trip first. Said it might be our last together."

Ellen looked across the beach to where Kate sat laughing and talking with some of the others. Will followed her gaze.

"She's very brave and of course she thinks everything will

come out all right. I'm more distraught than she is, or so it seems. I can't bear to think of her suffering, she's the only thing in life that matters to me. She's my soul, my conscience, the love of my life, the focus of my life, my dearest friend. She's the ear I talk to, the person who loves and listens and understands and accepts me completely. She thinks I'm a lot better than I really am, but then, she always thinks well of people. I don't know how I could live without her. There would be too great an emptiness in the universe, too great a gap in the world. What keeps me going now is my hope that the cancer will be arrested."

"No matter what happens," Ellen said, "you've been lucky. You've had something between you that few couples have." Her mind went back to how terribly alone she'd felt in the hospital. "I think you must be the happiest couple in EL."

"Thank you, honey," he said in his soft southern drawl. "I wouldn't be a bit surprised if that were true. We've been real lucky. I just pray our luck hasn't run out. But we both wanted you to know."

Ellen took his hand and held it between her own.

"You know what Kate said about you?" he asked. "She said when she met you, 'You know, you don't find a friend, you recognize one.' "

Ellen's eyes filled with tears. She and Will sat there recognizing each other.

7

*T*he trip to Japan seemed to take forever, with a stop for refueling at Guam, but they were all keyed up at the thought of seeing Japan. Because of the war, Jeff was the only one who had been there before. Tina chatted merrily to Ellen all through the trip, Kate looked drawn, and Myra Benson looked a little worried.

"Demented of her to have come on this trip," Tina said. "Can you imagine giving birth here? The baby will turn out with slanty eyes."

Marilyn was totally mute, Laura Pine gabbed away about the white man's burden in Central America, Heidi slept with her head in Samson's lap, and Candy whined about her fatigue. Ellen's eyes were so bleary after the trip that she noticed little on the drive from the airport. An old friend of Jeff's from the war, Kim, a Nisei doctor who had grown up in Ohio but resettled in Tokyo after the occupation, was waiting for them at the hotel.

Ellen enjoyed meeting him. Tired as she was, she was instantly aware that Kim was the first person she'd met since her marriage who really cared about Jeff as a human being, completely apart from his business role. He was grateful because Jeff had never once exhibited anti-Japanese prejudices, had seemed indifferent to racial matters, and always treated Kim as a complete equal. After the occupation, Jeff had regularly sent Kim money to help get him started in Japan.

Kim would have done anything to reciprocate Jeff's kindness. Now a prosperous doctor, he drove them around Tokyo in a limousine rented in their honor and he had assisted Jeff with local arrangements for the EL group. Enthusiastically, the two of them caught up with past events in a combination of Japanese and English.

At 3:00 A.M., Hawaii time, Ellen found herself being escorted into a tempura bar. Jeff had longed for good Japanese food since he'd returned from the occupation duty and he frequented the only two Japanese restaurants in New York which were good.

"Kim and I are thinking about starting a Japanese restaurant chain in New York," Jeff told her as he proceeded to devour the extraordinary tempura: turnips, zucchini, sweet potatoes, black mushrooms, giant shrimp, all downed with small cups of hot sake.

She found herself admiring Jeff's vitality. Here she was struggling to stay awake and he was already talking business. She had never seen him happier. Kim told her, "Do you know what the woman at the *furo* in Matsuyama said to me about Jeff? She said, 'He was the first American to come, he spoke the best Japanese, and he was the kindest.' " Ellen beamed with unaccustomed pride.

But as they continued to talk business, her thoughts started to wander and she felt lonely for Jennifer. Despite her delight at being in this legendary country of *The Mikado* and *Madame Butterfly,* she was a prisoner, totally dependent on Jeff, disoriented, unable to speak the language. She had not the slightest idea of where she was, of the name of the restaurant, of what the menu said.

"I have to go to the bathroom," she whispered. He had taught her the words *Benjo dokodeska* and she was directed to the ladies' room. When she entered, she was horrified. It contained a urinal which sat flat on the floor and she would have to squat to use it. She couldn't do it and while she stood gazing at it despairingly, a Japanese man, dressed Western-style in suit and tie, entered and unzipped, oblivious of her. She fled and finally convinced Jeff to take her back to the hotel, Frank Lloyd Wright's famous earthquake-proof structure, the Imperial. The other women had been able to go to their rooms and rest.

As soon as they reached their room, she fell into the bed with a deathlike sleep. When she awakened, it was a bright, sunny day. Jeff was not there, nor had he left a note. Typical, she thought. She picked up the room phone. "*Mushy, mushy,*" said the operator. She hung up. What should she say? If Jeff had thought to leave a message, he would have left it next to the bed, rather than with the hotel operator. She called each of the EL rooms but all of her friends were out. She wondered if she should get dressed, go down to the lobby, and wait there for Jeff. Well, she might as well go down to the lobby. Suppose Jeff phoned her here though? And where the devil was he?

She looked at her watch: 2:00 P.M. She had slept for sixteen hours and she was hungry and alone. A feeling of irrational panic swept through her. So this is what it would be like without Jeff. Filled with fear and homesickness she sat there until she heard the key in the door and Jeff entered, triumphant, a conquering hero.

Weeping, she ran to him and threw her arms around him.

"What the hell's wrong with you?" he asked.

"I was afraid," she said. "Where were you?"

"What were you afraid of?" he said irritably.

"I was afraid of being raped by a gang of Japanese," she said and he threw back his head and laughed uproariously.

"Nobody would dare to touch my wife," he joked, "and besides, you're taller than most of the men."

262

Now that she had calmed down, she was angry.

"Where were you?" she repeated. "How could you just go off that way without even leaving a note?"

"I thought you'd remember. I made my speech this morning."

"Oh, God, your speech. I missed your speech. Why didn't you awaken me?"

"No women," he said. "Anyway, the entire speech was in Japanese."

"I would have liked to see their reception of you," she said. "Was it a great success?"

"Piece of bean cake," he said, with a grin. "In Japan, wives are expected to stay home but if you had been there, you would have been mighty proud."

They gazed at each other with affection. It was one of the best moments of their marriage. She dressed quickly while Jeff explained the schedule to her. As she listened, she felt the same frustration as in San Francisco.

"Kim and I are taking the men on a tour of the Diet, then to the Yashica camera factory. Then the president of Yashica is hosting us at a geisha house. You and the other women are being taken to shop at the department stores. The chauffeurs will take you to dinner, then bring you back here."

"I don't want to go shopping," she said. "I want to go to the Diet and do what you're doing, exactly what you and the men are doing."

"Even Kate isn't going with the men, babes. I'd love to take you but things just don't work that way in Japan. It's a man's society. The women stay at home and keep quiet. Even the wife of the president of Yashica isn't coming to dinner with us tonight."

Ellen thought of Jeff's Japanese pornographic scroll. Forty-two positions and the women don't talk back. What a society! No wonder Jeff had been so happy here.

"You don't have to go along with their archaic ideas," she pointed out.

263

"If I want their accounts I sure as hell do," he said. "Come on, Ellen, be reasonable. You're always ranting about insensitive imperialists and now you want to step on Japanese traditions."

"I know you're right and I don't want to offend your hosts but I find it boring to always be in a women's ghetto. I don't want to be segregated. All women are not alike just because they're women. I hate pretending that I enjoy shopping. At least I should be able to do something that interests me, even if it's not with you."

"Tough," he said. "Just try to look at it as your part of the war effort. There are lots of times that I'm bored with what I have to do but I have to do it anyway. When we get back, Ellen, maybe you should have a little therapy to find out why you always insist on being different."

"I don't insist on being different," she said quietly, "I am different." They left it at that.

She put on her mask and went to meet the other women in the lobby, carefully scrutinizing the faces of these people she spent so much time with and really knew so superficially. Kate and Myra had both begged off to spend the day in bed but the others were filled with the excitement of the hunt. They were going to Mikimoto.

"Sammy said when I get in," Heidi said, "I should just say to them, 'Sell me your most expensive string of pearls.' He said if I did that I couldn't go wrong."

"Isn't this a fabulous opportunity," Tina squealed as their chauffeured Cadillacs drew up in front of the main store of the famed Mikimoto. "Thank God they all speak English."

"They're supposed to learn English in school," Candy said. "It's a requirement. But yesterday my waiter did not know English. I wanted only one egg and one slice of bread for breakfast. Thank God Jeff was there. You would have thought I was asking the waiter to commit hara-kiri. We'd all be dead without Jeff. He must be a genius to have mastered this peculiar language."

"Why do you think Japanese is peculiar?" Ellen shot out.

264

"To them, English is peculiar." Candy shrugged and turned away, leaving Ellen feeling rude.

Once inside the store, there was nothing to do but to buy. So Ellen bought pearls. Long pearls, short pearls, pearls for Jennifer, pearls for her mother, even a strand for Ursula. From Mikimoto they went to Takashimaya where Ellen bought a variety of dolls for Jennifer. She knew that what would delight Jennifer the most was not the most expensive doll in authentic kimono and obi but the doll within the doll within the doll, ending with the world's teeniest little wooden doll. As she bought, she felt so lonely for her daughter that she could have wept. If only she had been able to persuade Jeff to bring Jennifer, this entire trip would have been a delight. She would have had the joy of seeing things through a child's eyes and so much of what they had done was really designed for children.

From there, they went to a famous lacquerware shop where they bought jewelry boxes, serving trays, platters, wall plaques, rice boxes, soup bowls. The buying became automatic, things she didn't need or want or ever expect to use, but what the hell, there was nothing to do but buy. It was an Alice-in-Wonderland kind of shopping, dreamlike. The women would point to what they wanted, the items would be wrapped, and the bills presented to the chauffeurs. No cash was exchanged and Ellen had no clear idea of how much each item cost, of what she was spending as she went along, or of what the total came to.

Next they explored the basement of Watanabe's department store which was filled with exotic foods—strange fish, dried fruits, candies made from rice and bean paste, and extraordinary fresh loquats, as delicious as the mangoes had been in Hawaii. Jeff had warned them about the loquats, telling them how he had become violently sick from simultaneously eating loquats and drinking water. The combination made the eater swell up. Ellen and the other ladies sampled their loquats dry and loved them.

Then they were taken to dinner at an expensive Japanese restaurant where they ate, Japanese-style, sitting on the tatami mats, hiking up their short skirts, and giggling as they toyed with their chopsticks. Musicians played the samisen and Ellen imagined they all belonged to an emperor's harem, doing just what they had done today, moving as a group, carrying no money, watched over by eunuch chauffeurs.

Myra and Kate had made plans to join them at the restaurant and Ellen was relieved to be sitting next to Kate.

"How do you feel?" Ellen whispered to her.

"I'm feeling fine after sleeping all day," Kate whispered back. "I'm pretending there's nothing wrong with me. How could there be, really, if I feel so fine tonight? Maybe when we get back to New York the doctors will find they've made a mistake."

Ellen looked into her dear friend's drawn face and knew Kate really couldn't believe it was all a mistake, but if Kate wanted to pretend, she would pretend with her.

Myra was the only one who received a chair because of her advanced pregnancy. "He'll grow up with a fixation on Japanese food." She laughed, patting her stomach and drinking the plum wine.

"Jeff is a tremendous help to Leonard in his negotiating here," Myra confided to Ellen. "We're buying our first hotel in the Orient. It's so exciting, I'm glad I didn't listen to the people who told me not to come. I'm feeling fine and I really love that Japanese food."

The food temporarily dispelled Ellen's boredom with the group's activities. She loved the sukiyaki (pronounced *skee-yaki*) with the slippery devil's root, bean curd, and unfamiliar mushrooms. The eel in taro sauce, chicken teriyaki, and eggplant in ginger sauce were equally delicious. Only Tina didn't eat.

"I'm not going to let the Japanese spoil this gorgeous body that it's taken me a lifetime to achieve," she said proudly. She contented herself by sipping sake.

Ellen had given up the idea of simply taking a long walk around the city. Nobody wanted to go with her.

266

"Why should we walk?" Tina asked. "We'll get lost. Besides, we've already had a tour of the city in our limousines. What else is there to see? Local color is usually quite unsanitary. Besides, we don't have time to waste just walking."

So the next day the harem spent at fittings for magnificent brocade dresses and coats. Ellen picked a rich green with a blue dragon splashed across it. She thought it made her look like a hostess in a Chinese restaurant. The women were promised the dresses for the next day's festivities, a visit to the Grand Kabuki. Apparently, the shop would keep the humble little seamstresses working all night to accommodate the rich American ladies. Ellen shuddered, then pushed it from her mind.

But the Grand Kabuki experience was a rapturous one for Ellen. She was fascinated by the strange, raucous music, the sing-song words like inverted cries, starting loud and ending in guttural whispers and snarls, the tremendous impact of the traditional drama. Every gesture had been thought out and practiced for generations. She felt drawn into a religious mystery in which each detail of the costumes, each configuration of the extraordinary sets, each piercing wail had been ritualized into high art. Despite the language differences, the mime made it possible to have a vague idea of the story and when the lights came on for the first intermission, she sat there drugged with awe at the sheer perfection of the spectacle.

"What a bore," Tina said, breaking into Ellen's trance, "I wish we could leave. The shrieking is giving me a headache."

"Why, look, there's my cousin," Candy said, pointing to a tall, distinguished man walking up the aisle.

"Her cousin's the American ambassador," Tina whispered dramatically to Ellen. "I recognize his wife. She's had her hair done at Christopher's."

When Candy presented the EL'ers to the ambassador in the lobby, Ellen thought Michael would burst with pride. His wife's cousin, an ambassador. As simple as that.

"He invited us all back to the embassy," Candy said as they

returned to their seats, "and if we're too tired to go tonight, we can go tomorrow night."

"What a contact *he* can be for Japanese accounts," Jeff whispered to Ellen as they waited for the curtain to rise again for another enchanting act.

When it was over, the audience slowly filed out to find that a group of people were demonstrating in front of the theater. Ellen stood looking at them in dismay. The people in the group were horrible, deformed, sick, distorted, like the screaming figures in Picasso's *Guernica.*

"Hiroshima victims," someone murmured, "appealing to the American ambassador for medical help, for reparations."

"Don't look," Heidi said to Myra, "it's bad luck for your baby." Myra turned pale.

"Ignore that little moron," Tina said, putting an arm around Myra's shoulder and giving Heidi a dirty look. Leonard helped Myra into a limousine and Heidi, sniffling, snuggled in the shelter of Samson's arms.

Ellen watched from the car window as the police came and, none too gently and with disgust, herded off the victims.

"It's so horrible," Ellen said, close to tears. "The faces of those people. I don't think I'll ever forget the sight of them. That people should be so maimed and still live!"

"Oh, for Chrissake," Amos exploded, "they would have done the same to us if they could."

"Forget it," Jeff said. "It has nothing to do with us. Don't let this spoil our trip." But Amos was fulminating.

"Those people are at least alive," he snarled, "alive enough to come here and bother us. But my brother, killed at Guadalcanal, is stone cold dead. I've said it before and I'll say it again. I'm glad we bombed the Japs. Truman was one hundred percent right. He said he never hesitated and neither would I. I'd sacrifice a thousand of those yellow bastards for one American boy."

"Shussh," Ellen whispered, "the driver may understand English."

"Don't you tell me to shussh, young lady," Amos yelled, his

face reddening. "I don't give a damn what language he speaks. He's working for me right now and I can say whatever I like as long as I pay him. Jeff, why don't you tell your wife to shut up? She's giving me a headache."

"I can talk any time I want to, you Philistine," Ellen flared back. "You're not paying me. I don't work for you."

Marilyn gasped. Then there was dead silence all the way to the hotel.

"My cousin said we had better call it off for tonight," Candy said when they had returned to the lobby. "They may be demonstrating outside of the embassy."

Shivering, Ellen walked to their room with Jeff beside her, feeling like a condemned prisoner walking to her execution. He slammed the door behind him and turned to her, his face contorted with hate.

"This time," he said, "you've gone too far. I'm going to spend the night with Kim. If you've lost me Amos's account, so help me I'll file for divorce the minute we get home."

He slammed the door behind him and she sat down for a few minutes to wait until her knees stopped shaking. Then she walked down to the lobby to get some cigarettes. Her spirits were raised when she saw Will Sweet at the cigarette counter. "These Japanese cigarettes," he joked, "taste like death but they're called Hope. I look for symbolism in everything nowadays."

Will and Kate had been in another car so he didn't know about the conflagration. Kate had gone to bed and they sat down to have a drink together while Ellen told him the whole story.

"Brava," he chuckled when she had finished. "Kate will be so sorry we missed it. So somebody finally had the guts to talk back to that boor. Good for you, honey."

"A Pyrrhic victory," she said, shivering, "if Jeff loses the account because of me."

"Don't you worry none about that, honey. Jeff won't lose the account because of you. Amos is the kind of man who likes to pull wings off flies but he's also a smart businessman. I assure you he'll keep Jeff on just as long as Jeff keeps pulling in the profits and no matter how many faux pas Jeff's rebel wife makes. After all, you really are irrelevant to Amos's business. But Amos is a cruel man, a sadistic man, and he loves to turn the knife. You're so open Ellen, my dear, such a rotten actress, that Amos can see right through you and Amos hates women like you, women who think and who talk back to him. He feels the same way about Kate as about you, I assure you, but he doesn't dare to bait her. He's a smart man, that Amos, and he understands you and he understands Jeff, too. So he'll save all of this up as an extra bit of sadism for when he decides to dump Jeff, as inevitably he will. You know the turnover rate with PR agencies! Amos is a mean, rotten bully and he has the highest rate of executive turnover of any man in EL.

"The minute Amos's profits take a dip, Jeff will be sacrificed. But will he then be able to come to his loving wife for comfort? No, because Amos is fixing that. Amos will place much of the blame right on the intelligent shoulders of Jeff's tactless wife. Honey, men like Amos always hate intelligent women. They can only get it up with poor, humble, grateful little slaveys or with women they can buy. So the smartest thing you can do is to not let Amos get to you. Forget about him, try to set Jeff right, and go right ahead and be your own self. I mean, who the hell is Amos to go around censoring people's thoughts and conversations?"

"Are you sure Jeff won't lose the account because of me?" she asked, still needing more reassurance.

"If you had two heads he'd keep the account as long as Amos was flying high. Listen, honey, would you want me to talk to Jeff about Amos? I've been around these bullies a good time longer than he has. You know, I'm twenty years older than Kate, so I've seen a lot of these fellas in my lifetime."

"Better not," she said, "he'd be furious if he knew we'd talked about this. He'll just have to get over it on his own."

"Maybe you could try setting Jeff straight tomorrow," he said, "when he's cooled down."

270

"No," she said despondently, "we'll just have to let it fade. We never seem able to work things out. We just let them happen and wait to forget them or until a new thing comes up to quarrel about. You and Kate are so lucky, so happy together. It seems so wonderful to me to have a relationship with another rational person to whom you can talk as an equal. You two would have had such contented children. May I ask, please, if it doesn't seem an intrusion, why you never had any?"

"Perfectly all right to ask," he said. "As you know, Kate and I married after she'd had three other marriages, but that's not the reason."

"What is?" Ellen asked.

"You really have no idea?" he asked, looking at her closely. She shook her head.

"How curious," he said. "My dear girl, I'm homosexual." Ellen could not remember ever being more shocked. She had never before even met a homosexual who admitted it.

"Homosexual," she whispered, "but you're married."

"Yes, of course we're married and we love each other and are dear friends, but we do not sleep with each other."

"No sex," Ellen said, still dazed. "Then why did you get married?" She could hardly believe what he was telling her. The only marriage she had thought was perfect was as flawed as any other.

"We married for love," he said, "not for sex. I worked for Kate and we became companions, grew to love and respect each other. Our ideas, our perceptions, our values, were all similar. We enjoyed being with each other and missed each other when we were apart. We found we needed each other's companionship. So the only socially acceptable way we could live together as loving friends was to get married."

"Forgive me if I sound stupid or say the wrong thing," Ellen said, struggling to accept, "but when you found you loved each other, couldn't you then sleep together?"

"Because we love each other," he said, "we've never even

tried. It would be a travesty. It would fail and then we would always have that embarrassment between us. Instead, we've been married now for many years and it has been a glorious, loyal, constructive, learning relationship. I have felt privileged to exist in her presence and I believe she feels the same way about me."

"Do other people in EL know?" she asked.

"Perhaps," he said, "but even if they do, they would prefer not to know, so they just push the knowledge away. After all, Ellen, we don't know what goes on in anybody else's bedrooms, do we? Not even in yours and Jeff's."

She sat there thinking and sipping her drink.

"Why so quiet?" he asked. "What are you thinking?"

"I was thinking of how ironic everything is," she said. "Amos hates me for nonconformity, but I really am a conformist. I do everything I'm programmed for, just complain a little about it along the way. But you and Kate are the real nonconformists. That really delights me. Nonconformists in our midst and there's nothing Amos or anybody else can do about it."

"Anything else?" he asked.

She leaned over and hugged him. "I'm glad you two are my friends," she said. "You're worth more than the rest of them all together."

They sat there companionably for a while, drinking together, until Ellen looked up and saw Jeff appear. "Let me say something," Will said. "Don't worry. I'll be subtle and I won't get you in trouble."

Jeff ordered a Japanese beer and sat down at their table. She could see from his body language that he was still angry at her. Why had he come back? Probably Kim's house was too uncomfortable.

"This has been a grand trip, Jeff," Will said. Jeff grunted. "You seem to be upset about something," Will added. "Care to share it?"

"It's that Amos," Jeff said. "He's such a prima donna, keeps threatening to take away his account."

"You have to face the fact that eventually he will take his

272

account away," Will said. "Your agency has had it longer than any other one. You've got to relax about Amos. You can never do enough for him. Think he'll be grateful for this trip? Not a chance. There's no way to permanently please him, Jeff, so you should just stop trying. Do the best you can, expect him to leave, and then relax. Amos's way is to make people sweat and I don't think he will ever forgive you, Jeff, for being born so handsome."

Jeff looked at Ellen while this new perception penetrated. Then he smiled at her but she kept her face stony. He might forgive her but she was damned if she would forgive him. He treated her exactly the way Amos treated him but she was supposed to be something more than a PR account.

The next day the group left for the final part of the trip. They were going to Matsuyama and Hakone on a boat going down the Inland Sea. From Matsuyama they visited the city where Jeff had been during the occupation. He led the fascinated group around his old haunts. The *furo* where he used to bathe was still in operation and the gnarled old woman who owned it bowed before him. This was the woman who had spoken so highly of him to Kim.

All day, Jeff had been acting particularly nice to Ellen, his way of apologizing since he was incapable of ever saying "I'm sorry." Here he seemed more handsome than ever before, lit with a kind of radiance, concerned about the other members of the group, determined that they all have a good time. It was good to see him relaxed, not hustling an account. She wished this image could wipe out all of the negative ones.

Every night was spent with the EL'ers except one. Jeff and Ellen left the group for a private dinner in a little village near Matsuyama, a village of lacquermakers. Although fourteen years had passed since VJ-Day, there were still no street lights, no paved roads, no indoor plumbing. The limousine stopped outside the little village and they walked into it because the village roads were not wide enough for cars.

Jeff led her to a flimsy house which was occupied by the

family of a child whose life Jeff had saved during the occupation. Bending to keep his head from hitting the ceilings and low staircase beams, Jeff led her into the two-story house where the parents, still grateful to the embarrassed Jeff, bowed their heads to the floor in greeting.

His return to this town constituted a big news event. The newspapers were filled with the story and his picture, and everyone in the town wanted to pay homage to him. The child's family had prepared dinner for them on the open roof and the girl, now grown, waited on them herself but did not eat. The other members of the family, too, only watched.

"Why aren't they eating with us?" Ellen asked.

"Probably can't afford to," Jeff said. Their hosts brought in dish after exquisite dish; fishcakes arranged in a seascape, prawns large as small trout, vegetables cut like flowers, varied *sushi*, rolls of seaweed-wrapped rice filled with delicacies such as quail eggs.

"Can't we share?" Ellen asked uncomfortably.

"Of course not. They'd lose face. Look around you discreetly." All about them, hanging from trees and windows, squatting on adjacent rooftops, were villagers, watching them eat, as somberly attentive as if they were watching a coronation. "Eat," Jeff said, "and smile. Show that this is the best food you've ever eaten."

"Actually," Ellen said, "it is."

They ate course after course, forcing it down long after they were full. Night had fallen by the time they finished and when they went down to the street, their path to the car was lit by dozens of torches carried by singing townspeople.

How incredible that they were our enemies, Ellen thought, as all said a tearful farewell. Again, the parents and the girl prostrated themselves in the dust. Ellen felt tears running down her face. She and Jeff held hands in the limousine and she felt a thrill of renewal, as if somehow their marriage had been consecrated again by what they had shared in this country.

The next day they moved on to Hakone, where they could see Mount Fuji from the hotel balcony. Ellen was moved by the reverence of the local farmers for the majestic sight. They would stop in the midst of their labors just to contemplate the mountain.

"The Japanese have a particularly intense reverence for nature," Jeff explained to the group, "because they have so little land. Their crowded condition was probably the major reason for invading China—*Lebensraum*—the need for land. Notice how the terraced farms run right out to the highways, with not an inch wasted."

"You're really brilliant, Jeff," Candace caroled in her high voice.

At night, the hushed group stood on a balcony and watched the fabled mountain, glowing ghostly white. When the wisps of cloud floated across it, strange facelike shadows seemed to form.

All of the group with the exception of Kate and Myra were going to climb Mount Fuji the next day but Ellen awakened with a bad cold and sore throat, and Jeff advised her not to try it if she did not feel completely well. Disappointed, Ellen watched them leave without her.

Then she returned to the Japanese-style floor mats, which were surprisingly comfortable, and fell asleep again. She thought, at first, that rain was awakening her, until she sorted out the sound and realized that a light tapping was coming from her door. Her watch said almost noon, so she threw on a robe and opened the door.

A frightened young desk clerk stood there and in jerky pantomime conveyed a swollen stomach that could belong only to Myra. Ellen followed the clerk to Myra's room, where a Japanese doctor was already in attendance, preparing to move the expectant mother to the hospital over the mountain. Ellen knelt beside Myra and smoothed her damp bangs off her forehead.

"I never dreamed I'd go into labor early," Myra wept. "I feel like such a fool, a headstrong fool. I should never have come. Please don't leave me."

"I'll get dressed and go with you in the ambulance," Ellen said.

"Five minutes," she told the ambulance attendant. Then she knocked on Kate's door to tell her what was happening. Kate came to the door, looking wan and yellow.

"Do you want me to go with you?" she asked.

"No, it would be better for you to stay here," Ellen said. "Just send Leonard along as soon as they get back. You look as if you could benefit from a day in bed. You take care of yourself and I'll worry about Myra."

She dressed and got in back of the ambulance beside Myra, who looked bad, kind of blue, but the attendant had sedated her and she seemed to be sleeping comfortably.

"Used to be American hospital after war," the driver told Ellen. "Now fine Japanese hospital. Western equipment. Not worry."

As soon as they got to the hospital, Myra was whisked away and Ellen sat in the lobby reading one of the paperback books she automatically carried in every purse. But after two hours, she found it harder and harder to read. Her body ached and she could find no comfortable position on the hard, waiting-room bench. Thinking back fondly to Jennifer's birth and to the comforting presence of Jeff and even her mother, she hoped Myra wasn't frightened by the strangeness. After all, having a baby should be a fairly standardized procedure throughout the world.

A nurse came and brought her green tea and some rice. When she asked about Myra the nurse bobbed and simpered and smiled but didn't say anything so Ellen realized she couldn't speak English. She kept expecting Leonard to appear, and the time passed slowly.

Finally, just before 6:00 P.M., the little nurse walked briskly into the waiting room and beckoned to Ellen to follow. Ellen was thrilled at the idea that she would be seeing a new baby. They walked through several sets of swinging doors to the end of a long corridor where the nurse courteously held the door and Ellen was shown into a spare, white-walled office, furnished with a desk and two chairs.

It was a Spartan room without a diploma, a picture, or any

comforts, a room as bare as a cell. After several moments, the doctor entered. To her surprise he was Indian—very short, very dark. Extending his hand formally to Ellen, he said with a surprising Oxford accent, "I am Dr. Chatterjee."

"How do you do," Ellen said. "How is Mrs. Benson? How is the baby?"

"Mrs. Benson is fine," he answered. "The baby is a female." The words were all right. Why did they sound so foreboding to her? The doctor's face, although it strove to be impassive, was not pleased.

"Your name, please."

"Mrs. Ellen Sheldon."

"You are a relative? A sister perhaps?"

"No, just a friend."

"And Mr. Benson?"

"He is on the way," Ellen said. "I'm sure he will be here soon."

"Mrs. Sheldon, your friend Mrs. Benson, was she in or near Hiroshima?"

"No," Ellen said. "That wasn't on our itinerary."

"I do not mean on this trip. I mean during the war. Was she in Japan?"

"No," Ellen said. Her heart contracted anxiously, like a bird trapped in her chest. "My husband is the only one in our group who has ever been in Japan before. Why do you ask?"

Something was definitely wrong. "Why do you ask?" Ellen repeated.

Dr. Chatterjee rose. "Will you please for to come with me?"

He led her to a familiar glass-windowed nursery. One crib was closer to the windows than the others. A nurse looked out at them through the window. Her face was anguished. The doctor nodded to her and she walked to the crib. She picked up the tiny baby within and held it so they could see it clearly. Ellen looked intently at the tiny baby. Then, "Oh, my God," she whispered, closing her eyes.

"Are you fainting?" the doctor asked her.

Perspiration covered her. "No, no, I'm all right. Don't worry. I won't faint."

She turned her horrified face back to the baby. The newborn child had no arms or legs. Its appendages ended in flipperlike stumps. Ellen fought against nausea.

"How could this have happened?" she asked in a horrified whisper.

"We have seen such children born to survivors of Hiroshima," the doctor said; "that is why I asked about your friend. The child will not survive. Its internal organs are deformed as well; an incomplete digestive system."

The nurse replaced the baby in its crib, keeping her eyes averted. There was something unholy about the poor deformed infant whose unfinished limbs seemed to recapitulate a transitional evolutionary moment.

Dr. Chatterjee led her back to his office where she sank weakly into the chair.

"She was not in Hiroshima, not exposed to radiation?"

Ellen again shook her head, no.

"Was she under medication of any kind?"

Ellen thought about it. A dim memory of things Myra had said on the plane. What was it? "I think she was taking some kind of tranquilizer," Ellen said. "European, I believe. I have her purse here. I think it would be all right if we looked."

She opened Myra's exquisite Mark Cross purse which Myra had asked her to hold. Inside: lacy handkerchief, alligator wallet, atomizer of Joy perfume, comb in an alligator case, a few lipsticks, a solid gold compact, and two bottles of pills. She handed them to the doctor, who held them up to the light.

"The first," he said, "is merely a mild barbituate." Then he looked at the second bottle.

"Thalidomide," he said. "I am not familiar with this. Issued in West Germany. Thalidomide. Do you know what it is?"

Ellen shook her head. "I will keep these bottles for testing for the moment, if you have no objections," he said.

"May I see Mrs. Benson now?" she asked.

278

"I would not say anything about the baby," he cautioned.

"No, no, of course not," Ellen answered.

She followed him down the hall, past the nursery, where she turned her head away from the glass window behind which the horror lay, down a corridor, and then into a gloomy room where Myra was sleeping. Ellen was pleased that Myra slept, so she wouldn't have to say anything. Two nurses were in there, speaking Japanese. They kept their eyes on the floor, avoiding Ellen's glances.

The room seemed to reek with fear or superstition, with a fear that had gone beyond the rational to a kind of primeval terror. It was the shock of this unexpected, twisted historical visitation, the emergence of a freak from the petite, slender, rich American, whose husband was nowhere in sight.

Ellen sat beside the bed, waiting anxiously for Leonard and Jeff to get there. Myra looked so pale, so childlike sleeping there. Ellen dozed, thinking of Jennifer, remembering the moment the baby was brought to her, so tiny, so pink, fragrant as a flower. Myra would not have the joy of that first moment with this baby. Thank God she had others. What would they do? Would they show her the changeling? Well, Leonard would have to make that decision. Ellen hoped the baby would die before Leonard got there, to make things easier for both of the parents. Sitting in the chair there, beside Myra's bed, Ellen wept with terrible nostalgia, as if no pure, fragrant children would ever be born again, as if what had been done at Hiroshima had unleashed a horror for future babies that would touch them all.

When she opened her eyes, Jeff and Leonard stood there. She ran to Jeff and he put his arms around her. "I'm proud of you," he told her. Then he led her outside so Leonard could be alone with his wife.

"The baby just died," Jeff told her.

"Thank God," she said.

The next day, a sober group left for New York. Not even EL power and money could avert catastrophe. Nobody wanted to think about that. The Bensons had stayed behind in Japan, waiting for Myra to feel well enough to travel. No one discussed the birth of the freak, not even Tina. It was the same kind of primitive, superstitious avoidance that people had shown toward the Hiroshima victims. Throughout the trip home, husbands and wives sat together, speaking in hushed whispers and when they reached the airport they made their hurried goodbyes. It would be a while before they could meet each other's eyes and admit that horror could descend even on them unexpectedly and make havoc of their life plans.

When Jeff and Ellen finally arrived home, it was with great relief. Order was once more in their lives. The house was immaculate, more beautiful even than they had remembered. A service had waxed the magnificent old hardwood floors, gently laundered the Oriental rugs, waxed the wood-paneled walls, cleaned the cut-glass Baccarat chandeliers, polished the delft tiles in the kitchen, and made the house look as pristine as if no one lived in it.

Only Ursula was there to greet them since Jennifer was at camp in Maine. But Jeff and Ellen had plans to drive there to see her that weekend. They left early Friday morning and drove in silence. Ellen, who was driving, tried to make conversation, but Jeff was in one of his moods.

"I keep thinking about the Benson baby," Ellen said.

"Rotten shame," he agreed. "I have work to do."

He pulled out his briefcase, his little black book in which he incessantly made notes, a portable file, and he went to work. She drove until dinnertime, when they stopped at a charming old Maine lobster restaurant where they ate five-pounders, blueberry muffins, corn on the cob, and blueberry pie with homemade ice cream.

"Now I know we're home," Ellen joked.

"We'll stay at the first motel that has a vacancy," Jeff said. One hour later, they looked at each other with mounting irritation and dismay. Not a room to be found anywhere. Jeff squared his jaw. It seemed incredible to him that if he were able to pay for any room, he still could not get one. "We're going to the police station," he said.

The Yankee police were polite but unimpressed with Jeff and the Cadillac. Jeff was sure they could find him a room and he held out one of his crisp twenty-dollar bills. It didn't help. People just didn't do things that big city way around there. No matter what he paid, there was no way he could get anybody else's reservation. And there was no room in the jail. Only one cell there and it was in use. Ellen could see how furious he was and prayed that he would control his anger.

"I'll call up to the hospital for you," the policeman told them. They waited while he lazily talked to someone at the hospital about family and mutual friends. Finally, he asked about a room and told them, "You can have a room. Just pray no emergency cases come in during the night. They'll wake you at six tomorrow morning, same as other patients. Give you breakfast and charge you the usual rate."

They found the hospital and a pleasant receptionist signed them in and took them up to a standard, sterile, functional semiprivate room with two beds and a small bathroom. "It's so cold in here," Ellen whispered, "it reminds me of my operation and of sitting there in Japan with Myra. I hate hospitals. They give me the creeps, Jeff."

A nurse brought them apple juice and Saltines. Silently, they undressed and got into the cold, separate hospital beds. He fell asleep instantly but she got out of her bed after hours of sleeplessness and squeezed in beside him, grateful for the warmth. I still need him, Ellen thought to herself, before she fell asleep.

They left after breakfast and made for Jennifer's camp. Some early risers were meandering around the camp like little ghosts in the early morning mists. No one was in the camp office but one of the children told them she'd find the director. "I think Jennifer's feeding the goats," the girl said. Jeff's reaction was unpleasant.

"This place is a shithouse," he said irritably, looking about.

"How did you find it? Who recommended it?"

"The Mozers," she answered nervously. "All the kids in their family, their nephews and nieces go here. They said it was individualized, child-centered . . . really cared about self-actualization."

"It's too bad they don't care about neatness," he said contemptuously. "This place is a pigsty, just like the Mozers' house. Why does a child-centered place have to be so sloppy?"

She followed his gaze to a large living room next to the camp office in which a few children played. Books, coloring books, parts of toys, pieces of puzzles, and maimed dolls littered the floor. Next to a crumpled tricycle was a popcorn-covered coffee table. The whole place presented the impression of intense disorder. Ellen didn't dare to explain further to him that self-expression was considered more important here than rules and repression. An advantage of this camp was that kids *could* be messy, but she had to admit to herself that the messiness was somewhat disturbing. It seemed more like an orphanage than an expensive private camp which accepted new children only through recommendations.

Another camper came along and offered to take Ellen and Jeff to find Jennifer. Disapprovingly, they followed the child, who looked as if he hadn't washed since camp began. When they reached the herd of goats they saw a fat, ragged girl sitting on a rock nearby. "Is that Jennifer?" Ellen whispered, shocked at the girl's appearance. Her hair was matted with leaves and burrs, the filthy laces on her sneakers were untied, and she was biting her nails. "I'm afraid it is," Jeff said in disgust.

"Jennifer," Ellen called, ran to her, kneeled down in front of her, and grabbed her child in her arms.

"Mommy," Jennifer screamed. She threw her arms around Ellen and grabbed her so tight that they lost their balance and rolled over in the dirt together, kissing and hugging. They cried and hugged and hugged and cried, and finally disentangled themselves from each other. Jeff, perfectly neat, impeccably dressed, watched disapprovingly.

282

"Daddy," Jennifer cried, reaching out her arms to him.

"No, you don't," he snapped. "You're filthy. What's that all over your mouth? Impetigo or strawberry jam? Don't you ever wash? My God, you're seven years old. You're supposed to know how to brush your hair and tie your shoelaces. I want to see your counselor. Where is she?"

"In the bunk," Jennifer faltered, putting down her arms.

"Some greeting," Ellen snapped, "after a month's absence."

"Lead us to your bunk," Jeff said grimly. "We're going to see about this. Fifteen hundred dollars to have you look neglected? Not on your life."

Jennifer walked ahead holding Ellen's hand while Jeff followed in fury. The bunk was also a shambles.

"What's that smell?" Jeff asked.

"It's the toilet, Daddy," Jennifer said. "It's all stuffed up, doesn't flush. That's what you smell."

"Oh, wonderful, wonderful," he said.

The beds were unmade and possessions dotted the bunk. Piles of clothes had been dropped on the floors and flies clustered around empty soda bottles in the waste basket. In one bed, still asleep, lay a teenage girl.

"Get out of that bed," Jeff roared, in a voice like doom. Bewildered, terrified, the girl sat up, clutching the blanket against her.

"What is the meaning of this pigsty?" Jeff thundered. Shocked, her teeth chattering, the girl said nothing.

Jennifer threw herself on the bed and put her arms around the girl. "Don't yell at her," she said, "this is Marylou, the junior counselor. It's her day off. She's allowed to sleep."

"Not while I'm here," Jeff scolded. "Marylou, you get up and get busy. I want Jennifer's possessions packed carefully and I want her dressed and cleaned up in one hour. We're taking her home with us today."

Jennifer started to wail. "I don't want to go home. I love it here. Camp isn't over yet. Why do I have to go home?"

"Because I say so," Jeff said. "Now shut up and get ready,

I'm going to see the camp owner. You come with me, Ellen."

"Get moving, both of you," he said to Jennifer and Mary-lou, as he and Ellen walked out.

"I should have known better than to let you handle anything," he said as they walked back to the main building. "You're totally incompetent. Look at the way Ursula had the house looking when we got home. You would be incapable of having a house that clean or orderly. And now this camp! Why didn't you ask Marilyn where she sent their kids. You can be sure Amos's kids wouldn't go to a place that lets them look this dirty."

"She loves it here," Ellen pleaded.

"Then she's as stupid as you," he snarled.

They returned to the office of Mrs. Gresham, the director, a round, dumpy, unprepossessing middle-aged woman whose gray hair was up in a bun. She wore old jeans and a faded T-shirt and sneakers. Jeff's eyes flicked across her the way Amos's eyes had flicked across Ellen and dismissed her that first night of the EL installation.

"May I offer you some herb tea?" she asked kindly.

"We don't have time for tea," Jeff said. "I want to talk to you."

"I'd like some tea," Ellen defied him. She drank the tea while Jeff paced about like a raging animal.

"You seem perturbed, Mr. Sheldon," Mrs. Gresham said in an understatement that was almost funny to Ellen. "Is there some problem?"

"You bet your sweet life there is, and it starts right with the fact that you don't *know* there's a problem," Jeff raged. "The problem is that this camp is one big shithouse. There's no supervision, the kids are filthy and ragged, the toilet in the bunk is stuffed up, there are piles of dirty clothes all over the bunk floor, the junior counselor was asleep, and no other counselor was in sight."

"I can see how it looks to you, Mr. Sheldon," Mrs. Gresham

said, trying to neutralize his anger. "But let me try to explain. I must remind you that it is only 8:30 A.M. on a Saturday. Saturday mornings we usually sleep a little later, then spend the rest of the morning cleaning. But the camp is so well protected, so safe, that we don't mind if early risers wander around. We also have flexible meal times so they can eat earlier if they wish, then go out to pick blueberries or feed the goats.

"On Saturdays, after the bunks are cleaned, everyone's hair is washed and dried in the sun. As for the toilet, it's hard to get plumbers here but one is coming this morning to look at the toilet. It's only been stuffed up since yesterday. That kind of thing is unavoidable, much as we regret it. Little children throw all kinds of things down the toilet.

"Laundry service also comes on Saturday mornings so the piles of clothing you saw are probably waiting to be listed and put into laundry bags. By lunchtime today, you will see a totally different place and you'll just love lunch here. We grow all our own vegetables and serve local fish. Jennifer's group made blueberry cobbler yesterday, which we're serving for dessert today."

"That sounds delicious," Ellen said, sipping her herb tea.

"We won't be here for lunch," Jeff said, "and neither will Jennifer. We're leaving just as soon as we can get Jennifer cleaned up and packed."

"Do you think that's wise?" Mrs. Gresham asked in that same mild, unruffled voice. Ellen admired her control. It was probably essential for the owner of a children's camp.

"Don't worry," he said nastily, "I won't ask you to reimburse me for the rest of August."

"I assure you, Mr. Sheldon," she said, still calm, "I wasn't thinking of the money. I'm just wondering if this is wise for Jennifer. You know, she is a child with many problems and it's taken her a month to adjust, to come out of herself, to laugh and play and not worry about her appearance. It would be a shame to stop her progress so precipitously."

"What kind of problems?" Ellen asked, suddenly frightened.

285

"I'm not interested in her problems," Jeff said rudely. "The only problem I can see is that for my fifteen hundred dollars she looks like a filthy, fat, diseased gypsy. Now it's a long trip home and I'd like to get underway immediately. If it isn't too much trouble, in exchange for my not suing for a refund, would you zip down to her bunk and help her counselor get her ready?"

"Of course," Mrs. Gresham said. "I'm very fond of Jennifer. I couldn't let her go without speaking to her."

"Jeff," Ellen said, "maybe we should reconsider. I mean, let's at least ask Jennifer what *she* wants."

"Get her," he snapped. "I'll be in the car." He stormed out, letting the screen door slam behind him.

"I'm terribly sorry," Ellen said, close to tears, "Jeff doesn't really mean to sound rude. I think he's tired." And she told Mrs. Gresham the story of sleeping in the hospital, trying to make it responsible for Jeff's behavior.

"We all have our off moments, don't we?" Mrs. Gresham murmured kindly.

"Please," Ellen whispered, "before we go. What did you mean about Jennifer's problems?"

"When she arrived," Mrs. Gresham told her, "she didn't relate well to other children. She was a frightened child, compulsive about her possessions, about cleanliness, about performing just right. She was given to certain rituals. At the beginning of the summer she had to go through a ritual before she would go to sleep at night. It was unvarying. On one side of the top of her trunk, she would arrange her dolls, always in the same order: one, two, three, four. Then she would arrange her books on the other side. They had to be perfectly symmetrical, not extending even one inch out over another.

"Then her pillow had to be in the exact center, with the same bed margin on either side. The shutters behind her bed had to be a certain way, slanted just to an exact angle, or she couldn't sleep. If she was interrupted in the middle of her routine, she couldn't just pick it up again. She would have to start all over, from the very beginning.

"She had a terror of getting messy. She wouldn't play or dig or work with clay. She would sit, instead, perfectly neat, all by herself. If Jennifer looks messy now, it's an accomplishment."

Mrs. Gresham suddenly had tears in the corners of her eyes. She quickly brushed them away and walked with Ellen to Jennifer's bunk.

"Mrs. G.," Jennifer squealed with delight, when they entered. She threw her arms around the woman, who picked her up and hugged her, despite her weight.

"They want to take me home," Jennifer complained. "But I want to stay with you. Do I have to go, Mrs. G.?"

"Yes, you do," Mrs. Gresham said, holding her. "I've been lucky enough to have you all this past month. Now it's your parents' turn. I know how much they must have missed you."

"That's a lie," Jennifer scowled. "They don't miss me. They're never home. They leave me with that Ursula and I hate her."

"They do miss and love you, or they wouldn't have driven so far to get you," Mrs. Gresham told her. Then she made a funny story out of their previous night at the hospital. Gradually, she made Jennifer accept the idea of leaving.

"Can I come back next summer?" she begged.

"Of course, Jenny, dear," Mrs. Gresham said. "I promise you that if your parents want you to come, I'll make room for you. I'll always have a place for you."

"I love you," Jennifer said.

"I love you, too," Mrs. Gresham said, looking as if she were about to cry.

Jennifer ran around saying goodbye to her friends, while Jeff honked impatiently. Then, unable to delay further, they were in the car, on their way home.

"Is Ursula still there?" Jennifer asked.

"You bet your sweet life she is," Jeff answered.

"I hate her," Jennifer said. "All she ever does is clean, clean, clean. I don't want to go home to Ursula. I want to stay at camp and be messy."

She started to cry noisily so Jeff turned the music up loud and finally the girl stopped crying and fell asleep across the back seat.

"If Ursula doesn't shape up that kid," Jeff said angrily, "I'll fire her."

"You should fire her anyway," Ellen said. "I don't like her and Jennifer hates her."

He didn't answer. Ellen sat there despising herself for her weakness. Jeff had been totally wrong. Jennifer had been happy at camp, was making progress, and it was absolutely wrong to pull her out that way. A bad shock for the child. But Ellen had stood by and let it happen. She'd been weak and passive and she was disgusted. "I swear," she told herself, "I swear that no matter what happens in the future, I will never again stand by and let something I think is wrong happen, not to Jennifer and not to anyone else." Something had happened to Ellen as well as to Jennifer. This was the final emotional rupture. Jeff could never find his way back to her again.

8

Despite Ellen's resolve, nothing changed. After their return home, life seemed to revert to its previous pattern. In the fall Jennifer entered the second grade. Ellen gave up the notion of going back to school and spent a lot of time reading. When Will called to tell her Kate would have her operation, it was the first time Ellen felt some energy. It seemed natural to ask if she could go to the hospital with them. The doctors removed one breast but the prognosis for the future looked good for Kate. "Why, they tell me women can live long, healthy, pain-free lives after an operation of this sort," Will told Ellen. "No reason at all to worry about it spreading." When Kate returned to their Fifth Avenue mansion from the hospital, Ellen visited her every day, chatting with her, reading to her, helping her with a few phone calls and letters, even staying over in one of the many guest rooms, from time to time.

Sometimes she thought how strange it was that this awe-inspiring mansion should have become so accessible to her. She hardly noticed its grandeur anymore. "You're my best friend outside of Will," Kate told her fondly. "I'm lucky to have you."

"You're seeing an awful lot of them, aren't you?" Tina asked one day when she phoned, not jealous, just curious. "Don't you find them terribly dull?"

"No," Ellen told her, "I'm terribly dull."

By the end of September, Kate was ready to return to work and she became as busy as before, leaving Ellen with too much spare time. With nothing to do, Ellen went back to her routine of reading and sitting home all day. She was always depressed and even Tina couldn't get her out. When she called her to have lunch or go shopping, Ellen refused. Life seemed increasingly dull and pointless. But one day Tina called with especially exciting news.

"Guess what?" she said. "All of the EL'ers are invited to celebrate New Year's Eve at Gabe and Laura Pine's plantation in Honduras. He's going to fly us down in his private plane. And listen, we're going from his own landing strip in Locust Valley so we'll also get to see his house there."

"Do you think I could take Jennifer?"

"Are you kidding? Of course not. What do you want to take a kid for, Ellen? It's terribly square. She would have nothing to do and she would inhibit everybody. She can come and spend New Year's Eve here with Jacques, if you like."

"I'll ask her," Ellen said, doubting that Jennifer would go.

"Jeff has certainly put Gabe on the map with that banana business," Tina said. "It's a good thing his Spanish is so good. I'll never forget how offended Heidi got when Gabe told her to shut up. Listen, I don't think he was the only one who wanted her to shut up. Word has it that Samson is going mad with boredom with his 'Petite.' What fools men are. What did he ever see in her in the first place? I give that marriage six months more. He would have been better off staying with Valerie. She has a new tennis instructor boyfriend and her crewelwork business is thriving. It worked out fine for her."

Ellen was most reluctant to leave Jennifer over the holidays but Jeff was adamant. And he would not go without Ellen.

"We have to go away over the New Year's Eve weekend," Ellen told Jennifer, "but we'll be here with you for Christmas and you can spend New Year's Eve with Jacques or go down to Florida to visit Grandma. Next Saturday we can buy out F.A.O. Schwarz."

"I'll visit one of my friends," Jennifer sighed. She had long since abandoned begging to be taken along.

The group met Gabe at his home in Locust Valley. To Ellen's delight, Kate was well enough to come. Nobody other than Ellen knew why Kate had been in the hospital. Heidi and Candace, both of them swathed in sable, were there with their husbands, as were Myra and Leonard Benson. Leonard had, unaccountably, taken his public relations to another company and Myra, looking brittle, thin, and haunted, stayed far away from Ellen.

"I think they resent the fact that we know exactly what happened in Hakone," Jeff said. "I don't mind losing their account. I've long since replaced it with Japanese accounts I got after my lecture at the trade association and Gabe's account is taking up most of my time. Thank God I know Spanish."

Tina had had an eye-lift operation and she looked beautiful as ever; young, firm, trim, exquisitely dressed. Harry, silent as usual, walked by her side, saying nothing while she chattered away vividly.

Jeff was overwhelmed by the Locust Valley estate. "His own landing strip," Jeff agonized. "This place makes our house look like a shack. The guy must have a couple of hundred acres. His own landing strip and did you see the size of the pool? An exact copy of Hearst's pool at San Simeon. And did you see the indoor pool, the tennis courts, and squash courts! It's like a hotel."

She could see the wheels churning behind Jeff's eyes and she looked away from him.

The plane took off to a round of popping champagne corks and everyone was pleasantly mellow by the time they landed on the field at the Pines' estate in the lush Central American country. The house was romantic and magnificent; with its balconies and white columns it looked like a misplaced southern plantation. "Tara," Tina joked.

Servants showed the group to their rooms, each one high-ceilinged, with large, screened lanais and graceful, scrolled furniture. Dressed in dinner gowns and jackets, the group filed in to a formal dinner in a room lit with hundreds of candles. Dozens of black servants waited on them and Ellen felt dreamy, thrown back to a costume drama in another century. After dinner, they moved from the dining room into a large ballroom set up like a cabaret. Small tables ringed a large central area for dancing. There was a raised platform for the small calypso band and a second platform in the center of the dance floor.

A flourish of drums and a hand-held spotlight focused on the second platform where a black man and two women, all dressed in brightly colored calypso clothes, stood posed, waiting to begin.

"Oh, God," Tina said, "local entertainment. How dull. I'd rather dance."

Another flourish of drums and the entertainment started. While the beautiful guests, dressed in their couturier clothes, watched with gradually mounting interest, the three began to gyrate wildly to the music. Slowly they divested themselves of the gaily colored calypso clothes. The pounding drums seemed to hypnotize the entertainers and the audience as well. Finally, the three of them stood there naked and the audience applauded the perfection of their glistening bodies.

Ellen thought that was the end of the show but, instead, that was when the performance began. She watched in shock. One of the women knelt down in front of the man and sucked and sucked his black penis until it was erect. It looked like the largest penis in the world and an ecstatic, admiring gasp swept through the audience like a passionate, unconscious sigh.

"I can't believe what I'm seeing," Ellen said to Jeff. "I think it's disgusting."

"Shut up," he said.

Ellen looked around at the others but she was the only one whose eyes were not riveted on the performers. Couples moved close together, gripping hands tightly, the way people do when watching spectacles of overwhelming excitement. Ellen gripped her own hands tightly in her lap. She didn't want to watch, was appalled at being in this congregation, and yet she shared the same breathless fascination they seemed to be feeling. Feeling difficulty breathing, Ellen turned her eyes back to the performers.

The woman had finished sucking the enormous penis and now the man pushed her back on the floor, straddled her, and began to brush his penis rhythmically across her stomach, back and forth, back and forth, forth and back. The audience moved in unconscious rhythm with him.

Jeff reached for Ellen's hand and she let him take it. His palm was sweating.

The brushing seemed to last for an unbearable time until finally, unable to wait any longer, someone in the audience called out savagely, "Fuck her, fuck her," but still he waited. The woman writhed and strained, seemingly unable to wait any longer and suddenly, when the suspense seemed unendurable, the man pulled her legs apart fiercely and easily entered her wetness. And then a rhythm began again and Ellen could feel the audience trying to restrain itself.

Rhythmically, as in a dance, he moved in and out of her, in and out of her, the spotlight clearly illuminating the length of his glistening penis and the perspiration that dripped from him. He moved and moved and finally, with a scream, she arched in climax after climax. But still he did not come. Perspiration dripped from his face onto the body beneath him.

In her mind, Ellen saw and remembered the ecstasy of her one encounter with Lenny, reliving it here, at this moment. Each member of the audience seemed lost in a private remembered dream.

Suddenly, still not having come, he drew himself out and

rolled his partner over onto her belly. Fiercely, brutally, he held apart her buttocks and thrust himself hard, deep into her, and he thrust and he thrust and he thrust, a wild horse, a stallion in heat, and the woman's moans grew louder and louder, and finally, with a gigantic groan, the man came and the woman screamed and still he came and came and then, with a proud smile at the audience, he pulled himself out of her, rolled over onto his back, and rested.

Again, Ellen looked around. The audience was hypnotized. Lips parted, scarcely breathing, they watched the performers.

Then the other woman came forward, carrying a swathed parcel. She turned the first exhausted woman on her back again and, from the sheath, she drew an enormous dildo which she held aloft for the audience. She lowered it and, spreading the other woman's legs, began to thrust the dildo into the woman on the floor, in and out, in and out, wildly, savagely. When the woman on the floor did not respond, she took the dildo out and with another savage movement, quickly pushed it up inside herself. Playing with her clitoris with one hand, she moved the dildo back and forth inside herself with the other, faster and faster, faster and faster, until at last, with an eerie scream that made the audience's hair stand on end and skins prickle, she shuddered and writhed in orgasm after orgasm, screaming and screaming, unable to stop until finally her body shuddered to a halt.

My God, my pants are wet, Ellen thought in embarrassment. But the woman was not through. Now she leaned forward to the other woman, the one who had been unresponsive to the dildo and still lay there in exhaustion and, parting the lips of the woman's vulva so that her clitoris stood erect, she licked and sucked the clitoris until the woman on the floor began to again writhe in ecstasy. As she bent intently to her work, the man, now big again from watching them, approached her from the rear and thrust into her as she sucked. All three now moved in feverish rhythm, wilder and wilder, each pushing the others on, moving and licking and thrusting and touching until, with screams and

294

shudders that seemed to split the night, they came in an earth-shaking three-way orgasm. The drums beat furiously, the three picked up their clothes and stiffly crept off the floor and out of sight, and the spotlight dimmed.

The room was in total darkness. "My God," Jeff muttered to her, "I've never seen anything like that before."

"Didn't you just love it?" Tina whispered.

The lights went on, but dimly, so that nobody could be seen too clearly. The evening was obviously over. Couple by couple, they said goodnight, averting their eyes from each other, and went to their own rooms. The circus had been depraved, degrading, and immoral but extraordinarily exciting, even for Ellen. But her vague stirrings evaporated as she and Jeff walked to their room.

"God, those people are animals," he said.

"Which?" Ellen asked in annoyance at his spoiling her mood. "The ones who performed or the ones who watched?"

"Very funny," he said. "You know, Gabe really has a little paradise here. But I think he's worried. The natives are restless and unfortunately, Castro has shown them they can make a revolution and get away with it."

"I'll bet there are no circuses like this in Cuba now," she said.

"Nobody can afford them," he joked, "not anymore."

"You know it's not the cost," she said. "I mean they don't have them in Cuba because they're degrading. The people tonight probably only submitted to such degradation because they're so poor."

"There's that liberal bullshit again. What a bore you can be, Ellen. The people tonight probably did it because it's an easy way to make money. Maybe they did it because they like sex. I didn't see anybody holding a gun to their heads and one thing that couldn't be faked was that erection. But forget about that. That's not important. What is important is if Gabe gets kicked out of here, I'll lose his account. He contributed half a million to the last presidential campaign but I don't think that can help him here anymore. The natives are too restless and the U.S. probably won't interfere, damn it, and I'll lose the account."

"Well," she joked, "the natives may think there are more important problems than putting bananas in the refrigerator."

"Very funny," he said. "When we lose the account you won't think it's so funny. Come on, let's go to sleep." The evening's circus had been wasted on him.

The next morning, as the guests assembled on the patio for breakfast, the circus seemed to Ellen like a surrealistic dream. She sat down at a table with Kate and Will.

"How are you feeling?" Ellen asked.

"Fine," Kate said. "I went to sleep early last night and had a good night's sleep. I understand I missed some excitement. Tina's just been telling me all about it, thrust by thrust." She and Ellen laughed together.

"I'm delighted that we missed it," Will said. "We saw one years ago and once is enough. Eventually, all pornography is repetitious."

Kate decided to change the subject. "Did you register for spring semester yet?" she asked Ellen.

"No, I was busy," Ellen excused herself. "I have until February to do it."

"With the way you keep putting it off," Kate said, "I get the feeling that you really don't want to do it at all. Why don't you drop that idea and come and work with me, Ellen? I'd teach you everything there is to know about the knitwear business."

"Maybe I will come and work with you someday," Ellen said. "But you really don't need me. You're just trying to be a good friend and I really do want to get my B.A. before doing anything else. If I came into the city and worked for you, I'd never see Jennifer. That's important to me. I like to be there afternoons when she gets home from school."

"If you ever change your mind," Kate said, "you know you have a job waiting."

296

Tina came and sat beside them. "God, what a scene last night," she said. "Harry had his fingers up me under the table-cloth, during the whole thing. I held back and almost fell apart coming when we reached our room. Good thing those rooms have thick walls. Best time we've had in years. I'll bet lots of the guys came while they were watching. Did you notice how stiffly some of them were walking at the end, when they limped to their rooms?"

Ellen looked at Tina with amusement. Every nail was perfectly manicured, every toenail was perfectly pedicured to match. Every part of her body was pounded, smoothed, buffed, made-up, every lovely red hair was in place. She wore a green shantung breakfast dress with matching open sandals. This was Tina, exquisitely groomed, and foul-mouthed. A perfect upper-class lady!

After breakfast, the group went on a tour of Gabe's vast plantation.

"What a building job I could do here," Amos boomed.

Ellen felt terribly uncomfortable as they drove, dressed in all of their magnificence, amid the ragged pickers. She felt a bond with the laborers, hypocritical as that might seem. Spiritually, she would always be with the pickers, with the have-nots. But by now she'd learned to completely repress any expression of these feelings.

The rest of the afternoon was spent in swimming, card playing, drinking, and talking. Dinner the second night was a South American version of a luau, with a whole pig roasted in the ground and people dressed in festive but informal clothes. Ellen had been drinking champagne all afternoon and she was feeling pleasantly relaxed as they dug in. She had wanted to taste a whole roast pig ever since high school when they had read Charles Lamb's "A Dissertation on Roast Pig" in a class in which not one of the students would dare to eat nonkosher meat. But now she could. Now she could eat or do or buy anything she wanted. The steel band played a gentle background accompaniment and the air was balmy and sweet-scented.

Suddenly, with a squeal of breaks, three cars, filled with men in uniform, hurtled to a halt in the circular driveway in front of the plantation. Gabe walked over to the men and all began to talk and gesticulate noisily and frantically. A hush fell. Laura walked across the lawn to Gabe and the men, listened to them for a few moments, then began to weep and wring her hands in agitation.

Several of Gabe's vice-presidents, who lived in houses near the plantation, ran over and joined the circle and soon became as agitated as Laura. Only Gabe remained calm; a dark-haired, short, round little man, whose poise indicated his unquestioned leadership. He snapped his fingers and servants brought drinks for the uniformed men. They drank them quickly, returned to their cars, the motors were kept running, and they waited.

Gabe walked over to the musicians and dismissed them. Then he turned to the guests, sitting there in complete silence, anxiously waiting to find out was was wrong.

"Dear guests," he said in a firm, calm voice, "it appears that our local guerrilla chieftain has advanced a good deal further than we had ever thought possible. We probably underestimated his ability. So my good friends in the cars here have come to suggest that it might be in the best interests of your comfort and safety to depart immediately. There is nothing to worry about but we must be cautious."

The men had now come back out of the cars with machine guns, had their backs to Gabe's guests, and had fanned out to make a protective semicircle around them.

"Those machine guns don't reassure me," Tina said.

"Listen carefully, everyone," Gabe continued, "I must ask you to do the following. Go to your rooms, pack your things, and return to the plane as soon as possible. Do not panic, but remember please that we have a maximum of one half-hour to leave, no more, absolutely no more, according to the calculations of my friends here, if we wish to avoid a possibly unpleasant confrontation. Remember. Do not panic. Just pretend that you are watching a movie. Do not change your clothes, do not try to pack neatly. Just throw your things in your suitcases and return here. If you cannot fit something in, just leave it. I will reimburse you for everything you forget or cannot pack. Is that clear?

"It would be unwise to minimize the necessity for haste. Ten minutes after the dinner gong sounds, we will take off."

He pointed to a servant standing next to the dinner gong, which looked like the trademark of J. Arthur Rank films.

"Listen," Gabe said. "This is how it sounds."

The servant struck the gong, which echoed in the stillness like a shiver, chilling them in the hot tropical night.

"Remember," Gabe repeated. "Ten minutes after the gong sounds we will go. Those not at the plane must be left behind. You may then be stranded here indefinitely and I could not guarantee your safety. My friends here tell me that the airport is jammed with frantic refugees. Therefore, I am certain you understand the necessity for haste. Any questions? No? Then, for God's sake, run."

As they tossed their expensive possessions into the new Mark Cross suitcases, Ellen had a dreamlike feeling that this could not be happening. She sat on the suitcases to push them shut, while Jeff flicked the latches, and then they raced out together to the landing strip. Gabe read the names on his invitation list. Everyone was there. These captains of industry were nothing if not efficient.

Ellen could see Gabe's top employees getting on another plane. Then Gabe shook hands with the leader of the military men, the door of their plane slammed shut, and they roared off immediately. Gabe looked around, saw that every one of his guests was all right, and then mopped his face and sank back exhausted.

The Pines were seated right in front of Jeff and Ellen. Laura had burst into tears on takeoff and wept noisily while Gabe attempted to console her.

"The most beautiful house in the world," she wept. "Why should those damned guerrillas get it? Did they build it? No, we built it. My blood went into it. It's ours. It was like a part of my body and now it's gone. It's not fair. We didn't take it from anyone. Why couldn't they have let us alone. We never hurt anybody. We increased employment in that damned country and now you see the result. Those ungrateful people!"

"There, there," Gabe comforted her. "It's only temporary. We'll be back there soon. You know these baby revolutions blow over. We've lived through this kind of thing before."

"We'll never have the house again," she wept. "My astrologer predicted this. We'll never have it back. It's lost, gone, defiled, lost. Every inch of our beautiful work of art." She continued to weep and speak to those sitting around them.

"Five years to carve the front door. Dozens of workmen. Starving before we got there. Every floor, every piece of wood paneling, especially selected. Not a creak in the entire house. Part of me, my heart, my soul. One whole room filled with my clothes. What would those monkeys need designer clothes for? They've just learned to use toilet paper. *If* they've learned that much. All I could take were my jewels. The house meant more to me than my jewels. All that effort, for nothing. No one will ever know what we went through supervising those local workmen. Back in the Stone Age. Neanderthal. The most beautiful house in the world. Those bathrooms, onyx. Onyx bathrooms for filthy savages.

"The front staircase was planned so that our children could be married from that house. All the years they've been growing up I could see, in my mind, each bride and groom in turn walking down those stairs. We built it. We made it. We own it. Why should we have to give it up?"

Ellen really didn't feel sorry for Laura; after all, they had many mansions. Gabe was a very rich man, still president of a worldwide fruit empire.

"Look," she wanted to say to Laura, "Hitler made millions of refugees. Every day in some part of the world—Korea, China, Vietnam—there are refugees. You're not the only ones and you won't really suffer at all. You can rebuild and replace everything you lost and chances are you really will get your property back. You're going home to an estate in Locust Valley. Stop acting as if this is the world's greatest tragedy." But she would not dare to say such words to a client.

Jeff had been sweating slightly beside her, agonizing over the possible loss of the banana account.

"Go sit with Harry, Jeff," Tina said, coming over to them. "I want to talk to Ellen." She sank down and went into one of her familiar hot whispers.

"What a marvelous weekend," she whispered, "like being in a movie. What did you think of that black guy? Unbelievable, wasn't he? I still feel excited at the thought of him. Best time I've had in years."

"Laura wouldn't agree," Ellen whispered back, motioning with her head to the seat in front of them where Laura sat weeping.

"Oh, pooh," Tina said. "The way she's carrying on. It's not such a catastrophe. If they lose the estate they'll have an unbelievable tax write-off. But Harry says they don't really have to worry. They'll be back in two weeks. There's no way the U.S. will let the guerrillas get another toehold in this hemisphere. After all, we know who's supplying their arms. Harry says it would be like having Russians in our backyard. He says if the U.S. can't interfere officially, big business has its own methods. There's no way they'll let that Communist puppet out. We own too much there. Harry says it will all blow over."

"Jeff doesn't think so," Ellen said, amused that a conversation between two somewhat intelligent women should consist of reporting their husband's ideas. "Jeff says their leader isn't just some ignorant peasant. He's a brilliant man, a lawyer, and an outstanding military strategist. Jeff says he's also getting expert advice from the Soviet Union in addition to arms. Jeff doesn't think it will ever blow over."

"Thank God we never opened any salons in these shaky countries," Tina said.

"A blessing." Ellen laughed. "But the situation may change

in the future. Revolutions come and revolutions go, but people will always need beauty parlors."

"You're being funny," Tina said, "but what you're saying is absolutely true. All any of these countries really want is American know-how, and staying beautiful is part of that."

Laura's noisy weeping interrupted them. "My only comfort," she cried, "is that Mr. Buttons is waiting for me at home. Thank God he wasn't with us. He's terribly sensitive."

"That's right, dear," Gabe answered, pleased that something had distracted her. "Mr. Buttons is waiting for you and he wouldn't like to see you cry.

"Many's the night she's sat up nursing that poodle," Gabe told the listeners.

"And I'd do it any time," Laura added. "You have to be ready to sacrifice for those you love."

"Oh, God," Tina moaned.

A short while afterward they reached Gabe's airstrip where cars were waiting to take them to their homes. Laura cried and kissed each of the guests goodbye and Gabe shook each hand soberly, warmly, thoughtfully, as if they were all British stiff-upper-lip aristocracy presiding over the retreat from India.

"It will all blow over in no time," Gabe cheerily told each guest, but his gloom and pessimism were evident behind his words.

Events seemed to happen quickly after that. They had been back from Central America less than a month when Jeff came home talkative for a change.

"Something's going on with Gabe," Jeff told Ellen. "He's gloomy, jumpy, uncommunicative. I went to his office and he just sat there smoking Havana cigars, not saying a word. He looked like he wanted to cry but didn't know how. I kept pulling out contracts and campaigns for him, but couldn't get him to sign anything. I think the guy's having some kind of breakdown.

"Today he kept me in his office all day without lunch while he carried on about the millions he had wasted on Batista, about the hundreds of thousands spent to overthrow a left-wing regime in Guatemala, and about the tremendous losses in Ecuador. The size of his payoffs alone was greater than the national budgets of those countries. One of his greatest worries is that the guerrillas will find the papers hidden under the house in his subterranean vault.

"It's our own U.S. government that the guy's really heart-broken about. He says the government let him down and I think he's right. It's a rotten shame."

One week later newspaper articles began to appear about the tremendous losses Gabe's company had undergone. The more articles that appeared, the more his stock plummeted. Finally, Jeff decided to write him off.

"The account's dead," Jeff said bitterly, "and I have no more time to waste. From now on, I'm not in to him anymore at the office and if he calls here, the answer is the same. I'm not in. He's under investigation by a congressional committee and one of my old buddies at the FBI tells me they can't save him. It's a shame but he's got to be the government's scapegoat."

That fact hit hard and Ellen told Tina about it the next day when they took Jennifer and Jacques to New York City to the Colonial Club for the children's weekly ballroom dancing class.

"Why does it upset you so much?" Tina asked. "You always thought he was an imperialist son of a bitch. Besides, it's nothing to worry about. He'll be investigated by a congressional committee, they'll slap his wrist, he'll cool it for a while, then business will go on as before. As far as I know, nobody has yet gone to jail for buying foreign governments."

"I know he's done terrible things," Ellen said, "and he should be punished. But it seems sad that everyone is deserting him."

"That's the way it is," Tina said. "That's the way it's always going to be."

"That's the way it shouldn't be," Ellen said.

"I see the world realistically," Tina said. "And I accept it."

"You wouldn't if it were you in the hot seat," Ellen said indignantly.

They watched the children for a while, looking so correct in their white gloves and regulation clothes, then went out to a nearby restaurant for coffee. On the way, they passed a newsstand where the afternoon papers had just been delivered. They both looked at the headlines and froze in horror. Plastered across the front page was a picture of Gabe Pine . . . a suicide. He had thrown his attaché case through a plateglass window in the twentieth-floor office and had gone through after it.

Ellen bought all the afternoon papers and they went into a little coffee shop to read them. Apparently, the congressional committee had received Gabe's buried papers which revealed to them the full extent of his bribery of governments so that his company could operate without hindrance. Unfortunately for Gabe, copies of his papers had also been given to the press. It appeared that Gabe had never paid income taxes on the money used for bribery.

"Wow," Tina said. "Buying foreign governments is one thing but not paying income taxes is another. They would have put him in jail for the rest of his life. Still, he was a fool to kill himself. He could have threatened to pull down three-quarters of Congress with him. Everybody knew what he was doing, and nobody blew the whistle. In a way, he was kind of a hero, a fighter against Communism. But this country is ungrateful and all those congressmen are so yellow."

"He's the second person I've known to commit suicide," Ellen said. "Davida was the first. It's so awful."

"It certainly is," Tina answered. "He was another idiot. He could have gone somewhere where there was no extradition and just waited things out."

"He must have been so frightened," Ellen sighed. "He was so cocky, so successful, so self-confident just a short time ago."

"But he lost his nerve," Tina said, "and I think that's unforgivable. He should just have disappeared for a while. He could have gone somewhere and written a book. The government would have overlooked that. He panicked."

"Well," Ellen sighed, "it's sad but I guess he's no great loss to society. It really isn't right to corrupt governments just for the sake of business."

"I can't think of any better reason," Tina said. "Anyway, everybody does it. He was just unlucky. There's not a big business in the U.S. that doesn't pay off these coffee-country governments."

Jeff's only concern was the account. "When I think of all the time I spent romancing that weakling," he said angrily, "I could kick myself. He was a weak *schmuck* to panic that way. He could have stonewalled, waited it out. He wasn't doing anything more crooked than what everybody else does for overseas investment."

"Should we go to the funeral?"

"What for?"

"Well, he was kind of a friend of yours. We did stay at his house."

"He was no friend. Strictly business, babes, and now that's over. No point in being photographed at the funeral. Might be bad publicity to be associated with him."

Ellen thought about Laura over the next few days and felt guilty about not calling her or going to the funeral until she opened the women's page of the *Times* a few weeks later and saw a picture of a big charity ball in Palm Beach. And there was Laura, resplendent in diamonds, carrying Mr. Buttons with her, looking as gay and well kept as the rest of the Palm Beach set. Apparently, she had survived. Poor Gabe, Ellen thought, remembering how sympathetic he had been to his wife on the plane. Then they both slipped from her thoughts.

The whole experience left Ellen depressed. Life seemed more hollow than ever. The registration deadline passed and she made up a dozen excuses why she again couldn't go back to school. She even talked to Tina about seeing Dr. Bloom to help her understand her apathy, why she couldn't seem to get started on what she wanted to do. Tina thought it would be a great idea for her to see Dr. Bloom and kept pushing her but this was another beginning Ellen resisted. And after a while, Tina told her wisely, "When the emptiness hurts enough, you'll go."

The next EL'er to fall from the solid gold circle was Michael Stewart. Ellen was sitting at breakfast with Jeff when he opened the *Times* and let out a moan. "Jesus Christ," he wailed, "another account."

Michael had been arrested and was out on bail for receiving pirated records and tapes for his vast record business. He claimed that an underling had bought them without checking the source and that he had not known they were counterfeit.

"Is he telling the truth?" Ellen asked.

"Of course not," Jeff said. "Don't be stupid."

His wife, Candace, the article continued, noted socialite, was quoted as saying, "There's been some terrible misunderstanding."

"Some misunderstanding." Jeff laughed wryly. "Her father's the underling in charge of purchasing and he's rarely sober. And his assistant is Candace's brother, another drunk incompetent. Between them, they've really fixed the poor bastard. Damn! I don't know how this will affect the account." He was sweating. "Call you later," he said, taking off for his office.

The phone rang as soon as Jeff had gone. It was Tina. "Isn't it simply marvelous," she panted. "Davida must be laughing like crazy in heaven, or wherever she is. You know both of the kids have left Michael and they're living on a commune out west somewhere. What could be crazier than that? Still, I guess they preferred it to living with the sugar stiletto. That Candace is a real killer, a barracuda. Harry says she probably planned the whole debacle to get Michael out of the way and get control of the business."

"Tina, that's ridiculous. People don't do things like that. You're fantasizing."

"There you go again," Tina said. "You still haven't grown up. People do things like that every day in business . . . especially if they're smart. Off to Dr. Bloom now. *Ciao!*"

"What do you still find to talk about?" Ellen teased.

"Oh, I'm endlessly fascinating," Tina answered. "Most of the time we talk about why I feel I still have to see him. What the hell. It's something to do."

Ellen sat there drinking her third cup of coffee feeling she would go mad with boredom. She had nothing to do. Jennifer was in school, the house was immaculate, it was too cold to horseback ride, she had seen most of the plays and movies in the city, seen every good art show, had nothing to shop for, and was totally trapped by her freedom. Her classes with Helen had ended and she saw Alain only once a week. Life was passing by and still she did nothing. She had never registered for courses, had never become pregnant again, had accomplished nothing with her life. How did some women seem to feel contentment with lives such as hers. She didn't know, but the emptiness and loneliness within were becoming unbearable.

She called Tina back. "Want to have lunch after your appointment?" she asked.

"Sorry, sweetie," Tina said, "but we're meeting a new investor after my appointment with Dr. Bloom. You can spend the day at Christopher's as my guest if you like or else call Dr. Bloom. I used to feel the emptiness you're feeling a lot before I started to see him. Now he keeps me feeling good. I couldn't live without him."

Ellen sat on the chair, her hand on the phone, and repressed a desire to scream or weep at the pain of loneliness. She could no longer bear it. It was too much for her. She picked up the phone and dialed Dr. Bloom before she had a chance to reconsider her actions. She was in luck. He had a cancellation and could fit her in if she'd make it by eleven. Oh, well! Why not? She took the hour. Seeing an analyst would, if nothing else, give her a focus for the day.

His office was in a quietly expensive building on Park Avenue and Sixty-seventh Street. It had the traditional waiting room: good magazines, leather couches, thick carpet, good paintings. But the walls bothered her. Dark green, gloomy, enveloping, they depressed her. She was ready to flee.

A distant door shut. There were different exits and entrances to avoid embarrassment, like a speakeasy or maybe a whorehouse. The doctor, an ordinary-looking man in his fifties, wearing a hearing aid and smoking a pipe, sat behind a desk making notes. She had always disliked pipes. They seemed like props for phony academics. The most inadequate professors at college had been the ones who puffed their pipes incessantly and hid behind the smoke. Funny, Tina had never mentioned to her that he wore a hearing aid. She imagined he turned it off lots of times when Tina was there.

"Have a seat, Ellen," he said. "I'll be right with you." She bristled. What gave doctors and cops who stopped you for speeding, the right to call you by your first name? Was she calling him by his first name? If she did, she would break up in laughter. His first name was Barrymore, Barry for short. Apparently his mother had worshiped John Barrymore. Barrymore Bloom! No wonder the kid had become an analyst. How could a mother saddle a kid with a name like that? There he sat now, grown-up Barrymore Bloom in his hearing aid, making his face look pontifical and wise. He sat there writing on her time, probably making notes on his last session, while she sat there bristling, unwillingly reduced to childhood status.

Angrily, she took a paperback book out of her purse and started to read. She looked up after a few minutes to find that he was watching her with a probing gaze. Flushing, she closed the book.

"Hiding behind your book?" he asked.

Hiding behind your pipe? she thought, not daring to say it. He sat there waiting with an all-forgiving smile until, in confusion, she said, "Sorry, didn't realize you were ready."

"That's perfectly all right." He smiled expansively. He forgave her and gave her his blessing. Round one to the doctor.

"Do you mind if I tape you?" he asked, turning it on.

She wanted to scream, I certainly do. But what she said was, "If you think best." Nearly nine years of marriage to Jeff had taught her to control her thoughts, her feelings, the words that came naturally to her. Why was she afraid to tell the doctor that she didn't want to be taped? Was she afraid that if she didn't give him exactly what he wanted, he'd turn her out?

"I'd prefer that you didn't tape me," she forced herself to whisper. Why was she whispering? Why was she worried about pleasing him? Wasn't she the one he was supposed to be pleasing? She was paying, she was the client. Jeff had always said the client is always right. Of course, Bloom had a reputation for being one of the best analysts in New York. Surely, someone with such a reputation must be a master at dealing with people, would not want to make her ill at ease. No, if she were acting and feeling this way, it must be her problem, not his.

"I'll be glad to turn the tape off this time," he said. "But I'm certain that if we continue to see each other you would not want to interfere with my procedures. Isn't that so?"

"Oh, of course, of course," she said, simultaneously apologizing and promising.

"Now suppose we start with your telling me exactly why you're here," he said.

"Has Tina told you anything about me?"

He looked pained, aggrieved, as if she had accused him of unethical behavior. She immediately apologized again. Round two for the doctor.

They talked for a while, then Ellen told him her most recent, remembered dream. She had just had all four of her wisdom teeth removed, a horrendous operation, and she was lying in bed in agony when Jeff came in. To her amazement, it was Jeff who had been the oral surgeon, Jeff who had pulled her four wisdom teeth. Now, right after the operation, he wanted to make love. Not wanting to offend him, for after all she needed his help to recover from the operation, she showed him that the Venetian blinds were raised and that it was daytime. Somebody might see them. He closed the blinds but said that even if people did see them, it would be acceptable because he was the doctor. Then, after the blinds were down, he reached for her and she mentioned her terrible pain and her concern lest the stitches be pulled out. To this complaint, he assured her that he wouldn't do anything not good for her, that the stitches wouldn't pull out, that he wouldn't hurt her in any way, that she should just lie back and relax because, after all, it was he who had done the operation and he wouldn't do anything to jeopardize his handiwork.

Dr. Bloom listened and made notes. "Aha," he said, when she had finished, "teeth and the fear of losing them is often a symbol that reflects fear of aging. Do you feel undue concern about growing old?"

"I never think about it at all," she said.

"Now, now, Ellen, I don't know if you really mean 'never.' Most people feel concern about growing old. You cannot set yourself apart from the rest of mankind. Every conscious human being worries about the aging process."

"Well," she said weakly, "maybe I worry about it on the subconscious level, but on the conscious level I never think about it. After all, I'm less than thirty years old."

"Ah, yes, but then again, there's the over-thirty syndrome. To some people, becoming thirty is more traumatic than becoming forty. There is no doubt but that thirty is a highly significant age. Difficult any longer to get away with being childlike. It is highly significant that it is only now, as you approach twenty-nine, that you've been impelled to seek out psychoanalytical help. No, you can't convince me that you're not concerned about losing your teeth, symbolically, of course."

"Well, maybe you're right," she sighed. "I'll have to think about it."

"That's better, my dear," he beamed. "Mustn't have a

closed mind. Growth is only possible through the development of distance from the self. Not let us talk further about your dream. How do you interpret it?"

"Jeff is pulling my wisdom teeth. I think that means he's making me stupid."

"Aha," he said. "That's a rather hostile interpretation, isn't it. Let me offer some other perceptions. When wisdom teeth become infected, they have to be pulled and patients are usually quite grateful to their oral surgeons for performing the operation. Is it possible that you are telling yourself in your dream that your husband is your doctor, your source of strength, the person who would take care of you in every situation? I'm sure you realize that the doctor is often viewed as a father figure."

"Well," she said, "I can understand what you're saying, but I don't think the Jeff figure was a positive one in the dream. After all, what normal beneficent doctor in his right mind would want to make love to a patient right after an operation? I mean, doesn't it show unbelievable insensitivity to the feelings and needs of the patient?"

"Only if that's how you choose to interpret it," he said. "The way I see it is that your subconscious is showing you that even when you're sick and ailing, bandaged and toothless, your husband will still take care of your physical needs, will still want to make love to you. Your subconscious is reminding you of how fortunate you are to have such a husband."

"No," she insisted, "I just can't see it that way. The dream had a negative feeling. It had a tone that was not favorable to Jeff. It wasn't a pleasant picture of a warm and loving and protecting man. It was a picture of a man who wanted to make love to me, to satisfy himself, regardless of how sick I was, how exposed I was, or how fearful I was."

"My dear child, if you are going to argue with everything I say, why are you here? Why pay my high prices to listen to yourself? Why negate my expertise? You can interpret your dreams at home, alone, and not pay for it. Why will you not listen?"

311

"I am listening," she bristled. "I just thought you wanted to know my feelings, too. After all, it's my dream."

"Of course, of course," he said, puffing out clouds of smoke. "It's your dream and there is no doubt but that you want to perceive your husband as exploitive. Can you explain that?"

"It's not that I want to perceive him that way. He is an exploitive person."

"You sit there before me," Dr. Bloom said, "bursting with health, with wealth, with well-being. You say you do not work, that all that you have comes to you from your husband. Explain to me then, how it is that you perceive him as exploitive."

"I don't know," she said. She sat there confused, trying to remember what it was she wanted, what it was she was lacking, why she felt Jeff had failed her. She had money, a beautiful home, the EL social world, a secure place in the solid gold circle, servants, and Jeff never even bothered her much anymore for sex. So how did he exploit her actually? Why was she so disappointed and disapproving of him?

The hour was over and she left. She asked herself if she felt better after seeing Dr. Bloom and had to say she did not. She suddenly felt an overwhelming need to indulge herself. She walked to Rumpelmayer's, where she ordered a grilled bacon and cheese, hot chocolate with whipped cream, and a hot fudge sundae. Despite her lack of appetite, she wolfed them down, paid the bill, felt increasingly depressed, then wandered down Fifth Avenue trying to figure out what to do with the rest of her life, and for that matter, what to do with the rest of her day.

Only one o'clock in the afternoon. Jeff was at work, Jennifer was at school. Servants were cleaning her house and cooking her food. Everyone seemed purposeful except for her. She continued to walk down Fifth, past the stores, but she didn't need anything. She didn't want anything. She walked on, now leaving the chic part of the city frequented by EL members behind her.

The streets became grimier, the people no longer so well dressed. She walked through the garment district, through Chelsea, and finally she reached Greenwich Village, turned down Eighth Street, and walked along it to University Place, enjoying the displays in the little boutiques, the crafts shops with their handmade leather, Indian silver, pottery; the clothing shops displaying deliberately mismatched gypsylike clothes which made her matching purse and shoes and white gloves look out of place.

With waves of nostalgia sweeping through her, making the past seem better than it ever was, she finally reached Washington Square and sat on a bench looking at New York University, where she had once trained to be an elementary schoolteacher. How far she had come. But to what? She was the wife of a rich man, the well-dressed wife of a rich man, but what more had she become than that?

There, on the corner of Waverly and University Place was Chock full o'Nuts, the only restaurant she and Saul had been able to afford as commuting undergraduates. Nothing had ever tasted as good to her in those days as their coffee, raisin bread and cream-cheese sandwiches. She went in, sat down, and ordered them. The waitress's eyes flicked over her, fastened on her jade and diamond pin, moved to her pear-shaped diamond engagement ring which had long ago replaced the original one Jeff had given to her. The waitress's eyes lingered on Ellen's mink jacket, designed to look casual, and thereby looking especially expensive.

"Fifty-two cents," the waitress snapped, unable to forgive Ellen for her appearance.

One sip of coffee, one bite of sandwich, and Ellen got up. She had been spoiled. Her palate had been educated and she could no longer enjoy the food of her youth. The waitress's eyes followed her accusingly as if to say "food waster." Ellen fled.

She wandered south another block to the college bookstore and lost herself for a pleasurable half-hour in the paperback section, remembering the days when she had so hungrily looked at all the books she could not afford to buy. She had been reading about Hermann Hesse so she bought everything they had by him

313

and paid with a hundred dollar bill which the cashier changed with annoyance.

It was three o'clock. My God, only three o'clock. What was she to do with the rest of the day? She'd already seen the movies playing at the Art, the Eighth Street, and the Waverly Theater. Half-consciously, she drifted to the south building where the Elementary Education Department was located. She would ask about registering for that final year of courses. She was a bit embarrassed at her mink and jewelry, but was determined to act, since fate had brought her there. She quickened her step, suddenly purposeful.

"Yes?" the secretary asked.

"I would like to see somebody about finishing my B.A.," Ellen said, shyly. The clerk looked at her with hostility, as the waitress had. Don't you have enough, the glance seemed to ask. Why must you also invade our territory?

"Undergraduate, you say?"

"Yes."

"First door on the right."

The individual cubicles didn't have ceilings, just partitions between them. She knocked.

"Come in," said a man's voice. She opened the door, the man spun around and they grinned at each other in astonishment.

"I can't believe it," the man said, "it's Lady Bountiful from San Francisco."

"Are you Todd?" Incredible that she should remember him so clearly.

"I certainly am. Ellen, my God, I've been sitting here in this city for one semester, wondering how to see you again, afraid to call your house, afraid you wouldn't remember me. And now, here, what luck"—he threw back his head with a joyous laugh—"you walk into my office."

"But what are you doing here? Where do you live? Is your family with you?" she asked.

314

"We can't talk here," he whispered, "the partitions have ears. Let's go for a drink and I'll tell you all about it.

"I should tell you," he said, immediately reestablishing their intimacy, "that I don't need anybody to pay for my drinks."

"With this office," she joked back, "I wouldn't think so." The months fell away.

Ellen walked along at his side, elated beyond memory. Serendipity! That was what made it especially lovely. She kept stealing glances at him as they walked, amazed at what she saw. He was beautifully dressed in a fine suede jacket, turtle-necked shirt, gray flannel trousers, and short, highly polished, fine wine-leather boots. He seemed to have put on some weight, developed, matured, flowered, and turned, with the help of a good tailor, into an exceptionally handsome man. His body was lean, erect, and firm. Who would ever have thought that the skinny, anxious, poverty-stricken little professor from Berkeley could change this way in less than a year. Wonder of wonders.

They sat in a dark little corner at the Cedar Street Tavern and began to talk. How handsome he had become with his curly hair, blue eyes, ruddy, rosy cheeks and white skin, not more handsome than Jeff or Giovanni, but a different type, more midwestern-looking, rangier, less formal, a kind of California look. Jeff was an Arrow-collar ad and Giovanni was a dark, Italian matinee idol, but Todd was apple pie, a frontiersman, the rugged western cigarette man celebrated in the commercials.

"Even lovelier than I remembered," he said to her. He gently touched her straightened, smooth, shimmering hair, the soft fur of her jacket, and the smooth cheeks labored over by Arden technicians.

"You may have trouble believing this," he said, "but I've never forgotten you. You were the dark lady of the sonnets, La Belle Dame Sans Merci, Circe, the Lorelei. It was your image that gave me the strength to go on and make changes after you left. I cursed myself for days for having let you slip through my arms. I realized that I had never been in love with anybody in my

315

entire life, that when they played romantic songs, songs like 'Shangri-La,' those songs were meant for other people, not for me. Sometimes I'd fantasize that we were together; flying down to Rio, lying on beaches in the Caribbean, looking over Paris from the Eiffel Tower, dancing the bossa nova to a steel-drum band somewhere in the tropics. I built up a whole fantasy life with you and I knew that somehow I had to get to New York."

Then he told her about the fantastic luck that had brought him there. His wife and children had remained in California, where she was finishing her B.A., but he had come to NYU because of the tremendous amounts of money the government had been setting aside for education because of the challenge of the Russian Sputnik I, and also because of the increased push for civil rights. He discovered that he had a previously untapped ability and facility for writing grant proposals, for getting money, for putting together packages which united the federal government, state governments, colleges, and the surrounding public schools. He had become one of a new breed of jet-set professors ... professors who lectured and consulted on the Washington-New York-California axis.

From his base at NYU, where he taught an occasional class and helped out with advisement, he administered these grants: grants to desegregate public school classrooms, grants to provide models of education for ghetto (now called "inner city") youth, grants to study the psychology of alienated black children, grants to study the effects of the maltreatment of young black children who were integrating previously all-white schools, grants to do with anything about black-white relations. Apparently, there was no end to the study of what it meant in America to be poor and black.

"Does it help the blacks?" Ellen asked.

"It sure as hell helped me," he joked. But then he suddenly turned serious. "You can't imagine how many times I've gone to the phone to call you," he said, "but I couldn't face the end of my fantasy life."

"Well, here I am," she said.

316

"Yes, here you are and I can't believe it."

He took her hand and his beautiful blue eyes looked into hers. She'd had two whiskey sours and she was unusually swoony and romantic.

"I don't have anything to do for the rest of today," he said, "what about you?"

"I can make a call," she answered, her heart beating wildly.

"Make the call," he said in a voice that made her heart turn over, "so we can take up where we left off last summer."

Walking along the street, too tense and wound up to talk, brushing shoulders with little electric shocks, they hurried to his apartment.

"It isn't much," he said, "considering the way you live. Just a two-room walkup on Jane Street."

"It's a lot," she answered huskily, "considering the way I live." She could have wept for joy at feeling some emotion after so many arid years.

Never losing contact with each other's body, they walked up the stairs and entered his apartment. He locked the door and reached for her with a joyous laugh. Oh, my God, how good I feel, she thought as she held out her arms to him. There was no strain, no awkwardness, no pretending, no worrying, no standing above or away or apart. They gamboled, played, touched, teased, stroked, and melted toward each other, delaying, delaying, delaying . . . oh, delicious torture. Naked, they lay on his narrow bed, loving each other. And finally, when they could wait no longer, he mounted her, looked down at her with those beautiful eyes and said, "All right, love, here we go." And effortlessly and beautifully, it was right for both of them.

This is the high point of my life, she told herself. She wanted to weep, to kiss his hand in gratitude. Oh, Todd, life, hope, change, feeling, the future. Oh, Todd, purpose and excitement and love of my own body. Todd, Todd, make love to me, again and again and again. Life wasn't over. There was still wine to sip and he had brought her the glass.

He shifted his weight, afraid he might be too heavy. "No,

don't go," she said. "You're not heavy. Stay, stay a while longer, love." She could not get enough of the feel of his skin, of the smell of his neck, the taste of his lips, and the inside of his mouth. She could not let him go.

Finally, she realized it was time to go home. But not without making plans to see him the following week. The week's wait seemed endless. She worried that Jeff would be able to sense a change in her, note that she seemed happy, cheerful, optimistic, alive. But Jeff had his own life. He was terribly busy now assisting Candy with Michael's account. Michael was awaiting trial and was, Jeff said, a broken man. "It's a lucky thing he has a wife like Candy at his side to take over. She's quite a girl. I thought she was just some kind of dumb deb but she hasn't missed a stroke. Pure steel, that's what she has in her backbone."

"Davida probably would have agreed."

"Aren't you ever going to forget about Davida?"

"Probably not."

Jennifer came drifting past them on her way to the refrigerator. Jeff followed. "Get out of the kitchen," he yelled. "I thought you promised to lose weight."

"I'm hungry."

"Tough," he snapped. "You just finished dinner. Don't you feel any shame at being so fat? My God, I've got one kid and she's a blimp."

Ignoring him, Jennifer took a half-gallon of ice cream out of the freezer. Jeff stomped after her and knocked the ice cream out of her hands. The container smacked on the floor with a bang and ice cream splattered all over. Ursula came creeping in to clean it up and Jennifer went into a tantrum screaming, "I hate you, I hate you. I'm running away."

"Wonderful," Jeff snarled. "Don't come back until you're thin. I can't stand to look at you. I want to be able to show you off to people, not to feel ashamed."

"I hate you, I hate you," Jennifer screamed again. "I wish you'd die. I'd like to kill you."

318

"You really scare me," Jeff said. "How about going up to your room and hating me more quietly."

Ellen stepped forward and put her arms around Jennifer. "You don't make this expensive abode particularly pleasant for her," Ellen said dryly.

"You don't make it particularly pleasant for me," he mimicked her. "You should see how Candy runs her home. Elegant dinner parties every Saturday night, a salon on Sunday afternoons. Everything she does shows her breeding. Michael's house is a warm, pleasant place because of her and she knows everybody. Every time I'm there I meet celebrities, people like that guy Dalway we met at her wedding. I meet people in government, actresses, writers. And she carries on all of this social activity while running Michael's business and suffering and worrying about the publicity of the trial. She's the kind of woman I admire. Everybody adores her."

"Apparently Michael's children didn't," Ellen said, feeling hurt. "But in any event, Jeff, I'm not Candy and I never can be. If you wanted someone like Candy, you married the wrong person."

"That's for sure," he said. They stood there glaring at each other. Her arms were still around Jennifer and she wanted to change the subject to a more peaceful one.

"Jeff," she said, "I've registered for one course at NYU. I have to go there next Thursday night. I won't be able to go to the opera."

"I thought registration was over," he said.

"This isn't a regular course," she lied, "just a workshop."

"On what?" he asked.

"Changing life-goals," she said. And before he could ask her any more questions, she continued, "Why don't you take Jennifer to the opera instead of me? She can go in to school late the next day and I think she'd love the experience."

"I would like it," Jennifer said.

"Not on your life," Jeff said. "Not the way you look. Other

kids come to the opera with straight, neat, blond hair and thin little legs inside their patent pumps. And they're little ladies. I'm not going to be seen publicly with you until you shed some weight and start to behave politely. I'll be damned if I'm going to take someone who hates me to the opera."

"How can you be so cruel?" Ellen said.

"I'll take Candy if it's okay with you," he said, ignoring her remark. "She needs some distraction from her troubles with Michael."

"Why does she need distraction?" Ellen snapped. "I thought you said she was made of steel." He turned away and she took Jennifer upstairs to comfort her.

"I always knew he was ashamed of me," Jennifer said. "I really do hate him. He acts like I want to be fat. Who would want to be fat?"

"He didn't really mean it, darling," Ellen said, trying to hug her, but Jennifer pulled away in misery. "People just say mean things when they're upset."

"And he's always upset," Jennifer said. "If you don't mind, Mommy, I don't feel like talking anymore tonight." She turned her radio on to deafening loudness and waited for Ellen to leave. Ellen felt as if her heart were breaking.

"Do you know that I love you?" she called above the noise.

Jennifer nodded and Ellen left her room. God, life was depressing. Things always seemed to go so wrong. Almost twenty-nine years old and she felt like an amateur at living. Maybe Jennifer should have some therapy. Tina's son Jacques had been in therapy since grade one. Of course, Ellen didn't know how a kid whose mother disliked him so much could help but be neurotic, but she loved Jennifer. Tina thought all children should be kept in cages until they were twenty-one. Well, if Jacques could survive Tina's hostility, maybe Jeff's would not damage Jennifer if Ellen did everything to balance it.

On the following Thursday, she went for her last visit to Dr. Bloom to tell him she wouldn't be taking the hour after all. He wanted to discuss with her the two tests she had taken for him: the Rorschach and the Thematic Apperception Test, which he referred to familiarly as the TAT. Her interpretation of one picture especially interested him. This was a picture of a farm girl in pigtails and apron, standing outside a farmhouse, looking at the men in the fields. Ellen had said the girl didn't want to be in the kitchen in her apron but out there in the fields, working alongside the men.

"Your problem," Dr. Bloom told her, "is that you are suffering from sexual ambivalence. Half of you wants to be feminine; you want to be the girl but also to be out with the men in the fields. Your rejection of the normal feminine role is at the base of your frigidity with your husband. In addition, you have a repressed jealousy of your husband's success. You want that success to be yours. You are not content to be in the house doing the normal feminine tasks, practicing a logical division of labor and it is evident, also, that you do not wish to relinquish your femininity. You want it both ways. You wish to be simultaneously dependent and independent, feminine and masculine, in the home and out at work in the fields with the men.

"It is no wonder, my poor child, that you are conflicted, frigid, restless, discontented, and unhappy and it is this same conflict that has resulted in your avoidance of a second child, which would be the normal path.

"We must work hard in the months ahead to get to the roots of your rejection of your own femininity, to find out why you do not wish to be a woman and a mother, to enable you to see emotionally what undoubtedly you do perceive intellectually . . . that you cannot be both a man and a woman, that you must be only a woman. Through therapy you will eventually come to welcome your normal female role. You will end your attempts to emasculate your husband, refrain from subconscious desires to sabotage his work, become happy in your predestined role, and rush to have some more children."

"How can you tell all that about me from a few pictures,"

she said angrily. "Why do you make everything my fault instead of Jeff's?"

"I assure you, my dear child, given your inner conflicts, you would not be happy with any man. But nobody forced you to marry your husband or to stay with him. As for judging from a few pictures, that is not true. It was you, yourself, who provided me with this information."

"I don't accept anything you've said," she said indignantly. "It's all just ridiculous clichés, formulas, stereotypes."

"It's hard to face the truth," he said. "You'll feel differently about this in time."

"I'm never coming back," she said.

"As you wish. I fitted you in as a favor to Tina; there's a long waiting list. But if you leave now, I may not be able to fit you back in."

"I will never want to come back. Why should you call me Ellen or my poor child, while I have to call you Dr. Bloom?"

"Would you like to explore your feelings about that?"

"Oh, nonsense," she said, standing up.

"You will not receive a refund for the remainder of the month," he said.

"I don't care about that."

"You will never find inner peace without therapy."

"I'll take my chances," she said. "I may not find your kind of inner peace but whatever I do find will be my own. I'll have my own mind. Thank God, I can think for myself. I don't need anyone to interpret pictures for me."

She walked out of his office feeling liberated. What nonsense it all was. All he'd done for Tina, after so many years and the fortune she'd paid him, was to make her completely dependent on him. Imagine, seeing that old quack four times a week. Imagine being unable to make a decision without Svengali's advice. Euphoric, free, gloriously happy, she drove down to see Todd.

The next months were the happiest in her memory. New York was her city. She loved it and she loved showing it to Todd.

322

Together they walked across the Brooklyn Bridge and explored Brooklyn Heights. They went to Chinatown, the Lower East Side, Little Italy, the Cloisters, and the Morgan Library. All the things that had palled when she was alone were filled with joy with him. He was so open in his ability to appreciate, so full of praise, so sensitive to beauty. He seemed to feel things with her and she never had to ask or to explain. They spent one glorious day at the Bronx Botanical Garden and she was aware that it cost them very little money to be so happy together. He was the kind of friend and companion she had not known since the days of Saul. But he was more than that. He was her lover, her love, and her affection and desire for him grew every time they met.

One day she invited him to her house, feeling slightly guilty about it. They had tea with Jennifer, who adored him instantly as he admired her drawings and told her how pretty she was. She showed him slowly through the house and afterward, sipping brandy in the living room and looking out at the pool through the bay window, he said, "Yes, yes, this was how I pictured you living. This was the kind of setting I saw you in, Ellen, the way I dreamed about you. But, Ellen, with all this, what do you see in me?"

"See in you?" she exclaimed. "All of this is dead without a feeling of love."

"The happiest time of my life," he often said.

"Of mine, too," she would echo.

Jeff was so busy with Candy's affairs that he was unaware of Ellen's absences. They were going through a period of peace. They would meet at night in their bedroom, talk briefly, then fall asleep in the large king-sized bed, as remote as if they were in different cities.

It was sheer agony in May when Todd's semester was over and he was due to fly home to his family. Finally, one night he said it, the words she had been waiting for and longing for, the words she had known in her heart must come.

"We have to get married," he said, "to be together all the time."

323

"I know," she said, as contentment spread through every cell of her body. All of her past life, all of the sadness and loneliness and emptiness and despair, all of it had served a purpose, if it had brought her to this man. She had even told him about the rape. He had reacted as casually as Kate had.

"Forget it," he had said. It was no stigma, not something she had caused or willed and it had not defiled her. She was loved, loving, able to make good love, able to be loved. Forget it. Forget it. Goodbye sadness, she had thought.

"It will mean changing your style of living radically," he had told her. "Will you mind?"

"Nothing matters except being with you," she told him in a delirium of love. "I don't care about these things."

She took him to the airport and wept. "I'll ask my wife for a divorce," he promised her. "I've only been waiting until after she got her degree so that she wouldn't mess up on her exams. I didn't want to interfere with that. Don't do anything until I get back. I'll come back in July and then you can tell your husband."

She felt sad, empty, drained, and lonely when she went down to breakfast the next morning. Jeff was already eating, being clucked over by Ursula, and Jennifer had gone to school.

"Is your workshop over?" he asked.

"Yes," she said.

"Then your summer will be free?"

"I expect so," she answered. They had never done much in summers but to lie beside the pool. "Why do you ask?"

"Because I have plans for you," he said. "I want a divorce."

A divorce! She could feel her knees shaking and waves of nausea surged through her. All very well to talk of it to Todd but terribly shocking and frightening when presented this way. She decided not to say anything about Todd. "May I ask why?" she said, her teeth chattering.

"I'm in love with someone else. I want to marry her."

"Someone else? Who?"

"Candace."

"Candace. You must be kidding. She's married."

"Not for long. Michael's going to be sent to jail. There's no way he can get out of a sentence. And Candace is going to divorce him."

"Jeff, you can't be serious. Tina said she's a barracuda. She probably isn't even in love with you. She's divorcing Michael, dumping him because of his business problems. What would happen if you ever fell on bad times? She wouldn't be good for you."

"Are you?"

"No," she said soberly, feeling guilty about Todd. "I'm not really good either, but she would be worse."

"I'm in love," he said, "and it feels wonderful. Suddenly, life has purpose and meaning for me again. I'm thirty-six but Candace is only twenty-four. It's like starting over. She'll have kids, lots of kids. She promised me."

"She'd probably promise you anything at this point," Ellen said.

"Ellen, there's no point in discussing it further. You've never been right for me. I tried to improve you, but there was only so far I could go with the original material. You can never be a Candace. There's nothing you can do for me socially or financially. It's a dead-end with you. There Candace is introducing me to the leaders of the country and you're fooling around with education. Let's face it, Ellen. That's your natural habitat. That's where you should have stayed."

She sat there stunned, terrified, all of her shelter yanked away without warning. But, thank God, there was Todd.

"I hope you won't kill yourself over this, like Davida," he said.

"Kill myself." Ellen burst out into laughter that surprised her. The egotistical son of a bitch. "Kill myself over you and the baby monster. Kill myself? By the time Candace gets through milking you, you may be the one wanting to commit suicide. I can still see that little nit at Disneyland, looking up and saying, 'This really is a magic kingdom.'

"Jeff, you have to believe that what I'm saying now I'm saying with disinterest. I may not be the right wife for you, I know I'm not, but Candy isn't either. She probably doesn't love you the way you love her. I don't think she's capable of it. She's only using you to bail her out. Why don't you take your time and think about it. There's no rush. I'm sure she's just using you because you're a far better bet at this point than Michael is."

"I'm not the good bet," he said bashfully, "*she* is. Who would ever think she'd be marrying a once poor Jewish boy?"

"Certainly not the once poor Greek boy she married two years ago," Ellen said.

"Spare me your sarcasms, Ellen," he said. "I don't have to put up with them anymore. That's one of the things I've liked least about you. Your sarcasm. Thinking you're funny with those ironic remarks. The other thing is your frigidity. Candy thinks I'm the greatest in bed."

"Well, maybe you don't make phone calls and notes in your little black book during sex with her. I hope she'll continue to think you're great for at least a week after the wedding."

"I don't have to listen to you anymore," Jeff said. "You'll hear from my lawyer. I suggest that you start to look for a place to live."

A place to live? Was he kicking her out? Why, even Michael had left Davida in their house with his kids. A place to live? What did that mean? Where did he intend to put Jennifer?

"I'm going to sell this house," he said, "and most of the furniture. I'll move right in with Candy. I've been wanting to be in New York City for some time now."

"I see," she said, "you have it all thought out, haven't you?"

"Yes," he said seriously, "we've been planning for some time. You take Jennifer and we get Ursula."

"Ursula?" Ellen giggled. "I'll try to make that sacrifice."

"You never liked her anyway," Jeff said, "and she doesn't like or respect you. She adores Candy, recognizes a real lady. Of course, everyone likes Candy."

"Everyone liked Willy Loman, too," Ellen said. He ignored her.

"When is all this change supposed to occur?" Ellen asked.

"As soon as Jennifer's school ends and she goes off to camp. That gives you six weeks to find an apartment and move. All household expenses will be paid until you leave, but don't try to use any of the credit cards or you'll find yourself in jail. I have informed all of the companies that I will no longer be responsible for your purchases. There's enough money for food and Jennifer's expenses in our joint checking account but you'll get no more money from me until our lawyers have made an agreement."

"Just like this?" Ellen asked. So this was all he had ever been, the cold FBI man standing before her. "After almost nine years of marriage, this is all there is. I'm dismissed like an employee, without even getting severance pay?" Who was this hard stranger standing in front of her, who would rather take a competent maid than his daughter?

"No point in discussion," he said, "cold turkey is always best, the least messy. My mind is made up, I know what I want, I know what I intend to do, so no further discussion is necessary. Our lawyers will arrive at some equitable income for you. Of course, it will be nothing like what you had here, but there's no reason why you shouldn't go to work full-time now. You'll get enough to get by."

He was right. Conversation would be pointless, had, in fact, been pointless for years. She straightened up and looked at this stranger with whom she had lived all these years. This stranger she had never really known or liked.

"All right," she said. "I guess there is nothing further to say."

"I certainly like the way you're taking this, Ellen," he said. "You really are a good sport."

"A good sport?" She broke into hysterical peals of laughter and he walked out. It was only as she heard his car moving out of

327

the driveway that she realized she had ten dollars in her purse. She ran down to the garage, but he was gone. In the kitchen, Ursula, hands on hips, head thrown back triumphantly, regarded her with undisguised triumph. She had never thought Ellen paid the proper deference to Jeff.

"Did Mr. Sheldon leave me any cash?" she asked, breathlessly.

"*Nein,*" Ursula said, remembering how Ellen had wanted to ship her back to Germany. "But I safe my money. I vill lend, if you vish."

"No, no," Ellen said, and she fled up to her room to think about the future.

PART
THREE

9

llen had always played along with Jeff and repressed her true ideas, feelings, and desires through the years in order to gain security. And now, suddenly, she was double-crossed. Everything she had done had been a waste. It had bought her time but at too great a price and now, here she was, as defenseless as if she had never gone along with him at all. Their ninth anniversary was approaching. Nine years and she was going out of the marriage with as little as she had entered. No, she couldn't say that. She had Jennifer and she had Todd and together they would help her to be strong. The two of them prevented the sentence she had served from being a total waste.

For she had wasted those years when she could have been learning a trade, could have become licensed as a schoolteacher. Over and over again she had been warned. Tina had warned her to be realistic and Davida's fate had been another warning but she had ignored them. Why had she been so blind, so foolish? Why had she squandered her time?

She couldn't blame Jeff for wanting out. He was entitled to the same happiness as she. But she was absolutely terrified at the way he had done it. She could not remember being more frightened. It had been easy enough to renounce material possessions in her romantic discussions with Todd, but that was a totally different reality from the one she now saw before her. She was a fool, a romantic fool, and she had not really faced all of the details involved in ending a relationship. In her imagination, she and Jennifer had just gently flowed from her home to Todd's. The one thing she had never considered was that she might have to accomplish everything with ten dollars in her purse. She had to be out at the end of June and Todd had not planned to be back until July, and she had no way of knowing how long it would take for them each to be divorced, find an apartment, and remarry. She would have to find a place to move to.

She needed a friend to talk to so she called Kate. The butler, in a grave voice, told her that Kate and Will had just gone to a clinic in Switzerland.

"Is Miss Evans sick again?" Ellen asked.

"I'm not at liberty to divulge any information, madam," he said, "but they did ask me to inform you about their departure. They will be back in a few weeks and will phone you."

Next, she called Tina. Tina, of course, knew about Jeff and Candace.

"I've known for some time," Tina told her. "Just a minute, sweetie. I was just about to get into my tub. I'll pick up the tub phone in half a sec.

"Okay, I'm on," Tina said a few seconds later. "I'm using the most unbelievably fragrant bath oil. I bought it when we were in Japan but haven't had a chance to try it before. Would you like the name? It's fabulous. Hold on a second. Marie is bringing my coffee and I don't want to talk in front of her. Okay. She's gone now and I'm all ears."

"If you knew about Jeff and Candace before now," Ellen said through tight, angry lips, "why didn't you tell me? You tell me every other little bit of gossip that blows your way."

"I figured it would blow over," Tina said, "as soon as he got to know her, so there was no point in upsetting you. It never occurred to me that little Candy would want to marry somebody in the gold circle. Honestly, sweetie, with her credentials, she could marry right up there in the platinum circle. I never dreamed she'd be serious about Jeff, gorgeous as he is. I just assumed, as did everybody else, that she was simply using him, leaning on him until things got settled with Michael. How could I ever have dreamed they'd want to get married? And if I had told you, what good would that have done? You couldn't have locked him in his room. So it was just as well that I spared you a few months of worry. And I don't want to be prying, but you haven't been around much yourself these past few months. I just figured you were being equally entertained."

"He's left me with ten dollars, Tina. What should I do?"

"There's nothing you can do," Tina said, "so don't panic. Call Jim Anthony, you know, the lawyer I once mentioned to you, and start to look for a place to live. Rotten luck that Jeff's selling the house. But I warned you years ago. You should have insisted that he put it in both your names. Now it's too late."

"I'm feeling a little shaky," Ellen said, "and I need some support. May I come over and visit now?"

"It wouldn't be a good idea," Tina said.

"Not a good idea?" Ellen echoed.

"Listen, sweetie," Tina said, "we've been good friends all these years and I'll always be very fond of you, but I've never lied to you and I'm not going to start now. Harry and I can't be friendly both with you and with Jeff and Candy. Harry and Jeff are involved in too many deals together. You won't be a member of EL any longer. You're out of the circle. So what would be the point of our seeing each other? Our lives will pull us in different directions. Let's just say goodbye in a friendly way. Then we can remember happy days in the past and you'll be able to concentrate on meeting new friends wherever you go."

Ellen replaced the receiver and wept. She was surprised at how much the betrayal hurt. Without missing a beat, Harry and

Tina would switch from Jeff and Ellen to Jeff and Candy. She felt as if she were drowning. She dreaded calling Todd at his home but she felt desperate. What would she do if his wife answered? She would just have to hang up. Feverishly she dialed his home in California. Her heart was beating wildly. She could have fainted with relief when he answered the phone himself.

"Forgive me for calling you at home," she said, "but something terribly important has come up. Can you talk?"

"Not exactly," he answered.

"Can you listen? Is it all right to talk?"

"Yes," he said, "for a moment or so."

"Jeff wants a divorce," she said.

"Why?" he asked and he sounded nervous.

"Oh, don't worry," she said. "He doesn't know about us. That's not it. He's in love with someone else."

"I'm glad that's the reason," Todd said. "I don't think there is any necessity to give him that other information."

"Don't worry," she said, "I won't."

"Anything else?" he asked.

"I'm scared, Todd," she said. "I have no money and no one to depend on but you. When are you coming back?"

"That has not yet been decided," he said. "I'll have to let you know."

"I love you," she said.

"Thank you," he answered, and hung up the phone.

She ended the conversation with him feeling terribly uneasy. Obviously he couldn't talk. But suppose he backed out. That would be the last straw. But she was sure he wouldn't do it. She remembered the way they had clung to each other at the airport, and she tried to convince herself that there was nothing to worry about. She was alone now but soon he would be back. They would marry, love, live together happily forever. Terrible as this period was, it was best that the long illness was finally ending. The chronically ill patient would finally get well. Still, her heart leaped up when she heard the car in the driveway. Maybe Jeff

334

had come back and things would be as before. Maybe she wouldn't have to lose her beautiful home after all. She dashed down the stairs but Ursula had already opened the door to admit a town policeman and Jennifer. The policeman introduced himself and began to explain.

"Drinking," Ellen gasped. "But she's not even nine years old. Beer? Behind the school? No, officer, never before and I promise you never again. Thank you for being so understanding this time. I really appreciate it. I assure you, never again. Thank you very much."

Ursula showed the officer out. Jennifer stood there, fat, pimply, ragged.

"I don't want to discuss it, Mom," she said, running to her room, slamming the door, locking it, and turning on the radio.

Ellen would have to get Jennifer some therapy, she realized. But right now, she was overcome with fatigue. Too tired to force Jennifer to open the door, she crept into her bed with the magnificent down comforter on it, and sank into blessed sleep.

She awakened the next morning, heart pounding, dimly remembering that something was terribly wrong. She staggered downstairs to the breakfast room; looked at the table and found it empty. No coffee brewing, no croissants or brioches, no fresh strawberries and *crème-suisse* in the Staffordshire dish. Ursula entered, dressed in street clothes, arrogant, now that Ellen was no longer in command.

"Jennifer is gone to a frient's," she hissed. "Mr. Sheldon my salary has payt me. This is my veekend off. He has dischart the housekeeper so you vill haff to make your own breakfast. I vill pick up Jennifer ven I return tomorrow night."

She left and Ellen struggled for equilibrium. Oh, God, where was the coffee kept? Too much of an effort to locate it. Wearily, she climbed the stairs and crept back into bed, where she stayed until late Sunday afternoon when she heard Ursula and Jennifer and smelled cooking. She was ravenous.

She walked down to the breakfast room, gave Jennifer a hug.

Ursula ignored her. Damn it, this was still her home and she was still mistress here.

"My dinner," she barked at Ursula and in a few minutes she received her first hot meal that weekend. She wondered if she should say anything to Jennifer about the divorce, then decided to wait. What was the rush? She said nothing about the drinking either, simply too worn out to confront that problem at this time. Perhaps being brought home once by a policeman would do the trick. Why would Jennifer drink? She certainly didn't see that example at home. In any event, discussion of the situation would have to wait until she was stronger.

Monday, as soon as Jennifer went off to school, Ellen went to the savings bank and, blessing Tina's practicality, Ellen took out her few thousand dollars and put them into a checking account. She had made an appointment with Jim Anthony for the afternoon. She felt insecure as she walked into the sumptuous office waiting room. Strange how overnight the trappings of wealth had become intimidating to her. Incredible to think that with one blow she had sunk to a lower income level than a blue-collar worker. She was now unemployed and unsupported, in a lower economic class than a garbage collector, a trucker, or an automobile assembly-line worker. Lower than a woman who packaged chicken parts. She waited and waited in the elegant room, restless and irritated, having learned enough about corporate workings from Jeff to understand that the rich and important were not kept waiting this way.

She was surprised, when she was finally shown in, at how young the lawyer was. "Mr. Anthony?" she queried softly.

"I'm afraid not," the chinless young man said. "Mr. Anthony is snowed under right now, but he's asked me to meet with you. Now, let's discuss why you're here."

"I'm getting a divorce," she said, "and I wanted Mr. Anthony to represent me."

"But surely, Mrs. Sheldon, you must know that would be impossible. It's really rather unfair of you to put us in this position."

"What's unfair? What position?" she asked, bewildered.

"We are already representing your husband and Candace Stewart," he said. "Now we may seem a bit incestuous at times," he sighed, "but we do have our limits. We could not do anything unethical, not even for you at this time. We do have our limits."

"I see," she said. "And I'm the limit?"

"I'm afraid so," he said blandly. "Besides, Mrs. Sheldon, let's not beat around the bush. You can't afford our firm. Could you afford twenty-five big ones?"

"Not even twenty-five little ones," she joked, pretending poise. With false apologies, he instantly edged her out.

She went to the public ladies' room on that floor and stood there having hysterics. The secretaries dashing in and out to chatter didn't even look at her. They'd come across lots and lots of ladies who were getting divorces.

Finally, she calmed down and was able to leave the building. She started to walk, without direction, trying to forget the humiliation of Anthony's office boy, forcing herself to examine all aspects of her situation.

First, she would need to find a lawyer. For the moment, this would have to wait. Kate and Will would be back in a few weeks and she was sure they could recommend her to a fine one who would treat her well merely because she was their friend.

Second, there was the question of money. Her paramount need was for money immediately and she racked her brains as she walked for ways to get some. Her rings. Of course! Her engagement and wedding rings were worth at least twelve thousand dollars. Diamonds really are a girl's best friend. Better to pawn or to sell? She had no idea of where to find a pawn shop and the very idea made her shudder. She would go back to the diamond center, to the very shop where Jeff had bought her new rings when they'd traded in the originals. She started to hail a cab, then lowered her hand and continued to walk. She had acquired a set of habits that she would have to now unlearn.

When she reached the shop the very same salesman was there. Yes, he remembered her quite well, remembered that Jeff had paid twelve thousand. Yes, she had kept them well, easy to see that she wasn't one of those women whose hands were always in dishwater. He offered her three thousand dollars.

"Three thousand!" she exclaimed indignantly. "Diamonds appreciate."

"They're secondhand," he said. "Four thousand and my boss will kill me."

"No."

"Five thousand and you're killing me."

"No," she repeated.

"So how much?"

"Twelve thousand. The original price. You can sell it for more."

"You're out of your mind, lady. Six thousand and that's my final price. That's the top."

She wavered for a moment, knowing she was being taken, but lacking energy to bargain further.

"Done," she said. "I want cash."

"I don't keep that kind of money here."

"Then go with me to your bank."

Forcing herself not to feel emotion, she slipped the rings off, gave them to him, and then they walked across the street to his bank for a cashier's check. She opened an account with the check and left, feeling surprisingly proud of herself. It was the first independent thing she could remember doing in years. The good life had rendered her an infant, incompetent at life. But now she was taking control and some of her panic subsided. With a new sense of well-being, she could now face going home.

When she let herself in through the door that connected the house to the garage, all of her good feelings abruptly left her. Not believing what she saw, she let out a gasp. The entire downstairs, with the exception of the kitchen and the breakfast room, was empty. Gone from the living room were the soft couches, the Oriental rugs, antique carriage lamps, paintings, objets d'art, bibelots, Canton china, Lowestoft, American pewter. Gone from the dining room were the magnificent Queen Anne chairs and table, the sets of Royal Crown Derby, Spode, and Wedgwood. Gone were the sets of sterling flatwear, the Jensen serving pieces, the antique sterling tea service. Everything was gone, empty, cleaned out.

Shaking, she went upstairs. Jennifer's room was intact. The guest bedrooms were empty, but her bedroom was still intact. The enormous king-sized bed remained there like an ironic joke. She heard footsteps behind her and turned, still shaking, to face Ursula.

"Jennifer is sleeping by her frent. Do you vish dinner?"

She shook her head, exhausted. Now she would not be able to put off telling Jennifer. She sank into her bed and slept.

She had hoped to send Jennifer off to camp not knowing about the sudden change in their lives, but Jeff's precipitous cruel removal of the furniture made the discussion imperative. The next day she picked Jennifer up at school, where she had gone directly from her friend's house that morning, and the two of them drove to Steppingstone Park, where they sat on the grass, looked at the Sound, and talked.

"I'm glad, Mommy," Jennifer said, awkwardly putting her arms around Ellen, who could not hold back her tears. "I want to be alone with you, without Daddy or Ursula. I hate them both. And Daddy hates me."

"No, no, honey," Ellen responded automatically, "Daddy loves you. It's just his way."

"He hates me," Jennifer said. "Please don't lie to me anymore. All he ever wanted was a son. He hates me and I hate him and I'm glad we're leaving. Where will we live?"

"We'll move to Manhattan," Ellen said, "so I can finish school and get a job."

"I think I'd like that," Jennifer said. "How big will our new place be?"

"Probably pretty small," Ellen said, "especially in comparison with our house."

"Where will we sleep?"

"I'll get two bedrooms. You and I will sleep in rooms right next to each other."

"With the doors open?"

"Whenever you like. All the time if you wish."

"And if I got scared, could I pop right into your room?"

"Any time, all the time, whenever you wish. I expect to be scared sometimes myself. But never too scared, because you'll be with me."

"Yippee," Jennifer caroled. She took her mother's hand between her own two plump grubby ones, with her nails bloody and ragged and the cuticles rough and uneven, and gently she kissed her mother's hand. Ellen felt such a weight of sadness, she thought she could hear her heart cracking. Ah, if only somehow, some way, she could undo, repair, change the past.

"Don't cry, Mom," Jennifer said. "Everything will be all right. We'll be together. We'll have a lot of good times. You'll see. I promise. I'm sorry about that thing with the policeman. I'll even try to lose weight so you can be proud of me."

"I've always been proud of you," Ellen said. "I love you."

"And I love you," the girl answered.

Her next task was to get that apartment she had promised to Jennifer. In a way, it was quite pleasant to be so busy, so purposeful. She went into Manhattan to see a real estate agent whom she had once met at a party. The agent, a hard but attractive middle-aged woman, explained that the most Ellen could afford for rent was two hundred dollars a month and that would not include garage, telephone, or utilities.

"What about paying less than that?" Ellen asked.

"Forget it," the agent said, "or go to Brooklyn." Ellen shuddered.

"On top of that," the agent continued, "you'll have to put your daughter in private school, another one hundred a month. If you eat a lot of macaroni and cheese, you two can eat on another one hundred a month, bringing your base total to five hundred dollars. Mind you, that's the base, without any clothes, entertainment, medical, dental, or extras. Your husband will have to pay all of this eventually, but if it takes you six months to get some money from him, you'll need, conservatively, about five thousand because you'll have moving expenses, first and last month's rent, plus security on the apartment, the deposit to the telephone company and assorted miscellaneous expenses."

Panic again filled Ellen. Her money, which had seemed like a lot, she suddenly realized was nothing. Well, six months was all she needed. Thank God she had Todd. Poor as he was he would help her.

"According to what you've been telling me," the agent continued, "you don't even know what furniture you'll have. If your husband doesn't give you any and you have to furnish, you're up shit's creek. Of course, you can always go to the Salvation Army."

"Salvation Army?" Visions of gaunt, red-nosed people singing in the streets at Christmastime!

"People donate their old furniture."

"I don't think I could use that kind of furniture."

"Suit yourself. Baby, I'm divorced, too. There's lots of things we don't think we can do that we end up doing. Ask any divorced woman. One lightning flash and we sink to the bottom of the economic heap. Now let's get a few things straight. If you're going to waste my time asking for a modest little duplex off Twelfth and Fifth, let's knock it off right now. I don't like to waste my time. Understood?" Ellen nodded, staggered at her disastrous economic slide.

Their first stop was what the agent called a not-bad neighborhood. "We won't even bother with the East Side," she said, "forget about going east right now. There's no value at all and even a sublet closet would cost five hundred. So let's stick to the West Side, unpleasant as that may be. Now this here is Seventy-second Street, one of the better West Side streets. There are doormen right along the street, so you don't have to worry about getting mugged. Rape is never a problem here, but sometimes mugging is. But this street, because it's wide and because of the doormen, is pretty safe. Not absolutely, though. One poor old lady I know was mugged right in front of Fine and Shapiro, a kosher delicatessen, which should theoretically be perfectly safe.

"I'm taking you to a new building only because I just had a one-bedroom open up that's within your price range. And this house, I swear it, is completely safe. You drive into the garage and you need keys to get into the house from the garage. Also, there's lots of taxicabs around all the time. A disadvantage is that the garage costs twenty-five a month, but it's worth it for safety.

"Note this elegant lobby. The help's been here since it opened. A lovely lobby. They redo it all the time. Wish I made what the employees get in tips alone. Christmas they turn into tycoons with the tips. The apartment's on the fifth floor. Traffic noises may bother you at first, you coming from the suburbs, but you'll get used to it. Each floor up, the rent is higher for the same size apartment. But heavy soundproofed drapes will shut out everything except the sirens and the fire engines. Another advantage is this house is centrally air-conditioned. The help's marvelous. Lots of old ladies here because it's safe. Lots of kids in the building too. They go to Dalton, good for your kid, too."

They stepped off on the fifth floor and even in this nice apartment house Ellen was immediately assailed by the smell in the halls of food cooking, a smell that reminded her of Saul's Brooklyn tenement, so many long years ago. She shuddered, then stood inside the apartment, stunned.

"This is two hundred dollars?" she exclaimed. "Why, the entire apartment isn't as big as my bedroom at home. One bathroom? And where is the storage space? Only two closets? My God, I can't move into this tiny coffin."

"Okay, okay," the agent said, trying to soothe her, "just hang on. I'm getting a feel of what you want. If space is your thing, let's go further uptown toward Columbia. Not as safe, of course, but more space if that's your thing."

They took a cab to 110th Street. "Subway stops right at the

342

corner," the agent said, "but you'd better take cabs. This is a wide street too, and the wider streets are always better for women alone. Everything is more visible on them. Now there are lots of Puerto Ricans in these buildings, but the low academic salaries keep some people from Columbia here also. There are also lots of students and a solid underpinning of older Jewish people who've been here for years. They get away with murder on their rents, let me tell you. The buildings are old, but here you'll get space. A few cockroaches, too. Ha, ha. No, I'm only kidding. Not a roach on the block. I'm going to show you one apartment that's a real prize and if you don't take it, you might as well give up, because there's no agent in the city who can show you anything better or different. How come you don't want to get an apartment in Westchester where it's familiar at least?"

"Nothing to do there," Ellen said. "Besides, I want to go to college full-time. I have to be in the city."

They stepped out of the cab, in front of a grimy, gray old stone building, defaced with Spanish phrases written all over the front.

"This building has its own tenant protection society," the agent told Ellen. "All of the tenants chip in to have someone at the door on duty at all times. But honestly, it's a really safe building."

"If it's so safe," Ellen asked, between chattering teeth, "why do they have to pay to have someone on duty?"

"Smart girl," the agent chuckled. "it's safe precisely *because* they have someone on duty. Even if you have to go down to the laundry room, you just stop off here and tell the guy on duty and if you're not back in fifteen minutes, he comes looking for you."

I'm going to be sick, Ellen thought. She felt dazed, confused. She had married and stayed with Jeff to be protected, safe from assault, and now she had messed up her life and ended up with the very vulnerability she had struggled to escape. She had managed to be reduced to a situation in which she was totally vulnerable to the world; emotionally, economically, physically vulnerable . . . doubly, triply vulnerable because she was a woman.

They entered the creaky elevator ("only has broken down

343

twice in the past three years") in which Ellen read a notice from the tenants' association which stated that uncovered garbage must not be left in halls because of cockroaches and rats. The agent saw Ellen reading the notice.

"You live in New York, you get cockroaches and rats," the agent said breezily, "but don't worry. They don't come out during the day, they're afraid of the light."

Ellen wrapped her arms around herself and held on tightly, held on to keep from flying apart in hysteria.

"The previous tenants are still here," the agent said, "but they fixed the place up beautiful."

She rang and after identifying herself, Ellen heard one, two, three locks being turned. Then there was the sound of a heavy metal object being dragged away from the door, and finally the door opened, still held in place by a chain. A girl's face looked out over the chain, then the door opened to reveal the apartment.

"Sorry to keep you waiting," the girl said sunnily, with complete acceptance of the exigencies of New York living, "but it's always a bitch to move this metal bar. I'll leave you all the locks. They've kept us completely safe."

The apartment wasn't impossible. It did have space; a large kitchen, dining room, living room, two bedrooms and one bathroom. The bathroom and kitchen were in bad shape, with large gaps of plaster showing where tiles were off, but the girl assured Ellen that someday soon the apartment was due to be painted.

"You just have to keep after them," she said, "but one good thing is that the apartment has plenty of hot water. Good water pressure, too, if you like bubble baths. I do."

Ellen had forgotten there were apartments in which hot water was a problem. She looked in the tub: metal showing through the rubbed-off enamel. The windowsills were grimy, one window was cracked. The living room looked out on 110th Street, but all of the other windows looked out on a narrow back courtyard, strewn with garbage.

"There's a peeper across the way with binoculars," the girl said, "so you have to be careful to pull the shades."

"You mean somebody watches you and you don't do anything about it?"

"Can't do anything about it. Everybody's screwed up in this neighborhood, and the police won't even bother with a peeper. So sometimes, just to torture him, we leave the shades up and drive him crazy. I'll leave you the shades."

"How much is this apartment?" Ellen asked the agent, clenching her teeth to stop that damned shaking.

"One hundred and eighty and you'll be able to afford it if you get rid of your car. You don't need a car in Manhattan, anyway. You can always rent one. You see, this building has no garage and you're better off taking cabs directly here from wherever you are, than using your own car, putting it in the garage on Amsterdam and 118th, and then walking home alone from the garage at night. A car in New York is really just a burden. So? What do you say? You want it? Yes or no?"

Ellen hesitated.

"By tomorrow it will be gone. You won't do better for the price."

"All right, all right," Ellen said. "I'll take it."

They went to the agent's office where Ellen went through the dreary business of signing the lease, paying the deposit, paying the first and last month's rents, and paying the agent's fee. The girls would move out the first of June, so she'd have a month for the landlord to paint.

"Come on, I'll buy you a drink," the agent said, patting her hand sympathetically. They sat in the elegance of the Carlyle bar and Ellen felt as if her heart were breaking. Overnight she was deposed royalty: Anastasia, Davida, Marie Antoinette, Laura Pine, Anatevka. She had now joined the company of those forever exiled from the Garden of Eden. Now she understood the myth of the Fall. She, too, was truly exiled, through her own complicity, her own stupidity, her own refusal to really contemplate her life, never realizing how precious her life with Jeff would seem in the midst of urban rot.

All the way home she kept revolving in her mind how she

could have made things different. But could she have made things different? She had tried. She had repressed her true self and tried to be what Jeff had wanted. She had chopped off her breasts, changed her speech, given up friends like the Mozers, always been at Jeff's beck and call, accepted Ursula. Was she guilty? Well, yes and no. By the time Todd had come along, the marriage was only a hollow shell. Hadn't she planned to leave Jeff, too? Had that been her intention? Would she have gone through with it? She didn't know. What she did know was that she could never have been so cruel to him. But what did you expect, she could almost hear Tina's voice in her mind, Jeff's a businessman and you stopped being a client. One thing she did know. Whatever there had been between her and Jeff, it hadn't been love. With Todd there could be a new start and it would be better for Jennifer, too, to live in a home in which the adults loved each other.

By the time Jennifer was due to leave for camp, Ellen was practically ready to move. Jeff had found this summer's camp for Jennifer. It was a camp that specialized in riding and tennis and boasted a *Social Register* clientele. Probably Candy had recommended it. Ursula had shopped for Jennifer's camp wardrobe, sewn on labels, and packed her trunk and duffel bag. Jennifer didn't really want to go to camp.

"Must I go, Mom," she begged. "I would rather be with you. I could help you move."

"The city is too unpleasant and hot during the summer," Ellen told her. "There's no place to swim and you would have nothing to do. I'm going to try to attend summer session, besides. I'd love to have you with me, my darling, but I don't want to be selfish. You'll be much better off in the country and I'll visit you as soon as I move."

The following Saturday the moving men came for Jennifer's camp things. Jennifer paced up and down through the empty rooms, waiting for them.

"For heffen's sake," Ursula said, "already to your frents go. I vill take care of the movers."

346

"My things have to be watched," Jennifer said. "See this little red crayon X mark here. Well, this end of the trunk has to go out first. Then the duffel has to go out with the string end first. Otherwise, my summer will be spoiled."

"You must be kidding," Ellen said, looking at her in concern. She certainly had some strange ideas. Well, wasn't imagination wonderful though? The Brontës, for example. Hadn't they suffered from strange fancies? She'd heard child psychologists talk about how dangerous it was to suppress the fantasies of childhood and many fanciful children grew up to be adult geniuses. But Jennifer was almost nine years old.

She certainly was somewhat peculiar. But they were all peculiar at this age, weren't they? Maybe Jennifer was a latent creative genius. She was smart enough. And although she'd been brought home that one time because of drinking, there had been no evidence since that it had been more than a childish, peer-induced prank. There had been no complaints from Jennifer's teachers and she never gave Jennifer enough money for beer.

Probably, everything was all right. Jennifer had many friends, many more than Ellen did. She was always staying somewhere and her manners with strangers were excellent. After all, she had to have some reaction to the break-up of the family. That was normal. Lack of reaction wouldn't have been normal. No matter what she said, Ellen was sure, Jennifer loved Jeff and longed for his love. She felt confused. The truth of it was, despite all the books she had read, Ellen couldn't distinguish between normal childhood craziness and real trouble. Regardless, there was nothing to be done now.

The moving men arrived and Ursula gave them the check Jeff had sent for this. Two of the men went over to the trunk and started to move it toward the door.

"No, no," Jennifer screamed suddenly. "You're turning it around in the wrong direction. You can't do that. It's bad magic."

"This kid nuts?" one of the men asked.

They started to move it again and then, with sudden fury,

Jennifer was attacking the first man, biting and scratching and kicking him in the shins like a mad demon, all the time wailing like a banshee.

"Stop that, stop that, Jennifer. I said stop it this minute," Ellen yelled. She flew to the girl and started to pull her away from the man but she was no match for the hysteria of the girl. Ursula dashed over to help Ellen and they managed to pull her away from the terrified man. But it wasn't over. Jennifer broke free and began to bang her head on the polished wood parquet floor. Ellen tried to stop her while Ursula supervised the movers. Finally Jennifer sat up and hunched her shoulders like a cat and moved to the corner of the room, hissing and spitting and crying until she finally wound down. Then, exhausted, she lay on the floor, immobile, staring out at space, breathing in deep, agonized rasps. It was the worst thing Ellen had ever seen, ever felt. Then, suddenly, Jennifer pulled herself together and dashed off to her friends, without a word. Ellen went upstairs, sat on her bed and wept. It was beyond her at this time to help her daughter. Camp would, she hoped, straighten Jennifer out. Perhaps she should call the camp and talk to them. She wouldn't have to describe this terrible scene but she might just inform them of the divorce and ask them to give Jennifer some extra consideration. But just as she was about to pick up the phone, she heard a car in the driveway and looked out her window. Jeff! She was filled with terror at the idea of facing him. What else did he want? She dried her eyes and put on some makeup. When she went down to the breakfast room, he was sitting there, chatting away to Ursula, who was serving him coffee.

"Hi, babes," he said, cheerfully.

"What do you want?" Ellen asked, filled with rage. "You've taken most of the furniture. Would you like my bed?"

"You can keep your bedroom furniture and Jennifer's furniture," he said. "But don't take anything else from the house or the kitchen because I've sold the house *with* the refrigerator, freezer, washer, and dryer. I'd like the king-sized bed when you move, if you don't need it, and in return, I'll give you back one of the guest room beds."

"Sold? So soon?"

"Well," he let slip, "it's not so soon. It's been on the market for six months."

She gasped. Six months! All this time she'd been living in false security. Behind her back, all this time, the plot had been hatching. No wonder he had never noticed how little she had been home.

"You can have the king-sized bed," she said. "I don't want any reminder of the hundreds of unpleasant nights I spent in it with you."

"When are you moving?" he asked, ignoring her remarks. He didn't care. Why should he when he was holding all the cards?

"Jennifer leaves June thirtieth and I'll be out as soon as possible after that."

"You'll have to leave that same day," he said. "The people want possession by July first."

"If you're telling me when I have to be out," she snapped, "why did you ask me?"

"I have to go," he said.

"Just a minute," she said. "I'm not leaving on June thirtieth until we have a few things settled."

"Speak to my lawyers."

"No, either you listen to me or I'll barricade myself in the house."

"All right, damn it. What do you want?"

"I want certain things that will later be Jennifer's."

"Such as?"

"I want the china sets back, the Canton china, the Royal Crown Derby, the Tuttle sterling, the Baccarat glasses, the capiz mats from Gump's, the Pratesi linens, all of the Mark Cross luggage, the Copco pots and pans, and all of the kitchen equipment. I can't keep house without the equipment I'm used to."

"You're becoming a conniving little bitch, aren't you? Who's your lawyer?"

"You'll find out." She kept her voice from trembling.

"Listen, Ellen, I paid for all of those things originally."

"I don't want to discuss that," she said. "I'm simply telling you what I want, Jeff, if you want me out. You've already moved out a hundred thousand dollars' worth of furniture that should be split with me."

"That's just too bad," he sneered. "I'm not bringing back the things you want unless I get something for it. What do I get if I give you all those things?"

"But they're for Jennifer," she said.

"In the meantime," he retorted, "they're for you. So what do I get out of it?"

She put on a big act, as if she were wrestling with herself, and finally, as if she had just seen light dawn, she said, "You can have my car the day after I move."

He and Ursula glanced quickly at each other. Poor Ellen, they were probably thinking, she doesn't even know the worth of a Mercedes. But what good would the car do her? She couldn't even afford to garage it. Jeff rushed to take her up on the offer before, as he probably thought to himself, she got smart.

"Ursula," he said, "remember what she said. You're witness to this."

"Ya, ya," Ursula said, flashing him a triumphant glance. She, too, obviously thought poor Ellen was demented. But Ellen knew what she was doing. She didn't need a car but she was determined to hold on to a dowry of beautiful things for Jennifer.

"All right," Ellen said, "now that all that's settled, we have to have a little talk about Jennifer." She told Jeff about the scene that had happened just before he came home that day.

"The kid's a little screwed up," Jeff said. "Most kids are nowadays. The problem is you've always been too soft on her. Don't expect me to mop up now."

"That's all you have to say?"

350

"It's not my problem," he answered.

"It's both our problem," she said. "Jeff, I don't even know if she should go away to camp. I think she needs professional help."

"She's going to camp," he said, "because I paid for it. Candy raved about the camp. It really puts a little polish on kids. As for professional help, you know I think that's a crock. Most analysts are more screwed-up than their patients. I mean, all that Jacques's analyst has been able to do is to explain why he keeps shoplifting but not to stop him. When Jen comes back from camp, you can do what you like. She's your responsibility now. But don't expect me to shell out a hundred and fifty dollars a week for an analyst. If you want it, sell the flatwear."

He was still there when Jennifer came storming in. "Hiya, fatso," he called after her. She walked up the stairs to her room without acknowledging his presence.

"See you at the train," he called after her. "Candy and I are coming to see you off." Receiving no answer, he left, with a strict reminder to Ellen that Ursula had witnessed her promise.

By the time Jennifer left, Ellen was frankly glad that she was going. There had been no more outbursts of peculiar behavior, but Ellen was wary, nervous, on edge about the girl. She hoped that Jennifer would get straightened out at camp and would return to her in September as a pretty, thin, regular kid.

Jeff and Candace also showed up at the train to say goodbye to Jennifer. Jeff handed her a five-pound box of chocolates and said, "Share this with your friends on the train, and for God's sake come back from camp skinny."

Jennifer kissed him coldly, sidestepped Candace's embrace, and hugged Ellen. "I'll be up first visiting day," Ellen said. "I'll write to you every day and you write to me a lot too, okay?" And then she was gone.

Despite her overwhelming depression, Ellen could not go to bed. She had to spend the rest of the day and all the following day packing. The sooner she was in her own place, be it ever so humble, the better it would be for her. Soon, everything would be better. Todd would come back with his wife's promise of divorce, pleased that things had also been set in motion with Ellen and Jeff, and Kate and Will would also soon be back and perhaps Kate would give Ellen that job she'd been talking about for so many years. She had looked at Jeff and Candy standing there together and didn't feel a thing. The only slightly recognizable feeling was actually one of relief. Somebody else would have to put up with Jeff's difficult moods now.

The moving company came early in the morning, a day and a half after Jennifer had gone, and Ellen was ready for them. Actually, there wasn't a great deal to move. Her possessions looked huddled and minimal, filling up only one small corner of the truck. She still had a few good pieces, however. The two Queen Anne highboys (probably worth about five thousand dollars), the antique grandfather clock from the bedroom alcove (with the authentic wooden works and original gold filial), the crewel-covered easy chairs, the pie-crust table, the fireplace accessories, the antique bed warmer, the antique chestnut roaster, and andirons. They were all good and someday Jennifer would want them.

Ursula stood in the kitchen, as stony-faced as ever. Jeff had brought back the sets of dishes, sterling, and glassware and now they were also loaded on the van. Ellen gave one set of her car keys and the name of the nearest garage to a triumphant Ursula. She would mail the parking receipt to Jeff.

Poor fool, Ellen thought. She thinks it's Gotterdammerüng for me. She's so stupid, she really thinks Jeff cares for her. She doesn't understand that he'll squeeze every bit of juice out of her, then throw away the remains. Well, it's not my problem.

She drove into the city and the moving men were waiting for her when she got there. The previous tenants had left the apartment spotless and in the middle of the living room, on the floor, they had left a small plant with a note wishing her well. She was touched. Always so lovely to find the unexpected kindness. The men moved her possessions in and arranged them. She paid them, then sank down in a chair and looked about her. It really was not too bad. Jennifer's room, especially with all of her furnishings intact, looked quite nice.

This is all mine, she thought. I don't have to put up with Jeff or Ursula or anyone or anything I don't want. Somehow, I'll find a way to keep paying for this until I can get some money from Jeff. In any event, I'm safe for six to eight months. As she prepared for bed that night, she found she was singing a little song. How wonderful. She didn't remember the last time she had felt like singing. Jennifer would straighten out. Todd would return with the promise of love. She would go back to school and make something of her life. She was alive. She had survived. Curtain going up!

She had never really understood, despite the example of Davida, how completely a divorce wrecks the social machine for a woman. All those years of charity balls and EL weekends and dinner parties to attend and dinner parties to give and museum openings and play openings and weddings and bar mitzvahs and surprise parties and masquerade parties and horseback riding and hunt breakfasts and country clubs and charity balls and on and on and on. And now, with one stroke, it was all swept away as if it had never existed at all.

But during the days Ellen kept busy. She went down to NYU and registered for two August session classes, then went from job agency to job agency in the city, looking for a part-time job. To her surprise, it seemed more difficult to get part-time than full-time jobs. She registered at a number of agencies just to be on the safe side, then settled down to wait for Kate and Will. She had left her new number with their butler. Finally, they came back to town and immediately called her.

"Ellen, honey," Will said, "we heard about it in Switzerland from a friend of Candy's, but we couldn't get back any sooner. We saw a new doctor there and I really think he helped Kate. Come on over, honey, right away. We're dying to hear all about it."

"Oh, Will," her voice quavered, "thank you. I thought I

could count on you, but I wasn't completely sure. Tina dropped me right away."

"So Tina dropped you," he jested. "Well, honey, just count your blessings. Take a cab, honey. Martin will be waiting to pay the driver."

In twenty minutes she was there. Will met her at the door and held her in his arms while she cried softly for a few minutes. Then he took her in to Kate, who was seated on the brocade sofa, her feet up, the white lock stark against her face, her once strong, enameled nails broken and ragged. Her face was carefully made up and to a stranger, apart from a slightly tired look around her eyes and those broken nails, she might have seemed normal. Ellen ran to her, kneeled beside the couch, and the two women hugged and cried a little together.

"I felt so bad that I couldn't be here with you," Kate said.

"I felt bad that I couldn't be with you," Ellen answered. "But, of course, you had Will."

"Yes," Kate said, "my beloved Will." He took her hand, helped her up, and they walked into the dining room for dinner.

Then Ellen told them her entire tale and they listened intently, alternately aghast and amused.

"He's making a big mistake with that Candy," Will said, "'cause that Candy is sugar-coated poison."

"He's not the only one making the mistake," Kate added. "She's making one too."

"Why do you say that?" Ellen asked.

"I never would have said it while you were married to him," Kate said, "but Jeff is a limited talent. He's gone about as far as he has only because this has been a boom period. Most businesses have found it easy to grow since the war. In addition, there's his face and charm and the fact that he speaks so many languages. It's no longer enough for the president of a PR agency to be nothing but a salesman.

"Most of your new young presidents are creative guys, guys like Ogilvy, and when they handle an account, the client can assume there will be a certain creative stamp to it. But that's not so

354

with Jeff now. He thinks he's too big. He doesn't supervise any accounts, just sells, runs, and that's about all. Takes the money and runs. For a while, he could get away with that because he had no competition, but now he does, and he's going to have to develop more than charm to keep his clients."

"She's right," Will broke in. "How old is Jeff? Almost forty? One morning he's going to look in the mirror and realize that looks alone aren't going to get clients for him, and that's going to be a big shocker."

"He'll walk in to see a new client," Kate continued, "and the client won't drop dead because he's so gorgeous. The client will also want to know what Jeff can do for him in the creativity department and if Jeff can't come up with an original campaign, he'll never get the account. It's been a long time since 'Live a little with Amos,' and public relations gets more sophisticated, more subliminal every day. I've spoken to Jeff about all of this in terms of our account but he thinks he knows it all, still thinks charm is enough. Unless he starts to listen soon, he'll see a mass exodus of clients. That's why I said Candy was making a big mistake."

"It's a little premature to predict disaster," Will said. "From what I hear, Jeff is still doing all right and with Candy, he'll hold on to the Stewart account and that alone is almost enough to pay the rent."

"Well, he's not doing all right with me," Kate snapped. "He'll never do another campaign for me. I never liked him, only put up with him because of Ellen. But the way he's treated her! It's outrageous. Worst story I've heard in years. I don't mind his leaving her for Candy. That's common enough. But to leave her without a penny, to sell the house out from under her. Outrageous. I always found him so detestable I was sure you only stayed with him for the money, Ellen. And I think you earned your keep."

"No, it wasn't just the money I stayed for," Ellen said, almost thinking aloud.

"Then why?" Will asked, in his kindly fashion.

"Fear of the outside world," Ellen said. "Fear of the Mongol hordes sweeping down and raping me. You know, just the plain fear of being a stateless unperson."

They didn't laugh. "Lots of women stay married because of that," Kate said, "but usually they can't even articulate it that well. For some it's fear, for the rest it's apathy. Fear and apathy, the keys to most human relations, I'm afraid."

The butler announced dinner. Leaning slightly on her husband's arm, Kate led the way to the magnificent table, set as beautifully for Ellen, with its antique flatwear, Aynsley china, and Baccarat glasses, as if an ambassador were coming to dinner. Everything was lovely and muted, sparkling and comforting at the same time. Good red and white wines, quenelles light as meringue, filet mignon, salad, fresh raspberries, and florentines for dessert. During dinner they made light pleasant conversation, talking of the theater season in London, of the restaurants near Lyons, of sunning at Cap d'Antibes.

After dinner they returned to the living room, where the butler brought them espresso and brandy. They both looked at her and became serious. "Ellen, dear," Kate said, "we would like to help you. You say you don't need money because of the ring, so we won't offer money for the moment, although you know you can always call on us if you run out of money before things are settled. But there is something else I can do for you. I would like to offer you a job."

"I have no qualifications," Ellen said, "what kind of job could you give me?"

"I need someone here with me," Kate said.

"A housekeeper?" Ellen asked, her heart sinking. Would she have to become a maid, a servant like Ursula?

"Not a housekeeper," Will said seriously, "a life keeper."

"I don't understand," Ellen said.

"The time has come," Kate said, "for us to be very honest with each other. In Switzerland, Ellen, they removed my second breast. They think they've stopped the cancer. At least that's what the doctor in Switzerland told us. But we can't be sure until after the radiation and chemotherapy."

"Of course they've stopped it," Will said.

"Dear, dear Will. I don't think we should start to lie to each other now. Let's say, Ellen, that the doctors may be right and they may not be right. They know almost as little about cancer as we do. We won't know anything until after the chemotherapy. But I do know that I don't feel as energetic as in the past. I'm tired and weak much of the time and it may grow worse with the therapy.

"So what I need," Kate continued, "is not a housekeeper but a girl Friday. I need someone to go with me for my therapy, to assist me with my work here when I'm not feeling well, to discuss my work with me intelligently, to keep me company when Will is down South visiting our plants. Will must carry on the business and I don't want to be a burden to him. I need a combination secretary, friend, business assistant, and companion. I need a sister. Would you be interested in doing this?"

"It would save my life," Ellen said, "but there's only one thing I have to check out first."

Then she told them about Todd. "Are you shocked?" she asked. "Disappointed in me?"

"Of course not," Kate said. "Jeff's been having his affair with Candy for at least that long and everybody knew about it."

"You, too?" Ellen asked. "Why didn't you tell me?"

"Well," Kate said, trying to be delicate, "it wasn't the first time we had seen it. We felt the same way as Tina. We thought it would blow over. But Candy probably insisted on marriage. No, of course we're not disappointed in you. What would give us the right to judge you anyway? I'm glad if you've found a little joy, if you've found someone who really cares for you the way you deserve."

"And he does, doesn't he?" Will asked in a serious voice.

"Oh, of course," Ellen said. "He's gone home to ask his wife for a divorce. I don't feel good about that, but he told me his marriage has been over for years. I don't want to make any definite plans until he comes back and we've had a chance to talk."

"When is he coming back?" Kate asked.

"Any day now, I guess," Ellen said. "I haven't heard from his since I called him but I called his office and his secretary said he'd be back soon. So will you wait for me to decide on the job until I see him?"

"Of course we will," Kate said, "but don't let it be too long. I need you now."

Will sent her home in the limousine and the chauffeur escorted her to her door. She let herself in, then locked the locks to the apartment and sat down, feeling good. She had a man she loved and the promise of a good job. I feel pretty good about myself, she thought. Everything was turning out just fine. She spent the next few days helping Kate to sort the correspondence that had piled up during her absence. She couldn't understand why Todd was taking so long to return. Finally, she called his office again.

"But Dr. Howard *is* back," the secretary said. "He's been back for over a week. The first summer session starts Monday. He will not be here to teach the second one that begins in August, so if you wish to take his classes, you must come in on Monday and request late registration."

This was the worst shock of all. Back over a week? Impossible. Why hadn't he called her? She had mailed him her new number. She called him at his apartment.

"Ellen, love," he answered, "I just got back this morning. You caught me just as I was about to dial you. I've missed you terribly. When can I see you?"

"Right now," she said. "I'll be there in half an hour."

"I'll be waiting for you," he said in that thrilling sexy voice.

Then she called Kate. She didn't go into any explanation but simply told her, "I've made up my mind. I'd be proud and happy to have that job. I'd like to begin tomorrow."

"Oh, Ellen, dear," Kate said, her voice cracking slightly,

showing a kind of vulnerability Ellen had never seen before, "I'm so happy that you'll come. I really need you."

"Thank you for needing me," Ellen said. Thank you Kate dear for more than you know, she thought. Ellen hailed a cab and gave him Todd's address. This would be the last of her unfinished business.

He was waiting for her in the thick, ankle-length terry-cloth robe she had bought for him at Bergdorf's.

"We have to talk," she said coldly, as he reached for her.

"Later, darling," he said, nuzzling her.

"No," she said, "now, right away. We have to speak about my divorce and yours."

"Yes," he said nervously, "you told me a little about it on the phone. You said he didn't know anything about us."

"He doesn't," she reassured him. And then she told him the details.

"No money," he exclaimed. "But he'll never get away with that. He'll have to pay alimony and child support. How will you manage?"

"Well, of course," she said brightly, watching him sweat, "Jennifer and I couldn't move in here with you. It's too small. But the apartment I took has two bedrooms and is large enough for the three of us. So if you move in with us and help with the rent, I'll be able to manage just fine."

"I don't think I can do that," he said nervously.

"But, Todd, love. Didn't you tell me you wanted to be with me, to marry me, to live with me? Now we're getting exactly what we want. You should be very happy about it. Don't you love me?"

"Of course I love you," he said irritably, "it's just that I wasn't prepared for things to move this fast. I mean, Ellen, give a guy a break. You can't just spring this kind of thing on people. My wife still doesn't know about us."

"I thought you were going home to tell her," Ellen said quietly, wondering how she had ever loved this weak man who could not deliver what he could so easily promise.

"I didn't want to upset her," he said. "She's starting on her M.A."

"What about upsetting me?"

"Yeah, well, I can see your point of view, but you're a lot stronger than my wife."

"But, Todd," she said, "you told me your were going home to ask for a divorce. Suppose I had told my husband about us and you had come back and disappointed me? What kind of position would I be in?"

"It wouldn't be my fault," he said. "I told you not to say anything to your husband until I got back. And thank God you didn't. Now let's look at this practically, Ellen. I started to think about things while I was away and I realized there was no way I could support you in the fashion to which you're accustomed. And there's something else. I wasn't sure before I left, but I saw a few people out in California and I was able to work out a good deal back there. So I'm going back there to work. They're giving me my own staff and a beautiful office, not the dinky one I have now where you can't even make a phone call without everybody hearing you. So I took the job."

She was so disgusted she didn't answer.

"I know how this must look to you," he said nervously.

"How do you think it looks to me?" she asked.

"Well, I guess you're pretty teed off, Ellen, but honestly, I never wanted to do anything except to make you happy. I'll never stop loving you. We don't have to say goodbye. It will never be goodbye for us, my love. I'll be coming to New York and Washington lots of times. We'll see each other every time. Why, we'll be together more than I'm with my wife. Now, love, let's stop this arguing and get back to what's important."

Gently, he pulled her to him and started to deftly unbutton her blouse. "Just a minute," she said. He pulled back and looked at her tenderly. With all the force she could muster, with anger and frustration built up over a lifetime, she pulled her right hand back and smashed him across the face. It was the first time she had ever struck anyone. "That's what's really important," she said. She slammed the door thunderously behind her.

She took a cab back to Kate's. No reason to wait until tomorrow to start. "No contracts, no formal agreements," Will said. "We'll just go from week to week as long as you and Kate are happy."

And that's the way it was. Each morning she joyously sprang out of bed, dressed, listened to television, then went downstairs where Kate's chauffeur waited for her. She loved work, she breathed work. After a while she routinely ate her dinners with them so that she and Kate could return to business matters after dinner.

"You really should move in here," Will said a short time before she went up to visit Jennifer at camp. "We have so much room and we would dearly love to have you both."

"I'll discuss it with her," Ellen said. My God, to live here. What a joke on Jeff that would be.

She borrowed a car from Kate and drove to Vermont to visit Jennifer. Checking into a small motel near the camp she had a wholesome dinner in the dining room and went to sleep early, filled with loving thoughts of her daughter. How happy Jennifer would be that everything was going so well.

She stopped at the camp director's office the next morning, as she had been requested to do in his letter. Mr. Steiger was a pleasant, kind, rugged-looking man with the serious, civilized demeanor of a forest ranger. They made the customary chatter about the beds in the motel and the roads on the way up. It was evident that he was trying to put her at ease. "How is Jennifer doing?" she asked, trying to sound casual.

"Well, essentially fine," he told her, "but she does have a few little problems. Nothing to be overly concerned about, mind you. Just to be aware of. She has problems about herself physically. She's ashamed of her body and it's always a struggle to get her into a bathing suit. She has tantrums if anybody accidentally sees her when she's naked and she only dresses and undresses in privacy in the bathroom. This isn't terribly serious, of course, but it does diminish her pleasure in life. She agonizes constantly.

"I kid her. I say, 'Jenny, you're gorgeous. If you worry now, what will you do when you get really old, like me?'" He patted his paunch. "We had that very discussion only yesterday."

"What did she say to that?"

"She said, 'I'm not going to live to grow up.'"

Ellen felt an icy chill around her heart. She sat there, shocked.

"There, there," he said compassionately, "kids say lots of funny things."

"This isn't so funny," Ellen said. They sat quietly thinking for a few moments.

"Your husband visited her last week," Mr. Steiger said.

"Oh? I didn't know."

"I spoke with him about Jennifer and he seemed to regard it as a problem emanating from you. He said your focus on appearance might have communicated itself to her."

Why, that bastard, she thought. "It's not because of me," she protested. "I adore Jennifer and I adore her apart from her appearance and I always have and always will. It's her father who has tormented her all of her life."

"There, there," he said, "I didn't mean to upset you."

"It's all so damned unfair," she broke out, "so unjust. To blame me for what he knows damned well was caused by him."

"Well," he said, "no point in fighting over it, is there? I just wanted you to know. Don't worry. She'll grow out of these fancies."

Ellen left him and walked to Jennifer's bunk. Jennifer was waiting outside for her and when she saw her she was so deeply shocked that she could not control her reaction. Jennifer saw her face and saw the shock and Ellen realized that had been a strategic mistake. Jennifer looked as if she'd put on more than twenty pounds. In one month, she had passed from being slightly over-

362

weight to being an obese girl, waddling along, oozing sadness from every sausage roll of fat.

Ellen's expression of shock became a barrier between them for the rest of the visiting day. After their initial kiss, Jennifer had nothing to say, so Ellen just chattered away mindlessly. She told her about Kate and Will's offer to let them live there. Jennifer was furious. "But, Mommy," she said, "you promised that we could have a place of our own."

"I know I did," she answered, "and if that's what you want, that's what we'll have. But honestly, love, it doesn't make sense. Why should we live in an apartment where I'm afraid to get a glass of water at night because of the roaches, instead of in one of the last remaining mansions in New York City? Most of the good schools are on the East Side, too. It would even be convenient for the Dalton School."

"Would you really rather live there than to live alone with me, Mommy?"

"I *would* live alone with you there, darling. The house is so large we could have our own wing. We would still sleep right next door to each other every night, the way I promised you."

"I don't want to go there, Mommy."

"Why not?"

"Because it will be full of people like Ursula and because I'll always have to be thinking about everything the way I did with Daddy, what I eat, how I look, what I say. I mean, would I be able to just go down to their refrigerator and help myself? You might say yes, Mommy, and mean it but it wouldn't work out that way."

"All right, love, then we'll live in the apartment on 110th Street the way I promised."

"I don't want to anymore."

"You mean you'll go to Kate's with me?"

"No, I don't want to do that either. I want to go away to school where there would be lots of other kids."

"You do?"

"Yes, I've been wanting to all summer but I didn't want to leave you alone."

"Are you sure, baby?"

"Absolutely, Mom. I even know the school I want to go to. One of the kids in my bunk goes to a school named Maplewood. It's only about two hours away from New York City so you and I can still see a lot of each other. She and her sister go there and they both like it."

"All right," Ellen said hesitantly, "if you're really sure. But I won't give up the apartment on 110th Street for a year. If you decide, during that time, that you want to come back, we'll move in there, just as I promised. All right?"

"Sure, Mom," Jennifer said.

"There's something else I want to talk about," Ellen said. "Remember the day you left for camp. That terrible scene. I've been worried about it."

"Oh, Mom, you don't have to worry about that. And I won't ever take a drink again. You don't have to worry."

"Why did you start? We don't drink."

"Oh, you know, other kids. But honestly, Mom, you don't have to worry."

"I thought maybe in the fall you'd like to see a doctor to discuss anything that is bothering you. Now that I'll be working for Kate, I'll be able to afford it."

"I'm not interested, Mom. I don't need it. Honestly, everything's going to be all right now. You don't have to worry."

"But your weight," Ellen said.

"That's one thing I don't want to discuss," Jennifer said angrily. "I lost a pound last week."

"All right," Ellen sighed. "It's your body." She didn't want to upset Jennifer now. Maybe, once she got to school she would take the weight off.

Ellen moved to Kate's the week after she returned from Vermont.

"We don't want Jeff to find out about this," Kate said. "He

would use it as a pretext to get out of giving you adequate alimony and child support. Use the apartment as your mailing address."

Ellen decided not to take the courses in August for which she'd registered. She didn't even go down to get her money back. She was still too bruised to risk running into Todd.

Kate sent Ellen to a laywer friend for her divorce. His office was as elegant as Anthony's but now she was treated with an extension of the respect accorded to Kate and Will.

"You're young," she told the eager, dark-haired man who rose to greet her.

"You're pretty young yourself." He grinned as he handed her a cup of coffee. Yes, she thought, I guess I still am. There's still time to make something of myself.

"Your big problem," he told her, "is not because everything is in Jeff's name. We could easily deal with that. You've got a problem because Jeff has witnesses to adultery, and because there's a lot of money involved, he's ready to go to court.

"I want you to be completely truthful with me," Peter Pfizer said. "To begin with, there's one Giovanni Lampedusa. Apparently, in a moment of anger, he informed his wife of your existence, and she went to your husband. The wife is convinced that you'll end up in hell and wants to personally begin that process on earth. In addition, there's your au pair girl, Ursula, who apparently overheard you telling your friend Tina about two men, this Lampedusa and a certain riding instructor, named Lenny. However, this last bit of information is the most damaging. Apparently, your husband has had an old FBI buddy of his follow you around for the past few months, and this man has sworn that what you were doing for your recent educational studies was not educational at all in the way assumed by your husband.

"Well, we could discredit Ursula by saying she was in love with your husband and this Giovanni thinks he could quell his wife, but there's one witness whose word *would* stand up in court."

"Who is that?" Ellen asked. She had never been more ashamed in her life.

"That witness, my dear woman, is the professor himself."

"I don't believe it," she said. "I don't believe he would do such a thing. He was supposed to be in love with me. Why would he try to hurt me?"

"I'm certain he would deeply regret it if he hurt you. I don't think he's doing this against you. He's probably been bought."

"I don't believe it."

"You'd better believe it. Are there any other infidelities that might be brought up?" She shook her head. "Nevertheless," he continued, "there's quite a lot here that would undoubtedly prejudice a judge. We may have to take a lot less than you should get because judges in general look with jaundiced eyes on unfaithful wives, especially those of the upper classes whose husbands, like yours, appear to slave away to give them everything. I heard one judge say in a case that resembled yours, 'The problem with these women is that they haven't enough to do with themselves. Give them a few floors to scrub and they won't be running around fornicating in all of that spare time.'

"So you can see what we're up against. We can protect Jennifer without difficulty. Alimony for you is another matter. And for heaven's sake, don't let anyone know you're living with Will and Kate or have a job. It sounds more pathetic for you to go from riches to rags and to be unemployable."

Ellen told Kate and Will about what had happened over dinner that night. Will burst into laughter, when she told him about Todd. "The absolute, sheer rottenness of the fellow! At least Jeff is rotten on a grand scale, not for a few pieces of silver."

"Don't cry, Ellen, dear," Kate said. "Laugh. Please laugh. It's really funny. Someone once told me," she went on, "that growing up was the process of accepting the possibility of betrayal as a fact of life. I don't remember where I once read the story of a father who puts his child up on a table, holds out his arms and says, 'Jump. Don't worry, I'll catch you.' The child jumps, the father folds his arms, and lets the child fall to the ground with a thud. When the child stands up aggrieved and yells, 'Why didn't you catch me?' the father responds, 'Let that be a lesson to you. Don't ever trust anybody.' "

"That's awful," Ellen said, but suddenly all three friends were laughing.

"Champagne," Kate said, "this calls for champagne. Remember this maxim, Ellen. 'The worse the trouble, the better the vintage.' "

Toasting each other, toasting Kate's health, Ellen's divorce, and the success of their business undertakings, they drank.

10

The success of Kate's company was based on one major concept. She had been the first to understand that non-crushable knits were the answer to the modern woman's clothing needs.

"When I was a girl," she told Ellen in her lovely, throaty voice, "the only knits women wore were sweaters, Shetlands, cashmere if you were wealthy, Tyrolean sweaters for ice skating, wool which had to be dry-cleaned. So I started to think. If I went on a trip and decided to wear a sweater, the sweater would look fine when I unpacked but the skirt to go with it did not. It would be crushed, unlike the sweater. If I wanted to take two coats, unless I wore one and carried one, the one in my suitcase would get crushed and I'd be worried about having it pressed at my destination.

"Other factors also made the growth of knits essential. In the old days, travel was limited to the wealthy, a family could check into a hotel on the Lido for a month with their servants to clean and press their clothes. But after the war, travel opened up for the masses who traveled for shorter periods of time. They'd spend two days in Venice, two in Rome, go around the world in a month. And these people needed serviceable clothes.

"So we were the first to produce knit suits for women, three-piece suits, either slacks, blouses, and jackets, or skirts, blouses, and jackets. After a while we started to produce these pieces separately so women could coordinate their own wardrobes and not worry if their hips were two sizes larger than their waists or shoulders. A woman could coordinate Katie Knits such as the following: a pair of beige knit slacks, a matching jacket, a matching skirt, two matching blouses, one blue and one beige, and one pair of matching knit shorts. Then we started to produce coordinated long skirts so she could be dressed for evening, as well. We added to that knit halters, which could either be coordinated for evening with the long skirts or for daytime with the coordinated skirts, shorts, or slacks. Our slogan, which I have to admit was Jeff's inspiration, was 'Total Freedom with Katie Knits.' "

"I remember that campaign," Ellen said. "The ad I loved was the one that showed the girl surfboarding or skiing or skating, saying, 'Katie Knits give me more time for the things I love to do.' "

"God, yes," Kate reminisced. "Remember the trouble we had with the ad showing the girl sitting on the edge of a bed in a short knit nightgown, looking down at the man under the covers with only his magnificent, bare, but suggestive shoulders showing, saying, 'Katie Knits give me more time for the things I love.' "

"You can get away with a lot more now," Ellen said.

Kate, perceptive as ever, looked at Ellen's suddenly sad face. "Come now," she said gently, "so he thought up great campaigns. That doesn't mean he was the right husband for you." Ellen wiped away a tear. "I'm only crying," she said, "not for what it was but for what it might have been."

"All right," Kate said, "but now it's over and I'm going to give you the first advice someone once gave me and it's helped me to become a successful businesswoman. Don't waste time in unproductive thought, in posturing, in the striking of romantic attitudes. Don't waste thought on yesterday. Jeff is over. He's the past, he no longer can serve any purpose at all for you. I understand what you're doing because I did the same thing once. You go around and around like a rat in a maze, thinking about what he said and what you said and what he did and what you did. You keep thinking of how it could have been salvaged, of how it could have been made different. You go over each unsuccessful confrontation, each necessary and unnecessary quarrel, and the more you think the more depressed you get and the more depressed you get the more your present productivity falters. The more your productivity falters, the more unhappy you get, and so you enter that downward spiral which results in a complete impasse.

"Ellen, dear. I'm not saying people shouldn't grieve. Mourning and wailing are normal and they serve an important cathartic function. But then it's over and if you continue to grieve you start to go backward instead of forward. Then you're in decline. Take Will and me. For several weeks, after each operation, we grieved. Then, almost simultaneously, we looked at each other and I said, 'Okay, I may be dying but in the meantime, let's get on with the business of living.' "

"Oh, Kate, dear, I adore you," Ellen said. "You're the most admirable person I've ever known. You've saved my life. I don't know how I can ever show my gratitude."

"Hey, listen," Kate said, "I need you, too, and it's not just because of my illness. I never had a sister and all these years I've never had a woman friend. Those men in EL. They made me sick. Even without knowing the truth about us, they would say things like, 'Hey, Kate, if you're the president and Will is vice-president, who's in charge in bed?' They'd hint that I was masculine, domineering, dominating, and downright castrating. And all the while, Will was happier with me than they were with their supposedly docile wives. The real castrators, like Heidi and Candace, had them completely bamboozled.

"But the women weren't my friends either. They would say

dumb things to me like, 'My husband won't let me work,' or, 'I believe the man should wear the pants in the family.' Stupid, vulnerable, defenseless dolls! They never understood that in undermining me, they were undermining themselves. Miserable and unhappy as most of them were and are, they refused to believe that I had a better way to live. The only thing those women really admired about me was this house and it means nothing to us. Frankly, we purchased it only as a business investment and someday we'll sell it for a fortune to someone who wants to erect an apartment house here. So, all of these years I haven't had a friend. I need you every bit as much as you need me."

For the first time in her life Ellen was able to speak about anything she wished without fear of ridicule or censure. They talked incessantly while they worked. Ellen told Kate how troubled she was about Jennifer's camp report and Kate comforted her.

"What can your worrying do at this moment but depress you?" Kate asked. "Camp will soon be over and when she gets to school, if you think she needs extra counseling, you'll get it for her. Now let's get back to work."

"You're the most disciplined person I've ever known," Ellen said.

"I am well disciplined and you must be, too," Kate told her. "We want to *use* our problems, not let our problems use us. That's the only way to be successful in business. For example, right now I have our designers working on a knit bra with foam rubber inserts, for women who have had breast surgery." The teaching went on each day.

"After our meteoric success with women's knits," Kate told her, "we bought another mill and branched out into men's knits. Here, too, we became instantly successful because we filled a need. Men, as well as women, were tired of clothes that had to be pressed each time they were worn. With our 'Willknit Suits,' a man found that he could carry all of the clothing he needed for a trip right on the plane with him in an overnight bag.

"What gave our empire its greatest boost was the discovery

371

of synthetic fibers. With the help of our chemists, there was no stopping us. We learned to make synthetic fiber warm-weather knits—although I find cotton far cooler in warm weather because it can breathe—and, best of all, we developed knits with a memory, washable knits."

"It sounds to me as if you've done everything," Ellen said.

"It's only the beginning," Kate said. "I used to work eighteen hours a day. I want you to work that hard. I really worked to become a member of EL. Lots of tasks lie ahead, as you learn the business; new advertising slogans, new gimmicks, new ways of promoting; new uses for knits. I used to arrange for tie-ins; department store fashion shows, new jewelry lines, specials in fashion magazines, celebrity endorsements. I want you to learn how to do every one of those tasks. Right now, I can still think, plan, and project, but until I'm completely recovered, my energy will be limited. But you'll supply me with your energy. You'll be my staff, my assistant, my confidante. I need someone to trust in that Versailles out there." (Funny, Ellen thought, that's the way Jeff had seen the business world also.) "The more you help me, Ellen, dear, the more you will equip yourself for this business. You can start on my shoulders, probably rise to even greater heights in this business than I have done. During this next decade women will really start to come into their own and you will be in a perfect position to assume business leadership, if you listen to me. What do you say?"

"You're dreaming," Ellen said.

"I'll dream the dreams I had for myself for you from now on," Kate said somberly.

"Please don't say those things," Ellen pleaded, "you're going to get better. I know it." But in her heart she didn't believe it.

Ellen was able to get Jennifer admitted to Maplewood without difficulty and at the end of the summer she made plans to pick Jennifer up at camp and drive her directly to the school. When Ellen arrived at the camp, Jennifer didn't have much to say. She nodded coldly to her mother instead of running to her and kissing her, then said goodbye to her bunk mates without enthusiasm, and plunked herself down in the car after it was loaded with her stuff.

"Don't I get a kiss?" Ellen asked.

"Where'd ya get the station wagon?" Jennifer answered.

"I rented it," Ellen said, "so we could fit your bicycle and trunk in. After we check in to the school, we'll go shopping and I'll buy every lovely thing you want. I've been putting money aside every week so we could have a great shopping spree."

"Wonderful," Jennifer said, without enthusiasm. They drove along for a while in uneasy silence.

"Well, how was the end of camp?" Ellen asked.

"Fine."

"Do you want to tell me anything about it?"

"Nope."

"Would you like to hear about my job with Kate?"

"Nope. Can I listen to the radio?" She turned it on full blast and didn't say another word until they stopped for lunch.

"Cheeseburger with mayo, French fries, a chocolate malted, and French fried onion rings," Jennifer ordered. Ellen shuddered at the calorie count but repressed her comments. She didn't want to upset Jennifer at this time of transition. It was probably a very threatening time for her. Jennifer kept shoveling food into her mouth and simultaneously feeding quarters to the table jukebox. She finished what she had ordered, asked for pie and ice cream, listened to more music, and then they were off again.

They arrived at Maplewood shortly after two in the afternoon. Ellen loved the grounds immediately; long rolling fields and lawns, a group of boys playing soccer, four young girls working on the tennis court with an attractive young instructor, and a symmetry to the white, Federal-style buildings which made it resemble a small New England town.

"It's lovely," Ellen sighed. "I think you've made a wise choice. The catalog says that you can learn riding and tennis. Their academic standards are high, too. At the end of your time here, you'll be able to get into any college you want."

Jennifer had her own room, even though it had cost something extra. But that's what she had wanted and Ellen wanted to make her happy. After they unpacked the trunk and duffel, they put all the dirty clothes in the car, drove to a local laundromat that promised to have them ready by six, and went out to shop. Ellen bought Jennifer several deep, huge floor cushions to sit on, a moderately priced hi-fi, a throw rug for the floor, a bedspread, and some inexpensive batiks for the walls. They picked up the laundry, had dinner, then took the new items to Jennifer's room.

"Would you like to stay with me at the motel tonight?" Ellen asked, and was pleased when Jennifer agreed. She was happy that the school had given her a key to lock her room. "I was worried about that," she said.

That night in the motel was a renewal for both of them. They watched television, talked, laughed, and planned. "Let's go some place warm for Christmas," Jennifer said. "I haven't been to an ocean for years." Ellen promised to make arrangements and they fell asleep holding hands across the space between the beds. Ellen hated to leave her the next day.

"It's not too late to come back to New York with me, my love," she told her.

"No, Mom, I like it here. I'll be fine. Please don't worry."

Ellen kissed her goodbye and started to cry as soon as she had driven through the school gates. Happy as she was working with her friends, that didn't stop her terrible loneliness. But she mustn't depend on Jennifer to fill that void. It was probably for the best that Jennifer had made her decision to go away to school. Ellen simply had to build a social world of her own. It would be wrong to be dependent on her daughter.

Increasingly she threw herself into work when she returned. Every day she read endless books and journals about the knitwear business and she worked with Kate from morning till late at night. Kate seemed to be racing against time and Ellen had nothing else to do with herself. But at the back of Ellen's mind was always some anxiety about Jennifer. Two weeks after school began, she received a call that Jennifer was in the school infirmary and she went dashing up to visit her.

Jennifer lay in bed, passively watching television. Her arm was in a cast, and she had a bad cold. Gradually, Ellen wormed the entire story out of her. The night before she had been dusted. Dusted? What was that? What was another word that meant "dusted"? Well, it kind of meant being initiated.

"I was sound asleep, Mommy. It was about midnight, when I heard a knock on the door and somebody's voice said there was an urgent telephone call for me. At first, I wouldn't open the door because I didn't believe them and I had heard about the tricks here. But then they said my daddy was on the phone and he was calling from the hospital because he'd had a heart attack. So I went flying up to the second floor where the hall phone is and the receiver was hanging from the phone, so I picked it up and I said, 'Daddy. Daddy. Is this you?'

"Then they dusted me. From all four corners of the hall ice-cold pails of water were thrown on me and then the kids yelled, 'You're being dusted. Welcome to Maplewood!'

"Well, Mommy, the water was so cold and I was so shocked and sleepy that I was a little confused. I said, 'He's not on the line anymore,' and then they started to laugh and I understood that he hadn't called at all. So I started to stumble back to my room but I was so dizzy and confused that I fell down the stairs and broke my wrist."

"Oh, darling," Ellen wept, holding the girl tightly to her. "I'm so sorry you had such an awful experience."

"It's all right now, Mommy, honest. It happened but now it's over. They only do it once and then they leave you alone."

Finally Jennifer slept and Ellen went marching to the school guidance counselor in a towering rage. "I cannot believe," she shouted, when she entered the office, "that a school that costs five thousand dollars a year could let this kind of incident occur. What kind of place is this, anyway? You have a fine reputation and yet I find cruelty, sadism, lack of supervision. What kind of monstrous children do you harbor here? I don't only blame the kids who did this terrible thing. I blame all of you here. Children may do irrational things but the function of adults is to control and supervise. Have you any idea of how traumatic a stunt like that is? Why were those children wandering through the halls after midnight?"

The guidance counselor, a well-bred southern girl named Courtenay Bradley, put her arms around Ellen and patted her gently and let Ellen cry.

"You're absolutely right," Courtenay said.

"What?"

"I said you're absolutely right. It's an outrage. But there's something I'd like to tell you before you decide to take Jennifer away from here. I shouldn't be telling you but I know you'll respect my confidence."

Defused, Ellen sank down on a couch and Courtenay brought her coffee and Social Tea biscuits.

"The ringleader has been asked to leave," Courtenay said. "She's packing right now, has been on probation from last year but she's a senior and her father begged us to let her stay. He's a pretty powerful man, a big builder, and in return for our letting her stay, he rebuilt the Student Union at his own expense. Our school is over a hundred years old and many of the buildings are in disrepair. We can't use as much money as in the past for our building fund because we're committed to more scholarships for minority students. So when the girl's father offered to rebuild, our board of trustees overruled my desire to expel the girl. I almost lost my job over it.

"The girl is deeply disturbed. Last year she kept calling parents of students who were perfectly fine and telling them their kids had run away or been in auto accidents. In the middle of many nights I'd be awakened by hysterical parents. But the board kept her anyway.

"When I wanted her out, I was told that if I couldn't help her, I was not earning my salary. 'It's easy enough to work with normal young people,' they told me, 'but what separates the professional from the amateur is the ability to work with children with deep-set problems.'

376

"So, as I said, they kept her on and I was sorry then and I am sorry today. But she has finally gone too far. She's leaving and I promise you to take a personal interest in Jennifer and to make all of this up to her."

"A builder," Ellen said with some trepidation. "What's the name of the girl you're expelling?"

"Well, I really shouldn't say, but I guess it doesn't matter now that she's going. Her name is Georgina. Georgina Landor."

What an irony, Ellen thought. "I know the family," she said dryly. There was no way, it seemed, to escape from the octopus of EL. And now poor Jennifer had been caught in the web.

It took two years for Ellen and Jeff to be divorced and for Michael and Candace to be divorced. Jennifer started to like her school and there were no more crises there. Kate's cancer had not metastasized and she had returned to her office in the Evans Building, taking Ellen along with her. One morning, when they stepped out of the elevator on to the executive floor, Kate said to her, "Close your eyes."

"Don't be afraid of tripping, I'll lead you, honey," Will added.

"Now you can open," Kate said gleefully.

"I can hardly believe it," Ellen said, deeply touched. There on the door of the office she used, which was right next to Kate's, was the sign: *E. Sheldon, Assistant to the President.*

"Thank you, thank you both," she said, enthusiastically kissing her two friends.

"You deserve it, honey," Will said. "Nobody could work harder than you do."

"It was a lucky day that we hooked up together," Kate added.

"But now for some less pleasant news," she said, as they walked together into her office. "Jeff's getting married." She handed Ellen the invitation. "December 20."

"I couldn't care less," Ellen said, meaning it. Jeff was old business. The lawyers had come to an agreement and the divorce had been settled out of court. She was to get ten thousand a year for Jennifer until she finished graduate school, but that was it. Ellen was to get no alimony, no additional furnishings or accoutrements other than those she had insisted on for Jennifer. She was to receive no stocks, bonds, or savings.

"It's a rotten settlement," Will had said in fury when Peter Pfizer had come to the house to inform them.

"The lady has been rather indiscreet," the lawyer had said.

"It's all right," Ellen said. "I don't care about money. I don't care about those things. It's worth anything to be free of him."

"There's a difference between not caring about money and allowing oneself to be cheated," Will said.

"But, Will, I'm grateful to him for booting me out. My life started here with you and Kate."

The world had changed. Her way of life had changed. Camelots had a way of ending, but they also had a way of beginning again.

"Do you care if we go to the wedding?" Will asked.

"Of course I don't." Ellen laughed. "I want you to go. It's the only way I'll find out anything about it. I bet Candy will be pretty nervous wondering if I'm going to commit suicide during this wedding. I wonder if Jennifer is going." She called her daughter at school.

"I'm not invited," Jennifer said in anger. "That snob isn't inviting me. She said she doesn't want a repetition of her first wedding. I'm really disappointed, Mom. I've never been to a wedding. Well, I won't invite Daddy to my wedding either, if anybody ever marries me."

"I'm sure he wanted to invite you," Ellen said lamely, "but he probably didn't want to fight with Candace."

"I don't know why," Jennifer said. "He certainly fought a lot with you. He may blame her for this but I don't really think it's her fault. If he wanted me to be there, he'd insist. The real

378

reason he's not inviting me is that I'm too fat. He's always been ashamed of me and that's the truth of the matter. I'll show him. He'll be sorry. I'll stop eating completely and when I die he'll be sorry."

"I'm the one who would be sorry," Ellen said, "so just drop that idea fast." Every time she spoke to Jennifer, she came away depressed.

"I knew things were too good to last," Kate said to Ellen a few weeks later. "It looks like the cancer has metastasized and I have to undergo some more chemotherapy. Oh, damn it. The stuff makes me feel so sick." It was the first time Ellen had seen her really break down. So the chemotherapy began again and Kate and Ellen moved their offices back to the Fifth Avenue house.

After six weeks, Ellen was disturbed to see how much Kate had changed. The chemotherapy was taking a terrible toll. Her hair was all gone and she had to wear a wig. She was always tired and her nausea and weakness after each treatment resulted in additional responsibility being heaped on Ellen each day. When the date for Jeff's wedding arrived, Will decided to go alone. They could hardly wait for him to come home to tell them about it.

Jeff's and Candy's wedding, according to Will, hit a new low of vulgarity. The women's page of the *Times* carried a full report the next day. Six hundred family friends and retainers attended. There were five vocalists, five harps, four white baby grand pianos, ice sculptures that were six feet high, sixty giant plaster wedding bells, cloud-making machines, thirty waiters holding aloft flaming sabers, and a roster of EL and PR celebrities, in addition to Candy's socialite friends. Dalway had come alone, the Moranos were there, sitting far away from Amos, Tina and Harry were there, Myra and Leonard, almost the same cast of characters as for the last wedding.

With Dalway was Senator Dunstan, who was being spoken of as the next President, and a contingent of big-name politicians. Enid Taylor and Tim Scott had brought a Hollywood crowd.

Wedding guests entered the grand ballroom of the Pierre on a red carpet, cordoned off by red velvet ropes and guards in tuxedos.

They were married by the same minister as before, and after the ceremony, the guests tore into piles of smoked salmon, mounds of cream cheese, tiny lamb chops, prosciutto wrapped around white asparagus, hunks of roast beef, and seafood crêpes. Flaming baked Alaska was the dessert, brought in by a chorus line of waiters.

The decor had been done by a friend of Jeff's who designed shows for Madison Square Garden. "All that was missing were the elephants," Will reported.

"If it gives you any satisfaction," he chuckled, "Candy was nervous throughout. Maybe she thought you would show. And oh, yes, Dalway asked about you. He was there, incidentally, without his wife. Tina looked as pretty and merry as always, but Harry looked even more sour than usual; gray and tired."

"No wonder," Kate said, "after all those years of living with Tina's babble."

"He adores her," Ellen said.

"Well," Kate joked, "at least that's what she always says. But whoever knows what goes on inside silent Harry?"

"I think it's pretty sad," Ellen said, "that Jeff could spend a fortune feeding six hundred strangers and couldn't invite his own daughter. He has no heart."

"My dear girl," Will joked, "whoever thought he did?"

Two days later, they were having breakfast when Kate opened the newspaper to the obituary page and gasped. A third EL'er had broken the solid gold circle. Harry had died of a heart attack immediately after returning home from Jeff's wedding.

"Jeff killed him with all that food," Will said. "Jeff must be frantic. That might be another client down the drain. What bad timing for him. If he'd waited, he might have married Tina and he'd have a lot more fun with her than with Candace. Besides, Harry's empire is far larger than Michael's."

"Poor fellow," Kate said, "always so silent. I never really knew what he was like."

"I guess none of us did," Ellen answered. "But he and Tina certainly had a good, workable marriage arrangement."

Her first impulse was to rush to the phone, but she could never forget Tina's betrayal, the way Tina had cut all connection at the very moment Ellen most needed a friend. Ellen decided to do nothing but she felt guilty at the thought of Tina all alone in that enormous mansion in Scarsdale. It would be easy for her to forgive Tina; she understood why they had broken off. It wasn't malice. Tina wasn't that way; Tina was realistic. That was the way she was. She had never pretended to be anything other than hedonistic and pragmatic. The next week, Ellen finally called, and after the housekeeper had carefully screened the call, Tina got on immediately.

"Oh, God, Ellen," she said, as if she had spoken to her yesterday, "do I need to talk to you! Where are you living?"

Not trusting Tina's discretion, Ellen arranged to meet her at the 110th Street apartment. She had held on to it for these past two years, waiting for the divorce to be final, although now, even when Jennifer came home on vacations, they stayed at Kate's house. Tina agreed to meet her there the next day so they could have dinner together. She came sweeping in a half-hour late and looked around the apartment as if she were smelling garbage.

"I can't believe that you would live in such a place," she said. "How can you live here, Ellen? Nobody lives on the West Side." Ellen grinned.

"You're looking pretty sensational," Ellen said. Tina wore a gray suede suit with matching gray suede boots, a small diamond pin, her usual assortment of extraordinary rings, and diamonds in each ear to match the pin. "You're lucky you didn't get murdered in the elevator for your jewels."

"I wish I could say you look well, Ellen, but you're not. You're certainly not holding up very well in life. Better take care of your looks, or you're going to lose them. It's no wonder your skin is abominable if you live in a sooty, dusty place like this. Let's go to Pavillon. My chauffeur's downstairs. He's probably horrified by the neighborhood."

381

"You'll have to pay for my dinner at Pavillon," Ellen said.

"I could pay for a hundred dinners," Tina answered gaily. "I'm probably the richest eligible widow around, at the moment."

Continuing to express her disgust at the neighborhood and the apartment, Tina led her downstairs and Ellen sank back against the marvelous leather of the familiar Rolls, and a flood of memories swept across her.

"Do you miss Harry terribly?" she asked in a sympathetic voice.

"Of course not," Tina said, as if Ellen were stupid to even raise so preposterous an idea. Then, to Ellen's amazement, Tina burst into tears. It was the first time she had ever seen Tina indifferent to the state of her makeup.

"There, there," Ellen said, patting her arm gently. "You're not as tough as you pretend. You really do miss him."

"Don't be an idiot," Tina wailed. "That's not why I'm crying."

"Then why, for heaven's sake?" Was Tina perhaps a little unbalanced by grief?

"I'm crying about Dr. Bloom."

"What are you crying about him for? He didn't have the heart attack."

"Worse!"

"What could be worse?"

"It was after the funeral," Tina sniffled, "right here in this very car, in Harry's beloved Rolls, that it happened. Dr. Bloom put his hand up right between my legs and started to passionately kiss and fondle me."

"Outrageous," Ellen said, trying to keep a straight face. Why, that old quack. Maybe he thought it was good therapy for a widow.

"How could he do such a thing?" Tina continued.

"I don't know," Ellen said.

"And on the very day of the funeral. If only he had waited, I could have responded. This way, I had to act indignant because after all you have to have some respect for the dead for a little while at least. So what could I do? I scolded him and he apologized and said he understood if I never saw him again. If only he could have waited until my next session. Then things could have happened normally. He has that couch in his office, you know the one, and we could just have drifted into it. Just think, Ellen, of all the men I've known well in my life, he's the only one I've never slept with."

"Who'd want to sleep with him?" Ellen grimaced.

"You may not think he's attractive," Tina said testily, "but that's only because you're so super defensive. Bloom said it was as hard to reach you as a virgin through a chastity belt."

"That's some great analogy for a cultured, trained, professional analyst. Well, he couldn't reach me, that's true, but apparently, he didn't think he'd have any difficulty in getting through to you."

"He still can," Tina said, sniffling again, "but suppose he doesn't try. I love him but I had to reject him. When I scolded him he burst into tears, apologized for letting his passion get out of hand, and that's when he said he would understand if I never saw him again. Then he had me stop the car. He got out and ran away. He fled into the crowd."

"What Byronic behavior for that scrunched-up little man."

"Will you stop that, Ellen? He's not scrunched-up. He's beautiful. He has a beautiful soul and I love him."

"For heaven's sake. So go and tell him."

"Do you really think I can convince him of my love?"

"He's been listening to you for fifteen years. You two were probably meant for each other. Don't worry."

Tina wiped her eyes and the storm was over. The chauffeur let them out at Le Pavillon, where the maitre d' greeted Tina, who was a regular, with the warmth reserved for the wealthy. The restaurant aroused the same nostalgia in Ellen that the Rolls had. It was a joy to live with Kate and Will and nothing could be more luxurious than their way of life, but this was the first time Ellen had been out at a fancy restaurant since the separation. She looked at the couples seated around them, and realized that she was terribly lonely. Friends could not substitute for love. I'd like a date, she thought. But how to begin? She would have to talk to Kate about it.

Ellen listened to Tina ramble on as they ordered the familiar *boeuf en croute,* quenelles, endive salad, and, for dessert, the floating island she had always loved. The wine was a fine Batard Montrachet and she felt herself floating in the air like a Chagall bride, temporarily free of all cares.

"How soon do you think I can marry Dr. Bloom?" Tina asked her.

"Isn't it too soon to think of that?" Ellen answered.

"Certainly not," Tina said, exasperated. "Harry's dead. I made him happy while he was alive but now he's dead. There's nothing at all that I can do about that so I don't see why I should be lonely."

Ellen listened to her and envied her. How well-armored against life the very selfish were.

"How's Jacques?" Ellen asked.

"I have no idea," Tina answered. "He went back to school right after the funeral. I haven't talked to that little bastard since he set fire to the tablecloth at La Caravelle because the service wasn't fast enough for him. I haven't been back there since. If Harry hadn't left that little bastard a trust fund I wouldn't give him a cent. But I don't want to talk about him. Let me bring you up to date, Ellen.

"First, I want to tell you about Amos. He's going out of his mind with frustration. He contributed half a million dollars to the President's campaign in hopes of getting an ambassadorship, but his candidate lost. Now, instead of the ambassadorship, he's being investigated by a congressional committee over kickbacks, shoddy construction, and most of all, misleading public relations. Jeff will be clean, of course. He can always claim he only did as

384

he was told. And Amos will get away with it too. But it may cost him another half-million.

"Meanwhile, Marilyn is getting crazy. She's going for instruction, wants to turn Catholic and become a nun. And guess what the reason is for her nuttiness. Amos is having an affair; the first one apparently. You know he was never a sexual guy. Power was his only drive. But now he's head over heels in love and guess with whom? Kimberly Clare Wein. Honest, it's like the princess and the toad. But apparently she sees in him the same kind of crude sexiness she saw in Lenny and that must be what she needs. Amos bought her a tiara of diamonds and rubies from Van Cleef and he also bailed her out of trouble."

"What kind of trouble could she ever be in?"

"Smuggling," Tina crowed gleefully. "She was attempting to smuggle Buccellati silver into the country and customs wanted to fine her ten thousand dollars and throw her in jail, so she called Amos. He knows those waterfront guys. A little *schmearing,* a few bucks under the table, and it was dropped. What an idiot! She could easily buy all the silver she wants. I think she just did it for kicks because Jon is so boring. Well, that's how she got to know Amos and since then it's been a wild affair. He's determined to marry her."

"I feel sorry for Marilyn," Ellen said. Whispering hadn't helped Marilyn any more than her example had helped Ellen.

"Oh, pooh. You're always feeling sorry for people, Ellen. It's so boring. Marilyn doesn't need sympathy. She's living on some other planet; really spooky and ethereal. And she probably will be happier as a nun, if Amos lets it happen. I don't think he would like even an ex-wife to seem ridiculous."

By the end of the evening the two women had established all of their past rapport and Ellen felt comfortable enough to tell Tina about her job.

"That's absolutely marvelous," Tina said. "If I'm going to marry Dr. Bloom instead of going to see him, I'll have lots of spare time. Do you think they'd give me a part-time job? You know I can't get up in the mornings but I would love to have something to do in the afternoons."

"Come back there with me after dinner," Ellen said, "and we'll ask them."

She telephoned Will, told him they would be there around ten, and he promised to wait up for them. The bill came to over three hundred dollars.

"Pretty expensive wines," she said to Tina.

"I can afford it," Tina said. "I could afford to do this every night of the week. My poor missionary parents should see me now. I'm sitting pretty financially but I need something to occupy my afternoons. Anyway, I'd like to prove to Dr. Bloom that I really am capable of doing something."

"When you finally go to bed with him, will you still call him Dr. Bloom?" Ellen laughed.

"Probably," Tina giggled, and they laughed together like two teenagers, all the way home.

Ellen led Tina into the living room where Kate and Will were waiting. She had not said anything to Tina about Kate's condition. To her credit, Tina did not react to the evident ravages in Kate and Ellen was pleased with her for that. She and Kate embraced and Kate offered condolences for Harry. After a while, they got down to business.

"If you think you can be reliable and work every day," Kate told her, "we can give you something to do. I have not been well lately, and until I recover, Ellen will have to shoulder a great deal of responsibility. Although her official title is assistant to the president, she is going to have to do certain tasks I would normally have done. She's going to need an assistant of her own and that's where you might fit in, Tina. The two of you would make a perfect combination. You're practical, a realist, and Ellen's still a bit of a romantic. You take action and never think about it, before or after. Ellen tends to worry, to agonize, to ask herself if she's doing the right thing and if she *did* the right thing. Ellen's still a little shy and insecure with people but nothing impresses or awes you, Tina. You have the ability to cut right through bull-shit, to call a spade a spade, to say what you see without worry-ing about someone's feelings. So I think the two of you would work well together. What about it, Tina? Would you like to assist Ellen?"

"What would I get paid?" Tina asked.

Will burst into laughter. "You see," he said, his eyes twin-kling affectionately at them both, "that's the difference between the two of you. You don't need the money and ask about salary. Ellen does need it but she sits there dreamy and reflective and hasn't even asked about a raise."

"I'm not dreamy and reflective," Ellen protested. "I'm scared. I'm scared about having to do the things Kate's done. It means going out and holding my own with the kind of men we knew in EL."

"You shouldn't be scared of that, Ellen," Tina said. "I al-ways thought most of the men in EL weren't as smart as Kate. I think you'll be able to hold your own with them. But if any of them give you a hard time, I'll be right along there at your side."

"You see," Will jested, "a combination made in heaven. Tina, you will get paid ten thousand and I hope you're worth it. Ellen, your salary will go up to twenty-five. In the spring, the two of you will accompany me on a tour of our southern factories. Until then, Tina, I will expect you here every day regularly."

"I can't get up early," she said.

"The hours will be one to five," Will said firmly, "and that's five days a week. Can you do that?"

"I'm really going to try," Tina said. "I'll have to discuss it with Dr. Bloom first, of course."

She called them later that night. "Dr. Bloom says I'm ready to work," she told them. "I'll be there tomorrow."

"What a quack," Kate said. "Fifteen years of analysis in or-der to get to work. If she'd had a job all these years, she probably wouldn't have needed the analyst."

Tina became part of their daily routine and Ellen had to admit that the woman she had once thought was only a shallow birdbrain was a lot smarter in many ways than she was.

And she was also a good friend. For Jennifer's eleventh birthday, Ellen and Tina drove to Maplewood to take her out to dinner for a celebration. They planned to stay overnight in a motel and take her shopping for some new spring clothes the next day. Afterward, Ellen realized she should have warned Tina to be tactful. Frankness and directness might be invaluable for hard-headed business dealings, but they were hell on sensitive adolescents who were vulnerable and defensive. When Jennifer came waddling out of her dorm to meet them, Ellen realized that Tina hadn't seen her for three years.

"Hi, Mom," Jennifer said, giving Ellen a little kiss. "Hi, Tina," she said uneffusively. "I didn't know you were coming."

"My God, Jennifer," Tina said with undisguised horror, "is that really you? How on earth could you have let yourself get in such a condition? Don't nudge me, Ellen. If you ignore the way she looks it's just like that father feeding his son drugs in that movie *A Hatful of Rain*. Do you think you're doing this girl any favor by pretending she looks all right?

"I have always been frank and open with Jacques, Jennifer, and I think your mother owes it to you to act the same way. You look terrible. How can you waste your youth looking so bad? You'll set a pattern for life if you do."

"Tina," Jennifer said, "fuck off. Nobody asked you to come or to comment. As far as I'm concerned, it looks a lot better to look natural the way I do than to wear a ton of makeup and two-inch fake eyelashes the way you do."

Tina was unabashed. "Well, of course nobody in the world would agree with you," she said. "I'll go back to the motel now and we'll come by and pick the two of you up for dinner. All right?"

Ellen followed Jennifer to her room, where she burst into tears. "Why did you bring that idiot," she said. "Is it too much to ask that my mother spend one day alone with me, one birthday dinner alone with me. I wanted to talk to you. It's my birthday and you brought that idiot along with you. How dare she tell me anything about my appearance? She doesn't know anything and she's a lousy mother. Jacques used to tell me how much he hated her. She's selfish. I don't know how you can associate with her. Aren't you afraid people will think birds of a feather flock together? I'd worry about that. First you found a rotten husband, then you found a rotten friend. Maybe there's something rotten about anybody who associates with rotten people. Do you know what she did to Jacques?

"This is the kind of thing she did. Once she was standing in the kitchen on the cook's day off, talking on the phone, smoking away the way she does with those long cigarette holders and having her fifth martini and Jacques wanted a bowl of chocolate pudding and he was a little kid and they had one of those cabinet kind of refrigerators and he couldn't reach it. So he kept asking her for chocolate pudding and she kept talking because all of her friends were always more important to her than Jacques. So finally, in exasperation, she said to the person on the phone, 'Hold on a minute,' and she went to the refrigerator, reached up, and got the bowl of chocolate pudding. He was pleased and smiling away because she was doing this for him. He walked over to his pretty mother, looked up at her, still smiling, and then, with one swift movement, she dumped the bowl over his head. Chocolate pudding stuck in his hair and the liquid rolled down his face, down his neck, into his collar. 'Let that teach you,' she said. 'Don't ever bother me when I'm on the phone.' That's the kind of person your friend is. Why did you let her talk to me that way? What does she have to do with me? Who the hell is she to talk to me like that? Would one of my friends start to tell her that she looks like she's a plastic doll with those disgusting long nails, long lashes, and plastic hair?

"I'll tell you something else she did. One day, Jacques took the Rolls and went out riding. I know he shouldn't have done it but he was crazy to see what it was like to drive a Rolls and she never let him. So what did she do? She called the police and said the Rolls had been stolen. They picked him up immediately and when he called home, she said she'd come and get him. Instead of that, she just let him sit in jail overnight. They put him in with some pretty creepy characters, too. That's the kind of person she is, Mom. I always hated her, all the years I was growing up, and now you've brought her to spoil my birthday."

"I'm sorry, honey, honestly I am. I never dreamed it would upset you so much. It's just that I do so many things alone, it seemed fine to me to have some company here and back. You don't know how lonesome I feel for you every time I leave here."

"Oh, bullshit," Jennifer said. "You just wanted everyone to see you getting out of that Rolls-Royce. Anyway, I think Rollses are disgusting. Don't ever expect me to set foot in one. I'd throw up all over it. I don't want to have dinner with her and I'm not driving to dinner in a Rolls-Royce."

"You have to do both," Ellen said. "There's no way out of it now."

"Oh, sure, sure," Jennifer exploded, "You dump me up here all year, send me on ski trips and to Washington, D.C., on my vacations, then dump me in camp during the summer. You've managed to avoid spending any time with me and now on my birthday you bring her with you."

"Darling, you must know I'd never intentionally do anything to make you unhappy," Ellen said. "You must know how much I love and miss you. I gave you the option of living with me in the city but you wanted to be here. If you don't want to go to camp in the summer, you're welcome to spend the summer with me. We could even take a trip. Would you like to go to Disneyland? I have a little money saved up and it's a long time since I've had a vacation."

"I'll think about it," Jennifer grumbled.

"Here, open your birthday gifts," Ellen said. She had brought her a large shopping bag of gifts: a portable typewriter, dozens of new records, Wallabee's and matching purse, and an envelope from Kate and Will with a hundred dollars in it.

"Not bad," Jennifer said, counting the money. After a while Ellen coaxed her to fix up somewhat for dinner and they waited outside the dorm until Tina returned with the Rolls. They drove to the best restaurant in the area and Ellen relaxed a little. Maybe the storm was over. Jennifer proceeded to anesthetize herself with food. Tina ate nothing, sipped her drink, smoked her cigarettes, and watched Jennifer disapprovingly.

"You remind me of your mother when I first met her," Tina said. "I had to warn her not to stuff herself. But she developed some self-control and now she has a beautiful body. Really, Jennifer, I advise you not to have that second piece of birthday cake."

Ellen had ordered an entire cake so that Jennifer could take the rest of it back to her friends. At Tina's words, Jennifer stood up, picked up the birthday cake, lifted it high above her head, then dashed it to the floor. "I'll wait for you outside," she said.

Tina calmly beckoned to the busboy, pointed her toe at the mess on the floor, and handed him a twenty-dollar bill. "I'd much rather see it on the floor than in her stomach," she told Ellen as they walked to the car.

They drove Jennifer back to the school in silence. When the chauffeur opened the door of the car, she stepped out and walked away from them to her dorm without a backward glance. Ellen started to follow but Tina stopped her. "Let her cool off. You'll see her in the morning." So Ellen and Tina returned to the motel.

All night, Ellen lay there worrying. Jennifer was eleven years old and still seemed like a disturbed, unhappy child. When would she grow out of this and what should Ellen be doing about it?

"She should be kept in a cage," Tina said at breakfast the next morning. "That's one fat, spoiled-rotten girl. Send her to military school."

Jennifer's mood seemed to have passed when Ellen knocked on her door after breakfast. She was cordial to Tina, seemed rational and eager to shop. But that turned out to be another nightmare. No local store had girls' clothes large enough for her so they were finally forced to take her to an Army and Navy store where she settled for several pairs of men's jeans and a few T-shirts.

"I'm humiliated that I had to shop in a men's store," Jennifer scowled on the way back to school. "I should never have let you two creeps talk me into going shopping. Now that you've both made me completely miserable, would you mind leaving?"

They dropped her at the school and headed back to New York. Ellen sat silently crying.

"Listen, my dear," Tina said, patting her hand. "Stop suffering. At our age, tears start to crease the face. That girl needs therapy badly and you should get her some help when she comes home this summer."

"Do you have any suggestions?" Ellen asked. "Maybe I should send her to Dr. Bloom. I know that he and I didn't hit it off well but he seems to have made you happy and maybe he could do something for Jennifer."

Tina giggled. "She won't be able to see Dr. Bloom this summer. I've been waiting for the right moment to tell you, Ellen, because you seemed to despise him, but now that you think he's done a good job with me, I'll tell you my news. Dr. Bloom and I are getting married this summer. Then we'll go on a honeymoon for four weeks."

"Married!"

"Married," Tina said happily. "But you don't have to worry about my work. We've discussed the job and he approves thoroughly. He wouldn't let me give it up even if I wanted to. Now that I've become accustomed to daily work, I love it. Well, come on, say something."

"It's wonderful," Ellen said. "I think it's right, Tina, and I hope you'll be very happy. Every time my mother calls me from Florida she tells me how much she wishes I would remarry. She's getting a little senile. Of course, she's never forgiven me for the divorce. She insists on thinking that it was I who left Jeff."

Ellen kept the smile pasted on her face but inside she felt

392

cold. Six months a widow, and now Tina was getting settled again. But in the two and a half years since she and Jeff had separated, Ellen hadn't met anyone at all she liked. Occasionally she'd meet a single man but the vast volume of what she had to learn in business in so short a time had left her little spare time. The truth was, she was not yet ready to get involved. The first thing she had to do in life was to become secure in this field so that she could always support herself and Jennifer. Later, she would think about finding a second husband. She was not yet ready. At this time of her life, after so many wasted years, the thing that made her happiest was work.

It was Tina who came up with the idea of stretch knits for plump preadolescents. She got the idea from Jennifer really. They could develop knit clothes for teenagers, clothes that had the stretch built in so that they could be worn for several sizes; 6–8, 8–10, 12–14, 14–16, and so on. "You see," Tina pointed out, "the clothes Jennifer tried on had no stretch, so she couldn't even get into them. If they had stretched, she could have pushed into them and that would have given her some incentive. I bet there's an army of fat teenaged girls out there who would devour stretch knits."

Kate and Will loved the idea. They sat for one week in consultation with their new PR agency, trying to dream up a name for the new line. Ellen felt a little guilty that Kate had switched from Jeff's agency but Kate assured her that Ellen was not the cause. "We just thought it was time for a change," Kate said. "I never mix business with friendship. If I still thought Jeff's agency was the best one for us, he'd have the account. But I hear he wants to get out of the PR business anyway and take over the running of Michael's business. So please don't feel responsible."

Ellen found the brainstorming fascinating. She had never really understood before how difficult it is to come up with a good name for a line of clothes. Finally, at the end of the day, they had one they thought would work. The new line of fatty

393

knits would be called, Thinline Knits, and the advertising slogan would be, "To make you look as thin as you've always longed to be."

"Can't you see the headlines," Tina joked, "when you put out a call for fat models?"

By the time they had arranged for all aspects of the campaign, the television commercials, the talk show appearances, the magazine coverage, and the designs themselves, July had passed. Tina was off on her honeymoon with Dr. Bloom, Will and Kate had flown to their house on Martha's Vineyard, and Ellen was left to keep things running. She went to the Evans Building every day to learn more about the business operation from Will's assistant, a caustic British woman who had resented Ellen at first as an arriviste upstart but gradually became more friendly as she saw how hard Ellen worked.

Late every night, Ellen would take a taxi to Kate's house, eat dinner served to her by the reduced summer staff, get into bed and watch television. She made arrangements to pick Jennifer up on August 7, two weeks before the end of camp, and to take her to Tanglewood. She made reservations at the Curtis Hotel and bought tickets for many concerts, a few dance recitals at Jacob's Pillow, and tickets for summer stock at Williamstown and Stockbridge. She looked forward to sightseeing, the mansion Naumkeag, the home of Church, the sculptor, and the Clark Museum.

Filled with optimism and pleasure in sharing these experiences with Jennifer, she took off in one of Kate's cars, pleased that she had run Kate's empire that summer without any problem. All of her intellect, emotion, and energy had been devoted to learning the field and as she drove she was filled with a sense of her own usefulness and worth. Would she go back to being the appendage of a wealthy man? Not a chance, she told herself. There was no greater luxury than her present freedom. She need never again tremble before Jeff's moods, or any man's, for that matter. She did not need a man to provide for her. She had money in the bank, a good salary, and she could provide for herself and Jennifer.

She reached Jennifer's camp in four hours and walked immediately to Jennifer's bunk, where they had arranged to meet. When she entered, she saw a girl sitting on her bed in semidarkness. "I beg your pardon," she said, "can you tell me where Jennifer is?"

"Mom," Jennifer shrieked, "don't you recognize me? Surprise!" She switched on the bunk light and Ellen looked at her.

"Why, darling," she said, "how marvelous. You must have lost ten pounds this past month."

"Fifteen," Jennifer said proudly. She looked thinner but not actually better than before. Her face was broken out, her greasy hair hung lankly about her face, and her coloring was too white for summer.

"How did you do it?" Ellen asked, hugging her.

"I simply stopped eating," Jennifer said proudly. "Daddy and Candy came up to visit and Daddy promised me a vacation with them next winter if I'm thin enough."

"I see," Ellen said. Somehow it irritated her that Jennifer had so easily forgiven them for not inviting her to the wedding.

"Are you pleased with me, Mommy?"

"My darling, I'm always pleased with you. I love you completely, fat or thin. 'Love is not love that alters when it alteration finds.' That's by Shakespeare, honey, but it exactly expresses my feelings. I love you and I'm excited that we're going away on vacation together."

"I don't want to go, Mom."

"Honey, you can't mean that." Ellen found her voice cracking and she couldn't hold back the sudden tears. "I've made all the reservations. I've bought the tickets."

"I don't care. I still don't want to go."

"But why? Just explain why to me."

"You'll make me eat."

"I won't, darling. Honestly, I promise. I'll leave you alone. Of course I won't make you eat."

"But it will be very hard. You'll want me to go to meals with you to keep you company and then I won't be able to sit there doing nothing while you eat, so I'll start to eat again and before you know it, I'll have gained all my weight back. No, Mom. I'm not going with you. It's better for you to go by yourself anyway. Maybe you'll meet a man and get married again. Most of the parents up here are on their second or third marriages already.

"Please don't cry, Mom. I know you're disappointed but I have to do what's best for me. Please don't cry. Please don't be selfish. You have to try to understand what I want to do."

"But we spend so little time together," Ellen said.

"None of the kids up here spend any time with their parents," Jennifer answered.

"I don't exactly know what to do," Ellen said. "Do you want me to stay for the evening?"

"No, Mom. I think you should just go ahead and do what you planned to do with me. I'll see you in two weeks anyway when you come to pick me up. Okay?"

"All right," Ellen said, bending to kiss her goodbye. She hurried out so Jennifer would not see her crying again. She went to the guest bathroom to finish crying, then wiped her face, powdered her nose, and went to the director's office.

He greeted her warmly. "Another year has passed," he said, offering her a chair, "and let's see where we are." He took out his notes on Jennifer. "I think she's made progress," he said. "It's not a lot, but it's definitely there. You will remember that two years ago she was so ashamed of her body that she would not participate in normal activities like group swimming. By the end of the second summer, however, she was participating fairly well, was losing some of her self-consciousness, was getting a little more athletic. This summer, she swims a lot, is more social, comes to breakfast but skips the other two meals. She reads a lot, strums her guitar, and seems much more relaxed."

"She doesn't look well," Ellen said.

"I wouldn't worry about that," he told her. "She's had the regulation check-up and is in good health."

"I don't know," Ellen said. "There's something unhealthy-looking about her."

396

"There are no drugs here," he said. "I hope you don't communicate any worries to her. The summer has passed most uneventfully and there's nothing to worry about."

Ellen left feeling neurotically oversolicitous and a bit disloyal for perhaps putting ideas into his head. Unable to face the vacation alone, she returned to New York City and her eighteen hours a day of work. Thank God for work. She read endlessly; fashion in medieval times, fashion in the seventeenth century, the eighteenth century, the nineteenth century. Fashion and society, society's attitude toward fashion, fashion and women's rights, fashion and religion, fashion and role stereotypes, the history of fashion, the origin of weaving, hand and machine knitting, clothing labor unions, big business and fashion, fashion as big business, and on and on.

She stopped working only long enough to pick up Jennifer two weeks later.

"What do you think, Mom," Jennifer asked proudly, "twenty pounds."

"You look fine," Ellen said, "but I don't think you should continue to lose weight so fast. If you want to lose any more, do it gradually."

"Who asked you?" Jennifer snapped in one of her frightening shifts in mood that often reminded Ellen of Jeff. "Do I tell you how much weight to gain or lose?"

"I was only trying . . ." Ellen faltered.

"I know what you were trying," Jennifer said angrily. "Always looking for a way to get at me, to pick on me, criticize me."

"That's ridiculous," Ellen snapped back. "And it's not fair."

"Oh, isn't it," Jennifer said sarcastically. "People have different ideas of what's fair. Daddy and Candy visited me last week. She weighs a hundred and ten pounds and they both think I could weigh that much too. So I have thirty pounds to go."

"But, honey," Ellen said, wondering why she was even bothering to go on with the conversation, "that's ridiculous. Candy is only five feet tall. You're three inches taller."

"Stop using that word, 'ridiculous.' It makes you sound like your brilliant friend, Tina. I'm not interested in what you think, Mom. Daddy told me a lot about you that I never understood before. The reason he left was not, as you always let me believe, that I was too fat. He left because you were seeing someone else, some professor. So that's why he left."

For the first time in her life Ellen felt as if she was going to faint. She staggered to Jennifer's bed and sat down.

"All this time," Jennifer said, "I thought it was Daddy's fault the marriage broke up and now I find that it was your fault. For years you've tried to come between me and my father and I'm not going to let you do it anymore. He's the one who really loves and understands me. He got married again but I notice nobody's rushing to marry you."

"I can't believe you're saying these things," Ellen said. "It's I who have been concerned and involved with you all your life. I who have picked you up and driven you and cared about you. If Daddy loves you so much, why hasn't he ever been with you?"

"I would think that would be obvious to you, Mother. He doesn't like to be with me because I remind him of you."

"Oh, for heaven's sake, I give up. You just need somebody to kick."

"I think, Mother, you gave up years ago."

They rode to the school in angry silence. Wordlessly, Ellen helped Jennifer unload her belongings and then helped her shop for the essentials for the fall semester. Ellen decided not to stay overnight since she and Jennifer were barely talking to each other. They coolly said their goodbyes and Ellen left the school. She couldn't help feeling angry and hurt. Nothing Jeff did could surprise her but she had expected more loyalty from Jennifer. If she thinks Jeff is so great, Ellen thought, let him take over for a while. But she knew he never would and that no matter how badly Jennifer acted she would never stop loving or caring for her daughter.

Ellen called her the following week at school and they spoke cordially on the telephone and although Jennifer had not apologized, Ellen acted as if the cruel scene had never happened. Tina came back from her honeymoon raving about Dr. Bloom's sexual prowess. "Honestly," she said, "his penis is no bigger than my little finger but he does wonderful things with it. Anyway, a small penis is great for anal intercourse."

Will and Kate returned from Martha's Vineyard and it was immediately evident to Ellen that Kate had deteriorated further. She had lost more weight and was beginning to seem feeble. Now, when they worked she lay on the couch at all times, wrapped in a cashmere throw. Ellen felt tortured by her daily decline.

"Ellen, we have to talk about the future," Kate said to her one day when Tina wasn't there.

"I don't want to," Ellen said, dreading what she knew she would hear.

"But we have to," Kate insisted. "Will says that you've been wonderful for the business, that you've made it your life. We've never had a summer as good as this past one with you at the helm. Promise me that you'll stay on and keep working with Will after I'm gone. I worry about him. I don't want him to be lonely."

"You're not going," Ellen said, trying to hide her despair, "and I have no place in the world other than here. I'll always be here. You don't have to worry about that. All I want you to think about is getting well."

"God knows I want to." Kate's voice was a sob. "It's that damned chemotherapy that's killing me. The cure is killing me. Isn't that a joke? Oh, Ellen, what rotten luck this is. Just when things seem to be going so well, life zings you with something like this."

"I know," Ellen said, kissing Kate's hand. "I know."

"You've made me very happy these past years," Kate said, "and I want to thank you for everything. You're the only woman I have ever loved."

"I love you, too," Ellen said.

At the end of the evening, Kate kissed Ellen goodnight and Will carried her up to her bedroom. That was the last time Ellen ever saw her alive. Will came down to tell her at breakfast. Tired of suffering, Kate had swallowed a month's supply of sleeping pills.

"Did you know?" Ellen wept. "Did you have any idea she would do this?"

"Yes, I knew," he said, tears running down his face. "I sat with her while she took them and then I held her hand until she was gone."

He and Ellen put their arms around each other and wept for the woman they had loved.

11

*N*ow Tina and Ellen worked together the way
Ellen had worked with Kate. Ellen was supervising all aspects of
the soon-to-be launched Thinline campaign and Tina was working hard on another idea she had come up with because of her
impending grandchild. Jacques had, to everyone's surprise, married a nice girl and settled down. Tina was supervising the design
and production of a line of baby stretch knitwear called Baby
Saver Knits.

After working with the agency for weeks, Tina finally came
to Ellen and Will for the final approval. "How do you like this
one?" she asked. " 'This will cost you less than you thought,
Mommy, because my Baby Saver clothes stretch with me.' "

"That's absolutely terrible." Ellen laughed. "What do you
think, Will?"

"It is a little long," he said. "I think you should take it back
to the agency, Tina, honey. Ask them to come up with something
short and snappy."

"Maybe just show a baby reaching for something," Ellen
said, "kind of a cute picture, like a baby in a playpen reaching up

to a mobile. Something like that. And under it you can have a caption like, 'Stretch clothes for baby.' "

"That's not a bad idea," Will said. "It might really go if we find the world's most adorable baby and build the campaign around it."

"What about this one?" Tina asked, showing a drawing to them. It showed a grandmother holding a baby and the grandmother was saying: "My how you've grown." A balloon coming out from the baby said, "Goo-goo, but I still fit into those marvelous Baby Saver Knits you bought me last year."

"That one really stinks," Ellen said harshly. "Listen, Tina, tell that ad agency that I'm getting impatient. Either they come up with better slogans than we can devise ourselves or we'll start looking for a new agency."

"Yes, sir," Tina saluted. She gave Will a cheery wave and marched out.

"My, my, my," Will said. "Is this shy, retiring little Ellen?"

"Not any more it isn't." She grinned back.

Every day Will delegated more responsibility to her; each day he gave her another kind of problem to solve. He never interfered but at the end of the day they would discuss her actions and decisions and she grew in perception daily, as to whether her decisions had been right or wrong. When Ellen had a free minute during the eighteen-hour days she imposed on herself, she realized with surprise that she was quite contented. Work filled her life, satisfied all of her needs and desires.

Tina had tried to arrange dates for her but they had never progressed beyond the first night.

"Don't you miss sex?" Tina had asked her.

"I don't have time to think about it," Ellen said, and that was the truth.

Her appearance was changing. She grew more comfortable with herself, more confident about her opinions. People in the company now listened to her with respect and nobody challenged her right of inheritance. She was a model of fairness, of forethought, of wisdom. Nobody had ever seen her get excited or cry.

The knitwear craze continued to grow. In 1947, wool and cotton had accounted for eighty-four percent of all United States fiber production. "But now," Will told her, "seventy percent of the fabrics are man-made. Alongside our tanks of cotton and wool are Fiberglas, polyester, nylon, acrylic, rayon, and acetate. Katie Knits is going to be the largest and most diversified manufacturer of textiles and related products for apparel, home, and industry in the whole United States. And it's knits and man-made fibers that are doing it, Ellen. Of course, some Paris couturiers, like Chanel and Vionnet, have been using knitted jerseys since the twenties, but knitted fabrics just weren't used much in ready-made clothes till we came along."

"I worry about Captiva Knits catching up," Ellen said, mentioning a competitor. "Captiva's woolen knit bathing suits and dresses are becoming fashionable with the avant-garde. They're even making knit culotte suits, body sweaters, and blouses without bust darts, so they fit especially close to the body."

"Don't you worry," Will said. "We can make everything they make and then some. Right now, we have the tight leotard knit fabric dresses and they're just as popular as those culotte suits. Next month we come out with our line of knit miniskirts that can double for tennis and sports. Our knit slacks are doing exceptionally well, too. We're still number one."

Who would ever have thought that women could start to wear pants anywhere, Ellen thought, even to the finest restaurants. Teachers and students were wearing them to school, although some principals and men teachers were making awful fusses. Women were wearing them to work everywhere. It really made good sense for women to be able to wear pants wherever they wished, especially through cold eastern winters, and because of this, business was booming.

"We're in the middle of a style revolution," Will said, "and Katie Knits is right on the cutting edge. We have all of the new synthetics and the sales on our polyester and acrylic clothes are skyrocketing. Captiva's mills aren't even ready for this conversion. But we've got it all and our research department tells me that no other fiber can match synthetics for lightweight warmth. And they're comfortable. That's the big selling point. They're cheap and comfortable. Now we're going to start to make tailored jackets and suits for men and boys from the new synthetics. Polyester is going to make us the kings of the garment industry.

"One thing is certain, Ellen. Haute couture is dead and ready-to-wear is in. St. Laurent is opening a series of ready-to-wear shops and he's calling them Rive Gauche. And look at Mary Quant. I don't like her designs but it's the accessibility and mod quality that gets the consumer. Quant's branching out now into a line of cosmetics and there's no reason why we can't do the same. Why don't you ask Tina to take on the cosmetic line for now, Ellen, and this summer we can have Jennifer work with her. Then someday you can give it to Jennifer. And, honey, just wait till you see our new line of po'boy sweaters. You'll just love them."

Ellen was so excited about Will's idea that she called Jennifer, who was now a junior in high school. Jennifer seemed almost as excited as Ellen and in her heart she thanked Will for this wonderful idea.

"I'd love to work with a makeup line, Mom," Jennifer said. "I'd rather do that than go to summer school."

"Well, you don't have to make any decisions now," Ellen said. "Just try it out. It would be wonderful to have you working here with me."

Eventually, the new line of Thinline Knits ("Clothes to make you look thin") was in every major store in the country and a tremendous publicity campaign was underway to make these clothes available for summer. To Ellen's surprise, preliminary reports informed them that ordinary-sized women were buying these clothes designed for fat women and girls. After all, no woman in America ever thinks she's thin enough.

"It's incredible," Ellen crowed as the orders poured in.

404

"The comfort does it," Tina rejoiced with her. "That's why they all want them. This is the age of comfort, sports, movement, and we're riding the crest of the wave. Honestly, I could scream."

"Get ready for another first, Ellen," Will told her soon after. "You and I, honey, are set to appear on television to talk about our revolutionary new line of clothes."

It should have been Will and Kate, Ellen thought sadly. She wasn't sure she could do it.

"Maybe you should take Tina," she said, "I'm afraid of saying the wrong thing."

"Tina would be far more likely to say the wrong thing than you," Will told her. "Don't you worry, Ellen. I'll be there beside you and you'll do just fine. Once you start talking, your nervousness will disappear. You don't have to worry at all. Besides, honey, think what a shock it will be to Jeff and to that fellow Todd, if they happen to see you."

Will was right, as usual, although the morning of the show, she felt lobotomized with fatigue. Fearful of oversleeping, she had been up all night and was lightheaded from lack of sleep. The studio sent a limousine for them and as soon as they reached the studio they were whisked from room to room to talk to the hosts, to see makeup men, to meet various other functionaries, and there was hardly enough time to be nervous. Ellen looked at her professionally made-up face in the illuminated mirror.

Not bad. She smiled at herself. Who would believe this is little Ellen Graetz from Brooklyn?

Then they were on the air. At first, Will did most of the talking as he explained the growth of the textile industry in the United States.

"The basic steps of spinning, weaving, knitting, and dyeing have not changed since colonial days," he told the interviewer. "But the development of power machinery has made it possible to perform these tasks with greater efficiency . . . and with higher quality results. Our search for improvements in machine technology goes on continuously. These advances, combined with the development of new fibers, have helped to make quality textiles available to everybody at affordable prices.

"You know," he went on, "we Americans are probably the best-dressed people in the world today. If we need an item of clothing, all we have to do is go to a store and buy it. I like to think that Katie Knits has played no small part in this development."

Then it was Ellen's turn. The interviewer asked her to talk about the exciting new Thinline Knits.

"I was a fatty myself as a girl," the interviewer gushed, "and getting clothes then was a terrible problem."

"It still is." Ellen smiled. "That is, it *was* until we developed Thinline."

"How did you happen to think about it? What gave you the impetus to develop this line?"

"It was my dear daughter," Ellen said. "She's really quite slim now and doesn't need Thinline clothes, but last spring, when I went shopping with her when she was a little overweight, we couldn't find anything pretty, flattering, and feminine. That was when my assistant, Tina Bloom, suggested that there was a need for this new line, and we proceeded from there."

"So your own daughter was the inspiration for the line."

"Yes, my daughter, Jennifer."

A few more generalities, some information about the number of items available in the line, stores, outlets, price ranges, and their time was over. "Well done," the interviewer said to Ellen as they shook hands, "done like a real pro."

"I'm proud of you, my dear," Will said, as the limousine took them back to the house.

Tina and Dr. Bloom were waiting for them and they all sat down to a large, celebration breakfast together. They toasted each other with champagne. Then, misty-eyed, they toasted Kate. The phone never stopped ringing. "My God," Tina said, "it was the best publicity we could ever get."

406

The next phone call was for Ellen. It was Jeff, in a towering rage.

"You little bitch," he yelled, "vice-president of a knitwear empire. How dare you take money for Jennifer from me when you have such a good job! Do you know that paying you ten thousand dollars means I have to make twenty because of my tax bracket? Now I'm beginning to understand why I lost Kate's account. You planned it very carefully, very cagily indeed. And now I see why you pushed me to a divorce."

"I pushed you?" Ellen burst out laughing.

"You won't get away with it, Ellen," he snarled. "First I'm going to court to get you to contribute half of that ten thousand for Jennifer, and second, I'm going to sue you for half a million dollars for the loss of the Katie Knits account."

Ellen hung up and burst into tears. Jeff still had the power to upset her.

"Just calm down, honey," Will said, patting her hand. "He doesn't have a leg to stand on with either complaint. He's just trying to upset you. Probably can't stand the fact that you turned out so much better than Candy. He's just mad 'cause he bet on the wrong horse. How does it feel to be successful?" Will asked. "Bitter or sweet?"

"Oh, sweet, sweet," she said, "but bitter because of Kate. Bittersweet."

"That's the way life is," Will said.

"I must say, my dear girl," said Dr. Bloom, "you apparently have developed a dimension that was completely latent when I tested you."

"Maybe your tests weren't adequate," Ellen said.

"Aha, my dear girl," he pontificated, "there you go again. Still argumentative."

"Do me a favor, Barry," Ellen said. "Just fuck off."

"You don't mean that," he said.

"You're right," she answered, "I don't."

Ellen's feelings toward Dr. Bloom had changed. She really

liked him now. He was good for Tina, and a good friend to her and to Will.

"It makes me feel almost disloyal to Kate for this happiness to be mine," Ellen said.

"Enjoy it, Ellen, dear," Will said gently. "How much happiness have you had?" Sudden tears of gladness scalded her eyes. When the phone rang again it was her mother calling from Florida, where she was living with a housekeeper and nurse. Her mother's senses were failing but she was not yet completely senile. "Why did you have to wear such an ugly dress?" her mother asked her.

"Because the company I work for makes them," Ellen answered.

"That's a good reason," her mother said. "When are you coming to visit me?"

"Soon," Ellen said, tolerant and indifferent. Nothing had changed between her mother and herself but as Ellen said goodbye she realized that nothing her mother said could bother her anymore.

"Okay," Ellen said to Tina, "breakfast is over. Let's get to work."

I'm happy, I'm happy, her heart sang as they drove to work. This is the first pure happiness I've ever had in my life. I picked myself up from nothing. I knew nothing and now I know about an entire industry. There's no end to what I can learn and accomplish. And now, I might even try to find a husband.

They worked all day and at five they went back to the mansion where Dr. Bloom was meeting them for dinner. Ellen and Will were completely exhausted. They had been up since 4:00 A.M. Will had given instructions that they were not to be disturbed by calls but the butler told him that there was an urgent call and the expression on the man's face was enough to get Will scurrying to the phone. He picked it up, stood there, listened, and his entire face and body seem to droop.

"All right," he said, "we'll be there in about two hours, as fast as we can drive. It would take us as long as that to get a helicopter."

"What is it?" Ellen asked, her skin prickling, knowing almost instinctively in her gut that the call had been for her. "What's wrong?"

Will walked over to the bar, downed a fast shot of Scotch, then filled a tumbler with it and walked over to Ellen. He stood there before her, holding it out to her, and she knew. She let out a terrible scream that filled the house. "It's Jennifer," she screamed. "I know it's Jennifer. What is it? Tell me. What is it?"

Will made her sit down between Tina and Dr. Bloom. Tears were streaming down his face. "Oh, dear God," he wept, "it isn't fair. It isn't fair. Oh, dear God, how I wish I could spare you, Ellen, honey, but there's no way I can. There's no way I can be merciful, no way I can spare you. Ellen, honey, Jennifer is dead."

Ellen slumped back in a faint, welcoming the rush of unconsciousness blacking out the pain. When she came to, she was lying on the couch while Will, Tina, the butler, and Dr. Bloom hovered sadly around her.

"Are you strong enough to go?" Will asked. "Or do you want Tina and me to go without you?"

"I have to go, of course," Ellen said in an unnaturally calm zombielike voice emanating out of some hollow distance. "Someone should call Jeff."

"I already did," Tina said, "but he's out of town. I spoke to Candy and she said she'd try to reach him."

In the car, Will put his arm around her. "You're not alone, honey," he said, "we all love you." She sat in the car paralyzed. In a dream, the two hours passed until they were finally there. A police car was waiting for them at the gate and led them to the infirmary. Clutching Will, with Tina and Barry behind them, she entered the building. All conversation stopped as they came through the doors. A nurse stepped out and beckoned to them. They followed her inside to where they saw the school hospital bed, that bed accustomed to nothing worse than hockey bruises.

There, lying on the bed, looking only asleep, lay Jennifer, slim, white, peaceful.

Ellen knelt beside the bed and took her daughter's hand in her own. "She looks pretty," Tina said, for once saying the right thing. Dazed, Ellen knelt there holding on to the familiar hand, with its bitten nails and cuticles. She pressed it to her lips and leaned her head wearily on the bed.

"The policeman wants to ask you a few questions, honey," Will said. "Shall I tell him you can't talk now?"

"No," Ellen said, standing up. "I'll talk to him. What happened?" she asked, turning to the officer.

"Your daughter died of an overdose of drugs," the policeman said. "It was probably an accident. Did you know she was on drugs?"

"No." Ellen shook her head. "It must be some mistake. She doesn't take drugs. How would she get them? There must be some mistake. Maybe she's not really dead."

"She is dead," Will said gently, his hand on her shoulder.

Ellen could say nothing. The horror that had enveloped her was so cataclysmic that no words could express her loss. But somehow, deep inside her, she wasn't surprised. She felt as if all her life she had been waiting for this ultimate horror. She had not been born lucky. So many terrible things had happened to her. Now everything was gone, destroyed, down the drain. Her only happiness to come out of that terrible marriage had been destroyed. The marriage was gone, her offspring was gone. All gone, gone, dead, gone without a trace.

After the coroner had ruled that Jennifer's death was due to accident, they made arrangements for her body to be brought back to a funeral home in New York City, and then they returned together.

"What a shame," Tina said, "just when she was beginning to get so pretty."

"I'm being punished," Ellen said, "for having had one child."

"That's not so," Barry said. "You are not to think that even for a minute."

"You know that's ridiculous," Tina said. "There's nobody up there to reward or punish."

Ellen moved through the next two days in a dream. "No tranquilizers please," she told Barry, "this is my grief. I want to feel every moment of it. It's my way of saying goodbye to Jennifer."

She did not notify her mother. Ellen saw no point in upsetting her, would figure out a way to tell her later. Maybe she'd never have to know. The phone call after the broadcast had confirmed Ellen's idea that her mother was not quite all there.

Jeff and Candace came to the funeral looking tanned and chic and followed by about fifty EL friends. Many of them had seen Ellen and Will on television and they mentioned this to her with approbation when they filed past to express their condolences. She insisted that Will, Tina, and Barry sit with her in the first row usually reserved for family. "You're all the family I have," she told them. Will kept his arm around her shoulders throughout. Jeff kept giving them angry looks.

Ursula sat beside Candy and Jeff. Poor girl, Ellen thought. In the past years the rosy cheeks she had brought from Germany had faded and she looked tired and bitter. She wept throughout and at the end of the service she came up to Ellen and said, "I luffed her." Ellen answered despairingly, "I know." They looked at each other sadly before Ursula turned away, her life, too, a wasted life.

Afterward, the long line of limousines rode to the cemetery. Dazed, Ellen stood there watching the coffin as it was lowered into the ground, thinking, This is not happening. I am not here. This is just a nightmare, a terrible dream. I do not believe this. I must be asleep.

Throughout her agony she was conscious of the goodness and devotion of Will and Tina. How strange the world was! Here was Will, a man who had lived his life as a lie to avoid persecution, a man who belonged to a mocked and reviled minority, a man who was the best person she had known since Saul. And beside him stood Tina, brazen, tactless, foolish, thoughtless, selfish, but another good friend to Ellen in her moment of need. I love them, Ellen thought. I love them more than anyone else on earth and terrible as this is, it would be worse if they were not at my side.

Finally, it was over. The cars of friends moved away and only two limousines remained, Ellen's and Jeff's. They stood outside their cars for a moment.

"I hope you're satisfied now." Jeff's voice cut across her like a whip. "You drove her to this."

"Have you gone crazy?" Will broke in, shielding Ellen.

"She was mighty upset about the way you discussed her on TV," Jeff said. "Telling the whole world she had once been fat. She called me immediately and told me how embarrassed she was. I think she deliberately took that overdose. She committed suicide because of you."

"Jeff," Tina's voice broke in, "you always were a *schmuck* and now you're a worse *schmuck* than ever before. This may seem like a strange place for a business decision but let me tell you something, Jeff. After what you just said, you will never work on Harry's accounts again. His board of directors will hear from me tomorrow."

"You can keep your account," Jeff said, "in fact you can shove it. I know what she's done. She poisoned Kate against me and now she's poisoned you against me. Worst of all, she poisoned Jennifer against me."

"Just a minute," Barry said, raising his voice for the first time since Ellen had known him. "I had seen Jennifer several times recently and she was doing very well, was on an even keel. I had recommended her to a psychiatrist near her school and she saw him regularly. He was very pleased with her progress. Nobody could have expected this. She may have been slightly embarrassed, but not enough to do this intentionally."

412

"I'm not interested in anything you have to say, you quack," Jeff shouted, entering his limousine and slamming the door.

"Let's go," Will said, and he helped Ellen and Tina into the car. Then Barry got in and shut the door behind him.

"It strikes me," he said mildly, "that your husband is a very angry man."

"My genius," Tina said, giving her husband a fond hug.

"Thank you for helping me, Barry," Ellen said.

"Don't you dare blame yourself for this, Ellen," Will raged. "Everyone knows that you were a devoted mother to that girl. She was having problems long before the interview. You did everything anyone could do. Jeff is just blaming you to avoid facing himself."

"I think that what Will says is correct," Barry said.

"If Jeff's so concerned," Tina said, "how come he didn't offer to chip in for the funeral?" Her attempt at humor fell flat and everyone remained quiet for the rest of the ride home. The chauffeur let them out at the mansion and Tina and Barry came inside with them. Ellen just wanted to get away from everyone.

"I want to go to sleep," Ellen said. "Barry, I want some sleeping pills."

"I'll bring them to you," Will said. "You get into bed and I'll bring up some cocoa."

"Do you want me to help?" Tina asked. Ellen nodded and Tina came with her to her room. She ran a hot tub for Ellen and then sat and talked to her while she waited for her to come out.

"You're not going to try anything stupid, are you?" Tina asked.

"Such as?" Ellen called from the tub.

"Such as suicide," Tina called back. "Honestly, Ellen, you have to think of Will and me and the business. We couldn't go on without you. Barry's going to come up with Will and give you a sedative."

Ellen came out, put on her nightgown, and got into bed. She hadn't answered Tina's question about suicide.

"You didn't answer my question," Tina said. "I mean, you have to try to hang on, Ellen. Kate's whole business is riding on your shoulders. So promise me you won't commit suicide. I mean, if you did, just think of how much satisfaction that would give Jeff. He would tell everybody that you just couldn't stand your guilt, or something like that. I once heard somebody say, 'Living well is the best revenge.' That's what you have to do, Ellen. You have to live so well and do so well that you get your revenge on all the awful things in life. I think that's what Jennifer would have wanted you to do, too."

Ellen vaguely saw Barry and Will come into the room and the last words she heard before she fell asleep were Tina's. "We're staying here tonight, tomorrow's a workday."

Will was standing there looking at her when she opened her eyes the next morning to the remembered horror. She lay there listlessly, apathetically, the tears running from her eyes.

"Get up," Will said.

"Up?"

"Up," he said, as firmly as he had ever spoken. "We need you at the office. Breakfast is in half an hour." Tina and a maid came in and started to put Ellen together.

"Not even a day to mourn?" Ellen asked.

"You can mourn while you work," Tina said.

They were right, of course. Dragging herself up, Ellen tightened her mouth and resolved not to let them down. She couldn't eat but had another cup of coffee and then the chauffeur drove them to the Evans Building.

"We can leave as early as you like, honey," Will said.

"No," she answered. "We'll leave at five as usual." And they returned to the schedule they had followed before the tragedy.

"I want to make some changes," Will told them one night at dinner. "I don't need this house. I want to turn each floor into a separate apartment and the first floor into a private boutique. I thought maybe Tina would like to run it. We could carry everything Katie Knits makes. People would come only by appoint-

414

ment. There would be no display windows, of course."

"I'd like to develop a new, ultrachic line for it," Tina said, "and call it Tina Fashions. What do you think of that? Do you like that name? Maybe Tinabloom Fashions. Tinabloom? It has sort of a melodious ring, doesn't it? Or maybe I could call my line T-Blooms. 'T-Bloom Knits for those who love high fashion.' What do you think?"

"It sounds fine to me," Will said.

"In one year," Tina added, "we can have T-blooms sweeping the country. The sky's the limit. There's no stopping us. I have another idea. Katie Knits for astronauts. What do you think?"

So on they worked; day after day, night after night, working, growing, producing, extending, and acquiring.

"You do know, I'm sure," Will said to her one day, "that you and I are not leading normal lives. Each of us is totally celibate."

"I don't care," Ellen said. "That's fine with me. I only care about working."

"Well, it's not fine with me," Will said. "It's time for both of us to stop mourning and find a little love."

"You go right ahead," Ellen said. "I'm not ready yet. It takes all my energy just to survive each day."

"I'm going hunting," Will said, "and you should do the same."

"No time," Ellen said, "and less interest. Just go ahead and do what makes you happy, Will. And please don't worry about me."

The next time Ellen heard from Jeff was when he saw a news item in the *Times* that she had won the Coty Fashion Award.

"I want to congratulate you," he said.

"Thank you very much," she answered coldly.

"You've certainly surprised me," he said. "You know, you really owe me a lot. You should thank me. If we'd stayed married, you'd still be a housewife instead of a lady tycoon."

"Thank you, Jeff."

"Still sore at me about what I said at the cemetery?"

"Why, Jeff, how perceptive of you."

"Yeah, yeah, you're still sore. Listen, Ellen, I was pretty upset and all, losing my only daughter that way. Sometimes a guy needs something to strike out against."

She didn't answer him.

"I think I was probably wrong," he said, "that it was an accident."

"I'm very busy, Jeff. I'll have to get off now."

"Wait, wait," he said, "don't hang up."

"What is it?" she asked.

"It's about Jennifer," he said. "I kind of miss her. I think about her every day."

"Please, Jeff, I can't talk about it," she said, scalding tears running down her face. "It still hurts too much."

She listened to the phone incredulously. It sounded as if Jeff might be crying. She had never seen Jeff cry, didn't actually know if he possessed the capacity. She felt friendlier to him than ever before.

"There's something else I want to talk to you about." He broke into her feelings of affection.

"Something else?" He had something on his mind, he was trying to sell her something. He was "romancing" her. She should have known. She let out a rueful laugh. "What is it, Jeff?"

"I was thinking," he said, as if he'd had a sudden revelation that would enchant her, "that maybe you'd let me pitch Katie Knits again. I did damned well for Kate all those early years. It wasn't fair of you to make her take away the account. So, by rights, it really should be mine if you have any sense of fairness. Listen, Ellen, I did pretty well for you while we were married. You had a mink coat before you were twenty-five and I never asked anything from you in return. So now I'm asking. It wouldn't cost you anything and it would be a chance for you to repay me a little for all I did for you. Hey, listen, why are you laughing, Ellen? I'm serious."

416

"I thought you were giving up public relations, Jeff, and going into Michael's business. Wasn't that one of the reasons you married Candy?"

"Sure it was," he said, "but that's not the way it worked out. Candy and her family have such a stranglehold on that business that all I would be is a minor flunky. They'd dole out pennies to me and I'm not about to give up my independence. Besides, one of these days Michael's going to get out of jail and I wouldn't like to be around when he finds out he doesn't own his business anymore."

"Trouble in paradise?" Ellen teased. Had she ever really been so afraid of this pathetic man?

"I don't understand those people," Jeff continued. "They're always figuring, planning, squeezing the dollar. Amos was a monster but at least you knew where you stood with him. But these *Social Register* people kill you while they're smiling. They're so terrified that somebody's going to screw them that they spend their lives figuring how to get there first. On top of that, they're anti-Semitic. Oh, they would deny it, but you should hear the way they talk when they're off guard."

"Poor Jeff," she said. "Looks like you've made a lot of bad choices."

"Well," defensively, "so have you, Ellen."

"My choices seem to be working out at the moment," she said firmly.

"All right, all right, you don't have to rub it in. You know damned well, Ellen, that I gave you everything when I had it. Isn't that true? Didn't I fix you up so you looked pretty? Didn't I buy you nice clothes? Didn't you have a magnificent house? Didn't I give all of that to you?"

"And didn't you take it all away when you married Candy?" she couldn't help saying, although she had stopped caring a long time ago.

"You never used to be the kind of person to carry grudges," he said.

"I'm not the same person."

417

"Come on, Ellen, how about it? Be a good sport. Forget about the past and give me your account."

He was so outrageous. "Oh, Jeff," she said, bursting into laughter, "you never change. All right, all right, I'll talk to Will about it. If he says we can't give you the entire account, perhaps you can at least handle Tina's boutique line. I'll have Tina call you back after we speak to Will."

"At's a ma girl," he said. She winced, then grinned. She had just hung up when Tina came into Ellen's office with a large portfolio of drawings. "Prepare to see the most beautiful knits you've ever seen," she said gaily.

Ellen sat at her desk while Tina flipped through the drawings of knit blouses out of bouclé, knit blouses with sequins knit right in, beautiful long-cut knit sweaters, and dresses knitted of gold and silver thread.

"I think those will have mass appeal," Ellen said. "They probably shouldn't be limited to your boutique. Congratulations on them. I think they're absolutely sensational."

Tina beamed, then sat down to have a cigarette with her.

"Jeff just called," Ellen told her. "Would you mind if he handled PR for the boutique line?"

"Are you nuts? After the way he acted at the funeral? I took him off all of Harry's accounts the next day. Now you want me to forgive him?"

"Strange as it seems, yes, I do."

"Sometimes you really are a dope, Ellen. Why should you forgive him? He was absolutely lousy to you."

"So were you," Ellen said soberly.

Tina thought about it for a moment, then laughed with Ellen.

"Well, sweetie," she said, "if you put it that way, I can see your point. Okay, I'll speak to Will and if it's okay with him and you, it's okay with me. I'll call him then and tell him he can come back to the fold. You and Will didn't seem to like the other PR agency anyway.

"Now look closely at me," she continued. "Do you notice anything different?"

"Give me a clue."

"I had an estrogen pill injected under my skin yesterday," Tina said.

"Injected how?"

"It's this special doctor upstate. Nobody in New York City is willing to do it. He makes a little slit in my back, puts in the tablet, and sews me up with a stitch. It takes three or four months for the pill to dissolve and circulate through the bloodstream. Then I'll go back for another. He guarantees it will make me look ten years younger. I can see it working already."

"That's absolutely insane," Ellen said, "won't you have scars?"

"They won't show. He puts the stitch right under where my bathing suit or brassiere straps would be. Want to go with me next time?"

"Ycch," Ellen said. "I'd rather look old."

"You're only thirty-eight," Tina said, "but I'm forty-two. I don't know how we got so old so quickly. You could at least color your hair. Nobody has gray hair."

"I have gray hair," Ellen said, "and I'm certainly somebody. Out, please, I have work to do."

"You certainly have changed," Tina said.

"Thank you," Ellen answered.

Katie Knits continued to grow. Will became chairman of the board and Ellen became acting president. Their lives assumed a pleasant pattern. During the week she and Will worked from 8:00 A.M. to 7:00 P.M. Usually they had dinner together, occasionally they had a few guests to one or the other's apartment, on weekends they attended auctions at Parke Bernet, visited art galleries, went to the theater, ballet, opera, symphony, visited friends, and spent the day with Tina and Barry at their country club. Although the mansion had been divided into apartments, living just beneath Will gave her a feeling of family, of security.

Every day she could feel herself grow stronger, grow in self-esteem, in self-confidence, in self-forgiveness. His mind expanded hers, he was always full of new ideas, new plans, new activities. They were as compatible as two good friends could be. He was the friend Jeff had never been; her only compatible friend since Saul. She hadn't thought about Saul for many years. What did he look like? Where was he? Would she recognize him if their paths ever crossed?

But after six months of this idyllic existence with Will, she could sense a change. Will was as unfailingly courteous as ever but something had come between them. She let it pass, thinking that perhaps she was imagining something. Then, finally, he broached it himself.

"Do you remember Enid Taylor's first husband?" Will asked her one evening after his butler had served them coffee, and gone.

"Old oil wells?" Ellen asked. "Very well indeed. I used to think he was the most attractive man in EL."

"He's a lovely man," Will said, "and I have loved him for many years."

"I didn't know," Ellen said in a small hurt voice. Will was silent, waiting for her to come to terms with her hurt. She sat there struggling to be rational. Just because she was celibate, did that mean Will had to be also? He wasn't her husband. He was her dearest friend but that didn't mean she owned him. Did it? He had never accounted to her for all of his time and she had never dreamed of asking him to. Maybe with a lover you could ask exclusivity but it wasn't rational to demand this of a friend. But reason was one thing and emotion was another and she couldn't control the feeling of abandonment that swept through her now, reminding her of the past.

"Why are you telling me this now?" Ellen asked. No change please, the silent cry tore through her body, no more change, she begged. I need you, Will. I don't care if you're in love with him but please, no more change. Please, please don't abandon me.

"I'll tell you because I want to spend my weekends with

420

him," Will said. "I've been wanting to for some time but I didn't feel you could be left alone after Jennifer's death. So I've been waiting. It hasn't been so bad. I've been waiting all my life. Ron's family cottage in Southampton is empty now and we want to spend weekends and summers there. If we enjoy living together, we both want to retire and move out there permanently."

"Wouldn't you miss New York?" Ellen asked.

"I've had it all," he said. "Every play, every restaurant, every party, every museum. I've had everything all of my adult life except what I need the most."

"But what will I do?" Ellen cried. "What will I do with my weekends?"

"That, of course, is another point. It's time, my dear Ellen, for you to be weaned. Time for you to stop viewing yourself as a defenseless victim. You're a leader, president of a big corporation, admired, respected, loved. You're thirty-eight years old and you're letting yourself look fifty. You think it's been good for you, this dependence on me but it isn't. It's time for you to find your own kind, too.

"Entertain. You have a beautiful apartment, good help, plenty of money. People would be honored to come to your parties. Contribute and get on the boards of directors of art organizations, or museums. You love theater and ballet. Contribute and start to help the arts grow and survive. No more working seven days a week. On Fridays, you leave the office and plan for other kinds of enjoyment. It's time to reach out, Ellen. You'll still have me during the week. You still have Tina and Barry. Please don't view this as abandonment. Be happy. It's the beginning of a new era."

"Every other weekend?" She gave it a last try.

"Every weekend," he said. "I'm getting old. No time left to wait anymore. Wish me happiness!"

"Oh, I do, my dear Will. Every happiness. I wish you everything you deserve. You've spent your life taking care of Kate and me. Now live for yourself."

Her life assumed a different kind of pattern. She started to spend Saturdays at Elizabeth Arden's, taking care of her nails, her hair, working in an exercise class, getting a massage. Saturday nights she'd hold dinner parties for twelve that were soon discussed as perfect parties, desirable invitations.

She bought a box at the opera on Thursday nights at Lincoln Center, a new, shiny opera house where she could enjoy the experience without memories of the past. She met many people, extended her circle of acquaintances each week, flirted with a few men, but never got to the bedroom stage with any of them.

"I've become rusty, sexually," she told Tina.

"It will come back," Tina said, "but you have to work at it. It's like a sport, Ellen. The less you do it, the less you *can* do it."

Ellen began to find herself hungering for touch, not necessarily for orgasm but for touch, for the smell and taste of a man, for the excitement of waiting through dinner to finally get to bed, for the feel of long, smooth thighs against her own, for warming herself in the small of a man's back, for burying her face in his neck. Convalescent, all of her senses seemed to be returning.

She still had not met a man she wanted, but the month that she turned thirty-nine something wonderful happened to her. She received an invitation to join EL. At first her only emotion was euphoria. After that, she sat at her antique desk, looking west over Central Park, holding the invitation and feeling a certain wry amusement. Nobody had proposed her. So successful had she become that the EL board had taken it upon themselves to invite her. The solid gold circle had finally invited her in.

She remembered when Jeff had joined EL. And now, fifteen years later, Jeff had turned forty-five and was no longer a member and she had been invited to join. The cut-off age had been changed from forty to forty-five.

What a triumph! She had been invited to join not as a wife, not as an appendage whose only function was to look pretty and not screw-up her husband's accounts, not as someone to be shut up and whipped into shape, but as a businesswoman in her own right. Silently, she blessed Kate and Will. They had done this for her, shown her that she could be herself and still become an EL member. They had shown her that she was good and smart and the stuff of success.

The first person she told was Tina, who would appreciate the irony.

"You should join," Tina said, "just to give Jeff some bad moments. Can't you just see Candy's face?"

"I'm not going to join," Ellen said.

"Not going to join? Why not? How can you throw away this opportunity? Why wouldn't you join?"

"Because I have no interest in the organization," she said. What did they have to offer her beside an empty kind of triumph. How frightened and insecure she had been fifteen years ago. How desperately she had wanted to conform; the breast operation, the exercises with Alain, the speech lessons, the repression of her opinions.

"I'll tell you something else," she said with an impish grin. "That organization isn't good enough for me." And that was that.

The Solid Gold Circle. Where were they, all of them who had shone within it? Harry dead of a heart attack, Davida a suicide, Kate dead of cancer, Michael just getting out of jail, Jeff struggling to rebuild his business and trying to survive a second wife who was a worse enemy than Ellen had ever been. And the endless divorces: hers, the Bensons', the Landors', the Taylors', the Weins', the Plaris'. And now other deaths.

Marilyn had never become a nun. She had, perhaps accidentally, taken an overdose of barbituates, existed in a coma for several months, then finally died. Ellen felt particularly sorry for her. Marilyn also had seemingly played the game the right way but there was no way to win with Amos. Sad to think of Marilyn existing as an unconscious vegetable, hooked up to life-support machines for so many months. It was a blessing that she had finally died. Better to have it fast and terrible, as with Jennifer, than to linger that way. Oh, Jennifer, Jennifer. No, she mustn't let herself think of her daughter. Someday perhaps she could come to terms with her devastating loss, but not yet. Then, one month after Marilyn's death, Amos and Kimberly had died in a car crash in the south of France.

How glamorous EL had seemed fifteen years ago and how empty it seemed to her now. "Thank you for the invitation," she dictated to her secretary, "but I must respectfully decline. I really am not the kind of person you want."

Six months later, an invitation arrived which was much more important to her. When her secretary brought it in, Ellen was pleased.

"The first of many such invitations," Will assured her.

She was to be given an honorary degree and had been invited to serve as commencement speaker for Harrison College the following June, at the suggestion of Professor Emeritus Benjamin Dalway.

She read the letter to Will.

"In an era of developing women's rights," the letter stated, "your exceptional success stands as an inspiration to all young women, both in this graduating class and in society."

The letter then discussed the degree and honorarium, and closed with a paragraph of flowery compliments.

"I haven't seen you this tickled in a long time," Will told her.

"It's because I never went back to finish my degree," she told him. "I didn't give a rap about EL; that was no honor to me. But this is the greatest honor I've had in my entire life. How kind of Dalway to propose me."

It was the first time she had felt happy since Jennifer's death. Her pulse quickened. Here she was: Ellen, the despised, the Queen of Greenwich Village. Ellen, who had never finished college; Ellen, who always seemed to put her foot in her mouth. She was a VIP, a commencement speaker, and they would be honored to have her. She stood up in the middle of her office and let out one joyous "Yippee."

Tina pushed her way into Ellen's office just in time to hear the shout. "It's no wonder, you're getting crazy without sex," Tina said, and the two women hugged each other.

424

The days passed quickly and finally commencement weekend was there and like a young girl before the senior prom, Ellen selected, discarded, selected, and discarded, and finally decided on the right clothes and had her maid pack them in the Vuitton cases. At first she had thought she would drive, but a late business emergency forced her to take a plane. On the plane, she looked at her speech once again. She had worked on it for months. "This is ridiculous," Tina had told her, "get a ghost."

"No," Ellen had answered, "this is all mine."

Dalway was waiting at the airport and they hugged each other like old friends, without a shred of strangeness between them.

"Sorry to hear about your daughter," he said after he had escorted her into the waiting limousine.

"Thank you," she said. "Please don't refer to it or I'll spend the weekend weeping and spoil the image of the self-possessed career woman."

"Sorry," he said. "One never really knows what to say."

"Congratulations on the Pulitzer," she said.

"I was rather pleased about it," he said with that WASP restraint. "And congratulations to you on being the first woman commencement speaker here."

"Did you have to fight hard for that?" she asked.

"Not at all. They jumped at my suggestion."

"That makes me feel good," she told him.

He was as witty and intelligent as she remembered and she found herself laughing and enjoying his company as they drove. He told her that they were training prisoners at a local prison to teach reading and writing to other inmates.

"Of course," he said dryly, "we don't want to waste the training so we pick only prisoners with run-on sentences."

"I don't meet people with witty minds like yours in my field," she told him, half-seriously.

"I don't even meet them in academe," he laughed, his old arrogance intact but not offensive in any way.

He told her that his wife, Linda, had joined Alcoholics

Anonymous and had been sober now for all of the years since the Stewart wedding.

"I'll never forget"—Ellen laughed—"the sight of you, kneeling beside her in all of that cake icing. You must have ruined your beautiful dinner suit."

"That was when the marriage hit bottom," Dalway said. "I told her she either joined AA or I was through. She joined and, much to my surprise, we've had some fairly good years since then."

Dalway had also been at Jeff and Candy's wedding. "That circus," he called it. "And after all that investment, I've heard their marriage is on the rocks."

"I didn't know," Ellen said. Funny that the news evoked no more emotion in her than if they were total strangers.

"Poor Candy," Dalway said. "She certainly has peculiar taste in men. First Michael, when she could have married someone from a good family, and then Jeff. The same mistake twice."

"Hey, hold on," Ellen said. "I'm not from what you'd term a 'good family' either." What a snob he was.

"I'm not saying it in a pejorative way," Dalway covered smoothly. "I'm just saying that unless you marry within your own class, the marriage is doomed to failure."

"Then Jeff and I should have been perfectly suited," she teased him. "Your theory is no good, Dalway. What matters is character, not class." He was a friend of Candy's family and it amused her to see how perspective shifts according to affiliation. He didn't see Candy as a scheming little barracuda.

"What matters," he teased back, "is character *and* class. And Jeff was deficient in the character area. You're lucky to be rid of him. He was so transparent, such a con man. Even that one time we met I thought you deserved better."

Funny that he should say that. All those years she had lived under the delusion, fostered by Jeff, that people felt sorry for him for being saddled with so undistinguished a wife.

"Maybe I do deserve better," Ellen said lightly, "but I don't

426

seem to know how to find someone 'better.' For many years I haven't wanted someone, but now I think I'm ready." And she really meant it.

"If you're ready," he said, "you should have no difficulty at all. Many men would want a woman like you."

Feeling a surge of self-confidence, she said goodbye to him at the hotel where he was to pick her up for cocktails. The presidential suite had been reserved for her and in her room she found the VIP perks that still delighted her: a basket of perfect fruit, a few bottles of good liquor, and a large cut-glass vase of American Beauty roses. She was excited, elated, and felt none of her usual loneliness at not having anyone with whom to share the good things.

A small select dinner was to be held at the home of the college president in her honor, and she took particular pains with her appearance. Her body was still firm, her face looked pretty enough for someone of thirty-nine, and she wore a lovely dress from Tina's boutique. It was a machine-woven lace knit which in past generations would have taken hordes of workers years to make. Around her neck was the famous Marie Antoinette necklace which Kate had left to her.

"Someday you will give it to Jennifer," Kate had written in her will, "because I have no children. Your daughter will be my daughter." Oh, Jennifer, Jennifer.

"Don't you dare to cry," Ellen admonished herself severely. "You'll ruin your makeup. Come on, grow up. Captains of industry don't cry." She popped a Valium in her mouth, gave one final spray of Cabouchard, then went down to the lobby to meet Dalway.

"My word, Ellen, you're smashing," Dalway said. "What an extraordinary necklace."

"It belonged to Marie Antoinette."

"Is it real?"

"It's real all right." Ellen grinned. "The copy is me."

The night was so beautiful that Dalway dismissed the car

and they walked the few blocks to the president's house and entered the main gate of the college. Ellen had never been there before and now, suddenly, spread out before her like a movie set of Old Ivy, stood the college. Her skin prickled, gooseflesh in the warm, quiet night, gooseflesh at the traditional beauty, the calm, the substance, the understated wealth of endless endowments, the magnificent symmetry which was so well planned that it looked inadvertent.

This is the country where I belong, Ellen thought, hugging her prickled arms against herself. She thought of Kate and Will's words, "You don't find a friend. You recognize one." Ellen recognized a country.

"My God," she caroled joyously to Dalway, "I feel high."

Groups of laughing, erect, proud, sheltered students passed her. They moved in privilege, knowing that forever afterward, throughout their lives, people would say in hushed voices, "She went to Harrison, she's a Harrison girl, a typical Harrison product."

"Oh, Dalway, I love it here," burst from her lips. "I wish that I could stay forever."

"Do you mean that?"

"As much as I've ever meant anything in my life."

"I wouldn't want you to romanticize this place," he said. "Colleges are as cutthroat as business. But if you'd like to teach a course here occasionally, I think I could arrange it."

"But how? I never even finished college."

"With your credentials you don't need a degree. But are you forgetting that we're giving you an honorary one? That would suffice. However, the fact is that you are a leader of industry, one of the very few such women in the country, and our School of Business often appoints people without degrees who have been successful in the business world. Frankly, I think it makes far more sense than to hire business professors who may have their doctorates but have never worked in the real world of business. Would you really like to teach a course here?"

428

"I'd love it," she said weakly.

When she entered the president's drawing room, to her delight and surprise the assembled people stood up and applauded. The president shook her hand and thanked her for accepting. "Our academic vice-president regrets that he cannot be with us," the president told her. "His wife has just passed away after a long siege of cancer." Then he proceeded to introduce her to all of the other administrators and distinguished guests.

The food was excellent, spare but of good quality and beautifully served. Everyone was polite, courteous, receptive, and endlessly admiring. She asked to be excused early to go over her speech. Dalway escorted her back to the hotel.

"Would you like me to stay the night?" he asked casually.

"I want to rehearse my speech," she said, equally insouciant. "Thanks anyway."

He didn't care, of course; it was just a routine gesture of politeness. He gave her a little goodnight kiss on the brow and she went to her room to practice, blessing Helen Fern for all those lessons.

The next day, she quailed momentarily when she looked out at the sea of faces but she quickly began her speech and almost forgot about the audience except for the times they interrupted with spontaneous applause. They like me, she thought, and her heart quickened. As from a distance, she heard the words over which she had labored, and she was pleased by what she heard.

"It is never easy for a woman to head a large corporation," she told the attentive audience. "I do not think prejudice against us will disappear for a generation. We have to try harder, be better, be more rational, be better prepared, make fewer mistakes. If you cry easily as I do, this is one of the hurdles you must overcome. We cannot show emotion because the role model in industry is the stoic, hard-headed leader."

Then she told them a little about the history of the textile industry in the United States. Spellbound, they listened to her descriptions of spinning wool, spinning flax, making linen, weaving, dyeing, sewing, quilting, the development of style, class distinctions in the colonies based on clothing, the development of made-to-order clothes, and the nature of the textile industry in the present world.

"If you follow the development of the American textile industry," she said, just before closing, "you follow the birth and growth of America itself.

"And now," she continued, "I would like to pay homage to Kate Evans, the founder of Katie Knits, the first woman president in Executive Leaders, the first person to conceptualize the impact of man-made fibers on the entire world. And in her honor, the company she left behind, Katie Knits, has arranged for the following. We will provide funds to Harrison for a Kate Evans Research Institute which is to be staffed completely by women and which will train from ten to twenty-five young women each year to work in the textile field. In addition, Katie Knits will select five of those young women each year to serve as interns in the vast empire of Katie Knits. This training will be on the graduate level, and I hope that the first young woman to work with us will come from this graduating class before me.

"In closing, I salute and congratulate you all and ask that you move forward with me to show the world how great a contribution the modern woman can make to all of society."

She could hardly believe what happened then. The cheering continued for ten minutes as the waves of young women stood to pay honor to the slim, plain-beautiful, proud-humble, young-worn woman on the platform before them. Oh, Jennifer, she thought. You should have been among them. But good, warm, cleansing tears suddenly coursed from her eyes and she stood there unashamed, her head held proudly, letting them flow down her face without embarrassment.

She stood there for a half-hour afterward and individuals pushed forward to tell her how much they had liked her speech and how excited they were about the new program. When the people finally let her go, Benjamin Dalway drove her to the airport.

"The president was thrilled by your speech," he told her. "He congratulated me for having recommended you and I owe you my thanks for that."

"I know." Ellen laughed. "He kept pressing and pressing my hand and thanking me."

"He would have driven you to the airport himself but he has the traditional tea for parents this afternoon and he always uses that occasion for some subtle fund-raising. But he did authorize me to ask you to become the first head of the Kate Evans Research Institute and to ask if you could possibly combine it with your business next September."

She thought for a moment. "I don't want to combine it," she said. "I wouldn't be able to give either job my best. But I'd like to take a year off from my business and try it. I've been working awfully hard for a long time. I need a change. Please give him my consent and I'll send him an official letter."

She thought about it with great pleasure and excitement as he drove. "I would have the entire summer to make my preparations," she said. "I'd appreciate it if you would line up a few houses for me to look at and let me know when I can see them. I'm quite willing to buy because I can always rent it out when I return to New York. Can you find one with a swimming pool or else with enough land to put one in? A tennis court would be good, too."

"No problem in finding what you want," he said. "Most of the people around here don't have that much money.

"I can't get over the change in you, Ellen," he said while they waited for the plane. "When I knew you, you were a frightened housewife. Now you're one of the most successful women I know. That was the finest commencement speech I've ever heard: factual, inspirational, practical. You're quite a role model for young women." She kissed him goodbye, pleased that she had so good a friend, pleased that this famous man treated her as an equal.

Immediately after her return she met with Will and Tina and told them of her offer.

"I think it's just what you need," Will said. "A wonderful opportunity."

"But how will we manage?" Tina wailed. "Who will help you, Will? Who will take over Ellen's duties?"

Will looked across at Tina and twinkled at Ellen.

"Why, you, my dear," he said to Tina.

"Me?" and for the second time in all those years Ellen saw Tina cry. But this time, Tina did not care at all about how she looked.

"Remember," she wept to Ellen, "when we first met and I couldn't even get up in the mornings. I admired you so much for being able to work, even in that nursery school. I thought that all I was good for was to look pretty. And now Will thinks I'm good enough to take on your work." She burst into tears again.

"The only thing that bothers me about your taking over," Ellen said with pretended gruffness, "is that Barry's going to claim it's all due to his work with you. I bet he takes all the credit for this."

"He did help," Tina said, "and so did both of you. I won't let you down. When you get back, Ellen, you'll find everything going as well as when you left. Frankly, I think you're crazy to go. You'll be bored to death so far from New York City. Nobody lives in . . ."

"I will," Ellen stopped her, and they laughed together.

"Well," Tina conceded, "I suppose it's all right for a year. Colleges are really boring places and all those college professors smoke pipes and wear white socks with everything. Still, I suppose you have to get it out of your system. But you'll never stay."

"Maybe she'll never come back," Will said quietly.

"No, it will only be for a short time," Tina said. "Nobody even wants to teach college anymore. All those scruffy students eating peanut butter. It's a real loser occupation."

"Oh, Tina." Ellen laughed. Some things never change.

Ellen flew to Harrison again, found a beautiful house with a swimming pool and formal gardens, engaged a housekeeper-

432

cook, and hired a decorator to get some furniture in there as soon as possible. Then she called Jeff to visit Jennifer's grave with her.

"Sorry to hear about your marriage," she told him on the drive out.

"It's all right," he said. "I'm seeing someone else. Nobody you know . . . Maybe this time will be the right one."

"I'm glad," she said, really meaning it.

They walked from the car to Jennifer's grave. Standing there, with their arms around each other, they wept together.

"I don't hate you anymore," she said.

"Nor I you," he answered.

The old life was over.

She spent August getting settled in her new house. Each evening she walked around the campus at dusk, her skin prickling in delight, in the pleasure of having come home. She wanted to run and jump and turn cartwheels across the beautiful lawns. She watched the young girls walk past and thought, I'll be able to help many Jennifers.

Over and over her thoughts rioted joyously. I'm home, I'm home, I'm home.

Dalway had been in India when she arrived but he called her when he returned and asked her to meet him for lunch the next day at the Faculty Club. The academic vice-president would be joining them since he was anxious to meet the newest faculty member.

She was delighted that she was finally beginning her involvement with other members of the faculty. It was the beginning of a magnificent autumn and she dressed to blend with nature, in a brown tweed suit with yellow silk blouse, and high suede boots. She brushed her hair and put on an extra dab of color on her cheeks. Not bad, she thought, and she set off.

She had already met the maitre d', who greeted her warmly and asked her to follow him to her group. Dalway sat at a spacious table in front of the leaded windows with the academic vice-president, whose back was to her. All that she could see was a dark-haired man who was slightly bald. Dalway saw her and stood up, as did the other man. Dalway held out his hand to her and pulled her around to face the man. The surprise was so great that she felt dizzied and a rush of blood flashed to her face. It couldn't be, she thought. It was impossible. The man wore glasses and had an intense, intelligent look to him. A smile played around the corner of Dalway's mouth.

The man reached his hands across to Ellen and took her shaking, cold hands between his warm, comforting ones. She could feel the warmth radiate out from his hands and fill her entire being with comfort, like the sun on a wintry day.

"I'd like you to meet our academic vice-president," Dalway said, that little smile still playing around his mouth. "He thinks he knew you in another life."

The man looked at her and smiled. "Hello, Ellen," Saul said. "Welcome back."